I0764665

Pearl-Maiden

Pearl-Maiden

H. Rider Haggard

A Tale of the Fall of Jerusalem

Waking Lion Press

To
Gladys Christian
a dweller in the East
this Eastern tale is dedicated
by her own and her father's friend
The Author
Ditchingham: September 14, 1902

ISBN 978-1-4341-1741-0

Published by Waking Lion Press, an imprint of The Editorium

The Editorium, LLC
West Valley City, UT 84128-3917
wakinglionpress.com
wakinglion@editorium.com

Contents

Chapter 1

The Prison at Cæsarea

It was but two hours after midnight, yet many were wakeful in Cæsarea on the Syrian coast. Herod Agrippa, King of all Palestine—by grace of the Romans—now at the very apex of his power, celebrated a festival in honour of the Emperor Claudius, to which had flocked all the mightiest in the land and tens of thousands of the people. The city was full of them, their camps were set upon the sea-beach and for miles around; there was no room at the inns or in the private houses, where guests slept upon the roofs, the couches, the floors, and in the gardens. The great town hummed like a hive of bees disturbed after sunset, and though the louder sounds of revelling had died away, parties of feasters, many of them still crowned with fading roses, passed along the streets shouting and singing to their lodgings. As they went, they discussed—those of them who were sufficiently sober—the incidents of that day's games in the great circus, and offered or accepted odds upon the more exciting events of the morrow.

The captives in the prison that was set upon a little hill, a frowning building of brown stone, divided into courts and surrounded by a high wall and a ditch, could hear the workmen at their labours in the amphitheatre below.

These sounds interested them, since many of those who listened were doomed to take a leading part in the spectacle of this new day. In the outer court, for instance, were a hundred men called malefactors, for the most part Jews convicted of various political offences. These were to fight against twice their number of savage Arabs of the desert taken in a frontier raid, people whom to-day we should know as Bedouins, mounted and armed with swords and lances, but wearing no mail. The malefactor Jews, by way of compensation, were to be protected with heavy armour and ample shields. Their combat was to last for twenty minutes by the sand- glass, when, unless they had shown cowardice, those who were left alive of either party were to receive their freedom. Indeed, by a kindly decree the King Agrippa, a man who did not seek unnecessary bloodshed, contrary to custom, even the wounded were to be spared, that is, if any would undertake the care of them. Under these circumstances, since life is sweet, all had determined to fight their best.

In another division of the great hall was collected a very different company. There were not more than fifty or sixty of these, so the wide arches of the surrounding cloisters gave them sufficient shelter and even privacy. With the exception of eight or ten men, all of them old, or well on in middle age, since the younger and more vigorous males had been carefully drafted to serve as gladiators, this little band was made of women and a few children. They belonged to the new sect called Christians, the followers of one Jesus, who, according to report, was crucified as a troublesome person by the governor, Pontius Pilate, a Roman official, who in due course had been banished to Gaul, where he was said to have committed suicide. In his day Pilate was unpopular in Judæa, for he had taken the treasures of the Temple at Jerusalem to build waterworks, causing a tumult in which many were killed. Now he was almost forgotten, but very strangely, the fame of this crucified demagogue, Jesus, seemed to grow, since there were many who made a kind of god of him, preaching doctrines in his name that were contrary to the law and offensive to every sect of the Jews.

Pharisees, Sadducees, Zealots, Levites, priests, all called out against them. All besought Agrippa that he would be rid of them, these apostates who profaned the land and proclaimed in the ears of a nation awaiting its Messiah, that Heaven-born King who should break the Roman yoke and make Jerusalem the capital of the world, that this Messiah had come already in the guise of an itinerant preacher, and perished with other malefactors by the death of shame.

Wearied with their importunities, the King listened. Like the cultivated Romans with whom he associated, Agrippa had no real religion. At Jerusalem he embellished the Temple and made offerings to Jehovah; at Berytus he embellished the temple and made offerings there to Jupiter. He was all things to all men and to himself—nothing but a voluptuous time-server. As for these Christians, he never troubled himself about them. Why should he? They were few and insignificant, no single man of rank or wealth was to be found among them. To persecute them was easy, and—it pleased the Jews. Therefore he persecuted them. One James, a disciple of the crucified man called Christ, who had wandered about the country with him, he seized and beheaded at Jerusalem. Another, called Peter, a powerful preacher, he threw into prison, and of their followers he slew many. A few of these were given over to be stoned by the Jews, but the pick of the men were forced to fight as gladiators at Berytus and elsewhere. The women, if young and beautiful, were sold as slaves, but if matrons or aged, they were cast to the wild beasts in the circus.

Such was the fate, indeed, that was reserved for these poor victims in the prison on this very day of the opening of our history. After the gladiators had fought and the other games had been celebrated, sixty Christians, it was announced, old and useless men, married woman and young children whom nobody would buy, were to be turned down in the great amphitheatre. Then thirty fierce lions, with other savage beasts, made ravenous by hunger and mad with the smell of blood, were to be let loose among them. Even in this act of justice, however, Agrippa suffered it to be seen that he was gentle-hearted, since of his kindness he had decreed that any whom the lions refused to eat were to be given clothes, a small sum of money, and released to settle their differences with the Jews as they might please.

Such was the state of public feeling and morals in the Roman world of that day, that this spectacle of the feeding of starved beasts with live women and children, whose crime was that they worshipped a crucified man and would offer sacrifice to no other god, either in the Temple or elsewhere, was much looked forward to by the population of Cæsarea. Indeed, great sums of money were ventured upon the event, by means of what to-day would be called sweepstakes, under the regulations of which he who drew the ticket marked with the exact number of those whom the lions left alive, would take the first prize.

Already some far-seeing gamblers who had drawn low numbers, had bribed the soldiers and wardens to sprinkle the hair and garments of the Christians with valerian water, a decoction which was supposed to attract and excite the appetite of these great cats. Others, whose tickets were high, paid handsomely for the employment of artifices which need not be detailed, calculated to induce in the lions aversion to the subject that had been treated. The Christian woman or child, it will be observed, who was to form the *corpus vile* of these ingenious experiments, was not considered, except, indeed, as the fisherman considers the mussel or the sand-worm on his hook.

Under an arch by themselves, and not far from the great gateway where the guards, their lances in hand, could be seen pacing up and down, sat two women. The contrast in the appearance of this pair was very striking. One, who could not have been much more than twenty years of age, was a Jewess, too thin-faced for beauty, but with dark and lovely eyes, and bearing in every limb and feature the stamp of noble blood. She was Rachel, the widow of Demas, a Græco-Syrian, and only child of the high-born Jew Benoni, one of the richest merchants in Tyre. The other was a woman of remarkable aspect, apparently about forty years of age. She was a native of the coasts of Libya, where she had been kidnapped as a girl by Jewish traders, and by them passed on to Phœnicians, who sold her upon the slave market of Tyre. In fact she was a high-bred Arab without any admixture of negro blood, as was shown by her copper-coloured skin, prominent cheek bones, her straight, black, abundant hair, and untamed, flashing eyes. In frame she was tall and spare, very agile, and full of grace in every movement. Her face was fierce and hard; even in her present dreadful plight she showed no fear, only when she looked at the lady by her side it grew anxious and tender. She was called Nehushta, a name which Benoni had given her when many years ago he bought her upon the market-place. In Hebrew Nehushta means copper, and this new slave was copper-coloured. In her native land, however, she had another name, Nou, and by this name she was known to her dead mistress, the wife of Benoni, and to his daughter Rachel, whom she had nursed from childhood.

The moon shone very brightly in a clear sky, and by the light of it an observer, had there been any to observe where all were so occupied with their own urgent affairs, could have watched every movement and expression of these women. Rachel, seated on the ground, was rocking herself to and fro, her face hidden in her hands, and praying. Nehushta knelt at her side, resting the weight of her body on her heels as only an Eastern can, and stared sullenly at nothingness.

Presently Rachel, dropping her hands, looked at the tender sky and sighed.

"Our last night on earth, Nou," she said sadly. "It is strange to think that we shall never again see the moon floating above us."

"Why not, mistress? If all that we have been taught is true, we shall see that moon, or others, for ever and ever, and if it is not true, then neither light nor darkness will trouble us any more. However, for my own part I don't mean that either of us should die to-morrow."

"How can you prevent it, Nou?" asked Rachel with a faint smile. "Lions are no respecters of persons."

"Yet, mistress, I think that they will respect my person, and yours, too, for my sake."

"What do you mean, Nou?"

"I mean that I do not fear the lions; they are country-folk of mine and roared round my cradle. The chief, my father, was called Master of Lions in our country because he could tame them. Why, when I was a little child I have fed them and they fawned upon us like dogs."

"Those lions are long dead, Nou, and the others will not remember."

"I am not sure that they are dead; at least, blood will call to blood, and their company will know the smell of the child of the Master of Lions. Whoever is eaten, we shall escape."

"I have no such hope, Nou. To-morrow we must die horribly, that King Agrippa may do honour to his master, Cæsar."

"If you think that, mistress, then let us die at once rather than be rent limb from limb to give pleasure to a stinking mob. See, I have poison hidden here in my hair. Let us drink of it and be done: it is swift and painless."

"Nay, Nou, it would not be right. I may lift no hand against my own life, or if perchance I may, I have to think of another life."

"If you die, the unborn child must die also. To-night or to-morrow, what does it matter?"

"Sufficient to the day is the evil thereof. Who knows? To-morrow Agrippa may be dead, not us, and then the child might live. It is in the hand of God. Let God decide."

"Lady," answered Nehushta, setting her teeth, "for your sake I have become a Christian, yes, and I believe. But I tell you this—while I live no lion's fangs shall tear that dear flesh of yours. First if need be, I will stab you there in the arena, or if they take my knife from me, then I will choke you, or dash out your brains against the posts."

"It may be a sin, Nou; take no such risk upon your soul."

"My soul! What do I care about my soul? You are my soul. Your mother was kind to me, the poor slave-girl, and when you were an infant, I rocked you upon my breast. I spread your bride-bed, and if need be, to save you from worse things, I will lay you dead before me and myself dead across your body. Then let God or Satan—I care not which—deal with my soul. At least, I shall have done my best and died faithful."

"You should not speak so," sighed Rachel. "But, dear, I know it is because you love me, and I wish to die as easily as may be and to join my husband. Only if the child could have lived, as I think, all three of us would have dwelt together eternally. Nay, not all three, all four, for you are well-nigh as dear to me, Nou, as husband or as child."

"That cannot be, I do not wish that it should be, who am but a slave woman, the dog beneath the table. Oh! if I could save you, then I would be glad to show them how this daughter of my father can bear their torments."

The Libyan ceased, grinding her teeth in impotent rage. Then suddenly she leant towards her mistress, kissed her fiercely on the cheek and began to sob, slow, heavy sobs.

"Listen," said Rachel. "The lions are roaring in their dens yonder."

Nehushta lifted her head and hearkened as a hunter hearkens in the desert. True enough, from near the great tower that ended the southern wall of the amphitheatre, echoed short, coughing notes and fierce whimperings, to be followed presently by roar upon roar, as lion after lion joined in that fearful music, till the whole air shook with the volume of their voices.

"Aha!" cried a keeper at the gate—not the Roman soldier who marched to and fro unconcernedly, but a jailor, named Rufus, who was clad in a padded robe and armed with a great knife. "Aha! listen to them, the pretty kittens. Don't be greedy, little ones—be patient. To-night you will purr upon a full stomach."

"Nine of them," muttered Nehushta, who had counted the roars, "all bearded and old, royal beasts. To hearken to them makes me young again. Yes, yes, I smell the desert and see the smoke rising from my father's tents. As a child I hunted them, now they will hunt me; it is their hour."

"Give me air! I faint!" gasped Rachel, sinking against her.

With a guttural exclamation of pity Nehushta bent down. Placing her strong arms beneath the slender form of her young mistress, and lifting her as though she were a child, she carried her to the centre of the court, where stood a fountain; for before it was turned to the purposes of a jail once this place had been a palace. Here she set her mistress on the ground with her back against the stonework, and dashed water in her face till presently she was herself again.

While Rachel sat thus—for the place was cool and pleasant and she could not sleep who must die that day—a wicket-gate was opened and several persons, men, women, and children, were thrust through it into the court.

"Newcomers from Tyre in a great hurry not to lose the lions' party," cried the facetious warden of the gate. "Pass in, my Christian friends, pass in and eat your last supper according to your customs. You will find it over there, bread and wine in plenty. Eat, my hungry friends, eat before you are eaten and enter into Heaven or—the stomach of the lions."

An old woman, the last of the party, for she could not walk fast, turned round and pointed at the buffoon with her staff.

"Blaspheme not, you heathen dog!" she said, "or rather, blaspheme on and go to your reward! I, Anna, who have the gift of prophecy, tell you, renegade who were a Christian, and therefore are doubly guilty, that *you* have eaten your last meal—on earth."

The man, a half-bred Syrian who had abandoned his faith for profit and now tormented those who were once his brethren, uttered a furious curse and snatched a knife from his girdle.

"You draw the knife? So be it, perish by the knife!" said Anna. Then without heeding him further the old woman hobbled on after her companions, leaving the man to slink away white to the lips with terror. He had been a Christian and knew something of Anna and of this "gift of prophecy."

The path of these strangers led them past the fountain, where Rachel and Nehushta rose to greet them as they came.

"Peace be with you," said Rachel.

"In the name of Christ, peace," they answered, and passed on towards the arches where the other captives were gathered. Last of all, at some distance behind the rest, came the white-haired woman, leaning on her staff.

As she approached, Rachel turned to repeat her salutation, then uttered a little cry and said:

"Mother Anna, do you not know me, Rachel, the daughter of Benoni?"

"Rachel!" she answered, starting. "Alas! child, how came you here?"

"By the paths that we Christians have to tread, mother," said Rachel, sadly. "But sit; you are weary. Nou, help her."

Anna nodded, and slowly, for her limbs were stiff, sank down on to the step of the fountain.

"Give me to drink, child," she said, "for I have been brought upon a mule from Tyre, and am athirst."

Rachel made her hands into a cup, for she had no other, and held water to Anna's lips, which she drank greedily, emptying them many times.

"For this refreshment, God be praised. What said you? The daughter of Benoni a Christian! Well, even here and now, for that God be praised also. Strange that I should not have heard of it; but I have been in Jerusalem these two years, and was brought back to Tyre last Sabbath as a prisoner."

"Yes, Mother, and since then I have become both wife and widow."

"Whom did you marry, child?"

"Demas, the merchant. They killed him in the amphitheatre yonder at Berytus six months ago," and the poor woman began to sob.

"I heard of his end," replied Anna. "It was a good and noble one, and his soul rests in Heaven. He would not fight with the gladiators, so he was beheaded by order of Agrippa. But cease weeping, child, and tell me your story. We have little time for tears, who, perhaps, soon will have done with them."

Rachel dried her eyes.

"It is short and sad," she said. "Demas and I met often and learned to love each other. My father was no friend to him, for they were rivals in trade, but in those days knowing no better, Demas followed the faith of the Jews; therefore, because he was rich my father consented to our marriage, and they became partners in their business. Afterwards, within a month indeed, the Apostles came to Tyre, and we attended their preaching—at first, because we were curious to learn the truth of this new faith against which my father railed, for, as you know, he is of the strictest sect of the Jews; and then, because our hearts were touched. So in the end we believed, and were baptised, both on one night, by the very hand of the brother of the Lord. The holy Apostles departed, blessing us before they went, and Demas, who would play no double part, told my father of what we had done. Oh! mother, it was awful to see. He raved, shouted and cursed us in his rage, blaspheming Him we worship. More, woe is me that I should have to tell it: When we refused to become apostates he denounced us to the priests, and the priests denounced us to the Romans, and we were seized and thrown into prison; but my husband's wealth, most of it except that which the priests and Romans stole, stayed with my father. For many months we were held in prison here in Cæsarea; then they took my husband to Berytus, to be trained as a gladiator, and murdered him. Here I have stayed since with this beloved servant, Nehushta, who also became a Christian and shared our fate, and now, by the decree of Agrippa, it is my turn and hers to die today."

"Child, you should not weep for that; nay, you should be glad who at once will find your husband and your Saviour."

"Mother, I am glad; but, you see my state. It is for the child's sake I weep, that now never will be born. Had it won life even for an hour all of us would have dwelt together in bliss until eternity. But it cannot be—it cannot be."

Anna looked at her with her piercing eyes.

"Have you, then, also the gift of prophecy, child, who are so young a member of the Church, that you dare to say that this or that cannot be? The future is in the hand of God. King Agrippa, your father, the Romans, the cruel Jews, those lions that roar yonder, and we who are doomed to feed them, are all in the hand of God, and that which He wills shall befall, and no other thing. Therefore, let us praise Him and rejoice, and take no thought for the morrow, unless it be to pray that we may die and go hence to our Master, rather than live on in doubts and terrors and tribulations."

"You are right, mother," answered Rachel, "and I will try to be brave, whatever may befall; but my state makes me feeble. The spirit, truly, is willing, but oh! the flesh is weak. Listen, they call us to partake of the Sacrament of the Lord—our last on earth"; and rising, she began to walk towards the arches.

Nehushta stayed to help Anna to her feet. When she judged her mistress to be out of hearing she leaned down and whispered:

"Mother, you have the gift; it is known throughout the Church. Tell me, will the child be born?"

The old woman fixed her eyes upon the heavens, then answered, slowly:

"The child will be born and live out its life, and I think that none of us are doomed to die this day by the jaws of lions, though some of us may die in another fashion. But I think also that your mistress goes very shortly to join her husband. Therefore it was that I showed her nothing of what came into my mind."

"Then it is best that I should die also, and die I will."

"Wherefore?"

"Because I go to wait upon my mistress?"

"Nay, Nehushta," answered Anna, sternly, "you stay to guard her child, whereof when all these earthly things are done you must give account to her."

Chapter 2

The Voice of a God

Of all the civilisations whose records lie open to the student, that of Rome is surely one of the most wonderful. Nowhere, not even in old Mexico, was high culture so completely wedded to the lowest barbarism. Intellect Rome had in plenty; the noblest efforts of her genius are scarcely to be surpassed; her law is the foundation of the best of our codes of jurisprudence; art she borrowed but appreciated; her military system is still the wonder of the world; her great men remain great among a multitude of subsequent competitors. And yet how pitiless she was! What a tigress! Amid all the ruins of her cities we find none of a hospital, none, I believe, of an orphan school in an age that made many orphans. The pious aspirations and efforts of individuals seem never to have touched the conscience of the people. Rome incarnate had no conscience; she was a lustful, devouring beast, made more bestial by her intelligence and splendour.

King Agrippa in practice was a Roman. Rome was his model, her ideals were his ideals. Therefore he built amphitheatres in which men were butchered, to the exquisite delight of vast audiences. Therefore, also, without the excuse of any conscientious motive, however insufficient or unsatisfactory, he persecuted the weak because they were weak and their sufferings would give pleasure to the strong or to those who chanced to be the majority of the moment.

The season being hot it was arranged that the great games in honour of the safety of Cæsar, should open each day at dawn and come to an end an hour before noon. Therefore from midnight onwards crowds of spectators poured into the amphitheatre, which, although it would seat over twenty thousand, was not large enough to contain them all. An hour before the dawn the place was full, and already late comers were turned back from its gates. The only empty spaces were those reserved for the king, his royal guests, the rulers of the city, with other distinguished personages, and for the Christian company of old men, women and children destined to the lions, who, it was arranged, were to sit in full view of the audience until the time came for them to take their share in the spectacle.

When Rachel joined the other captives she found that a long rough table had been set beneath the arcades, and on it at intervals, pieces of bread and cups and vases containing wine of the country that had been purchased at a great price from the guards. Round this table the elders or the infirm among the company were seated on a bench, while the rest of the number, for whom there was not room, stood behind them. At its head was an old man, a bishop among the Christians, one of the five hundred who had seen the risen Lord and received baptism from the hands of the Beloved Disciple. For some years he had been spared by the persecutors of the infant Church on account of his age, dignity, and good repute, but now at last fate seemed to have overtaken him.

The service was held; the bread and wine, mixed with water, were consecrated with the same texts by which they are blessed to-day, only the prayers were extempore. When all had eaten from the platters and drunk from the rude cups, the bishop gave his blessing to the community. Then he addressed them. This, he told them, was an occasion of peculiar joy, a love-feast indeed, since all they who partook of it were about to lay down the burden of the flesh and, their labours and sorrows ended, to depart into bliss eternal. He called to their memory the supper of the Passover which had taken place within the lifetime of many of them, when the Author and Finisher of their faith had declared to the disciples that He would drink no more wine till He drank it new with them in His kingdom. Such a feast it was that lay spread before them this night. Let them be thankful for it. Let them not quail in the hour of trial. The fangs of the savage beasts, the shouts of the still more savage spectators, the agony of the quivering flesh, the last terror of their departing, what were these? Soon, very soon, they would be done; the spears of the soldiers would despatch the injured, and those among them whom it was ordained should escape, would be set free by the command of the representative of Cæsar, that they might prosecute the work till the hour came for them to pass on the torch of redemption to other hands. Let them rejoice, therefore, and be very thankful, and walk to the sacrifice as to a wedding feast. "Do you not rejoice, my brethren?" he asked. With one voice they answered, "We rejoice!" Yes, even the children answered thus.

Then they prayed again, and again with uplifted hands the old man blessed them in the holy Triune Name.

Scarcely had this service, as solemn as it was simple,

been brought to an end when the head jailer, whose blasphemous jocosity since his reproof by Anna was replaced by a mien of sullen venom, came forward and commanded the whole band to march to the amphitheatre. Accordingly, two by two, the bishop leading the way with the sainted woman Anna, they walked to the gates. Here a guard of soldiers was waiting to receive them, and under their escort they threaded the narrow, darkling streets till they came to that door of the amphitheatre which was used by those who were to take part in the games. Now, at a word from the bishop, they began to chant a solemn hymn, and singing thus, were thrust along the passages to the place prepared for them. This was not, as they expected, a prison at the back of the amphitheatre, but, as has been said, a spot between the enclosing wall and the podium, raised a little above the level of the arena. Here, on the eastern side of the building, they were to sit till their turn came to be driven by the guards through a little wicket-gate into the arena, where the starving beasts of prey would be loosed upon them.

It was now the hour before sunrise, and the moon having set, the vast theatre was plunged in gloom, relieved only here and there by stray torches and cressets of fire burning upon either side of the gorgeous, but as yet unoccupied, throne of Agrippa. This gloom seemed to oppress the audience with which the place was crowded; at any rate none of them shouted or sang, or even spoke loudly. They addressed each other in muffled tones, with the result that the air seemed to be full of mysterious whisperings. Had this poor band of condemned Christians entered the theatre in daylight, they would have been greeted with ironical cries and tauntings of "Dogs' meat!"

and with requests that they should work a miracle and let the people see them rise again from the bellies of the lions. But now, as their solemn song broke upon the silence, it was answered only by one great murmur, which seemed to shape itself to the words, "the Christians! The doomed Christians!"

By the light of a single torch the band took their places. Then once more they sang, and in that chastening hour the audience listened with attention, almost with respect. Their chant finished, the bishop stood up, and, moved thereto by some inspiration, began to address the mighty throng, whom he could not see, and who could not see him. Strangely enough they hearkened to him, perhaps because his speech served to while away the weary time of waiting.

"Men and brethren," he began, in his thin, piercing notes, "princes, lords, peoples, Romans, Jews, Syrians, Greeks, citizens of Idumæa, of Egypt, and of all nations here gathered, hearken to the words of an old man destined and glad to die. Listen, if it be your pleasure, to the story of One whom some of you saw crucified under Pontius Pilate, since to know the truth of that matter can at least do you no hurt."

"Be silent!" cried a voice, that of the renegade jailer, "and cease preaching your accursed faith!"

"Let him alone," answered other voices. "We will hear this story of his. We say—let him alone."

Thus encouraged the old man spoke on with an eloquence so simple and yet so touching, with a wisdom so deep, that for full fifteen minutes none cared even to interrupt him. Then a far-away listener cried:

"Why must these people die who are better than we?"

"Friend," answered the bishop, in ringing tones, which in that heavy silence seemed to search out even the recesses of the great and crowded place, "we must die because it is the will of King Agrippa, to whom God has given power to destroy us. Mourn not for us because we perish cruelly, since this is the day of our true birth, but mourn for King Agrippa, at whose hands our blood will be required, and mourn, mourn for yourselves, O people. The death that is near to us perchance is nearer still to some of you; and how will you awaken who perish in your sins? What if the sword of God should empty yonder throne? What if the voice of God should call on him who fills it to make answer of his deeds? Soon or late, O people, it will call on him and you to pass hence, some naturally in your age, others by the sharp and dreadful roads of sword, pestilence or famine. Already those woes which He whom you crucified foretold, knock at your door, and within a few short years not one of you who crowd this place in thousands will draw the breath of life. Nothing will remain of you on earth save the fruit of those deeds which you have done—these and your bones, no more. Repent you, therefore, repent while there is time; for I, whom you have doomed, I am bidden to declare that judgment is at hand. Yes, even now, although you see him not, the Angel of the Lord hangs over you and writes your names within his book. Now while there is time I would pray for you and for your king. Farewell."

As he spoke those words "the Angel of the Lord hangs over you," so great was the preacher's power, and in that weary darkness so sharply had he touched the imagination of his strange audience, that with a sound like to the stir of rustling trees, thousands of faces were turned upwards, as though in search of that dread messenger.

"Look, look!" screamed a hundred voices, while dim arms pointed to some noiseless thing that floated high above them against the background of the sky, which grew grey with the coming dawn. It appeared and disappeared, appeared again, then seemed to pass downward in the direction of Agrippa's throne, and vanished.

"It is that magician's angel," cried one, and the multitudes groaned.

"Fool," said another, "it was but a bird."

"Then for Agrippa's sake," shrilled a new voice, "the gods send that it was not an owl."

Thereat some laughed, but the most were silent. They knew the story of King Agrippa and the owl, and how it had been foretold that this spirit in the form of a bird would appear to him again in the hour of his death, as it had appeared to him in the hour of his triumph.[1]

Just then from the palace to the north arose a sound of the blare of trumpets. Now a herald, speaking on the summit of the great eastern tower, called out that it was dawn above the mountains, and that King Agrippa came with all his company, whereon the preaching of the old Christian and his tale of a watching Vengeance were instantly forgotten. Presently the glad, fierce notes of the trumpets drew nearer, and in the grey of the daybreak, through the great bronze gates of the Triumphal Way that were thrown open to greet him, advanced Agrippa, wonderfully attired and preceded by his legionaries. At his right walked Vibius Marsus, the Roman President of Syria,

1. See Josephus, "Antiquities of the Jews," Book XVII., Chap. VI., Sec. 7; and Book XIX., Chap. VIII., Sec. 2.

and on his left Antiochus, King of Commagena, while after him followed other kings, princes, and great men of his own and foreign lands.

Agrippa mounted his golden throne while the multitude roared a welcome, and his company were seated around and behind him according to their degree.

Once more the trumpets sounded, and the gladiators of different arms, headed by the equites who fought on horseback, numbering in all more than five hundred men, were formed up in the arena for the preliminary march past—the salutation of those about to die to their emperor and lord. Now, that they also might take their part in the spectacle, the band of Christian martyrs were thrust through the door in the podium, and to make them seem as many as possible in number, marshalled two by two.

Then the march past began. Troop by troop, arrayed in their shining armour and armed, each of them, with his own familiar weapon, the gladiators halted in front of Agrippa's throne, giving to him the accustomed salutation of "Hail, King, we who are about to die, salute thee," to be rewarded with a royal smile and the shouts of the approving audience. Last of all came the Christians, a motley, wretched-looking group, made up of old men, terrified children clinging to their mothers, and ill-clad, dishevelled women. At the pitiful sight, that very mob which a few short minutes before had hung upon the words of the bishop, their leader, now, as they watched them hobbling round the arena in the clear, low light of the dawning, burst into peals of laughter and called out that each of them should be made to lead his lion. Quite heedless of these scoffs and taunts, they trudged on through the white sand that soon would be so red, until they came opposite to the throne.

"Salute!" roared the audience.

The bishop held up his hand and all were silent. Then, in the thin voice with which they had become familiar, he said:

"King, we who are about to die—forgive thee. May God do likewise."

Now the multitude ceased laughing, and with an impatient gesture, Agrippa motioned to the martyrs to pass on. This they did humbly; but Anna, being old, lame and weary, could not walk so fast as her companions. Alone she reached the saluting-place after all had left it, and halted there.

"Forward!" cried the officers. But she did not move nor did she speak. Only leaning on her staff she looked steadily up at the face of the king Agrippa. Some impulse seemed to draw his eyes to hers. They met, and it was noted that he turned pale. Then straightening herself with difficulty upon her tottering feet, Anna raised her staff and pointed with it to the golden canopy above the head of Herod. All stared upward, but saw nothing, for the canopy was still in the shadow of the velarium which covered all the outer edge of the cavea, leaving the centre open to the sky. It would appear, however, that Agrippa did see something, for he who had risen to declare the games open, suddenly sank back upon his throne, and remained thus lost in thought. Then Anna limped forward to join her company, who once more were driven through the little gate in the wall of the arena.

For a second time, with an effort, Agrippa lifted himself from his throne. As he rose the first level rays of sunrise struck full upon him. He was a tall and noble-looking man, and his dress was glorious. To the thousands who gazed upon him from the shadow, set in that point of burning light he seemed to be clothed in a garment of glittering silver. Silver was his crown, silver his vest, silver the wide robe that flowed from his shoulders to the ground.

"In the name of Cæsar, to the glory of Cæsar, I declare these games open!" he cried.

Then, as though moved by a sudden impulse, all the multitude rose shouting: "The voice of a god! The voice of a god! The voice of the god Agrippa!"

Nor did Agrippa say them nay; the glory of such worship thundered at him from twenty thousand throats made him drunken. There for a while he stood, the newborn sunlight playing upon his splendid form, while the multitude roared his name, proclaiming it divine. His nostrils spread to inhale this incense of adoration, his eyes flashed and slowly he waved his arms, as though in benediction of his worshippers. Perchance there rose before his mind a vision of the wondrous event whereby he, the scorned and penniless outcast, had been lifted to this giddy pinnacle of power. Perchance for a moment he believed that he was indeed divine, that nothing less than the blood and right of godhead could thus have exalted him. At least he stood there, denying naught, while the people adored him as Jehovah is adored of the Jews and Christ is adored of the Christians.

Then of a sudden smote the Angel of the Lord. Of a sudden intolerable pain seized upon his vitals, and Herod remembered that he was but mortal flesh, and knew that death was near.

"Alas!" he cried, "I am no god, but a man, and even now the common fate of man is on me."

As he spoke a great white owl slid from the roof of the canopy above him and vanished through the unroofed centre of the cavea.

"Look! look! my people!" he cried again, "the spirit that brought me good fortune leaves me now, and I die, my people, I die!" Then, sinking upon his throne, he who a moment gone had received the worship of a god, writhed there in agony and wept. Yes, Herod wept.

Attendants ran to him and lifted him in their arms.

"Take me hence to die," he moaned. Now a herald cried:

"The king is smitten with a sore sickness, and the games are closed. To your homes, O people."

For a while the multitude sat silent, for they were fear-stricken. Then a murmur rose among them that spread and swelled till it became a roar.

"The Christians! The Christians! They prophesied the evil. They have bewitched the king. They are wizards. Kill them, kill them, kill them!"

Instantly, like waves pouring in from every side, hundreds and thousands of men began to flow towards that place where the martyrs sat. The walls and palisades were high. Sweeping aside the guards, they surged against them like water against a rock; but climb they could not. Those in front began to scream, those behind pressed on. Some fell and were trodden underfoot, others clambered upon their bodies, in turn to fall and be trodden underfoot.

"Our death is upon us!" cried one of the Nazarenes.

"Nay, life remains to us," answered Nehushta. "Follow me, all of you, for I know the road," and, seizing Rachel about the middle, she began to drag her towards a little door. It was unlocked and guarded by one man only, the apostate jailer Rufus.

"Stand back!" he cried, lifting his spear.

Nehushta made no answer, only drawing a dagger from her robe, she fell upon the ground, then of a sudden rose again beneath his guard. The knife flashed and went home to the hilt. Down fell the man screaming for help and mercy, and there, in the narrow way, his spirit was stamped out of him. Beyond lay the broad passage of the vomitorium. They gained it, and in an instant were mixed with the thousands who sought to escape the panic. Some perished, some were swept onwards, among them Nehushta and Rachel. Thrice they nearly fell, but the fierce strength of the Libyan saved her mistress, till at length they found themselves on the broad terrace facing the seashore.

"Whither now?" gasped Rachel.

"Where shall I lead you?" answered Nehushta. "Do not stay. Be swift."

"But the others?" said Rachel, glancing back at the fighting, trampling, yelling mob.

"God guard them! We cannot."

"Leave me," moaned her mistress. "Save yourself, Nou; I am spent," and she sank down to her knees.

"But I am still strong," muttered Nehushta, and lifting the swooning woman in her sinewy arms, she fled on towards the port, crying, "Way, way for my lady, the noble Roman, who has swooned!"

And the multitude made way.

Chapter 3

The Grain Store

Having passed the outer terraces of the amphitheatre in safety, Nehushta turned down a side street, and paused in the shadow of the wall to think what she should do. So far they were safe; but even if her strength would stand the strain, it seemed impossible that she should carry her mistress through the crowded city and avoid recapture. For some months they had both of them been prisoners, and as it was the custom of the inhabitants of Cæsarea, when they had nothing else to do, to come to the gates of their jail, and, through the bars, to study those within, or even, by permission of the guards, to walk among them, their appearance was known to many. Doubtless, so soon as the excitement caused by the illness of the king had subsided, soldiers would be sent to hunt down the fugitives who had escaped from the amphitheatre. More especially would they search for her, Nehushta, and her mistress, since it would be known that one of them had stabbed the warden of the gate, a crime for which they must expect to die by torture. Also—where could they go who had no friends, since all Christians had been expelled the city?

No, there was but one chance for them—to conceal themselves.

Nehushta looked round her for a hiding-place, and in this matter, as in others on that day, fortune favoured them. This street in the old days, when Cæsarea was called Strato's Tower, had been built upon an inner wall of the city, now long dismantled. At a distance of a few yards from where Nehushta had stopped stood an ancient gateway, unused save at times by beggars who slept under it, which led nowhere, for the outer arch of it was bricked up. Into this gateway Nehushta bore her mistress unobserved, to find to her relief that it was quite untenanted, though a still smouldering fire and a broken amphora containing clean water showed her that folk had slept there who could find no better lodging. So far so good; but here it would be scarcely safe to hide, as the tenants or others might come back. Nehushta looked around. In the thick wall was a little archway, beneath which commenced a stair. Setting Rachel on the ground, she ran up it, lightly as a cat. At the top of thirty steps, many of them broken, she found an old and massive door. With a sigh of disappointment, the Libyan turned to descend again; then, by an afterthought, pushed at the door. To her surprise it stirred. Again she pushed, and it swung open. Within was a large chamber, lighted by loopholes pierced in the thickness of the wall, for the use of archers. Now, however, it served no military purpose, but was used as a storehouse by a merchant of grain, for there in a corner lay a heap of many measures of barley, and strewn about the floor were sacks of skin and other articles.

Nehushta examined the room. No hiding-place could be better—unless the merchant chanced to come to visit his store. Well, that must be risked. Down she sped, and with much toil and difficulty carried her still swooning mistress up the steps and into the chamber, where she laid her on a heap of sacks.

Again, by an afterthought, she ventured to descend, this time to fetch the broken jar of water. Then she closed the door, setting it fast with a piece of wood, and began to chafe Rachel's hands and to sprinkle her face from the jar. Presently the dark eyes opened and her mistress sat up.

"Is it over, and is this Paradise?" she murmured.

"I should not call the place by that name, lady," answered Nehushta, drily, "though perhaps, in contrast with the hell that we have left, some might think it so. Drink!" and she held the water to her lips.

Rachel obeyed her eagerly. "Oh! it is good," she said. "But how came we here out of that rushing crowd?"

Before she answered, muttering "After the mistress, the maid," Nehushta swallowed a deep draught of water in her turn, which, indeed, she needed sorely. Then she told her all.

"Oh! Nou," said Rachel, "how strong and brave you are! But for you I should be dead."

"But for God, you mean, mistress, for I hold that He sent that knife- point home."

"Did you kill the man?" asked Rachel.

"I think that he died by a dagger-thrust as Anna foretold," she answered evasively; "and that reminds me that I had better clean the knife, since blood on the blade is evidence against its owner." Then drawing the dagger from its hiding-place she rubbed it with dust, which she took from a loop-hole, and polished it bright with a piece of hide.

Scarcely was this task accomplished to Nehushta's satisfaction when her quick ears caught a sound.

"For your life, be silent," she whispered, and laid her face sideways to a crack in the cement floor and listened. Well might she listen, for below were three soldiers searching for her and her mistress.

"The old fellow swore that he saw a Libyan woman carrying a lady down this street," said one of them, the petty officer in charge, to his companion, "and there was but a single brown-skin in the lot; so if they aren't here I don't know where they can be."

"Well," grumbled one of the soldiers, "this place is as empty as a drum, so we may as well be going. There'll be fun presently which I don't want to miss."

"It was the black woman who knifed our friend Rufus, wasn't it—in the theatre there?" asked the third soldier.

"They say so; but as he was trodden as flat as a roof-board, and they had to take him up in pieces, it is difficult to know the truth of that matter. Anyhow his mates are anxious to get the lady, and I should be sorry to die as she will, when they do, or her mistress either. They have leave to finish them in their own fashion."

"Hadn't we best be going?" said the first soldier, who evidently was anxious to keep some appointment.

"Hullo!" exclaimed the second, a sharp-eyed fellow, "there's a stair; we had better just look up it."

"Not much use," answered the officer. "That old thief Amram, the corn- merchant, has a store there, and he isn't one of the sort to leave it unlocked. Still, just go and see."

Then came the sound of footsteps on the stair, and presently a man could be heard fumbling at the further side of the door. Rachel shut her eyes and prayed; Nehushta, drawing the knife from her bosom, crept towards the doorway like a tigress, and placed her left hand on the stick that held it shut. Well it was that she did so, since presently the soldier gave a savage push that might easily have caused the wood to slip on the cemented floor. Now, satisfied that it was really locked, he turned and went down the steps.

With a gasp of relief Nehushta once more set her ear to the crack.

"It's fast enough," reported the man, "but perhaps it might be as well to get the key from Amram and have a look."

"Friend," said the officer, "I think that you must be in love with this black lady; or is it her mistress whom you admire? I shall recommend you for the post of Christian-catcher to the cohort. Now we'll try that house at the corner, and if they are not there, I am off to the palace to see how his godship is getting on with that stomach-ache and whether it has moved him to order payment of our arrears. If he hasn't, I tell you flatly that I mean to help myself to something, and so do the rest of the lads, who are mad at the stopping of the games."

"It would be much better to get that key from Amram and have a look upstairs," put in number two soldier reflectively.

"Then go to Amram, or to Pluto, and ask for the key of Hades for aught I care!" replied his superior with irritation. "He lives about a league off at the other end of the town."

"I do not wish for the walk," said the conscientious soldier; "but as we are searching for these escaped Christians, by your leave, I do think it would have been much better to have got that key from Amram and peeped into the chamber upstairs."

Thereon the temper of the officer, already ruffled by the events of the morning and the long watch of the preceding night, gave way, and he departed, consigning the Christians, escaped or recaptured, Amram and the key, his subordinate, and even the royal Agrippa who did not pay his debts, to every infernal god of every religion with which he was acquainted.

Nehushta lifted her head from the floor.

"Thanks be to God! They are gone," she said.

"But, Nou, will they not come back? Oh! I fear lest they should come back."

"I think not. That sharp-nosed rat has made the other angry, and I believe that he will find him some harder task than the seeking of a key from Amram. Still, there is danger that this Amram may appear himself to visit his store, for in these days of festival he is sure to be selling grain to the bakers."

Scarcely were the words out of her mouth when a key rattled, the door was pushed sharply, and the piece of wood slipped and fell. Then the hinges creaked, and Amram—none other—entered, and, closing the door behind him, locked it, leaving the key in the lock.

Amram was a shrewd-faced, middle-aged Phœnician and, like most Phœnicians of that day, a successful trader, this corn-store representing only one branch of his business. For the rest he was clad in a quiet-coloured robe and cap, and to all appearance unarmed.

Having locked the door, he walked to a little table, beneath which stood a box containing his tablets whereon were entered the amounts of corn bought and delivered, to come face to face with Nehushta. Instantly she slid between him and the door.

"Who in the name of Moloch are you?" he asked, stepping back astonished, to perceive as he did so, Rachel seated on the heap of sacks; "and you," he added. "Are you spirits, thieves, ladies in search of a lodging, or—perchance those two Christians whom the soldiers are looking for in yonder house?"

"We are the two Christians," said Rachel desperately. "We fled from the amphitheatre, and have taken refuge here, where they nearly found us."

"This," said Amram solemnly, "comes of not locking one's office. Do not misunderstand me; it was no fault of mine. A certain apprentice is to blame, to whom I shall have a word to say. In fact, I think that I will say it at once," and he stepped towards the door.

"Indeed you will not," interrupted Nehushta.

"And pray, my Libyan friend, how will you prevent me?"

"My putting a knife into your gizzard, as I did through that of the renegade Rufus an hour or two ago! Ah! I see you have heard the story."

Amram considered, then replied:

"And what if I also have a knife?"

"In that case," said Nehushta, "draw it, and we will see which is the better, man or woman. Merchant, your weapon is your pen. You have not a chance with me, an Arab of Libya, and you know it."

"Yes," answered Amram, "I think I do; you desert folk are so reckless and athletic. Also, to be frank, as you may have guessed, I am unarmed. Now, what do you propose?"

"I propose that you get us safely out of Cæsarea, or, if you prefer it, that we shall all die here in this grain-store, for, by whatever god you worship, Phœnician, before a hand is laid upon my mistress or me, this knife goes through your heart. I owe no love to your people, who bought me, a king's daughter, as a slave, and I shall be quite happy to close my account with one of them. Do you understand?"

"Perfectly, perfectly. Why show such temper? The affair is one of business; let us discuss it in a business spirit. You wish to escape from Cæsarea; I wish you to escape from my grain-store. Let me go out and arrange the matter."

"On a plank; not otherwise unless we accompany you," answered Nehushta. "Man, why do you waste words with us. Listen. This lady is the only child of Benoni, the great merchant of Tyre. Doubtless you know him?"

"To my cost," replied Amram, with a bow. "Three times has he overreached me in various bargains."

"Very well; then you know also that he is rich and will pay him liberally who rescues his daughter from great peril."

"He might do so, but I am not sure."

"I am sure," answered Nehushta, "and for this service my mistress here will give you a bill for any reasonable sum drawn upon her father."

"Yes, but the question is—will he honour it? Benoni is a prejudiced man, a very prejudiced man, a Jew of the Jew, who—does not like Christians."

"I think that he will honour it, I believe that he will honour it; but that risk is yours. See here, merchant, a doubtful draft is better than a slit throat."

"Quite so. The argument is excellent. But you desire to escape. If you keep me here, how can I arrange the matter?"

"That is for you to consider. You do not leave this place except in our company, and then at the first sign of danger

I drive this knife home between your shoulders. Meanwhile my mistress is ready to sign any moderate draft upon her father."

"It is not necessary. Under the circumstances I think that I will trust to the generosity of my fellow trader Benoni. Meanwhile I assure you that nothing will give me greater happiness than to fall in with your views. Believe me, I have no prejudice against Christians, since those of them whom I have met were always honest and paid their debts in full. I do not wish to see you or your mistress eaten by lions or tortured. I shall be very glad to think that you are following the maxims of your peculiar faith to an extreme old age, anywhere, outside the limits of my grain-store. The question is, how can I help you do this? At present I see no way."

"The question is—how will you manage to keep your life in you over the next twelve hours?" answered Nehushta grimly. "Therefore I advise you to find a way"; and to emphasise her words she turned, and, having made sure that the door was locked, slipped its key into the bosom of her dress.

Amram stared at her in undisguised admiration. "I would that I were unmarried," he said, "which is not the case," and he sighed; "for then, upon my word, I should be inclined to make a certain proposal to you—"

"Nehushta—that is my name—"

"Nehushta—exactly. Well, it is out of the question."

"Quite."

"Therefore I have a suggestion to make. To-night a ship of mine sails for Tyre. Will you honour me by accepting a passage on her?"

"Certainly," answered Nehushta, "provided that you accompany us."

"It was not my intention to go to Tyre this voyage."

"Then your intention can be changed. Look you, we are desperate, and our lives are at stake. Your life is also at stake, and I swear to you, by the Holy One we worship, that before any harm comes to my mistress you shall die. Then what will your wealth and your schemes avail you in the grave? It is a little thing we ask of you—to help two innocent people to escape from this accursed city. Will you grant it? Or shall I put this dagger through your throat? Answer, and at once, or I strike and bury you in your own corn."

Even in that light Amram turned visibly paler. "I accept your terms," he said. "At nightfall I will conduct you to the ship, which sails two hours after sunset with the evening wind. I will accompany you to Tyre and deliver the lady over to her father, trusting to his liberality for my reward. Meanwhile, this place is hot. That ladder leads to the roof, which is parapeted, so that those sitting or even standing there, cannot be seen. Shall we ascend?"

"If you go first; and remember, should you attempt to call out, my knife is always ready."

"Of that I am quite aware—you have said so several times. I have passed my words, and I do not go back upon my bargains. The stars are with you, and, come what may, I obey them."

Accordingly they ascended to the roof, Amram going first, Nehushta following him, and Rachel bringing up the rear. On it, projecting inward from the parapet, was a sloping shelter once made use of by the look-out sentry in bad or hot weather. The change from the stifling store below with its stench of ill-cured hides, to this lofty, shaded spot, where the air moved freely, was so pleasant to Rachel, outworn as she was with all she had gone through, that presently she fell asleep, not to wake again till evening. Nehushta, however, who did not go to sleep, and Amram, employed themselves in watching the events that passed in the city below. From this height they could see the great square surrounding the palace, and the strange scenes being enacted therein. It was crowded by thousands of people, for the most part seated on the ground, clad in garments of sack-cloth and throwing dust upon the heads of themselves, their wives and children. From all this multitude a voice of supplication rose to heaven, which, even at that distance, reached the ears of Nehushta and her companion in a murmur of sound, constant and confused.

"They pray that the king may live," said Amram.

"And I pray that he may die," answered Nehushta.

The merchant shrugged his shoulders. "I care nothing either way, provided that the peace is not disturbed to the injury of trade. On the whole, however, he is a good king who causes money to be spent, which is what kings are for—in Judæa—where they are but feathers puffed up by the breath of Cæsar, to fall if he cease to blow. But look!"

As he spoke, a figure appeared upon the steps of the palace who made some communication to the crowd, whereon a great wail went up to the very skies.

"You have your wish," said Amram; "Herod is dead or dying, and now, I suppose, as his son is but a child, that we shall be ruled by some accursed thief of a Roman procurator with a pocket like a sack without a bottom. Surely that old bishop of yours who preached in the amphitheatre this morning, must have had a hint of what was coming, from his familiar spirit; or perhaps he saw the owl and guessed its errand. Moreover, I think that troubles are brewing for others besides Herod, since the old man said as much.

"What became of him and the rest?" asked Nehushta.

"Oh! a few were trampled to death, and others the Jews stirred up the mob to stone, saying that they had bewitched the king, which they, who were disappointed of the games, did gladly. Some, however, are said to have escaped, and, like yourselves, lie in hiding."

Nehushta glanced at her mistress, now fast asleep, her pale face resting on her arm.

"The world is hard—for Christians," she said.

"Friend, it is hard for all, as, were I to tell you my own story, even you would admit," and he sighed. "At least you Christians believe in something beyond," he went on; "for you death is but a bridge leading to a glorious city, and I trust that you may be right. Is not your mistress delicate?"

Nehushta nodded.

"She was never very strong, and sorrow has done its work with her. They killed her husband at Berytus yonder, and—her trouble is very near."

"Yes, yes, I heard that story, also that his blood is on the hands of her own father, Benoni. Ah! who is so cruel as a bigot Jew? Not we Phœnicians even, of whom they say such evil. Once I had a daughter"—here his hard face softened—"but let be, let be! Look you, the risk is great, but what I can do I will do to save her, and you also, friend, since, Libyan or no, you are a faithful woman. Nay, do not doubt me. I have given my word, and if I break it willingly, then may I perish and be devoured of dogs. My ship is small and undecked. In that she shall not sail, but a big galley weighs for Alexandria to-night, calling at Apollonia and Joppa, and in it I will take you passages, saying that the lady is a relative of mine and that you are her slave. This is my advice to you—that you go straight to Egypt, where there are many Christians who will protect you for a while. Thence your mistress can write to her father, and if he will receiver her, return. If not, at least she will be safe, since no writ of Herod runs in Alexandria, and there they do not love the Jews."

"Your counsel seems good," said Nehushta, "if she will consent to it."

"She must consent who, indeed, is in no case to make other plans. Now let me go. Before nightfall I will return again with food and clothing, and lead you to the ship."

Nehushta hesitated.

"I say to you, do not fear. Will you not trust me?"

"Yes," answered Nehushta, "because I must. Nay, the words are not kind, but we are sadly placed, and it is strange to find a true friend in one whom I have threatened with a knife."

"I understand," said Amram gravely. "Let the issue prove me. Now descend that you may lock the door behind me. When I return I will stand in the open space yonder with a slave, making pretence to re- bind a burst bundle of merchandise. Then come down and admit me without fear."

When the Phœnician had gone Nehushta sat by her sleeping mistress, and waited with an anxious heart. Had she done wisely? Would Amram betray them and send soldiers to conduct them, not to the ship, but to some dreadful death? Well, if so, at least she would have time to kill her mistress and herself, and thus escape the cruelties of men. Meanwhile she could only pray; and pray she did in her fierce, half-savage fashion, never for herself, but for her mistress whom she loved, and for the child that, she remembered thankfully, Anna had foretold would be born and live out its life. Then she remembered also that this same holy woman had said that its mother's hours would be few, and at the thought Nehushta wept.

Chapter 4

The Birth of Miriam

The time passed slowly, but none came to disturb them. Three hours after noon Rachel awoke, refreshed but hungry, and Nehushta had no food to give her except raw grain, from which she turned. Clearly and in few words she told her mistress all that had passed, asking her consent to the plan.

"It seems good as another," said Rachel with a little sigh, "and I thank you for making it, Nou, and the Phœnician, if he is a true man. Also I do not desire to meet my father—at least, for many years. How can I, seeing the evil which he has brought upon me?"

"Do not speak of that," interrupted Nehushta hastily, and for a long while they were silent.

It was an hour before sunset, or a little less, when at length Nehushta saw two persons walk on to the patch of open ground which she watched continually—Amram and a slave who bore a bundle on his head. Just then the rope which bound this bundle seemed to come loose; at least, at his master's command, the man set it down and they began to retie it, then advanced slowly towards the archway. Now Nehushta descended, unlocked the door and admitted Amram, who carried the bundle.

"Where is the slave?" she asked.

"Have no fear, friend; he is trusty and watches without, not knowing why. Come, you must both of you be hungry, and I have food. Help me loose this cord."

Presently the package was undone, and within it appeared, first, two flagons of old wine, then meats more tasty then Nehushta had seen for months, then rich cloaks and other garments made in the Phœnician fashion, and a robe of white with coloured edges, such as was worn by the body-slaves of the wealthy among that people. Lastly—and this Amram produced from his own person—there was a purse of gold, enough to support them for many weeks. Nehushta thanked him with her eyes, and was about to speak.

"There, say nothing," he interrupted. "I passed my word, and I have kept it, that is all. Also on this money I shall charge interest, and your mistress can repay it in happier days. Now listen: I have taken the passages, and an hour after sunset we will go aboard. Only I warn you, do not let it be known that you are escaped Christians, for the seamen think that such folk bring them bad luck. Come, help me carry the food and wine. After you have eaten you can both of you retire here and robe yourselves."

Presently they were on the roof.

"Lady," said Nehushta, "we did well to put faith in this man. He has come back, and see what he has brought us."

"The blessing of God be on you, sir, who help the helpless!" exclaimed Rachel, looking hungrily at the tempting meats which she so sorely needed.

"Drink," said Amram cheerfully, as he poured wine and water into a cup; "it will hearten you, and your faith does not forbid the use of the grape, for have I not heard you styled the society of drunkards?"

"That is only one bad name among many, sir," said Rachel, as she took the cup.

Then they ate and were satisfied, and afterwards descended into the corn-store to wash with the remainder of the water, and clothe themselves from head to foot in the fragrant and beautiful garments that might have been made for their wear, so well had Amram judged their sizes and needs.

By the time that they were dressed the light was dying. Still, they waited a while for the darkness; then, with a new hope shining through their fears, crept silently into the street, where the slave, a sturdy, well-armed fellow, watched for them.

"To the quay," said Amram, and they walked forward, choosing those thoroughfares that were most quiet. It was well for them that they did this, for now it was known that Agrippa's sickness was mortal, the most of the soldiers were already in a state of mutiny, and, inflamed with wine, paraded the market-places and larger streets, shouting and singing obscene songs, and breaking into the liquor shops and private houses, where they drank healths to Charon, who was about to bear away their king in his evil bark. As yet, however, they had not begun killing those against whom they had a grudge. This happened afterwards, though it has nothing to do with our story.

Without trouble or molestation the party reached the quay, where a small boat with two Phœnician rowers was waiting for them. In it they embarked, except the slave, and were rowed out to the anchorage to board a large galley which lay half a mile or more away. This they did without difficulty, for the night was calm, although the air hung thick and heavy, and jagged clouds, wind-breeders as they were called, lay upon the horizon. On the lower deck of the galley stood its captain, a sour-faced man, to whom Amram introduced his passengers, who were, as he declared, relatives of his own proceeding to Alexandria.

"Good," said the captain. "Show them to their cabin, for we sail as soon as the wind rises."

To the cabin they went accordingly, a comfortable place stored with all that they could need; but as they passed to it Nehushta heard a sailor, who held a lantern in his hand, say to his companion:

"That woman is very like one whom I saw in the amphitheatre this morning when they gave the salute to King Agrippa."

"The gods forbid it!" answered the other. "We want no Christians here to bring evil fortune on us."

"Christians or no Christians, there is a tempest brewing, if I understand the signs of the weather," muttered the first man.

In the cabin Amram bade his guests farewell.

"This is a strange adventure," he said, "and one that I did not look for. May it prove to the advantage of us all. At the least I have done my best for your safety, and now we part."

"You are a good man," replied Rachel, "and whatever may befall us, I pray again that God may bless you for your kindness to His servants. I pray also that He may lead you to a knowledge of the truth as it was declared by the Lord and Master Whom we serve, that your soul may win salvation and eternal life."

"Lady," said Amram, "I know nothing of these doctrines, but I promise you this: that I will look into them and see whether or no they commend themselves to my reason. I love wealth, like all my people, but I am not altogether a time-server, or a money-seeker. Lady, I have lost those whom I desire to find again."

"Seek and you will find."

"I will seek," he answered, "though, mayhap, I shall never find."

Thus they parted.

Presently the night breeze began to flow off the land, the great sail was hoisted, and with the help of oars, worked by slaves, the ship cleared the harbour and set her course for Joppa. Two hours later the wind failed so that they could proceed only by rowing over a dead and oily sea, beneath a sky that was full of heavy clouds. Lacking any stars to steer by, the captain wished to cast anchor, but as the water proved too deep they proceeded slowly, till about an hour before dawn a sudden gust struck them which caused the galley to lean over.

"The north wind! The black north wind!" shouted the steersman, and the sailors echoed his cry dismally, for they knew the terrors of that wind upon the Syrian coast. Then the gale began to rage. By daylight the waves were running high as mountains and the wind hissed through the rigging, driving them forward beneath a small sail. Nehushta crawled out of the cabin, and, in the light of an angry dawn, saw far away the white walls of a city built near the shore.

"Is not that Appolonia?" she asked of the captain.

"Yes," he answered, "it is Appolonia sure enough, but we shall not anchor there this voyage. Now it is Alexandria for us or nothing."

So they rushed past Appolonia and forward, climbing the slopes of the rising seas.

Thus things went on. About mid-day the gale became a hurricane, and do what they would they were driven forward, till at length they saw the breakers forming on the coast. Rachel lay sick and prostrate, but Nehushta went out of the cabin to watch.

"Are we in danger?" she asked of a sailor.

"Yes, accursed Christian," he replied, "and you have brought it on us with your evil eye."

Then Nehushta returned to the cabin where her mistress lay almost senseless with sea-sickness. On board the ship the terror and confusion grew. For a while they were able to beat out to sea until the mast was carried away. Then the rudder broke, and, as the oars could not be worked in that fearful tempest, the galley began to drive shorewards. Night fell, and who can describe the awful hours that followed? All control of the vessel being lost, she drove onwards whither the wind and the waves took her. The crew, and even the oar- slaves, flew to the wine with which she was partly laden, and strove to drown their terrors in drink. Thus inflamed, twice some of them came to the cabin, threatening to throw their passengers overboard. But Nehushta barred the door and called through it that she was well armed and would kill the first man who tried to lay a hand upon her. So they went away, and after the second visit grew too drunken to be dangerous.

Again the dawn broke over the roaring, foaming sea and revealed the fate that awaited them. Not a mile away lay the grey line of shore, and between them and it a cruel reef on which the breakers raged. Towards this reef they were driving fast. Now the men grew sober in their fear, and began to build a large raft of oars and timber; also to make ready the boat which the galley carried. Before all was done she struck beak first, and was lifted on to a great flat rock, where she wallowed, with the water seething round her. Then, knowing that their hour was come, the crew made shift to launch the boat and raft on the lee side, and began to clamber into them. Now Nehushta came out of the cabin and prayed the captain to save them also, whereon he answered her with an oath that this bad luck was because of them, and that if either she or her mistress tried to enter the boat, they would stab them and cast them into the sea as an offering to the storm-god.

So Nehushta struggled back to the cabin, and kneeling by the side of her mistress, with tears told her that these black-hearted sailors had left them alone upon the ship to drown. Rachel answered that she cared little, but only desired to be free of her fear and misery.

As the words left her lips, Nehushta heard a sound of screaming, and crawling to the bulwarks, looked forth to see a dreadful sight. The boat and the raft, laden with a great number of men who were fighting for places with each other, having loosed from the lee of the ship, were come among the breakers, which threw them up as a child throws a ball at play. Even while Nehushta gazed, their crafts were overturned, casting them into the water, every one there to be dashed against the rocks or drowned by the violence of the waves, so that not a man of all that ship's company came living to the shore.

Like tens of thousands of others on this coast in all ages, they perished, every one of them—and that was the reward of their wickedness.

Giving thanks to God, Who had brought them out of

that danger against their wills, Nehushta crept back to the cabin and told her mistress what had passed.

"May they find pardon," said Rachel, shuddering; "but as for us, it will matter little whether we are drowned in the boat or upon the galley."

"I do not think that we shall drown," answered Nehushta.

"How are we to escape it, Nou? The ship lies upon the rock, where the great waves will batter her to pieces. Feel how she shakes beneath their blows, and see the spray flying over us."

"I do not know, mistress; but we shall not drown."

Nehushta was right, for after they had remained fast a little longer they were saved, thus: Suddenly the wind dropped, then it rose again in a last furious squall, driving before it a very mountain of water. This vast billow, as it rushed shorewards, caught the galley in its white arms and lifted her not only off the rock whereon she lay, but over the further reefs, to cast her down again upon a bed of sand and shells, within a stone's throw of the beach, where she remained fast, never to shift more.

Now also, as though its work were done, the gale ceased, and, as is common on the Syrian coast, the sea sank rapidly, so that by nightfall it was calm again. Indeed, three hours before sunset, had both of them been strong and well, they might have escaped to the land by wading. But this was not to be, for now what Nehushta had feared befell, and when she was least fitted to bear it, being worn out with anguish of mind and weariness of body, pain took sudden hold of Rachel, of which the end was that, before midnight, there, in that broken vessel upon a barren coast where no man seemed to live, a daughter was born to her.

"Let me see the child," said Rachel. So Nehushta showed it to her by the light of a lamp which burned in the cabin.

It was a small child, but very white, with blue eyes and dark hair that curled. Rachel gazed at it long and tenderly. Then she said, "Bring me water while there is yet time."

When the water was brought she dipped her trembling hand into it, and made the sign of the Cross upon the babe's forehead, baptising her with the name of Miriam, after that of her own mother, to the service and the company of Jesus the Christ.

"Now," she said, "whether she live an hour or an hundred years, this child is a Christian, and whatever befalls, should she come to the age of understanding, see to it, Nou, who are henceforth the foster-mother of her body and her soul, that she does not forget the rites and duties of her faith. Lay this charge on her also as her father commanded, and as I command, that should she be moved to marriage, she wed none who is not a Christian. Tell her that such was the will of those who begat her, and that if she be obedient to it, although they are dead, and as it seems strengthless, yet shall their blessing be upon her all her life's days, and with it the blessing of the Lord she serves."

"Oh!" moaned Nehushta, "why do you speak thus?"

"Because I am dying. Gainsay me not. I know it well. My life ebbs from me. My prayers have been answered, and I was preserved to give this infant birth; now I go to my appointed place and to one who waits for me, and to the Lord in Whose care he is in Heaven, as we are in His care on earth. Nay, do not mourn; it is no fault of yours, nor could any physician's skill have saved me, whose strength was spent in suffering, and who for many months have walked the world, bearing in my breast a broken heart. Give me of that wine to drink—and listen."

Nehushta obeyed and Rachel went on: "So soon as my breath has left me, take the babe and seek some village on the shore where it can be nursed, for which service you have the means to pay. Then when she is strong enough and it is convenient, travel, not to Tyre—for there my father would bring up the child in the strictest rites and customs of the Jews—but to the village of the Essenes upon the shores of the Dead sea. There find out my mother's brother, Ithiel, who is of their society, and present to him the tokens of my name and birth which still hang about my neck, and tell him all the story, keeping nothing back. He is not a Christian, but he is a good and gentle-hearted man who thinks well of Christians, and is grieved at their persecution, since he wrote to my father reproving him for his deeds towards us and, as you know, strove, but in vain, to bring about our release from prison. Say to him that I, his kinswoman, pray of him, as he will answer to God, and in the name of the sister whom he loved, to protect my child and you; to do nothing to turn her from her faith, and in all things to deal with her as his wisdom shall direct—for so shall peace and blessing come upon him."

Thus spoke Rachel, but in short and broken words. Then she began to pray, and, praying, fell asleep. When she woke again the dawn was breaking. Signing to Nehushta to bring her the child, for now she could no longer speak, she scanned it earnestly in the new-born light, then placed her hand upon its head and blessed it. Nehushta she blessed also, thanking her with her eyes and kissing her. Then again she seemed to fall asleep, and presently, when Nehushta looked at her, Rachel was dead.

Nehushta understood and gave a great and bitter cry, since to her after the death of her first mistress, this woman had been all her life. As a child she had nursed her; as a maiden shared her joys and sorrows; as a wife and widow toiled day and night fiercely and faithfully to console her in her desolation and to protect her in the dreadful dangers through which she had passed. Now, to end it all, it was her lot to receive her last breath and to take into her arms her new-born infant.

Then and there Nehushta swore that as she had done by the mother she so would do by the child till the day when her labours ended. Were it not for this child, indeed, they would have ended now, Christian though she was, since she was crushed with bitter sorrow and her heart seemed void of hope or joy. All her days had been hard—she who was born to great place among her own wild people far away, and snatched thence to be a slave, set apart by her race and blood from those into whose city she was sold; she who would have naught to do with base men nor become the plaything of those of higher birth; she who had turned Christian and drunk deep of the tribulations of the faith; she who had centred all her eager heart upon two beloved women, and lost them both. All her days had been hard, and here and now, by the side of her dead mistress, she would have ended them. But the child remained, and while it lived, she would live. If it died, then perhaps she would die also.

Meanwhile Nehushta had no time for grief, since the babe must be fed, and within twelve hours. Yet, as she could not bury her, and would not throw her to the sharks, she was minded to give her mistress a royal funeral after the custom of her own Libyan folk. Here was flame, and what pyre could be grander than this great ship?

Lifting the body from its couch, Nehushta carried it to the deck and laid it by the broken mast, closing the eyes and folding the hands. Then she loosened from about the neck those tokens of which Rachel had spoken, made some food and garments into a bundle, and, carrying the lamp with her, went into the captain's cabin amidships. Here a money- box was open, and in it gold and some jewels which this man had abandoned in his haste. These she took, adding them to her own store and securing them about her. This done she fired the cabin, and passing to the hold, broke a jar of oil and fired that also. Then she fled back again, knelt by her dead mistress and kissed her, took the child, wrapping it warmly in a shawl, and by the ladder of rope which the sailors had used, let herself down into the quiet sea. Its waters did not reach higher than her middle, and soon she was standing on the shore and climbing the sandhills that lay beyond. At their summit she turned to look, and lo! yonder where the galley was, already a great pillar of fire shot up to heaven, for there was much oil in the hold and it burnt furiously.

"Farewell!" she cried, "farewell!"

Then, weeping bitterly, Nehushta walked on inland.

Chapter 5

Miriam Is Enthroned

Presently Nehushta found herself out of sight of the sea and among cultivated land, for here were vines and fig trees grown in gardens fenced with stone walls; also patches of ripening barley and of wheat in the ear, much trodden down as though horses had been feeding there. Beyond these gardens she came to a ridge, and saw beneath her a village of many houses of green brick, some of which seemed to have been destroyed by fire. Into this village she walked boldly, and there the first sight that met her eyes was that of sundry dead bodies, upon which dogs were feeding.

On she went up the main street, till she saw a woman peeping at her over a garden wall.

"What has chanced here?" asked Nehushta, in the Syrian tongue.

"The Romans! the Romans! the Romans!" wailed the woman. "The head of our village quarrelled with the taxgatherers, and refused to pay his dues to Cæsar. So the soldiers came a week ago and slaughtered nearly all of us, and took such sheep and cattle as they could find, and with them many of the young folk, to be sold as slaves, so that the rest are left empty and desolate. Such are the things that chance in this unhappy land. But, woman, who are you?"

"I am one shipwrecked!" answered Nehushta, "and I bear with me a new- born babe—nay, the story is too long to tell you; but if in this place there is any one who can nurse the babe, I will pay her well."

"Give it me!" said the woman, in an eager whisper; "my child perished in the slaughter; I ask no reward."

Nehushta looked at her. Her eyes were wild, but she was still young and healthy, a Syrian peasant.

"Have you a house?" she asked.

"Yes, it still stands, and my husband lives; we hid in a cave, but alas! they slew the infant that was out with the child of a neighbour. Quick, give me the babe."

So Nehushta gave it to her, and thus Miriam was nurtured at the breast of one whose offspring had been murdered because the head of the village had quarrelled with a Roman tax-collector. Such was the world in the days when Christ came to save it.

After she had suckled the child the woman led Nehushta to her house, a humble dwelling that had escaped the fire, where they found the husband, a wine-grower, mourning the death of his infant and the ruin of his town. To him she told as much of her story as she thought well, and proffered him a gold piece, which, so she swore, was one of ten she had about her. He took it gladly, for now he was penniless, and promised her lodging and protection, and the service of his wife as nurse to the child for a month at least. So there Nehushta stayed, keeping herself hid, and at the end of the month gave another gold piece to her hosts, who were kindly folk that never dreamed of working her evil or injustice. Seeing this, Nehushta found yet more money, wherewith the man, blessing her, bought two oxen and a plough, and hired labour to help him gather what remained of his harvest.

The shore where the infant was born upon the wrecked ship, was at a distance of about a league from Joppa and two days' journey from Jerusalem, whence the Dead Sea could be reached in another two days. When Nehushta had dwelt there for some six months, as the babe throve and was hearty, she offered to pay the man and his wife three more pieces of gold if they would travel with her to the neighbourhood of Jericho, and, further, to purchase a mule and an ass for the journey, which she would give to them when it was accomplished. The eyes of these simple folk glistened at the prospect of so much wealth, and they agreed readily, promising also to stay three months by Jericho, if need were, till the child could be weaned. So a man was hired to guard the house and vines, and they started in the late autumn, when the air was cool and pleasant.

Of their journey nothing need be said, save that they accomplished it without trouble, being too humble in appearance to attract the notice of the thieves who swarmed upon the highways, or of the soldiers who were set to catch the thieves.

Skirting Jerusalem, which they did not enter, on the sixth day they descended into the valley of the Jordan, through the desolate hills by which it is bordered. Camping that night outside the town, at daybreak on the seventh morning they started, and by two hours after noon came to the village of the Essenes. On its outskirts they halted, while Nehushta and the nurse, bearing with them the child, that by now could wave its arms and crow, advanced boldly into the village, where it would appear men dwelt only—at least no women were to be seen—and asked to be led to the Brother Ithiel.

The man to whom they spoke, who was robed in white, and engaged in cooking outside a large building, averted his eyes in answering, as though it were not lawful for him to look upon the face of a woman. He said, very civilly, however, that Brother Ithiel was working in the fields, whence he would not return till supper time.

Nehushta asked where these fields were, since she desired to speak with him at once. The man answered that if they walked towards the green trees that lined the banks of Jordan, which he pointed out to them, they could not fail to find Ithiel, as he was ploughing in the irrigated land with two white oxen, the only ones they had. Accordingly they set out again, having the Dead Sea on their right, and travelled for the half of a league through the thorn-scrub that grows in this desert. Passing the scrub they came to lands which were well cultivated and supplied with water from the Jordan by means of wheels and long poles with a jar at one end and a weight at the other, which a man could work, emptying the contents of the jar again and again into an irrigation ditch.

In one of these fields they saw the two white oxen at their toil, and behind them the labourer, a tall man of about fifty years of age, bearded, and having a calm face and eyes that were very deep and quiet. He was clad in a rough robe of camel's hair, fastened about his middle with a leathern girdle, and wore sandals on his feet. To him they went, asking leave to speak with him, whereon he halted the oxen and greeted them courteously, but, like the man in the village, turned his eyes away from the faces of the women. Nehushta bade the nurse stand back out of hearing, and, bearing the child in her arms, said:

"Sir, tell me, I pray you, if I speak to Ithiel, a priest of high rank among this people of the Essenes, and brother to the dead lady Miriam, wife of Benoni the Jew, a merchant of Tyre?"

At the mention of these names Ithiel's face saddened, then grew calm again.

"I am so called," he answered; "and the lady Miriam is my sister, who now dwells in the happy and eternal country beyond the ocean with all the blessed"—for so the Essenes imagined that heaven to which they went when the soul was freed from the vile body.

"The lady Miriam," continued Nehushta, "had a daughter Rachel, whose servant I was."

"Was?" he interrupted, startled from his calm. "Has she then been put to death by those fierce men and their king, as was as her husband Demas?"

"Nay, sir, but she died in childbirth, and this is the babe she bore"; and she held the sleeping little one towards him, at whom he gazed earnestly, yes, and bent down and kissed it—since, although they saw so few of them, the Essenes loved children.

"Tell me that sad story," he said.

"Sir, I will both tell it and prove it to be true"; and Nehushta told him all from the beginning to the end, producing to his sight the tokens which she had taken from the breast of her mistress, and repeating her last message to him word for word. When she had finished, Ithiel turned away and mourned a while. Then, speaking aloud, he put up a prayer to God for guidance—for without prayer these people would not enter upon anything, however simple—and came back to Nehushta, who stood by the oxen.

"Good and faithful woman," he said, "who it would seem are not fickle and light-hearted, or worse, like the multitude of your sex—perchance because your dark skin shields you from their temptations—you have set me in a cleft stick, and there I am held fast. Know that the rule of my order is that we should have naught to do with females, young or old; therefore how can I receive you or the child?"

"Of the rules of your order, sir, I know nothing," answered Nehushta sharply, since the words about the colour of her skin had not pleased her; "but of the rules of nature I do know, and something of the rules of God also, for, like my mistress and this infant, I am a Christian. These tell me, all of them, that to cast out an orphan child who is of your own blood, and whom a cruel fortune has thus brought to your door, would be an evil act, and one for which you must answer to Him who is above the rules of any order."

"I may not wrangle, especially with a woman," replied Ithiel, who seemed ill at ease; "but if my first words are true, this is true also, that those same rules enjoin upon us hospitality, and above all, that we must not turn away the helpless or the destitute."

"Clearly, then, sir, least of any must you turn away this child whose blood is your blood, and those dead mother sent her to you, that she might not fall into the power of a grandfather who has dealt so cruelly with those he should have cherished, to be brought up among Zealots as a Jew and taught to make offering of living things, and be anointed with the oil and blood of sacrifice."

"No, no, the thought is horrible," answered Ithiel, holding up his hands. "It is better, far better that she should be a Christian than one of that fanatic and blood-spilling faith." This he said, because among the Essenes the use of oil was held to be unclean. Also above all things, they loathed the offering of life in sacrifice to God; who, although they did not acknowledge Christ—perhaps because He was never preached to them, who would listen to no new religion—practised the most of His doctrines with the greatest strictness.

"The matter is too hard for me," he went on. "I must lay it before a full Court of the hundred curators, and what they decide, that will be done. Still, this is our rule: to assist those who need and to show mercy, to accord succour to such as deserve it, and to give food to those in distress. Therefore, whatever the Court, which it will take three days to summon, may decide, in the meanwhile I have the right to give you, and those with you, shelter and provision in the guest- house. As it chances, it is situated in that part of the village where dwell the lowest of our brethren, who are permitted to marry, so there you will find company of your own sex."

"I shall be glad of it," answered Nehushta drily. "Also I should call them the highest of the brethren, since marriage is a law of God, which God the Father has instituted, and God the Son has blessed."

"I may not wrangle, I may not wrangle," replied Ithiel, declining the encounter; "but certainly, that is a lovely babe. Look. Its eyes are open and they are beautiful as flowers"; and again he bent down and kissed the child, then added with a groan of remorse, "Alas! sinner that I am, I am defiled; I must purify myself and do penance."

"Why?" asked Nehushta shortly.

"For two reasons: I have touched your dress, and I have

given way to earthly passion and embraced a child—twice. Therefore, according to our rule, I am defiled."

Then Nehushta could bear it no more.

"Defiled! you puppet of a foolish rule! It is the sweet babe that is defiled! Look, you have fouled its garments with your grimy hand and made it weep by pricking it with your beard. Would that your holy rule taught you how to handle children and to respect honest women who are their mothers, without whom there would be no Essenes."

"I may not wrangle," said Ithiel, nervously; for now woman was appearing before him in a new light; not as an artful and a fickle, but as an angry creature, reckless of tongue and not easy to be answered. "These matters are for the decision of the curators. Have I not told you so? Come, let us be going. I will drive the oxen, although it is not time to loose them from the plough, and do you and your companion walk at a distance behind me. No, not behind—in front, that I may see that you do not drop the babe, or suffer it to come to any harm. Truly it is sweet to look at, and, may God forgive me, I do not like to lose sight of its face, which, it seems to me, resembles that of my sister when she was also in arms."

"Drop the babe!" began Nehushta; then understanding that this victim of a rule already loved it dearly, and would suffer much before he parted with it, pitying his weakness, she said only, "Be careful that you do not frighten it with your great oxen, for you men who scorn women have much to learn."

Then, accompanied by the nurse, she stalked ahead in silence, while Ithiel followed after at a distance, leading the cattle by the hide loops about their horns, lest in their curiosity or eagerness to get home, they should do some mischief to the infant or wake it from its slumbers. In this way they proceeded to the lower part of the village, till they came to a good house—empty as it chanced—where guests were accommodated in the best fashion that this kind and homely folk could afford. Here a woman was summoned, the wife of one of the lower order of the Essenes, to whom Ithiel spoke, holding his hand before his eyes, as though she were not good to look at. To her, from a distance, he explained the case, bidding her to provide all things needful, and to send a man to bring in the husband of the nurse with the beasts of burden, and attend to his wants and theirs. Then, warning Nehushta to be very careful of the infant and not to expose it to the sun, he departed to report the matter to the curators, and to summon the great Court.

"Are all of them like this?" asked Nehushta of the woman, contemptuously.

"Yes, sister," she answered, "fools, every one. Why, of my own husband I see little; and although, being married, he ranks but low among them, the man is forever telling me of the faults of our sex, and how they are a snare set for the feet of the righteous, and given to the leading of these same righteous astray, especially if they be not their own husbands. At times I am tempted indeed to prove his words true. Oh! it would not be difficult for all their high talk; I have learned as much as that, for Nature is apt to make a mock of those who deny Nature, and there is no parchment rule that a woman cannot bring to nothing. Yet, since they mean well, laugh at them and let them be, say I. And now come into the house, which is good, although did women manage it, it would be better."

So Nehushta went into that house with the nurse and her husband, and there for several days dwelt in great comfort. Indeed, there was nothing that she or the child, or those with them, could want which was not provided in plenty. Messages reached her even, through the woman, to ask if she would wish the rooms altered in any way, and when she said that there was not light enough in that in which the child slept, some of the elders of the Essenes arrived and pierced a new window in the wall, working very hard to finish the task before sunset. Also even the husband of the nurse was not allowed to attend to his own beasts, which were groomed and fed for him, till at length he grew so weary of doing nothing, that on the third day he went out to plough with the Essenes and worked in the fields till dark.

It was on the fourth morning that the full Court gathered in the great meeting-house, and Nehushta was summoned to appear before it, bringing the babe with her. Thither she went accordingly, to find the place filled with a hundred grave and reverend men, all clad in robes of the purest white. In the lower part of that large chamber she sat alone upon a chair, while before her upon benches ranged one above the other, so that all could see, were gathered the hundred curators.

It seemed that Ithiel had already set out the case, since the President at once began to question her on various points of her story, all of which she was able to explain to the satisfaction of the Court. Then they debated the matter among themselves, some of them arguing that as the child was a female, as well as its nurse, neither of them could properly be admitted to the care of the community, especially as both were of the Christian faith, and it was stipulated that in this faith they should remain. Others answered that hospitality was their first duty, and that he would be weak indeed who was led aside from their rule by a Libyan woman of middle age and an infant of a few months. Further, that the Christians were a good people, and that there was much in their doctrines which tallied with their own. Next, one made a strange objection—namely, that if they adopted this child they would learn to love it too much, who should love God and their order only. To this another answered, Nay, they should love all mankind, and especially the helpless.

"Mankind, not womankind," was the reply; "for this infant will grow into a woman."

Now they desired Nehushta to retire that they might take the votes. Before she went, however, holding up the child that all could see it as it lay smiling in her arms, she implored them not to reject the prayer of a dead woman, and so deprive this infant of the care of the relative whom that departed lady had appointed to be its guardian, and of the guidance and directing wisdom of their holy Order. Lastly, she reminded them that if they thrust her out, she must carry the infant to its grandfather, who, if he received it at all, would certainly bring it up in the Jewish faith, and thereby, perhaps, cause it to lose its soul, the weight of which sin would be upon their heads.

After this Nehushta was led away to another chamber and remained there a long while, till at length she was brought back again by one of the curators. On entering the great hall her eyes sought the face of Ithiel, who had not been allowed to speak, since the matter having to do with a great-niece of his own, it was held that his judgment might be warped. Seeing that he smiled, and evidently was well pleased, she knew her cause was won.

"Woman," said the President, "by a great majority of this Court we have come to an irrevocable decision upon the matter that has been laid before it by our brother Ithiel. It is, for reasons which I need not explain, that on this point our rule may be stretched so far as to admit the child Miriam to our care, even though it be of the female sex, which care is to endure until she comes to a full age of eighteen years, when she must depart from among us. During this time no attempt will be made to turn her from her parents' faith in which she has been baptised. A house will be given you to live in, and you will be supplied with the best we have for the use of our ward Miriam and yourself. Twice a week a deputation of the curators will visit the house, and stay there for an hour to see that the health of the infant is good, and that you are doing your duty by it, in which, if you fail, you will be removed. It is prayed that you will not talk to these curators on matters which do not concern the child. When she grows old enough the maid Miriam will be admitted to our gatherings, and instructed also by the most learned amongst us in all proper matters of letters and philosophy, on which occasions you will sit at a distance and not interfere unless your care is required.

"Now, that every one may know our decision, we will escort you back to your house, and to show that we have taken the infant under our care, our brother Ithiel will carry it while you walk behind and give him such instruction in this matter as may be needful."

Accordingly a great procession was formed, headed by the President and ended by the priests. In the centre of the line marched Ithiel bearing the babe Miriam, to his evident delight, and Nehushta, who instructed him so vigorously that at length he grew confused and nearly let it fall. Thereon, setting this detail of the judgment at defiance, Nehushta snatched it from his arms, calling him a clumsy and ignorant clown only fit to handle an ox. To this Ithiel made no answer, nor was he at all wroth, but finished the journey walking behind her and smiling foolishly.

Thus was the child Miriam, who afterwards came to be called the Queen of the Essenes, royally escorted to her home. But little did these good men know that it was not a house which they were giving her, but a throne, built of the pure gold of their own gentle hearts.

Chapter 6

Caleb

It may be wondered whether any girl who was ever born into the world could boast a stranger or a happier upbringing than Miriam. She was, it is true, motherless, but by way of compensation Fate endowed her with several hundred fathers, each of whom loved her as the apple of his eye. She did not call them "Father" indeed, a term which under the circumstances they thought incorrect. To her, one and all, they went by the designation of "Uncle," with their name added if she happened to know it, if not as Uncle simply. It cannot be said, however, that Miriam brought peace to the community of the Essenes. Indeed, before she had done with them she rent it with deep and abiding jealousies, to the intense but secret delight of Nehushta, who, although she became a person of great importance among them as the one who had immediate charge of their jewel, could never forgive them certain of their doctrines or their habit of persistent interference.

The domiciliary visits which took place twice a week, and, by special subsequent resolution passed in full Court, on the Sabbath also, were, to begin with, the subject of much covert bitterness. At first a standing committee was appointed to make these visits, of whom Ithiel was one.

Before two years had gone by, however, much murmuring arose in the community upon this matter. It was pointed out in language that became vehement—for an Essene—that so much power should not be left in the hands of one fixed set of individuals, who might become careless or prejudiced, or, worst of all, neglectful of the welfare of the child who was the guest not of them only, but of the whole order. It was demanded, therefore, that this committee should change automatically every month, so that all might serve upon it in turn, Ithiel, as the blood-relation of Miriam, remaining its only permanent member. This proposal was opposed by the committee, but as no one else would vote for them the desired alteration was made. Further, to be removed temporarily, or for good, from its roster was thenceforth recognised as one of the punishments of the order.

Indeed, the absurdities to which its existence gave rise, especially as the girl grew in years, sweetness and beauty, cannot be numbered. Thus, every visiting member must wash his whole person and clothe himself in clean garments before he was allowed to approach the child, "lest he should convey to her any sickness, or impure substance, or odour." Then there was much trouble because some members were discovered to be ingratiating themselves with Miriam by secretly presenting her with gifts of playthings, some of them of great beauty, which they fashioned from wood, shells, or even hard stones. Moreover, they purveyed articles of food such as they found the child loved; and this it was that led to their detection, for, having eaten of them, she was ill. Thereupon Nehushta, enraged, disclosed the whole plot, using the most violent language, and, amidst murmurs of "Shame on them!" designating the offenders by name. They were removed from their office, and it was decreed that henceforth any gifts made to the child must be offered to her by the committee as a whole, and not by a single individual, and handed over in their name by Ithiel, her uncle.

Once, when she was seven years old, and the idol of every brother among the Essenes, Miriam fell ill with a kind of fever which often strikes children in the neighbourhood of Jericho and the Dead Sea. Among the brethren were several skilful and famous physicians, who attended her night and day. But still the fever could not be abated, and at last, with tears, they announced that they feared for the child's life. Then indeed there was lamentation among the Essenes. For three days and three nights did they wrestle in constant prayer to God that she might be spared, many of them touching nothing but water during all that time. Moreover, they sat about at a distance from her house, praying and seeking tidings. If it was bad they beat their breasts, if good they gave thanks. Never was the sickbed of a monarch watched with more care or devotion than that of this little orphan, and never was a recovery—for at length she did recover—received with greater thankfulness and joy.

This was the truth. These pure and simple men, in obedience to the strict rule they had adopted, were cut off from all the affections of life. Yet, the foundation-stone of their doctrine being Love, they who were human must love something, so they loved this child whom they looked upon as their ward, and who, as there was none other of her age and sex in their community, had no rival in their hearts. She was the one joy of their laborious and ascetic hours; she represented all the sweetness and youth of this self-renewing world, which to them was so grey and sapless. Moreover, she was a lovely maid, who, wherever she had been placed, would have bound all to her.

The years went by and the time came when, in obedience to the first decree, Miriam must be educated. Long were the discussions which ensued among the curators of the Essenes. At length three of the most learned of their body were appointed to this task, and the teaching began. As it chanced, Miriam proved an apt pupil, for her memory was good, and she had a great desire to learn many things, more especially history and languages, and all that has to do with nature. One of her tutors was an Egyptian, who, brought up in the priests' college at Thebes, when on a journey to Judæa had fallen sick near Jericho, been nursed by the Essenes and converted to their doctrine. From him Miriam learnt much of their ancient civilisation, and even of the inner mysteries of the Egyptian religion, and of its high and secret interpretations which were known only to the priests. The second, Theophilus by name, was a Greek who had visited Rome, and he taught her the tongues and literature of those countries. The third, all his life long had studied beasts and birds and insects, and the workings of nature, and the stars and their movements, in which things he instructed her day by day, taking her abroad with him that examples of each of them might be before her eyes.

Lastly, when she grew older, there was a fourth master, who was an artist. He taught Miriam how to model animals, and even men, in the clay of the Jordan, and how to carve them out in marble, and something of the use of pigments. Also this man, who was very clever, had a knowledge of singing and instrumental music, which he imparted to her in her odd hours. Thus it came about that Miriam grew learned and well acquainted with many matters of which most girls of her day and years had never even heard. Nor did she lack knowledge of the things of her own faith, though in these the Essenes did not instruct her further than its doctrines tallied with their own. Of the rest, Nehushta told her something; moreover, on several occasions Christian travellers or preachers visited this country to address the Essenes or the other Jews who dwelt there. When they learned her case, these showed themselves very eager to inform her of the Christian doctrine. Among them was one old man who had heard the preaching of Jesus Christ, and been present at His Crucifixion, to all of which histories the girl listened with eagerness, remembering them to the last hour of her life.

Further, and perhaps this was the best part of her education, she lived in the daily company of Nature. But a mile or two away spread the Dead Sea, and along its melancholy and lifeless shores, fringed with the white trunks of trees that had been brought down by Jordan, she would often walk. Before her day by day loomed the mountains of Moab, while behind her were the fantastic and mysterious sand-hills of the desert, backed again by other mountains and that grey, tormented country which stretches between Jericho and Jerusalem. Quite near at hand also ran the broad and muddy Jordan, whose fertile banks were clothed in spring with the most delicious greenery and haunted by kingfishers, cranes, wildfowl, and many other birds. About these banks, too, stretching into the desert land beyond, the flowers of the field grew by myriads, at different periods of the year carpeting the whole earth with various colours, brilliant as are those of the rainbow. These it was her delight to gather, and even to cultivate in the garden of her house.

Thus wisdom, earthly and divine, was gathered in Miriam's heart till very soon its light began to shine through her eyes and face, making them ever more tender and beautiful. Nor did she lack charm and grace of person. From the first, in stature she was small and delicate, pale also in complexion; but her dark hair was plenteous and curling, and her eyes were large and of a deep and tender blue. Her hands and feet were very slender, and her every gesture quick and agile as that of a bird. Thus she grew up loving all things and beloved by all; for even the flowers which she tended and the creatures that she fed, seemed in her to find a friend.

Now of so much learning and all this system of solemn ordered hours, Nehushta did not approve. For a while she bore with it, but when Miriam was about eleven years of age, she spoke her mind to the Committee and through them to the governing Court of Curators.

Was it right that a child should be brought up thus, she asked, and turned into a grave old woman whilst, quite heedless of such things, others of her age were occupied with youthful games? The end of it might be that her brain would break and she would die or become crazy, and then what good would so much wisdom do her? It was necessary that she should have more leisure and other children with whom she could associate.

"White-bearded hermits," she added with point, "were not suitable as sole companions to a little maid."

Thereon followed much debate and consultation with the doctors, who agreed that friends of her own years should be found for the child. This, however, proved difficult, since among these Essenes were no other girls. Therefore those friends must be of the male sex. Here too were difficulties, as at that time, of the lads adopted by this particular community which they were destined to join in after days, there was but one of equal birth with Miriam. Now so far as concerned their own order the Essenes thought little of social distinctions, or even of the differences of blood and race. But Miriam was not of their order; she was their guest, no more, to whom they stood in the place of parents, and who would go from them out into the great world. Therefore, notwithstanding their childlike simplicity, being, many of them, men experienced in life, they did not think it right that she should mix with those of lower breeding.

This one lad, Caleb by name, was born in the same year as Miriam, when Cuspius Fadus became governor on the death of Agrippa. His father was Jew of very high rank named Hilliel, who, although he sided from time to time with the Roman party, was killed by them, or perished among the twenty thousand who were trampled to death at the Feast of the Passover at Jerusalem, when Cumanus, the Procurator, ordered his soldiers to attack the people. Thereon the Zealots, who considered him a traitor, managed to get possession of all his property, so that his son Caleb, whose mother was dead, was brought in a destitute condition by one of her friends to Jericho. There, as she could not dispose of him otherwise, he was given over to the Essenes, to be educated in their doctrine, and, should he wish it, to enter their order when he reached full age. This lad, it was now decreed, should become the playmate of Miriam, a decision that pleased both of them very well.

Caleb was a handsome child with quick, dark eyes that

watched everything without seeming to watch, and black hair which curled upon his shoulders. He was clever also and brave; but though he did his best to control his temper, by nature very passionate and unforgiving. Moreover, that which he desired he would have, if by any means it could be obtained, and was faithful in his loves as in his hates. Of these hates Nehushta was one. With all the skill of a Libyan, whose only book is that of Nature and men's faces, she read the boy's heart at once and said openly that he might come to be the first in any cause—if he did not betray it—and that when God mixed his blood of the best, lest Cæsar should find a rival He left out the salt of honesty and filled up the cup with the wine of passion. When these sayings were repeated to Caleb by Miriam, who thought them to be a jest fit to tease her playmate with, he did not fly into one of his tempers, as she had hoped, but only screwed up his eyelids after his fashion in certain moods, and looked black as the rain-storm above Mount Nebo.

"Did you hear, Caleb?" asked Miriam, somewhat disappointed.

"Oh, yes! Lady Miriam," for so he had been ordered to call her. "I heard. Do you tell that old black woman that I will lead more causes than she ever thought of, for I mean to be the first everywhere. Also that whatever God left out of my cup, at least He mixed it with a good memory."

When Nehushta heard this, she laughed and said that it was true enough, only he that tried to climb several ladders at once generally fell to the ground, and that when a head had said good-bye to its shoulders, the best of memories got lost between the two.

Miriam liked Caleb, but she never loved him as she did the old men, her uncles, or Nehushta, who to her was more than all. Perhaps this may have been because he never grew angry with her whatever she might say or do, never even spoke to her roughly, but always waited on her pleasure and watched for her wish. Still, of all companions he was the best. If Miriam desired to walk by the Dead Sea, he would desire the same. If she wanted to go fishing in the Jordan, he would make ready the baits or net, and take the fishes off the hook—a thing she hated. If she sought a rare flower, Caleb would hunt it out for days, although she knew well that in himself he did not care for flowers, and when he had found it, would mark the spot and lead her there in triumph. Also there was this about him, as she was soon quick enough to learn: he worshipped her. Whatever else might be false, that note in his nature rang true. If one child could love another, then Caleb loved Miriam, first with the love of children, then as a man loves a woman. Only—and this was the sorrow of it—Miriam never loved Caleb. Had she done so both their stories would have been very different. To her he was a clever companion and no more.

What made the thing more strange was that he loved no one else, except, mayhap, himself. In this way and in that the lad soon came to learn his own history, which was sad enough, with the result that if he hated the Romans who had invaded the country and trampled it beneath their heel, still more did he hate those of the Jews who looked upon his father as their enemy and had stolen all the lands and goods that were his by right. As for the Essenes who reared and protected him, so soon as he came to an age when he could weigh such matters, he held them in contempt, and because of their continual habit of bathing themselves and purifying their garments, called them the company of washer-women. On him their doctrines left but a shallow mark. He thought, as he explained to Miriam, that people who were in the world should take the world as they found it, without dreaming ceaselessly of another world to which, as yet, they did not belong; a sentiment that to some extent Nehushta shared.

Wishing, with the zeal of the young, to make a convert, Miriam preached to him the doctrine of Christianity, but without success. By blood Caleb was a Jew of the Jews, and could not understand or admire a God who would consent to be trodden under foot and crucified. The Messiah he desired to follow must be a great conqueror, one who would overthrow the Cæsars and take the throne of Cæsar, not a humble creature with his mouth full of maxims. Like the majority of his own, and, indeed, of every generation, to the last day of his life, Caleb was unable to divine that mind is greater than matter, while spirit is greater than mind; and that in the end, by many slow advances and after many disasters seemingly irremediable, spirituality will conquer all. He looked to a sword flashing from thrones, not to the word of truth spoken by lowly lips in humble streets or upon the flanks of deserts, trusting to the winds of Grace to bear it into the hearts of men and thus regenerate their souls.

Such was Caleb, and these things are said of him here because the child is father to the man.

Swiftly the years went by. There were tumults in Judæa and massacres in Jerusalem. False prophets such as Theudas, who pretended that he could divide Jordan, attracted thousands to their tinsel standards, to be hewn down, poor folk! by the Roman legions. Cæsars rose and fell; the great Temple was at length almost completed in its glory, and many events happened which are remembered even to this day.

But in the little village of the Essenes by the grey shores of the Dead Sea, nothing seemed to change, except that now and again an aged brother died, and now and again a new brother was admitted. They rose before daylight and offered their invocation to the sun; they went out to toil in the fields and sowed their crops, to reap them in due season, thankful if they were good, still thankful if they were bad. They washed, they prayed, they mourned over the wickedness of the world, and wove themselves white garments emblematic of a better. Also, although of this Miriam knew nothing, they held higher and more secret services wherein they invoked the presence of their "angels," and by arts of divination that were known to them, foretold the future, an exercise which brought them little joy. But as yet, however evil might be the omens, none came to molest their peaceful life, which ran quietly towards the great catastrophe as often deep waters swirl to the lip of a precipice.

At length when Miriam was seventeen years of age, the first stroke of trouble fell upon them.

From time to time the high priests at Jerusalem, who hated the Essenes as heretics, had made demands upon them that they should pay tithe for the support of the sacrifices in the Temple. This they refused to do, since all sacrifices were hateful to them. So things went on until the day of the high priest Ananos, who sent armed men to the village of the Essenes to take the tithes. These were refused to them, whereon they broke open the granary and helped themselves, destroying a great deal which they could not carry away. As it chanced, on that day Miriam, accompanied by Nehushta, had visited Jericho. Returning in the afternoon they passed through a certain torrent bed in which were many rocks, and among them thickets of thorn trees. Here they were met by Caleb, now a noble-looking youth very strong and active, who carried a bow in his hand and on his back a sheath of six arrows.

"Lady Miriam," he said, "well met. I have come to seek you, and to warn you not to return by the road to-day, since on it you will meet presently those thieves sent by the high priest to plunder the stores of the Order, who, perhaps, will offer you insult or mischief, for they are drunk with wine. Look, one of them has struck me," and he pointed to a bruise upon his shoulder and scowled.

"What then shall we do?" asked Miriam. "Go back to Jericho?"

"Nay, for there they will come too. Follow up this gully till you reach the footpath a mile away, and by it walk to the village; so you will miss these robbers."

"That is a good plan," said Nehushta. "Come, lady."

"Whither are you going, Caleb?" asked Miriam, lingering, since she saw that he did not mean to accompany them.

"I? Oh, I shall hide among the rocks near by till the men are passed, and then go to seek that hyena which has been worrying the sheep. I have tracked him down and may catch him as he comes from his hole at sunset. That is why I have brought my bow and arrows."

"Come," broke in Nehushta impatiently, "come. The lad well knows how to guard himself."

"Be careful, Caleb, that you get no hurt from the hyena," said Miriam, doubtfully, as Nehushta seized her by the wrist and dragged her away. "It is strange," she added as they went, "that Caleb should choose this evening to go hunting."

"Unless I mistake, it is a human hyena whom he hunts," answered Nehushta shortly. "One of those men struck him, and he desires to wash the wound with his blood."

"Oh, surely not! Nou. That would be taking vengeance, and revenge is evil."

Nehushta shrugged her shoulders. "Caleb may think otherwise, as I do at times. Wait, and we shall see."

As it chanced, they did see something. The footpath by which they returned to the village ran over a high ridge of ground, and from its crest, although they were a mile or more away, in that clear desert air they could easily discern the line of the high priest's servants straggling along, driving before them a score or so of mules, laden with wine and other produce which they had stolen from the stores. Presently the company of them descended into that gully along which the road ran, whence a minute or two later rose a sound of distant shouting. Then they appeared on the further side, running, or riding their beasts hither and thither, as though in search of some one, while four of them carried between them a man who seemed to be hurt, or dead.

"I think that Caleb has shot his hyena," said Nehushta meaningly; "but I have seen nothing, and if you are wise, you will say nothing. I do not like Caleb, but I hate these Jewish thieves, and it is not for you to bring your friend into trouble."

Miriam looked frightened but nodded her head, and no more was said of the matter.

That evening, as Miriam and Nehushta stood at the door of their house in the cool, by the light of the full moon they saw Caleb advancing towards them down the road, a sight that made Miriam glad at heart, for she feared lest he might have come into trouble. Catching sight of them, he asked permission to enter through the door, which he closed behind them, so that now they stood in the little garden within the wall.

"Well," said Nehushta, "I see that you had a shot at your hyena; did you kill it?"

"How do you know that?" he asked, looking at her suspiciously.

"A strange question to put to a Libyan woman who was brought up among bowmen," she replied. "You had six arrows in your quiver when we met you, and now I count but five. Also your bow was newly waxed; and look, the wax is rubbed where the shaft lay."

"I shot at the beast, and, as I think, hit it. At least, I could not find the arrow again, although I searched long."

"Doubtless. You do not often miss. You have a good eye and a steady hand. Well, the loss of a shaft will not matter, since I noticed, also, that this one was differently barbed from the others, and double feathered; a true Roman war-shaft, such as they do not make here. If any find your wounded beast you will not get its hide, since it is known that you do not use such arrows." Then, with a smile that was full of meaning, Nehushta turned and entered the house, leaving him staring after her, half in wrath and half in wonder at her wit.

"What does she mean?" he asked Miriam, but in the voice of one who speaks to himself.

"She thinks that you shot at a man, not at a beast," replied Miriam; "but I know well that you could not have done this, since that would be against the rule of the Essenes."

"Even the rule of the Essenes permits a man to protect himself and his property from thieves," he answered sulkily.

"Yes, to protect himself if he is attacked, and his property—if he has any. But neither that faith nor mine permits him to avenge a blow."

"I was one against many," he answered boldly. "My life was on the hazard: it was no coward's act."

"Were there, then, a troop of these hyenas?" asked Miriam, innocently. "I thought you said it was a solitary beast that took the sheep."

"It was a whole company of beasts who took the wine, and smote those in charge of it as though they were street dogs."

"Hyenas that took wine like the tame ape whom the boys make drunken over yonder—"

"Why do you mock me," broke in Caleb, "who must know the truth? Or if you do not know it, here it is. That thief beat me with his staff, and called me the son of a dog, and I swore that I would pay him back. Pay him back I did, for the head of that shaft which Nehushta noted, stands out a span beyond his neck. They never saw who shot it; they never saw me at all, who thought at first that the man had fallen from his horse. By the time they knew the truth I was away where they could not follow. Now go and tell the story if you will, or let Nehushta, who hates me, tell it, and give me over to be tortured by the servants of the high priest, or crucified as a murderer by the Romans."

"Neither Nehushta nor I saw this deed done, nor shall we bear witness against you, Caleb, or judge you, who doubtless were provoked by violent and lawless men. Yet, Caleb, you told me that you came out to warn us, and it grieves me to learn that the true wish of your heart was to take the life of a man."

"It is false," he answered angrily; "I said that I came to warn you, and afterwards to kill a hyena. To make you safe—that was my first thought, and until you were safe my enemy was safe also. Miriam, you know it well."

"Why should I know it? To you, Caleb, I think revenge is more than friendship."

"Perhaps; for I have few friends who am a penniless orphan brought up by charity. But, Miriam, to me revenge is not more than—love."

"Love," she stammered, turning crimson to her hair and stepping back a pace; "what do you mean, Caleb?"

"What I say, neither more nor less," he answered sullenly. "As I have worked one crime to-day, I may as well work two, and dare to tell the lady Miriam, the Queen of the Essenes, that I love her, though she loves not me—as yet."

"This is madness," faltered Miriam.

"Mayhap, but it is a madness which began when first I saw you—that was soon after we learned to speak—a madness which will continue until I cease to see you, and that shall be soon before I grow silent forever. Listen, Miriam, and do not think my words only those of a foolish boy, for all my life shall prove them. This love of mine is a thing with which you must reckon. You love me not—therefore, even had I the power, I would not force myself upon you against your will; only I warn you, learn to love no other man, for then it shall go ill either with him or with me. By this I swear it," and, snatching her to him,

Caleb kissed her on the forehead, then let her go, saying, "Fear not. It is the first and last time, except by your own will. Or if you fear, tell the story to the Court of the Essenes, and—to Nehushta, who will right your wrongs."

"Caleb," she gasped, stamping her foot upon the ground in anger, "Caleb, you are more wicked than I dreamed, and," she added, as though to herself—"and greater!"

"Yes," he answered, as he turned to go, "I think that you are right. I am more wicked than you dreamed and—greater. Also, Miriam, I love you as you will never be loved again. Farewell!"

Chapter 7

Marcus

That night those of the curators who were engaged in prayer and fasting were disturbed by the return of an officer of those Jews that had robbed them, who complained violently that a man of his company had been murdered by one of the Essenes. They asked how and when, and were told that the man had been shot down with an arrow, in a gully upon the road to Jericho, by a person unknown. They replied that robbers sometimes met with robbers, and asked to see the arrow, which proved to be of a Roman make, such as these men carried in their own quivers. This the Essenes pointed out, and at length, growing angry at the unreasonableness of a complaint made by persons of the worst character, drove him and his escort from their doors, bidding them take their story to the high priest Ananos, with the goods which they had stolen, or, if they preferred it, to that still greater thief, the Roman procurator, Albinus.

This they did not neglect to do, with the result that presently the Essenes were commanded to send some of their head men to appear before Albinus to answer the charges laid against them. Accordingly they dispatched Ithiel and two others, who were kept waiting three months at Jerusalem before they could even obtain a hearing. At length the cause came on, and after some few minutes of talk was adjourned, being but a petty matter. That same evening Ithiel was informed by an intermediary that if his Order would pay a certain large sum of money to Albinus, nothing more would be heard of the question. This the Essenes refused to do, as it was against their principles, saying that they demanded nothing but justice, which they were not prepared to buy. So they spoke, being ignorant that one of their neophytes, Caleb, had in fact aimed the fatal arrow.

Then Albinus, wearying of the business and finding that there was no profit to be made out of the Essenes, commanded them to be gone, saying that he would send an officer to make inquiry on the spot.

Another two months went by, and at length this officer arrived, attended by an escort of twenty soldiers.

As it chanced, on a certain morning in the winter season, Miriam with Nehushta was walking on the Jericho road, when suddenly they saw approaching towards them this little body of armed men. Perceiving that they were Romans, they turned out of the path to hide themselves among the thorns of the desert. Thereon he who seemed to be the officer spurred his horse forward to intercept them.

"Do not run—stand still," said Nehushta to Miriam, "and show no sign of fear."

So Miriam halted and began to gather a few autumn flowers that still bloomed among the bushes, till the shadow of the officer fell upon her—that shadow in which she was destined to walk all her life-days.

"Lady," said a pleasant voice in Greek, spoken with a somewhat foreign accent—"lady, pardon, and I pray you, do not be alarmed. I am a stranger to this part of the country, which I visit on official business. Will you of your kindness direct me to the village of a people called Essenes, who live somewhere in this desert?"

"Oh, sir!" answered Miriam, "do you, who come with Roman soldiers, mean them any harm?"

"Not I. But why do you ask?"

"Because, sir, I am of their community."

The officer stared at her—this beautiful, blue-eyed, white-skinned, delicate-featured girl, whose high blood proclaimed itself in every tone and gesture.

"You, lady, of the community of the Essenes! Surely then those priests in Jerusalem lie more deeply than I thought. They told me that the Essenes were old ascetics who worship Apollo, and could not bear so much as the sight of a woman. And now you say you are an Essene—you, by Bacchus! you!" and he looked at her with an admiration which, although there was nothing brutal or even rude about it, was amusingly undisguised.

"I am their guest," she said.

"Their guest? Why, this is stranger still. If these spiritual outlaws—the word is that old high priest's, not mine—share their bread and water with such guests, my sojourn among them will be happier than I thought."

"They brought me up, I am their ward," Miriam explained again.

"In truth, my opinion of the Essenes rises, and I am convinced that those priests slandered them. If they can shape so sweet a lady, surely they must themselves be good and gentle"; and he bowed gravely, perhaps to mark the compliment.

"Sir, they are both good and gentle," answered Miriam;

"but of this you will be able to judge for yourself very shortly, seeing that they live near at hand. If you will follow us over yonder rise we will show you their village, whither we go."

"By your leave, I will accompany you," he said, dismounting before she could answer; then added, "Pardon me for one moment—I must give some orders," and he called to a soldier, who, with his companions, had halted at a little distance.

The man advanced saluting, and, turning aside, his captain began to talk with him, so that now, for the first time, Miriam could study his face. He was young—not more than five or six and twenty years of age—of middle height, and somewhat slender, but active in movement and athletic in build. Upon his head, which was round and not large, in place of the helmet that hung at his saddle-bow, he wore a little cap, steel lined and padded as a protection against the sun, and beneath it she could see that his short, dark brown hair curled closely. Under the tan caused by exposure to the heat, his skin was fair, and his grey eyes, set rather wide apart, were quick and observant. For the rest, his mouth was well-shaped, though somewhat large, and the chin clean-shaved, prominent and determined. His air was that of a soldier accustomed to command, but very genial, and, when he smiled, showing his regular white teeth, even merry—the air of one with a kind and generous heart.

Miriam looked at him, and in an instant was aware that she liked him better than any man—that is any young man—she had ever seen. This, however, was no great or exclusive compliment to the Roman, since of such acquaintances she had but few, if, indeed, Caleb was not the only one. However, of this she was sure, she liked him better than Caleb, because, even then and there, comparing them in her thoughts, this truth came home to her; with it, too, a certain sense of shame that the newcomer should be preferred to the friend of her childhood, although of late that friend had displeased her by showing too warm a friendship.

Having given his instructions, the captain dismissed the orderly, commanding him to follow at a distance with the men. Then saying, "Lady, I am ready," he began to walk forward, leading his horse by the bridle.

"You will forgive me," he added, "if I introduce myself more formally. I am called Marcus, the son of Emilius—a name which was known in its day," and he sighed, "as I hope before I have done with it, mine will be. At present I cannot boast that this is so, who, unless it should please my uncle Caius to decease and leave me the great fortune he squeezes out of the Spaniards—neither of which things he shows any present intention of doing—am but a soldier of fortune: an officer under the command of the excellent and most noble procurator Albinus," he added sarcastically. "For the rest," he went on, "I have spent a year in this interesting and turbulent but somewhat arid land of yours, coming here from Egypt, and am now honoured with a commission to investigate and make report on a charge laid at the door of your virtuous guardians, the Essenes, of having murdered, or been privy to the murder of, a certain rascally Jew, who, as I understand, was sent with others to steal their goods. That, lady, is my style and history. By way of exchange, will you be pleased to tell me yours?"

Miriam hesitated, not being sure whether she should

enter on such confidences at so short a notice. Thereon, Nehushta, who was untroubled by doubts, and thought it politic to be quite open with this Roman, a man in authority, answered for her.

"Lord, this maiden, whose servant I am, as I was that of her grandmother and mother before her—"

"Surely you cannot be so old," interrupted Marcus. He made it a rule to be polite to all women, whatever their colour, having noticed that life went more easily with those who were courteous to the sex.

Nehushta smiled a little as she answered—for at what age does a woman learn to despise a compliment?—"Lord, they both died young"; then repeated, "This maiden is the only child of the high-born Græco-Syrian of Tyre, Demas, and his noble wife, Rachel—"

"I know Tyre," he interrupted. "I was quartered there till two months ago"; adding in a different tone, "I understand that this pair no longer live."

"They died," said Nehushta sadly, "the father in the amphitheatre at Berytus by command of the first Agrippa, and the mother when her child was born."

"In the amphitheatre at Berytus? Was he then a malefactor?"

"No, sir," broke in Miriam proudly; "he was a Christian."

"Oh! I understand. Well, they are ill-spoken of as enemies of the human race, but for my part I have had to do with several Christians and found them very good people, though visionary in their views." Here a doubt struck him and he said, "But, lady, I understand that you are an Essene."

"Nay, sir," she replied in the same steady voice, "I also am a Christian, who have been protected by the Essenes."

He looked at her with pity and replied, "It is a dangerous profession for one so young and fair."

"Dangerous let it be," she said; "at least it is mine from the beginning to the end."

Marcus bowed, perceiving that the subject was not to be pursued, and said to Nehushta, "Continue the story, my friend."

"Lord, the father of my lady's mother is a very wealthy Jewish merchant of Tyre, named Benoni."

"Benoni," he said, "I know him well, too well for a poor man!—a Jew of the Jews, a Zealot, they say. At least he hates us Romans enough to be one, although many is the dinner that I have eaten at his palace. He is the most successful trader in all Tyre, unless it be his rival Amram, the Phœnician, but a hard man, and as able as he is hard. Now I think of it, he has no living children, so why does not your lady, his grandchild, dwell with him rather than in this desert?"

"Lord, you have answered your own question. Benoni is a Jew of the Jews; his granddaughter is a Christian, as I am also. Therefore when her mother died, I brought her here to be taken care of by her uncle Ithiel the Essene, and I do not think Benoni knows even that she lives. Lord, perhaps I have said too much; but you must soon have heard the story from the Essenes, and we trust to you, who chance to be Benoni's friend, to keep our secret from him."

"You do not trust in vain; yet it seems sad that all the wealth and station which are hers by right should thus be wasted."

"Lord, rank and station are not everything; freedom of faith and person are more than these. My lady lacks for nothing, and—this is all her story."

"Not quite, friend; you have not told me her name."

"Lord, it is Miriam."

"Miriam, Miriam," he repeated, his slightly foreign accent dwelling softly on the syllables. "It is a very pretty name, befitting such a—" and he checked himself.

By now they were on the crest of the rise, and, stopping between two clumps of thorn trees, Miriam broke in hastily:

"See, sir, there below lies the village of the Essenes; those green trees to the left mark the banks of Jordan, whence we irrigate our fields, while that grey stretch of water to the right, surrounded by a wall of mountain, is the Dead Sea."

"Is it so? Well, the green is pleasant in this desert, and those fields look well cultivated. I hope to visit them some day, for I was brought up in the country, and, although I am a soldier, still understand a farm. As for the Dead Sea, it is even more dreary than I expected. Tell me, lady, what is that large building yonder?"

"That," she answered, "is the gathering hall of the Essenes."

"And that?" he asked, pointing to a house which stood by itself.

"That is my home, where Nehushta and I dwell."

"I guessed as much by the pretty garden." Then he asked her other questions, which she answered freely enough, for Miriam, although she was half Jewish, had been brought up among men, and felt neither fear nor shame in talking with them in a friendly and open fashion, as an Egyptian or a Roman or a Grecian lady might have done.

While they were still conversing thus, of a sudden the bushes on their path were pushed aside, and from between them emerged Caleb, of whom she had seen but little of late. He halted and looked at them.

"Friend Caleb," said Miriam, "this is the Roman captain Marcus, who comes to visit the curators of the Order. Will you lead him and his soldiers to the council hall and advise my uncle Ithiel and the others of his coming, since it is time for us to go home?"

Caleb glared at her, or rather at the stranger, with sullen fury; then he answered:

"Romans always make their own road; they do not need a Jew to guide them," and once more he vanished into the scrub on the further side of the path.

"Your friend is not civil," said Marcus, as he watched him go. "Indeed, he has an inhospitable air. Now, if an Essene could do such a thing, I should think that here is a man who might have drawn an arrow upon a Jewish tax-gatherer," and he looked inquiringly at Miriam.

"That lad!" put in Nehushta. "Why, he never shot anything larger than a bird of prey."

"Caleb," added Miriam in excuse, "does not like strangers."

"So I see," answered Marcus; "and to be frank, lady, I do not like Caleb. He has an eye like a knife-point."

"Come, Nehushta," said Miriam, "this is our road, and there runs that of the captain and his company. Sir, farewell, and thank you for your escort."

"Lady, for this while farewell, and thank you for your guidance."

Thus for that day they parted.

The dwelling which many years before had been built by the Essenes for the use of their ward and her nurse, stood next to the large guest- house. Indeed, it occupied a portion of the ground which originally belonged to it, although now the plot was divided into two gardens by an irrigation ditch and a live pomegranate fence, covered at this season of the year with its golden globes of fruit. That evening, as Miriam and Nehushta walked in the garden, they heard the familiar voice of Ithiel calling to them from the other side of this fence, and presently above it saw his kindly face and venerable white head.

"What is it, my uncle?" asked Miriam running to him.

"Only this, child; the noble Roman captain, Marcus, is to stay in the guest-house during his visit to us, so do not be frightened if you hear or see men moving about in this garden—If, indeed, Romans care to walk in gardens. I am to bide here also, to play host to him and see that he lacks nothing. Also I do not think that he will give you any trouble, since, for a Roman, he seems both courteous and kindly."

"I am not afraid, my uncle," said Miriam; "indeed," she added, blushing a little in spite of herself, "Nehushta and I have already become acquainted with this captain"; and she told him of their meeting beyond the village.

"Nehushta, Nehushta," said Ithiel reprovingly, "have I not said to you that you should not walk so far afield without some of the brethren as an escort? You might, perchance, have met thieves, or drunken men."

"My lady wished to gather some flowers she sought," answered Nehushta, "as she has done without harm for many a year; and being armed, I did not fear thieves, if such men are to be found where all are poor."

"Well, well, as it chances, no harm has happened; but do not go out unattended again, lest the soldiers should not be so courteous as their captain. They will not trouble you by the way, since, with the exception of a single guard, they camp yonder by the streamlet. Farewell for this night, my child; we will meet to-morrow."

Then Miriam went to rest and dreamed of the Roman captain, and that he, she, and Nehushta made a journey together and met with many great adventures, wherein Caleb played some strange part. In that dream the captain Marcus protected them from all these dangers, till at length they came to a calm sea, on which floated a single white ship wherein they must embark, having the sign of the Cross woven in its sails. Then she awoke and found that it was morning.

Of all the arts she had been taught, Miriam was fondest of that of modelling in clay, for which she had a natural gift. Indeed, so great had her skill become, that these models which she made, after they had been baked with fire, were, at her wish, sold by the Essenes to any who took a fancy to them. As to the money which they fetched, it was paid into a fund to be distributed among the poor.

This art Miriam carried on in a reed-thatched shed in the garden, where, by an earthen pipe, water was delivered into a stone basin, which she used to damp her clay and cloths. Sometimes also, with the help of masons and the master who had taught her, now a very old man, she copied these models in marble, which the Essenes brought to her from the ruins of a palace near Jericho. At the time that the Romans came she was finishing a work more ambitious than any which she had undertaken as yet; namely, a life-sized bust cut from the fragment of an ancient column to the likeness of her great-uncle, Ithiel. On the afternoon following the day that she met Marcus, clad in her white working-robe, she was occupied in polishing this bust, with the assistance of Nehushta, who handed her the cloths and grinding-powder. Suddenly shadows fell upon her, and turning, she beheld Ithiel and the Roman.

"Daughter," said Ithiel, smiling at her confusion, "I have brought the captain Marcus to see your work."

"Oh, my uncle!" she replied indignantly, "am I in a state to receive any captain?" and she held out her wet hands and pointed to her garments begrimed with clay and powder. "Look at me."

"I look," said Ithiel innocently, "and see naught amiss."

"And I look, lady," added Marcus in his merry voice, "and see much to admire. Would that more of your sex could be found thus delightfully employed."

"Alas, sir," she replied, adroitly misunderstanding him, for Miriam did not lack readiness, "in this poor work there is little to admire. I am ashamed that you should look on the rude fashionings of a half- trained girl, you who must have seen all those splendid statues of which I have been told."

"By the throne of Cæsar, lady," he exclaimed in a voice that carried a conviction of his earnestness, staring hard at the bust of Ithiel before him, "as it chances, although I am not an artist, I do know something of sculpture, since I have a friend who is held to be the best of our day, and often for my sins have sat as model to him. Well, I tell you this—never did the great Glaucus produce a bust like that."

"I daresay not," said Miriam smiling. "I daresay the great Glaucus would go mad if he saw it."

"He would—with envy. He would say that it was the work of one of the glorious Greeks, and of no modern."

"Sir," said Ithiel reprovingly, "do not make a jest of the maid, who does the best she can; it pains her and—is not fitting."

"Friend Ithiel," replied Marcus, turning quite crimson, "you must indeed think that I lack manners who would come to the home of any artist to mock his work. I say what I mean, neither more nor less. If this bust were shown in Rome, together with yourself who sat for it, the lady Miriam would find herself famous within a week. Yes," and he ran his eye quickly over various statuettes, some of them baked and some in the raw clay, models, for the most part, of camels or other animals or birds, "yes, and it is the same with all the rest: these are the works of genius, no less."

At this praise, to them so exaggerated, Miriam, pleased as she could not help feeling, broke into clear laugher, which both Ithiel and Nehushta echoed. Now, so wroth was he, the face of Marcus grew quite pale and stern.

"It seems," he said severely, "that it is not I who mock. Tell me, lady, what do you with these things?" and he pointed to the statuettes.

"I, sir? I sell them; or at least my uncles do."

"The money is given to the poor," interposed Ithiel.

"Would it be rude to ask at what price?"

"Sometimes," replied Ithiel with pride, "travellers have given me as much as a silver shekel.[1] Once indeed, for a

1. About 2s. 6d. of English money.

group of camels with their Arabian drivers, I received four shekels; but that took my niece three months to do."

"A shekel! Four shekels!" said Marcus in a voice of despair; "I will buy them all—no, I will not, it would be robbery. And this bust?"

"That, sir, is not for sale; it is a gift to my uncle, or rather to my uncles, to be set up in their court-room."

An idea struck Marcus. "I am here for a few weeks," he said. "Tell me, lady, if your uncle Ithiel will permit it, at what price will you execute a bust of myself of the same size and quality?"

"It would be dear," said Miriam, smiling at the notion, "for the marble costs something, and the tools, which wear out. Oh, it would be very dear!" This she repeated, wondering what she could ask in her charitable avarice. "It would be—" yes, she would venture it—"fifty shekels!"

"I am poor enough," replied Marcus quietly, "but I will give you two hundred."

"Two hundred!" gasped Miriam. "It is absurd. I could never accept two hundred shekels for a piece of stonework. Then indeed you might say that you had fallen among thieves on the banks of Jordan. No. If my uncles will permit it and there is time, I will do my poor best for fifty—only, sir, I advise you against it, since to win that bad likeness you must sit for many weary hours."

"So be it," said Marcus. "As soon as I get to any civilised place I will send you enough commissions to make the beggars in these parts rich for life, and at a very different figure. Let us begin at once."

"Sir, I have no leave."

"The matter," explained Ithiel, "must be laid before the Court of Curators, which will decide upon it to-morrow.

Meanwhile, as we are talking here, I see no harm if my niece chooses to work a lump of clay, which can be broken up later should the Court in its wisdom refuse your request."

"I hope for its own sake that the Court in its wisdom will not be such a fool," muttered Marcus to himself; adding aloud, "Lady, where shall I place myself? You will find me the best of sitters. Have I not the great Glaucus for a friend—until I show him this work of yours?"

"If you will, sir, be seated on that stool and be pleased to look towards me."

"I am your servant," said Marcus, in a cheerful voice; and the sitting began.

Chapter 8

Marcus and Caleb

On the morrow, as he had promised, Ithiel brought this question of whether or no Miriam was to be allowed to execute a bust of the centurion, Marcus, before the Court of the Curators of the Essenes, who were accustomed thus to consider questions connected with their ward's welfare in solemn conclave. There was a division of opinion. Some of them saw no harm; others, more strait-laced, held that it was scarcely correct that a Roman whose principles, doubtless, were lax, should be allowed to sit to the lady whom they fondly called their child. Indeed, it seemed dubious whether the leave would be given, until a curator, with more worldly wisdom than the rest, suggested that as the captain seemed desirous of having his picture taken in stone, under the circumstances of his visit, which included a commission to make a general report upon their society to the authorities, it might be scarcely wise to deny his wish. Finally, a compromise was effected. It was agreed that Miriam should be permitted to do the work, but only in the presence of Ithiel and two other curators, one of them her own instructor in art.

Thus it came about that when Marcus presented himself for the second time, at an hour fixed by Ithiel, he found three white-bearded and white-robed old gentlemen seated in a row in the workshop, and behind them, a smile on her dusky face, Nehushta. As he entered they rose and bowed to him, a compliment which he returned. Now Miriam appeared, to whom he made his salutation.

"Are these," he said, indicating the elders, "waiting their turn to be modelled, or are they critics?"

"They are critics," said Miriam drily, as she lifted the damp cloths from the rude lump of clay.

Then the work began. As the three curators were seated in a line at the end of the shed, and did not seem to think it right to leave their chairs, they could see little of its details, and as they were early risers and the afternoon was hot, soon they were asleep, every one of them.

"Look at them," said Marcus; "there is a subject for any artist."

Miriam nodded, and taking three lumps of clay, working deftly and silently, presently produced to his delighted sight rough but excellent portraits of these admirable men, who, when they woke up, laughed at them very heartily.

Thus things went on from day to day. Each afternoon the elders attended, and each afternoon they sank to slumber in their comfortable chairs, an example that Nehushta followed, or seemed to follow, leaving Miriam and her model practically alone. As may be guessed, the model, who liked conversation, did not neglect these opportunities. Few were the subjects which the two of them failed to discuss. He told her of all his life, which had been varied and exciting, omitting, it is true, certain details; also of the wars in which he had served, and the countries that he had visited. She in turn told him the simple story of her existence among the Essenes, which he seemed to find of interest. When these subjects were exhausted they discussed other things—the matter of religion, for instance. Indeed, Miriam ventured to expound to him the principles of her faith, to which he listened respectfully and with attention.

"It sounds well," he said at length with a sigh, "but how do such maxims fit in with this world of ours? See now, lady, I am not old, but already I have studied so many religions. First, there are the gods of Greece and Rome, my own gods, you understand—well, the less said of them the better. They serve, that is all. Then there are the gods of Egypt, as to which I made inquiry, and of them I will say this: that beneath the grotesque cloak of their worship seems to shine some spark of a holy fire. Next come the gods of the Phœnicians, the fathers of a hideous creed. After them the flame worshippers and other kindred religions of the East. There remain the Jews, whose doctrine seems to me a savage one; at least it involves bloodshed with the daily offering of blood. Also they are divided, these Jews, for some are Pharisees, some Sadducees, some Essenes. Lastly, there are you Christians, whose faith is pure enough in theory, but whom all unite against in hate. What is the worth of a belief in this crucified Preacher who promises that He will raise those who trust in Him from the dead?"

"That you will find out when everything else has failed you," answered Miriam.

"Yes, it is a religion for those whom everything else has failed. When that chances to the rest of us we commit suicide and sink from sight."

"And we," she said proudly, "rise to life eternal."

"It may be so, lady, it may be so; but let us talk of something more cheerful," and he sighed. "At present, I hold that nothing is eternal—except perhaps such art as yours."

"Which will be forgotten in the first change of taste, or crumbled in the first fire. But see, he is awake. Come here, my master, and work this nostril, for it is beyond me."

The old artist advanced and looked at the bust with admiration.

"Maid Miriam," he said, "I used to have some skill in this art, and I taught you its rudiments; but now, child, I am not fit to temper your clay. Deal with the nostril as you will; I am but a hodman who bears the bricks, you are the heaven-born architect. I will not meddle, I will not meddle; yet perhaps—" and he made a suggestion.

"So?" said Miriam, touching the clay with her tool. "Oh, look! it is right now. You are clever, my master."

"It was always right. I may be clever, but you have genius, and would have found the fault without any help from me."

"Did I not say so?" broke in Marcus triumphantly.

"Sir," replied Miriam, "you say a great deal, and much of it, I think, you do not mean. Please be silent; at this moment I wish to study your lips, and not your words."

So the work went on. They did not always talk, for soon they found that speech is not necessary to true companionship. Once Miriam began to sing, and since she discovered that her voice pleased Marcus and soothed the slumbers of the elders, she sang often; quaint, sad songs of the desert and of the Jordan fishermen. Also she told him tales and legends, and when she had done Nehushta told others—wild stories of Libya, some of them very dark and bloody, others of magic, black or white. Thus these afternoons passed happily enough, and the clay model being finished, after the masons among the brethren had rough hewn it for her, Miriam began to fashion it in marble.

There was one, however, for whom these days did not pass happily—Caleb. From the time that he had seen Miriam walking side by side with Marcus he hated the brilliant-looking Roman in whom, his instinct warned him, he had found a dangerous rival. Oh, how he hated him! So much, indeed, that even in the moment of first meeting he could not keep his rage and envy in his heart, but suffered them to be written on his face, and to shine like danger signals in his eyes, which, it may be remembered, Marcus did not neglect to note.

Of Miriam Caleb had seen but little lately. She was not angry with him, since his offence was of a nature which a woman can forgive, but in her heart she feared him. Of a sudden, as it were, the curtain had been drawn, and she had seen this young man's secret spirit and learned that it was a consuming fire. It had come home to her that every word he spoke was true, that he who was orphaned and not liked even by the gentle elders of the Essenes, loved but one being upon earth—herself, whereas already his bosom seethed with many hates. She was sure also that any man for whom she chanced to care, if such an one should ever cross her path, would, as Caleb had promised, go in danger at his hands, and the thought frightened her. Most of all did it frighten her when she saw him glower upon Marcus, although in truth the Roman was nothing to her. Yet, as she knew, Caleb had judged otherwise.

But if she saw little of him, of this Miriam was sure enough—that he was seldom far from her, and that he found means to learn from day to day how she spent her hours. Indeed, Marcus told her that wherever he went he met that handsome young man with revengeful eyes, who she had said was named Caleb. Therefore Miriam grew frightened and, as the issue will show, not without cause.

One afternoon, while Miriam was at work upon the marble, and the three elders were as usual sunk in slumber, Marcus said suddenly:

"I forgot. I have news for you, lady. I have found out who murdered that Jewish thief whose end, amongst other things, I was sent to investigate. It was your friend Caleb."

Miriam started so violently that her chisel gave an unexpected effect to one of Marcus's curls.

"Hush!" she said, glancing towards the sleepers, one of whom had just snored so loudly that he began to awake at the sound; then added in a whisper, "They do not know, do they?"

He shook his head and looked puzzled.

"I must speak to you of this matter," she went on with agitation, and in the same whisper. "No, not now or here, but alone."

"When and where you will," answered Marcus, smiling, as if the prospect of a solitary conversation with Miriam did not displease him, although this evil-doing Caleb was to be its subject. "Name the time and place, lady."

By now the snoring elder was awake, and rising from his chair with a great noise, which in turn roused the others. Nehushta also rose from her seat and in doing so, as though by accident, overset a copper tray on which lay metal tools.

"In the garden one hour after sunset. Nehushta will leave the little lower door unlocked."

"Good," answered Marcus; then added in a loud voice,

"Not so, lady. Ye gods! what a noise! I think the curl improved by the slip. It looks less as though it had been waxed after the Egyptian fashion. Sirs, why do you disturb yourselves? I fear that to you this long waiting must be as tedious as to me it seems unnecessary."

The sun was down, and the last red glow had faded from the western sky, which was now lit only by the soft light of a half-moon. All the world lay bathed in peace and beauty; even the stern outlines of the surrounding mountains seemed softened, and the pale waters of the Dead Sea and the ashen face of the desert gleamed like silver new cast from the mould. From the oleanders and lilies which bloomed along the edge of the irrigation channels, and from the white flowers of the glossy, golden-fruited orange trees, floated a perfume delicious to the sense, while the silence was only broken from time to time by the bark of a wandering dog or the howl of a jackal in the wilderness.

"A very pleasant night—to talk about Caleb," reflected Marcus, who had reached the appointed spot ten minutes before the time, as he strolled from the narrow belt of trees that were planted along the high, outer wall, into the more open part of the garden. Had Marcus chanced to notice that this same Caleb, walking softly as a cat, and keeping with great care in the shadow, had followed him through the little door which he forgot to lock, and was now hidden among those very trees, he might have remembered a proverb to the effect that snakes hide in the greenest grass and the prettiest flowers have thorny stems. But he thought of no such thing, who was lost in happy anticipations of a moonlight interview with a lovely and cultured young lady, whose image, to speak truth, had taken so deep a hold upon his fancy, that sometimes he wondered how he would be able to banish it thence again. At present he could think of no better means than that which at this moment he was following with delight. Meetings in moonlit gardens tend proverbially to disenchantment!

Presently Marcus caught the gleam of a white robe followed by a dark one, flitting towards him through the dim and dewy garden, and at the sight his heart stood still, then began to beat again in a disorderly fashion. Had he known it, another heart a few yards behind him also stood still, and then began to beat like that of a man in a violent rage. It seems possible, also, that a third heart experienced unusual sensations.

"I wish she had left the old lady behind," muttered Marcus. "No, I don't, for then there are brutes who, if they knew, might blame her"; and, luckily for himself, he walked forward a few paces to meet the white robe, leaving the little belt of trees almost out of hearing.

Now Miriam stood before him, the moonlight shining on her delicate face and in her tranquil eyes, which always reminded him of the blue depths of heaven.

"Sir," she began——

"Oh, I pray you," he broke in, "cease from ceremony and call me Marcus!"

"Captain Marcus," she repeated, dwelling a little on the unfamiliar name, "I beg that you will forgive me for disturbing you at so unseasonable an hour."

"Certainly I forgive you, Lady Miriam," he replied, also dwelling on her name and copying her accent in a fashion that made the grim-faced Nehushta smile.

She waved her hand in deprecation. "The truth is, that this matter of Caleb's—"

"Oh, may all the infernal gods take Caleb! as I have reason to believe they shortly will," broke in Marcus angrily.

"But that is just what I wish to prevent; we have met here to talk of Caleb."

"Well, if you must—talk and let us be done with him. What about Caleb?"

Miriam clasped her hands. "What do you know of him, Captain Marcus?"

"Know? Why, just this: a spy I have in my troop has found out a country fellow who was hunting for mushrooms or something—I forget what—in a gully a mile away, and saw this interesting youth hide himself there and shoot that Jewish plunderer with a bow and arrow. More—he has found another man who saw the said Caleb an hour or two before help himself to an arrow out of one of the Jew's quivers, which arrow appears to be identical with, or at any rate, similar to, that which was found in the fellow's gullet. Therefore, it seems that Caleb is guilty, and that it will be my duty to-morrow to place him under arrest, and in due course to convey him to Jerusalem, where the priests will attend to his little business. Now, Lady Miriam, is your curiosity satisfied about Caleb?"

"Oh," she said, "it cannot be, it must not be! The man had struck him and he did but return a blow for a blow."

"An arrow for a blow, you mean; the point of a spear for the push of its handle. But, Lady Miriam, you seem to be very deep in the confidence of Caleb. How do you come to know all this?"

"I don't know, I only guess. I daresay, nay, I am sure, that Caleb is quite innocent."

"Why do you take such an interest in Caleb?" asked Marcus suspiciously.

"Because he was my friend and playmate from childhood."

"Umph," he answered, "a strange couple—a dove and a raven. Well, I am glad that you did not catch his temper, or you would be more dangerous even than you are. Now, what do you want me to do?"

"I want you to spare Caleb. You, you, you—need not believe those witnesses."

"To think of it!" said Marcus, in mock horror. "To think that one whom I thought so good can prove so immoral. Do you then wish to tempt me from my duty?"

"Yes, I suppose so. At least the peasants round here are great liars."

"Lady," said Marcus, with stern conviction, "Caleb has improved upon his opportunities as a playmate; he has been making love to you. I thought so from the first."

"Oh," she answered, "how can you know that? Besides, he promised that he would never do it again."

"How can I know that? Why, because Caleb would have been a bigger fool than I take him for if he had not. And if it rested with me, certainly he never would do it again. Now be honest with me, if a woman can on such a matter, and tell me true: are you in love with this Caleb?"

"I—I? In love with Caleb? Of course not. If you do not believe me, ask Nehushta."

"Thank you, I will be content with your own reply. You deny that you are in love with him, and I incline to believe you; but, on the other hand, I remember that you would naturally say this, since you might think that any other answer would prejudice the cause of Caleb with me."

"With you! What can it matter to you, sir, whether or no I am in love with Caleb, who, to tell you the truth, frightens me?"

"And that, I suppose, is why you plead so hard for him?"

"No," she answered with a sudden sternness, "I plead hard for him as in like case I would plead hard for you—because he has been my friend, and if he did this deed he was provoked to it."

"Well spoken," said Marcus, gazing at her steadily. Indeed, she was worth looking at as she stood there before him, her hands clasped, her breast heaving, her sweet, pale face flushed with emotion and her lovely eyes aswim with tears. Of a sudden as he gazed Marcus lost control of himself. Passion for this maiden and bitter jealousy of Caleb arose like twin giants in his heart and possessed him.

"You say you are not in love with Caleb," he said. "Well, kiss me and I will believe you."

"How could such a thing prove my words?" she asked indignantly.

"I do not know and I do not care. Kiss me once and I will believe further that the peasants of these parts are all liars. I feel myself beginning to believe it."

"And if I will not?"

"Then I am afraid I must refer the matter to a competent tribunal at Jerusalem."

"Nehushta, Nehushta, you have heard. What shall I do?"

"What shall you do?" said Nehushta drily. "Well, if you like to give the noble Marcus a kiss, I shall not blame you overmuch or tell on you. But if you do not wish it, then I think you would be a fool to put yourself to shame to save Caleb."

"Yet, I will do it—and to save Caleb only," said Miriam with a sob, and she bent towards him.

To her surprise Marcus drew back, placing his hand before his face.

"Forgive me," he said. "I was a brute who wished to buy kisses in such a fashion. I forgot myself; your beauty is to blame, and your sweetness and everything that is yours. I pray," he added humbly, "that you will not think the worse of me, since we men are frail at times. And now, because you ask me, though I have no right, I grant your prayer. Mayhap those witnesses lied; at least, the man's sin, if sin there be, can be excused. He has naught to fear from me."

"No," broke in Nehushta, "but I think you have much to fear from him; and I am sorry for that, my lord Marcus, for you have a noble heart."

"It may be so; the future is on the knees of the gods, and that which is fated will befall. My Lady Miriam, I, your humble servant and friend, wish you farewell."

"Farewell," she answered. "Yes, Nehushta is right, you have a noble heart"; and she looked at him in such a fashion that it flashed across his mind that were he to proffer that request of his again, it might not be refused. But Marcus would not do it. He had tasted of the joy of self-conquest, who hitherto, after the manner of his age and race, had denied himself little, and, as it seemed to him, a strange new power was stirring in his heart—something purer, higher, nobler, than he had known before. He would cherish it a while.

Of all that were spoken there in the garden, Caleb, the watcher, could catch no word. The speakers did not raise their voices and they stood at a distance, so that although he craned his head forward as far as he dared in the shadow of the trees, sharp and trained as they were, naught save a confused murmur reached his ears. But if these failed him, his eyes fed full, so that he lost no move or gesture. It was a passionate love scene, this was clear, for Nehushta stood at a little distance with her back turned, while the pair poured out their sweet speeches to each other. Then at length, as he had expected, came the climax. Yes, oh! shameless woman—they were embracing. A mist fell upon Caleb's eyes, in which lights flashed like red-hot swords lifting and smiting, the blood drummed in his ears as though his raging, jealous heart would burst. He would kill that Roman now on the spot. Miriam should never kiss him more—alive.

Already Caleb had drawn the short-sword from its hiding-place in his ample robe; already he had stepped out from the shadow of the trees, when of a sudden his reason righted itself like a ship that has been laid over by a furious squall, and caution came back to him. If he did this that faithless guardian, Nehushta, who without doubt had been bought with Roman gold, would come to the assistance of her patron and thrust her dagger through his back, as she well could do. Or should he escape that dagger, one or other of them would raise the Essenes on him, and he would be given over to justice. He wished to slay, not to be slain. It would be sweet to kill the Roman, but if he himself were laid dead across his body, leaving Miriam alive to pass to some other man, what would he be advantaged? Presently they must cease from their endearments; presently his enemy would return as he had come, and then he might find his chance. He would wait, he would wait.

Look, they had parted; Miriam was gliding back to the

house, and Marcus came towards him, walking like a man in his sleep. Only Nehushta stood where she was, her eyes fixed upon the ground as though she were reasoning with herself. Still like a man in a dream, Marcus passed him within touch of his outstretched hand. Caleb followed. Marcus opened the door, went out of it, and pulled it to behind him. Caleb caught it in his hand, slipped through and closed it. A few paces down the wall—eight or ten perhaps—was another door, by which Marcus entered the garden of the guest-house. As he turned to shut this, Caleb pushed in after him, and they were face to face.

"Who are you?" asked the Roman, springing back.

Caleb, who by now was cool enough, closed the door and shot the bolt. Then he answered, "Caleb, the son of Hilliel, who wishes a word with you."

"Ah!" said Marcus, "the very man, and, as usual, unless the light deceives me, in an evil humour. Well, Caleb the son of Hilliel, what is your business with me?"

"One of life and death, Marcus the son of Emilius," he answered, in such a tone that the Roman drew his sword and stood watching him.

"Be plain and brief, young man," he said.

"I will be both plain and brief. I love that lady from whom you have just parted, and you also love, or pretend to love, her. Nay, deny it not; I have seen all, even to your kisses. Well, she cannot belong to both of us, and I intend that in some future day she shall belong to me if arm and eye do not fail me now. Therefore one of us must die to-night."

Marcus stepped back, overcome not with fear, but with astonishment.

"Insolent," he said, "you lie! There were no kisses, and

our talk was of your neck, that I gave to her because she asked it, which is forfeit for the murder of the Jew."

"Indeed," sneered Caleb. "Now, who would have thought that the noble Captain Marcus would shelter thus behind a woman's robe? For the rest, my life is my own and no other's to give or to receive. Guard yourself, Roman, since I would kill you in fair fight. Had I another mind you would be dead by now, never knowing the hand that struck you. Have no fear; I am your equal, for my forefathers were nobles when yours were savages."

"Boy, are you mad," asked Marcus, "to think that I, who have fought in three wars, can fear a beardless youth, however fierce? Why, if I feared you I have but to blow upon this whistle and my guards would hale you hence to a felon's death. For your own sake it is that I pray you to consider. Setting aside my rank and yours, I will fight you if you will, and now. Yet think. If I kill you there is an end, and if by chance you should kill me, you will be hunted down as a double murderer. As it is, I forgive you, because I know how bitter is the jealousy of youth, and because you struck no assassin's blow when you might have done so safely. Therefore, I say, go in peace, knowing that I shall not break my word."

"Cease talking," said Caleb, "and come out into the moonlight."

"I am glad that is your wish," replied Marcus. "Having done all I can to save you, I will add that I think you a dangerous cub, of whom the world, the lady Miriam and I alike will be well rid. Now, what weapon have you? A short sword and no mail? Well, so have I. In this we are well matched. Stay, I have a steel-lined cap, and you have none. There it goes, to make our chances equal. Wind your cloak about your left arm as I do. I have known worse shields. Good foothold, but an uncertain light. Now, go!"

Caleb needed no encouragement. For one second they stood facing each other, very types of the Eastern and Western world; the Roman—sturdy, honest-eyed, watchful and fearless, his head thrown back, his feet apart, his shield arm forward, his sword hand pressed to his side from which the steel projected. Over against him was the Jew, crouched like a tiger about to spring, his eyes half closed as though to concentrate the light, his face working with rage, and every muscle quivering till his whole flesh seemed to move upon his bones, like to that of a snake. Suddenly, uttering a low cry, he sprang, and with that savage onslaught the fight began and ended.

Marcus was ready; moreover, he knew what he would do. As the man came, stepping swiftly to one side, he caught the thrust of Caleb's sword in the folded cloak, and since he did not wish to kill him, struck at his hand. The blow fell upon Caleb's first finger and severed it, cutting the others also, so that it dropped to the ground with the sword that they had held. Marcus put his foot upon the blade, and wheeled round.

"Young man," he said sternly, "you have learnt your lesson and will bear the mark of it till your death day. Now begone."

The wretched Caleb ground his teeth. "It was to the death!" he said, "it was to the death! You have conquered, kill me," and with his bloody hand he tore open his robe to make a path for the sword.

"Leave such talk to play-actors," answered Marcus. "Begone, and be sure of this—that if ever you try to bring treachery on me, or trouble on the lady Miriam, I will kill you sure enough."

Then with a sound that was half curse and half sob, Caleb turned and slunk away. With a shrug of the shoulder Marcus also turned to go, when he felt a shadow fall upon him, and swung round, to find Nehushta at his side.

"And pray where did you come from, my Libyan friend?" he asked.

"Out of that pomegranate fence, my Roman lord, whence I have seen and heard all that passed."

"Indeed. Then I hope that you give me credit for good sword-play and good temper."

"The sword-play was well enough, though nothing to boast of with such a madman for a foe. As for the temper, it was that of a fool."

"Such," soliloquised Marcus, "is the reward of virtue. But I am curious. Why?"

"Because, my lord Marcus, this Caleb will grow into the most dangerous man in Judæa, and to none more dangerous than to my lady Miriam and yourself. You should have killed him while you had the chance, before his turn comes to kill you."

"Perhaps," answered Marcus with a yawn; "but, friend Nehushta, I have been associating with a Christian and have caught something of her doctrines. That seems a fine sword. You had better keep it. Good- night."

Chapter 9

The Justice of Florus

On the following morning, when the roll of the neophytes of the Essenes was called, Caleb did not appear. Nor did he answer to his name on the next day, or indeed ever again. None knew what had become of him until a while after a letter was received addressed to the Curators of the Court, in which he announced that, finding he had no vocation for an Essenic career, he had taken refuge with friends of his late father, in some place not stated. There, so far as the Essenes were concerned, the matter ended. Indeed, as the peasant who was concealed in the gully when the Jew was murdered had talked of what he had witnessed, even the most simple-minded of the Essenes could suggest a reason for this sudden departure. Nor did they altogether regret it, inasmuch as in many ways Caleb had proved himself but an unsatisfactory disciple, and already they were discussing the expediency of rejecting him from the fellowship of their peaceful order. Had they known that when he vanished he left behind him a drawn sword and one of his forefingers, their opinion on this point might have been strengthened. But this they did not know, although Miriam knew it through Nehushta.

A week went by, during which time Miriam and Marcus did not meet, as no further sittings were arranged for the completion of the bust. In fact, they were not needful, since she could work from the clay model, which she did, till, labouring at it continually, the marble was done and even polished. One morning as the artist was putting the last touches to her labours, the door of the workshop was darkened and she looked up to see Marcus, who, except for his helmet, was clad in full mail as though about to start upon a journey. As it chanced, Miriam was alone in the place, Nehushta having gone to attend to household affairs. Thus for the first time they met with no other eyes to watch them.

At the sight of him she coloured, letting the cloth fall from her hand which remained about the neck of the marble.

"I ask your pardon, Lady Miriam," said Marcus, bowing gravely, "for breaking in thus upon your privacy; but time presses with me so that I lacked any to give notice to your guardians of my visit."

"Are you leaving us?" she faltered.

"Yes, I am leaving you."

Miriam turned aside and picked up the cloth, then answered, "Well, the work is done, or will be in a few minutes; so if you think it worth the trouble, take it."

"That is my intention. The price I will settle with your uncles."

She nodded. "Yes, yes, but if you will permit me, I should like to pack it myself, so that it comes to no harm upon the journey. Also with your leave I will retain the model, which by right belongs to you. I am not pleased with this marble; I wish to make another."

"The marble is perfect; but keep the model if you will. I am very glad that you should keep it."

She glanced at him, a question in her eyes, then looked away.

"When do you go?" she asked.

"Three hours after noon. My task is finished, my report—which is to the effect that the Essenes are a most worthy and harmless people who deserve to be encouraged, not molested—is written. Also I am called hence in haste by a messenger who reached me from Jerusalem an hour ago. Would you like to know why?"

"If it pleases you to tell me, yes."

"I think that I told you of my uncle Caius, who was proconsul under the late emperor for the richest province of Spain, and—made use of his opportunities."

"Yes."

"Well, the old man has been smitten with a mortal disease. For aught I know he may be already dead, although the physicians seemed to think he would live for another ten months, or perhaps a year. Being in this case, suddenly he has grown fond of his relations, or rather relation, for I am the only one, and expressed a desire to see me, to whom for many years he has never given a single penny. He has even announced his intention—by letter—of making me his heir 'should he find me worthy,' which, to succeed Caius, whatever my faults, indeed I am not, since of all men, as I have told him in past days, I hold him the worst. Still, he has forwarded a sum of money to enable me to journey to him in haste, and with it a letter from the Cæsar, Nero, to the procurator Albinus, commanding him to give me instant leave to go. Therefore, lady, it seems wise that I should go."

"Yes," answered Miriam. "I know little of such things, but I think that it is wise. Within two hours the bust shall be finished and packed," and she stretched out her hand in farewell.

Marcus took the hand and held it. "I am loth to part with you thus," he said suddenly.

"There is only one fashion of parting," answered Miriam, striving to withdraw her hand.

"Nay, there are many; and I hate them all—from you."

"Sir," she asked with gentle indignation, "is it worth your while to play off these pretty phrases upon me? We have met for an hour; we separate—for a lifetime."

"I do not see the need of that. Oh, the truth may as well out. I wish it least of all things."

"Yet it is so. Come, let my hand go; the marble must be finished and packed."

The face of Marcus became troubled, as though he were reasoning with himself, as though he wished to take her at her word and go, yet could not.

"Is it ended?" asked Miriam presently, considering him with her quiet eyes.

"I think not; I think it is but begun. Miriam, I love you."

"Marcus," she answered steadily, "I do not think I should be asked to listen to such words."

"Why not? They have always been thought honest between man and woman."

"Perhaps, when they are meant honestly, which in this case can scarcely be."

He grew hot and red. "What do you mean? Do you suppose—"

"I suppose nothing, Captain Marcus."

"Do you suppose," he repeated, "that I would offer you less than the place of wife?"

"Assuredly not," she replied, "since to do so would be to insult you. But neither do I suppose that you really meant to offer me that place."

"Yet that was in my mind, Miriam."

Her eyes grew soft, but she answered:

"Then, Marcus, I pray you, put it out of your mind, since between us rolls a great sea."

"Is it named Caleb?" he asked bitterly.

She smiled and shook her head. "You know well that it has no such name."

"Tell me of this sea."

"It is easy. You are a Roman worshipping the Roman gods; I am a Christian worshipping the God of the Christians. Therefore we are forever separate."

"Why? I do not understand. If we were married you might come to think like me, or I might come to think like you. It is a matter of the spirit and the future, not of the body and the present. Every day Christians wed those who are not Christians; sometimes, even, they convert them."

"Yes, I know; but in my case this may not be—even if I wished that it should be."

"Why not?"

"Because both by the command of my murdered father and of her own desire my mother laid it on me with her dying breath that I should take to husband no man who was not of our faith."

"And do you hold yourself to be bound by this command?"

"I do, without doubt and to the end."

"However much you might chance to love a man who is not a Christian?"

"However much I might chance to love such a man."

Marcus let fall her hand. "I think I had best go," he said.

"Yes."

Then came a pause while he seemed to be struggling with himself.

"Miriam, I cannot go."

"Marcus, you must go."

"Miriam, do you love me?"

"Marcus, may Christ forgive me, I do."

"Miriam, how much?"

"Marcus, as much as a woman may love a man."

"And yet," he broke out bitterly, "you bid me begone because I am not a Christian."

"Because my faith is more than my love. I must offer my love upon the altar of my faith—or, at the least," she added hurriedly, "I am bound by a rope that cannot be cut or broken. To break it would bring down upon your head and mine the curse of Heaven and of my parents, who are its inhabitants."

"And if I became of your faith?"

Her whole face lit up, then suddenly its light died.

"It is too much to hope. This is not a question of casting incense on an altar; it is a matter of a changed spirit and a new life. Oh! have done. Why do you play with me?"

"A changed spirit and a new life. At the best that would take time."

"Yes, time and thought."

"And would you wait that time? Such beauty and such sweetness as are yours will not lack for suitors."

"I shall wait. I have told you that I love you; no other man will be anything to me. I shall wed no other man."

"You give all and take nothing; it is not just."

"It is as God has willed. If it pleases God to touch your heart and to preserve us both alive, then in days to come our lives may be one life. Otherwise they must run apart till perchance we meet—in the eternal morning."

"Oh, Miriam, I cannot leave you thus! Teach me as you will."

"Nay, go, Marcus, and teach yourself. Am I a bait to win your soul? The path is not so easy, it is very difficult. Fare you well!"

"May I write to you from Rome?" he asked.

"Yes, why not, if by that time you should care to write, who then will have recovered from this folly of the desert and an idle moon?"

"I shall write and I shall return, and we will talk of these matters; so, most sweet, farewell."

"Farewell, Marcus, and the love of God go with you."

"What of your love?"

"My love is with you ever who have won my heart."

"Then, Miriam, at least I have not lived in vain. Remember this always, that much as I may worship you, I honour you still more," and kneeling before her he kissed first her hand, and next the hem of her robe. Then he turned and went.

That night, watching from the roof of her house by the light of the full moon, Miriam saw Marcus ride away at the head of his band of soldiers. On the crest of a little ridge of ground outside the village he halted, leaving them to go on, and turning his horse's head looked backward. Thus he stood awhile, the silver rays of the moon shining on his bright armour and making him a point of light set between two vales of shadow. Miriam could guess whither his eyes were turned and what was in his heart. It seemed to her, even, that she could feel his loving thought play upon her and that with the ear of his spirit he could catch the answer of her own. Then suddenly he turned and was lost in the gloom of the night.

Now that he was gone, quite gone, Miriam's courage seemed to leave her, and leaning her head upon the parapet she wept tears that were soft but very bitter. Suddenly a hand was laid upon her shoulder and a voice, that of old Nehushta, spoke in her ear.

"Mourn not," it said, "since him whom you lose in the night you may find again in the daytime."

"In no day that dawns from an earthly sun, I fear me, Nou. Oh, Nou! he has gone, and taken my heart with him, leaving in its place a throbbing pain which is more than I can bear."

"He will come back; I tell you that he will come back," she answered, almost fiercely; "for your life and his are intertwined—yes, to the end—a single cord bearing a double destiny. I know it; ask me not how; but be comforted, for it is truth. Moreover, though it be sharp, your pain is not more than you can bear, else it would never be laid upon you."

"But, Nou, if he does come back, what will it help me, who am built in by this strict command of them that begat me, to break through which would be to sin against and earn the curse of God and man?"

"I do not know; I only know this, that in that wall, as in others, a door will be found. Trouble not for the future, but leave it in the hand of Him Who shapes all futures.

Sufficient to the day is the evil thereof. So He said. Accept the saying and be grateful. It is something to have gained the love of such a one as this Roman, for, unless the wisdom which I have gained through many years is at fault, he is true and honest; and that man must be good at heart who can be reared in Rome and in the worship of its gods and yet remain honest. Remember these things, and I say be grateful, since there are many who go through their lives knowing no such joy, even for an hour."

"I will try, Nou," said Miriam humbly, still staring at the ridge whence Marcus had vanished.

"You will try, and you will succeed. Now there is another matter of which I must speak to you. When the Essenes received us it was solemnly decreed that if you lived to reach the full age of eighteen years you must depart from among them. That hour struck for you nearly a year ago, and, although you heard nothing of it, this decree was debated by the Court. Now such decrees may not be broken, but it was argued that the words 'full age of eighteen years,' meant and were intended to mean until you reached your nineteenth birthday; that is—in a month from now."

"Then must we go, Nou?" asked Miriam in dismay, for she knew no other world but this village in the desert, and no other friends than these venerable men whom she called her uncles.

"It seems so, especially as it is now guessed that Caleb fought the Captain Marcus upon your account. Oh! that tale is talked of—for one thing, the young wild-cat left a claw behind him which the gardener found."

"I trust then it is known also that the fault was none of mine. But, Nou, whither shall we go who have neither friends, nor home, nor money?"

"I know not; but doubtless in this wall also there is a door. If the worst comes to the worst, a Christian has many brothers; moreover, with your skill in the arts you need never lack for a living in any great city in the world."

"It is true," said Miriam, brightening; "that is, if I may believe Marcus and my old master."

"Also," continued Nehushta, "I have still almost all the gold that the Phœnician Amram gave us when I fled with your mother, and added to it that which I took from the strong box of the captain of the galley on the night when you were born. So have no fear, we shall not want; nor indeed would the Essenes suffer such a thing. Now, child, you are weary; go to rest and dream that you have your lover back again."

It was with a heavy heart that Caleb, defeated and shamed, shook the dust of the village of the Essenes off his feet. At dawn on the morning after the night that he had fought the duel with Marcus, he also might have been seen, a staff in his bandaged hand and a bag of provisions over his shoulder, standing upon the little ridge and gazing towards the house which sheltered Miriam. In love and war things had gone ill with him, so ill that at the thought of his discomfiture he ground his teeth. Miriam cared nothing for him; Marcus had defeated him at the first encounter and given him his life; while, worst of all, these two from whom he had endured so much loved each other. Few, perhaps, have suffered more sharply than he suffered in that hour; for what agonies are there like those of disappointed love and the shame of defeat when endured in youth? With time most men grow accustomed to disaster and rebuff. The colt that seems to break its heart at the cut of a whip, will hobble at last to the knacker unmoved by a shower of blows.

While Caleb looked, the red rim of the sun rose above the horizon, flooding the world with light and life. Now birds began to chirp, and beasts to move; now the shadows fled away. Caleb's impressionable nature answered to this change. Hope stirred in his breast, even the pain of his maimed hand was forgotten.

"I will win yet," he shouted to the silent sky; "my troubles are done with. I will shine like the sun; I will rule like the sun, and my enemies shall whither beneath my power. It is a good omen. Now I am glad that the Roman spared my life, that in a day to come I may take his—and Miriam."

Then he turned and trudged onward through the glorious sunlight, watching his own shadow that stretched away before him.

"It goes far," he said again; "this also is a very good omen."

Caleb thought much on his way to Jerusalem; moreover he talked with all whom he met, even with bandits and footpads whom his poverty could not tempt, for he desired to learn how matters stood in the land. Arrived in Jerusalem he sought out the home of that lady who had been his mother's friend and who gave him over, a helpless orphan, to the care of the Essenes. He found that she was dead, but her son lived, a man of kind heart and given to hospitality, who had heard his story and sheltered him for his mother's sake. When his hand was healed and he procured some good clothes and a little money from his friend, without saying anything of his purpose, Caleb attended the court of Gessius Florus, the Roman procurator, at his palace, seeking an opportunity to speak with him.

Thrice did he wait thus for hours at a time, on each occasion to be driven away at last by the guards. On his fourth visit he was more fortunate, for Florus, who had noted him before, asked why he stood there so patiently. An officer replied that the man had a petition to make.

"Let me hear it then," said the governor. "I sit in this place to administer justice by the grace and in the name of Cæsar."

Accordingly, Caleb was summoned and found himself in the presence of a small, dark-eyed, beetle-browed Roman with cropped hair, who looked what he was—one of the most evil rulers that ever held power in Judæa.

"What do you seek, Jew?" he asked in a harsh voice.

"What I am assured I shall find at your hands, O most noble Florus, justice against the Jews—pure justice"; words at which the courtiers and guards tittered, and even Florus smiled.

"It is to be had at a price," he replied.

"I am prepared to pay the price."

"Then set out your case."

So Caleb set it out. He told how many years before his father had been accidentally slain in a tumult, and how he, the son, being but an infant, certain Jews of the Zealots had seized and divided his estate on the ground that his father was a partisan of the Romans, leaving him, the son, to be brought up by charity—which estate, consisting of tracts of rich lands and certain house property in Jerusalem and Tyre, was still in their possession or in that of their descendants.

The black eyes of Florus glistened as he heard.

"Their names," he said, snatching at his tablets. But as

yet Caleb was not minded to give the names. First, he intimated that he desired to arrive at a formal agreement as to what proportion of the property, if recovered, would be handed over to him, the heir. Then followed much haggling; but in the end it was agreed that as he had been robbed because his father was supposed to favour the Romans, the lands and a large dwelling with warehouse attached, at Tyre, together with one- half the back rents, if recoverable, should be given to the plaintiff. The governor, or as he put it, Cæsar, for his share was to retain the property in Jerusalem and the other half of the rents. In this arrangement Caleb proved himself, as usual, prescient. Houses, as he explained afterwards, could be burned or pulled down, but beyond the crops on it, land no man could injure. Then, after the agreement had been duly signed and witnessed, he gave the names, bringing forward good testimony to prove all that he had said.

Within a week those Jews who had committed the theft, or their descendants, were in prison, whence they did not emerge till they had been stripped, not only of the stolen property, but of everything else that they possessed. Either because he was pleased at so great and unexpected a harvest, or perhaps for the reason that he saw in Caleb an able fellow who might be useful in the future, Florus fulfilled his bargain with him to the letter.

Thus it came about that by a strange turn of the wheel of chance, within a month of his flight from the colony of the Essenes, Caleb, the outcast orphan, with his neck in danger of the sword, became a man of influence, having great possessions. His sun had risen indeed.

Chapter 10

Benoni

A while later Caleb, no longer a solitary wanderer with only his feet to carry him, his staff to protect him, and a wallet to supply him with food, but a young and gallant gentleman, well-armed, clad in furs and a purple cloak, accompanied by servants and riding a splendid horse, once more passed the walls of Jerusalem. On the rising ground beyond the Damascus gate he halted and looked back at the glorious city with her crowded streets, her mighty towers, her luxurious palaces, and her world-famed temple that dominated all, which from here seemed as a mountain covered with snow and crowned with glittering gold.

"I will rule there when the Romans have been driven out," he said to himself, for already Caleb had grown very ambitious. Indeed, the wealth and the place that had come to him so suddenly, with which many men would have been satisfied, did but serve to increase his appetite for power, fame, and all good things. To him this money was but a stepping-stone to greater fortunes.

Caleb was journeying to Tyre to take possession of his house there, which the Roman commander of the district had been bidden to hand over to him. Also he had another object. At Tyre dwelt the old Jew, Benoni, who was

Miriam's grandfather, as he had discovered years before; for when they were still children together she had told him all her story. This Benoni, for reasons of his own, he desired to see.

On a certain afternoon in one of the palaces of Tyre a man might have been sitting in a long portico, or verandah as we should call it, which overlooked the Mediterranean, whose blue waters lapped the straight-scarped rock below—for this house was in the island city, not in that of the mainland where most of the rich Syrians dwelt.

The man was old and very handsome. His dark eyes were quick and full of fire, his nose was hooked like the beak of a bird of prey, his hair and beard were long and snowy white. His robes also were rich and splendid, and over them, since at this season of the year even at Tyre it was cold, he wore a cloak of costly northern furs. The house was worthy of its owner. Built throughout of the purest marble, the rooms were roofed and panelled with sweet-smelling cedar of Lebanon, whence hung many silver lamps, and decorated by statuary and frescoes. On the marble floors were spread rugs, beautifully wrought in colours, while here and there stood couches, tables and stools, fashioned for the most part of ebony from Libya, inlaid with ivory and pearl.

Benoni, the owner of all this wealth, having finished his business for that day—the taking count of a shipload of merchandise which had reached him from Egypt—had eaten his midday meal and now sought his couch under the portico to rest a while in the sun. Reclining on the cushions, soon he was asleep; but it would seem that his dreams were unhappy—at the least he turned from side to side muttering and moving his hands. At last he sat up with a start.

"Oh, Rachel, Rachel!" he moaned, "why will you haunt my sleep? Oh! my child, my child, have I not suffered enough? Must you bring my sin back to me in this fashion? May I not shut my eyes even here in the sunlight and be at peace a while? What have you to tell me that you come thus often to stand here so strengthless and so still? Nay, it is not you; it is my sin that wears your shape!" and Benoni hid his face in his hands, rocking himself to and fro and moaning aloud.

Presently he sprang up. "It was no sin," he said, "it was a righteous act. I offered her to the outraged majesty of Jehovah, as Abraham, our father, would have offered Isaac, but the curse of that false prophet is upon me and mine. That was the fault of Demas, the half-bred hound who crept into my kennel, and whom, because she loved him, I gave to her as husband. Thus did he repay me, the traitor, and I—I repaid him. Ay! But the sword fell upon two necks. He should have suffered, and he alone. Oh, Rachel, my lost daughter Rachel, forgive me, you whose bones lie there beneath the sea, forgive me! I cannot bear those eyes of yours. I am old, Rachel, I am old."

Thus Benoni muttered to himself, as he walked swiftly to and fro; then, worn out with his burst of solitary, dream-bred passion, he sank back upon the couch.

As he sat thus, an Arab doorkeeper, gorgeously apparelled and armed with a great sword, appeared in the portico, and after looking carefully to see that his master was not asleep, made a low salaam.

"What is it?" asked Benoni shortly.

"Master, a young lord named Caleb wishes speech with you."

"Caleb? I know not the name," replied Benoni. "Stay, it must be the son of Hilliel, whom the Roman governor"—and turning, he spat upon the ground—"has brought to his own again. I heard that he had come to take possession of the great house on the quay. Bring him hither."

The Arab saluted and went. Presently he returned and ushered in Caleb, now a noble-looking young man clad in fine raiment. Benoni bowed to him and prayed him to be seated. Caleb bowed in return, touching his forehead in Eastern fashion with his hand, from which, as his host noticed, the forefinger was missing.

"I am your servant, sir," said Benoni with grave courtesy.

"Master, I am your slave," answered Caleb. "I have been told that you knew my father; therefore, on this, my first visit to Tyre, I come to make my respects to you. I am the son of Hilliel, who perished many years ago in Jerusalem. You may have heard his story and mine."

"Yes," answered Benoni scanning his visitor, "I knew Hilliel—a clever man, but one who fell into a trap at last, and I see that you are his son. Your face proves it; indeed, it might be Hilliel who stands before me."

"I am proud that you should say so," answered Caleb, though already he guessed that between Benoni and his father no love had been lost. "You know," he added, "that certain of our people seized my inheritance, which now has been restored to me—in part."

"By Gessius Florus the procurator, I think, who on this account, has cast many Jews—some of them innocent—into prison."

"Indeed! Is that so? Well, it was concerning this Florus that I came chiefly to ask your advice. The Roman has kept a full half of my property," and Caleb sighed and looked indignant.

"You are indeed fortunate that he has not kept it all."

"I have been brought up in the desert far from cities," pleaded Caleb. "Is there no law by which I may have justice of this man? Cannot you help me who are great among our people?"

"None," answered Benoni. "Roman citizens have rights, Jews what they can get. You can appeal to Cæsar if you wish, as the jackal appealed to the lion. But if you are wise you will be content with half the carcase. Also I am not great; I am but an old merchant without authority."

Caleb looked downfallen. "It seems that the days are hard for us Jews," he said. "Well, I will be content and strive to forgive my enemies."

"Better be content and strive to smite your enemies," answered Benoni. "You who were poor are rich; for this much thank God."

"Night and morning I do thank Him," replied Caleb earnestly and with truth.

Then there was silence for a while.

"Is it your intention to reside in Hezron's—I mean in your house—in Tyre?" asked Benoni, breaking it.

"For a time, perhaps, until I find a tenant. I am not accustomed to towns, and at present they seem to stifle me."

"Where were you brought up, sir?"

"Among the Essenes by Jericho. But I am not an Essene—their creed disgusted me; I belong to that of my fathers."

"There are worse men," replied Benoni. "A brother of my late wife is an Essene, a kindly natured fool named

Ithiel; you may have known him."

"Oh, yes, I know him. He is one of their curators and the guardian of the lady Miriam, his great-niece."

The old man started violently, then, recovering himself, said:

"Forgive me, but Miriam was the name of my lost wife—one which it disturbs me to hear. But how can this girl be Ithiel's grand-niece? He had no relations except his sister."

"I do not know," answered Caleb carelessly. "The story is that the lady Miriam, whom they call the Queen of the Essenes, was brought to them nineteen or twenty years ago by a Libyan woman named Nehushta,"—here again Benoni started—"who said that the child's mother, Ithiel's niece, had been shipwrecked and died after giving birth to the infant, commanding that it should be brought to him to be reared. The Essenes consenting, he accepted the charge, and there she is still."

"Then is this lady Miriam an Essene?" asked Benoni in a thick, slow voice.

"No; she is of the sect of the Christians, in which faith she has been brought up as her mother desired."

The old man rose from his couch and walked up and down the portico.

"Tell me of the lady Miriam, sir," he said presently, "for the tale interests me. What is she like?"

"She is, as I believe, the most beautiful maiden in the whole world, though small and slight; also she is the most sweet and learned."

"That is high praise, sir," said Benoni.

"Yes, master, and perhaps I exaggerate her charms, as is but natural."

"Why is it natural?"

"Because we were brought up together, and I hope that one day she will be my wife."

"Are you then affianced to this maid?"

"No, not affianced—as yet," replied Caleb, with a little smile; "but I will not trouble you with a history of my love affairs. I have already trespassed too long upon your kindness. It is something to ask of you who may not desire my acquaintance, but if you will do me the honour to sup with me to-morrow night, your servant will be grateful."

"I thank you, young sir. I will come, I will come, for in truth," he added hastily, "I am anxious to hear news of all that passes at Jerusalem, which, I understand, you left but a few days since, and I perceive that you are one whose eyes and ears are always open."

"I try both to see and to hear," said Caleb modestly. "But I am very inexperienced, and am not sure which cause a man who hopes to become both wise and good, ought to espouse in these troubled days. I need guidance such as you could give me if you wished. For this while, farewell."

Benoni watched his visitor depart, then once more began to wander up and down the portico.

"I do not trust that young man," he thought, "of whose doings I have heard something; but he is rich and able, and may be of service to our cause. This Miriam of whom he speaks, who can she be? unless, indeed, Rachel bore a daughter before she died. Why not? She would not have left it to my care who desired that it should be reared in her own accursed faith and looked upon me as the murderer of her husband and herself. If so, I who thought myself childless, yet have issue upon the earth—at least there is one in whom my blood runs. Beautiful, gifted—but a Christian! The sin of the parents has descended on the child—yes, the curse is on her also. I must seek her out. I must know the truth. Man, what is it now? Can you not see that I would be alone?"

"Master, your pardon," said the Arab servant, bowing, "but the Roman captain, Marcus, desires speech with you."

"Marcus? Oh, I remember the officer who was stationed here. I am not well, I cannot see him. Bid him come to-morrow."

"Master, he bid me say that he sails for Rome to-night."

"Well, well, admit him," answered Benoni. "Perchance he comes to pay his debt," he added.

The Arab departed, and presently the Roman was ushered in.

"Greetings, Benoni," he said, with his pleasant smile. "Here am I, yet alive, for all your fears; so you see your money is still safe."

"I am glad to hear it, my lord Marcus," answered the Jew, bowing low. "But if it will please you to produce it, with the interest, I think," he added drily, "it may be even safer in my strongbox."

Marcus laughed pleasantly.

"Produce it?" he said. "What jest is this? Why, I come to borrow more to defray my costs to Rome."

Benoni's mouth shut like a trap.

"Nay," said Marcus, holding up his hand, "don't begin. I know it all. The times are full of trouble and danger. Such little ready cash as you have at command is out at interest in safer countries—Egypt, Rome, and Italy; your correspondent at Alexandria has failed to make you the expected remittance; and you have reason to believe that every ship in which you are concerned is now at the bottom of the ocean. So would you be so good as to lend me half a talent of silver—a thousand shekels in cash and the rest in bills of exchange on your agents at Brundisium?"

"No," said Benoni, sternly.

"Yes," replied Marcus, with conviction. "Look you, friend Benoni, the security is excellent. If I don't get drowned, or have my throat slit between here and Italy, I am going to be one of the richest men in Rome; so this is your last chance of lending me a trifle. You don't believe it? Then read this letter from Caius, my uncle, and this rescript signed by Nero the Cæsar."

Benoni perused the documents and returned them.

"I offer you my congratulations," he said. "If God permits it and you will walk steadily, your future should be brilliant, since you are of a pleasant countenance, and when you choose to use it, behind that countenance lies a brain. But here I see no security for my money, since even if all things go right, Italy is a long way off."

"Man, do you think that I should cheat you?" asked Marcus hotly.

"No, no, but accidents might happen."

"Well, I will make it worth your while to risk them. For the half- talent write a talent charged upon my estate, whether I live or die. And be swift, I pray you, for I have matters to speak of, of more importance than this miserable money. Whilst I was commissioner among the Essenes on the banks of Jordan—"

"The Essenes! What of the Essenes?" broke in Benoni.

Marcus considered him with his grey eyes, then answered:

"Let us settle this little matter of business and I will tell you."

"Good. It is settled; you shall have the acknowledgment

to sign and the consideration in cash and bills before you leave my house. Now what of these Essenes?"

"Only this," said Marcus; "they are a strange people who read the future, I know not how. One of them with whom I became friendly, foretold that mighty troubles were about to fall upon this land of yours—slaughter and pestilence, and famine, such as the world has not seen."

"That is an old prophecy of those accursed Nazarenes," broke in Benoni.

"Call them not accursed, friend," said Marcus, in an odd voice, "for you should do so least of all men. Nay, hear me out. It may be a prophecy of the Nazarenes, but it is also a prophecy of the Essenes, and I believe it, who watch the signs of the times. Now the elder told me this, that there will be a great uprising of the Jews against the strength of Cæsar, and that most of those who join in it shall perish. He even gave names, and among them was yours, friend Benoni. Therefore, because you have lent me money, although I am a Roman, I have come to Tyre to warn you to keep clear of rebellions and other tumults."

The old man listened quietly, but not as one who disbelieves.

"All this may be so," he said, "but if my name is written in that book of the dead, the angel of Jehovah has chosen me, and I cannot escape his sword. Moreover, I am aged, and"—here his eyes flashed—"it is a good end to die fighting one's country's enemies."

"How you Jews do love us to be sure!" said Marcus with a little laugh.

"The nation that sends a Gessius Florus, or even an Albinus, to rule its alien subjects must needs be loved," replied Benoni with bitter sarcasm. "But let us be done with politics lest we grow angry. It is strange, but a visitor has just left me who was brought up among these Essenes."

"Indeed," said Marcus, staring vacantly into the sea.

"He told me that a young and beautiful woman resides with them who is named the Queen of the Essenes. Did you chance to see her, my lord?"

Instantly Marcus became very wide awake. "Oh, yes, I saw her; and what else did he tell you?"

"He told me that this lady was both beautiful and learned."

"That is true," said Marcus with enthusiasm. "To my mind, although she is small, I never saw one lovelier, nor do I know a sculptor who is her equal. If you will come with me to the ship I will open the case and show you the bust she made of me. But tell me, did this visitor of yours lack the forefinger on one hand—his right?"

"He did."

"Then I suppose that he is named Caleb."

"Yes; but how do you know that?"

"Because I cut off his forefinger," said Marcus, "in a fair fight, and," he added savagely, "he is a young rascal, as murderous as he is able, whose life I did ill to spare."

"Ah," said Benoni, "it seems that I have still some discernment, for just so I judged him. Well, what more do you know of the lady?"

"Something, since in a way I am affianced to her."

"Indeed! Well, this is strange, for so, as he told me, is Caleb."

"He told you that?" said Marcus springing from his chair. "Then he lies, and would that I had time to prove it on his body! She rejected him; I have it from Nehushta; also I know it in other ways."

"Then she did accept you, my lord Marcus?"

"Not quite," he replied sadly; "but that was only because I am not a Christian. She loves me all the same," he added, recovering. "Upon that point there can be no doubt."

"Caleb seemed to doubt it," suggested Benoni.

"Caleb is a liar," repeated Marcus with emphasis, "and one of whom you will do well to beware."

"Why should I beware of him?"

Marcus paused a moment, then answered boldly:

"Because the lady Miriam is your granddaughter and the heiress of your wealth. I say it, since if I did not Caleb would; probably he has done so already."

For a moment Benoni hid his face in his hands. Then he lifted it and said:

"I thought as much, and now I am sure. But, my lord Marcus, if my blood is hers my wealth is my own."

"Just so. Keep it if you will, or leave it where you will. It is Miriam I seek, and not your money."

"I think that Caleb seeks both Miriam and my money—like a prudent man. Why should he not have them? He is a Jew of good blood; he will, I think, rise high."

"And I am a Roman of better blood who will rise higher."

"Yes, a Roman, and I, the grandfather, am a Jew who do not love you Romans."

"And Miriam is neither Jew nor Roman, but a Christian, brought up not by you, but by the Essenes; and she loves me, although she will not marry me because I am not a Christian."

Benoni shrugged his shoulders as he answered:

"All of this is a problem which I must ponder on and solve."

Marcus sprang from his seat and stood before the old man with menace in his air.

"Look you, Benoni," he said, "this is a problem not to be solved by you or by Caleb, but by Miriam herself, and none other. Do you understand?"

"I understand that you threaten me."

"Ay, I do. Miriam is of full age; her sojourn with the Essenes must come to an end. Doubtless you will take her to dwell with you. Well, beware how you deal by her. If she wishes to marry Caleb of her own free will, let her do so. But if you force her to it, or suffer him to force her, then by your God, and by my gods, and by her God, I tell you that I will come back and take such a vengeance upon him and upon you, and upon all your people, that it shall be a story for generations. Do you believe me?"

Benoni looked up at the man who stood before him in his youth and beauty, his eyes on fire and his form quivering with rage, and looking, shrank back a little. He did not know that this light-hearted Roman had such strength and purpose at command. Now he understood for the first time that he was a true son of the terrible race of conquerors, who, if he were crossed, could be as merciless as the worst of them, one whose very honesty and openness made him to be feared the more.

"I understand that you believe what you say. Whether when you are back at Rome, where there are women as fair as the Queen of the Essenes, you will continue to believe it, is another matter."

"Yes, a matter for me to settle."

"Quite so—for you to settle. Have you anything to add

to the commands you are pleased to lay upon your humble creditor, Benoni the merchant?"

"Yes, two things. First, that when I leave this house you will no longer be my creditor. I have brought money to pay you off in full, principal and interest. My talk of borrowing was but a play and excuse to learn what you knew of Miriam. Nay, do not start, though it may seem strange to you that I also can be subtle. Foolish man, did you think that I with my prospects should be left to lack for a miserable half-talent? Why, there at Jerusalem I could have borrowed ten, or twenty, if I would promise my patronage by way of interest. My servants wait with the gold without. Call them in presently and pay yourself, principal and interest, and something for a bonus. Now for the second, Miriam is a Christian. Beware how you tamper with her faith. It is not mine, but I say—beware how you tamper with it. You gave her father and her mother, your own daughter, to be slaughtered by gladiators and to be torn by lions because, forsooth, they did not think as you do. Lift one finger against her and I will hale you into the amphitheatre at Rome, there yourself to be slaughtered by gladiators, or to be torn by lions. Although I am absent I shall know all that you do, for I have friends who are good and spies that are better. Moreover, I return here shortly. Now I ask you, will you give me your solemn word, swearing it by that God whom you worship, first, that you will not attempt to force your granddaughter Miriam into marriage with Caleb the Jew; and secondly, that you will shelter her, treating her with all honour, and suffering her to follow her own faith in freedom?"

Benoni sprang from his couch.

"No, Roman, I will not. Who are you who dare to dictate to me in my own house as to how I shall deal with my own grandchild? Pay what you owe and get you gone, and darken my doors no more. I have done with you."

"Ah!" said Marcus. "Well, perhaps it is time that you should travel. Those who travel and see strange countries and peoples, grow liberal- minded, which you are not. Be pleased to read this paper," and he laid a writing before him.

Benoni took it and read. It was worded thus:

> "To Marcus, the son of Emilius, the captain, in the name of Cæsar, greetings. Hereby we command you, should you in your discretion think fit, to seize the person of Benoni, the Jewish merchant, a dweller in Tyre, and to convey him as a prisoner to Rome, there to answer charges which have been laid against him, with the particulars of which you are acquainted, which said particulars you will find awaiting you in Rome, of having conspired with certain other Jews, to overthrow the authority of Cæsar in this his province of Judæa.
>
> "(Signed) Gessius Florus, Procurator."

Benoni having read sank back upon his couch, gasping, his white face livid with surprise and fear. Then a thought seemed to strike him. Seizing the paper he tore it into fragments.

"Now, Roman," he said, "where is your warrant?"

"In my pocket," answered Marcus; "that which I showed you was but a copy. Nay, do not ring, do not touch that bell. See this," and he drew a silver whistle from his robe. "Outside your gate stand fifty soldiers. Shall I sound it?"

"Not so," answered Benoni. "I will swear the oath, though indeed it is needless. Why should you suppose that I could wish to force this maid into any marriage, or to work her evil on account of matters of her faith?"

"Because you are a Jew and a bigot. You gave her father and her mother to a cruel death, why should you spare her? Also you hate me and all my people; why, then, should you not favour my rival, although he is a murderer whose life I have twice spared at the prayer of Miriam? Swear now."

So Benoni lifted his hand and swore a solemn oath that he would not force his granddaughter, Miriam, to marry Caleb, or any other man; and that he would not betray the secret of her faith, or persecute her because of it.

"It is not enough," said Marcus. "Write it down and sign."

So Benoni went to the table and wrote out his undertaking and signed it, Marcus signing also as a witness.

"Now, Benoni," he said, as he took the paper, "listen to me. That warrant leaves your taking to my discretion, after I have made search into the facts. I have made such search and it seems that I am not satisfied. But remember that the warrant is still alive and can be executed at any moment. Remember also that you are watched and if you lift a finger against the girl, it will be put in force. For the rest—if you desire that the prophecy of the Essene should not come true, it is my advice that you cease from making plots against the majesty of Cæsar. Now bid your servant summon him who waits in the antechamber, that he may discharge my debt. And so farewell. When and where we shall meet again I do not know, but be sure that we shall meet." Then Marcus left the portico.

Benoni watched him go, and as he watched, an evil look gathered on his face.

"Threatened. Trodden to the dirt. Outwitted by that Roman boy," he murmured. "Is there any cup of shame left for me to drink? Who is the traitor and how much does he know? Something, but not all, else my arrest could scarcely have been left to the fancy of this patrician, favourite though he be. Yes, my lord Marcus, I too am sure that we shall meet again, but the fashion of that meeting may be little to your taste. You have had your hour, mine is to come. For the rest, I must keep my oath, since to break it would be too dangerous, and might cut the hair that holds the sword. Also, why should I wish to harm the girl, or to wed her to this rogue Caleb, than whom, mayhap, even the Roman would be better? At least he is a man who does not cheat or lie. Indeed, I long to see the maid. I will go at once to Jordan."

Then he sounded his bell and commanded that the servant of the lord Marcus should be admitted.

Chapter 11

The Essenes Lose Their Queen

The Court of the Essenes was gathered in council debating the subject of the departure of their ward, Miriam. She must go, that was evident, since not even for her, whom they loved as though each of them had been in truth her father or her uncle, could their ancient, sacred rule be broken. But where was she to go and how should she be supported as became her? These were the questions that troubled them and that they debated earnestly. At length her great-uncle Ithiel suggested that she should be summoned before them, that they might hear her wishes. To this his brethren agreed, and he was sent to fetch her.

A while later, attended by Nehushta, Miriam arrived, clad in a robe of pure white, and wearing on her head a wimple of white, edged with purple, and about her waist a purple scarf. So greatly did the Essenes love and reverence this maid, that as she entered, all the hundred of the Court rose and remaining standing until she herself was seated. Then the President, who was sorrowful and even shamefaced, addressed her, telling her their trouble, and praying her pardon because the ordinance of their order forced them to arrange that she should depart from among them. At the end of this speech he asked her what were her wishes as regarded her own future, adding that for her maintenance she need have no fear, since out of their revenues a modest sum would be set aside annually which would suffice to keep her from poverty.

In answer Miriam, also speaking sadly, thanked them from her heart for all their goodness, telling them she had long known this hour of separation to be at hand. As to where she should dwell, since tumults were so many in Jerusalem, she suggested that she might find a home in one of the coast cities, where perhaps some friend or relative of the brethren would shelter Nehushta and herself.

Instantly eight or ten of those present said that they knew such trusty folk in one place or another, and the various offers were submitted to the Court for discussion. While the talk was still going on there came a knock upon the door. After the usual questions and precautions, a brother was admitted who informed them that there had arrived in the village, at the head of a considerable retinue, Benoni, the Jewish merchant of Tyre. He stated that he desired speech with them on the subject of his granddaughter Miriam, who, he learned, was, or had been recently, in their charge.

"Here may be an answer to the riddle," said the President. "We know of this Benoni, also that he purposed to demand his granddaughter of us, though until he did so it was not for us to speak." Then he put it to the Court that Benoni should be admitted.

To this they agreed, and presently the Jew came, splendidly attired, his long white beard flowing down a robe that glittered with embroideries of gold and silver. Entering the dim, cool hall, he stared in amazement at the long half-circles of venerable, white-robed men who were gathered there. Next his quick eyes fell upon the lovely maiden who, attended by the dark-visaged Nehushta, sat before them on a seat of honour; and looking, he guessed that she must be Miriam.

"Little wonder," reflected Benoni to himself, "that all men seem to love this girl, since at the first sight of her my own heart softens."

Then he bowed to the President of the Court and the President bowed back in answer. But not one of the rest so much as moved his head, since already every man of them hated this stranger who was about to carry away her whom they called their Queen.

"Sirs," said Benoni breaking the silence, "I come here upon a strange errand—namely, to ask of you a maid whom I believe to be my granddaughter, of whose existence I learned not long ago, and whom, as it seems, you have sheltered from her birth. Is she among you here?" and he looked at Miriam.

"The lady Miriam sits yonder," said the President. "You are right in naming her your granddaughter, as we have known her to be from the beginning."

"Then why," said Benoni, "did I not know it also?"

"Because," answered the President quietly, "we did not think it fitting to deliver a child that was committed to our charge, to the care of one who had brought her father, and tried to bring her mother, his own seed, to the most horrible of deaths."

As he spoke he fixed his eyes indignantly upon Benoni; as did every man of all that great company, till even the bold-faced Jew dropped his head abashed.

"I am not here," he said, recovering himself, "to make defence of what I have done, or have not done in the past.

I am here to demand that my grandchild, now as I perceive a woman grown, may be handed over to me, her natural guardian."

"Before this can be considered," answered the President, "we who have been her guardians for so many years, should require guarantees and sureties."

"What guarantees, and what sureties?" asked Benoni.

"These among others—That money sufficient for her support after your death should be settled upon her. That she shall be left reasonable liberty in the matter of her daily life and her marriage, if it should please her to marry. Lastly, that as we have undertaken not to meddle with her faith, or to oppress her into changing it, so must you undertake also."

"And if I refuse these things?" asked Benoni.

"Then you see the lady Miriam for the first and last time," answered the President boldly, while the others nodded approval. "We are men of peace, but, merchant, you must not, therefore, think us men without power. We must part with the lady Miriam, who to every one of us is as a daughter, because the unbreakable rule of our order ordains that she, who is now a woman grown, can no longer remain among us. But wherever she dwells, to the last day of her life our love shall go with her and the whole strength of our Order shall protect her. If any harm is attempted to her, we shall be swift to hear and swifter to avenge. If you refuse our conditions, she will vanish from your sight, and then, merchant, go, search the world, the coasts of Syria, the banks of Egypt, and the cities of Italy—and find her if you can. We have spoken."

Benoni stroked his white beard before he answered.

"You talk proudly," he said. "Did I shut my eyes I might

fancy that this voice was the voice of a Roman procurator speaking the decrees of Cæsar. Still, I am ready to believe that what you promise you can perform, since I for one am sure that you Essenes are not mere harmless heretics who worship angels and demons, see visions, prophesy things to come by the help of your familiars, and adore the sun in huts upon the desert." He paused, but the President, without taking the slightest notice of his insults or sarcasms, repeated merely:

"We have spoken," and as with one voice, like some great echo, the whole hundred of them cried, "We have spoken!"

"Do you hear them, master?" said Nehushta in the silence that followed. "Well, I know them. They mean what they say, and you are right—what which they threaten they can perform."

"Let my grandchild speak," said Benoni. "Daughter, is it your wish that such dishonouring bonds should be laid upon me?"

"Grandsire," replied Miriam, in a pure, clear voice, "I may not quarrel with that which is done for my own good. For the wealth I care little, but I would not become a slave in everything save the name, nor do I desire to set my feet in that path my parents trod. What my uncles say—all of these"—and she waved her hand—"speaking in the name of the thousands that are without, that I do, for they love me and I love them, and their mind is my mind and their words are my words."

"Proud-spirited, and well spoken, like all her race," muttered Benoni. Still he stroked his beard and hesitated.

"Be pleased to give your answer," said the President, "that we may finish our discussion before the hour of evening prayer. To help you to it, remember one thing—we ask no new conditions." Benoni glanced up quickly and the President added: "Those of which we have received a copy, that you swore to and signed in the presence of Marcus the Roman, are enough for us."

Now it was Miriam's turn to look, first up and then down. As for her grandfather, he turned white with anger, and broke into a bitter laugh.

"Now I understand—"

"——that the arm of the Essenes is longer than you thought, since it can reach from here to Rome," said the President.

"Ay! that you can plot with Romans. Well, be careful lest the sword of these Romans prove longer than *you* thought and reach even to your hearts, O you peaceful dwellers in the desert!" Then, as though he feared some answer, he added quickly, "I am minded to return and leave this maiden with you to dispose of as you think fit. Yet I will not do so, for she is very fair and gracious, and with the wealth that I can give her, may fill some high place in the world. Also—and this is more to me—I am old and draw near my end and she alone has my blood in her veins. Therefore I will agree to all your terms, and take her home with me to Tyre, trusting that she may learn to love me."

"Good," said the President. "To-morrow the papers shall be prepared and signed. Meanwhile we pray you to be our guest."

Next evening signed they were accordingly, Benoni agreeing without demur to all that the Essenes asked on behalf of her who had been their ward, and even assigning to her a separate revenue during his lifetime. Indeed, now that he had seen her, so loth was he to part with this new-found daughter, that he would have done still more had it been asked of him, lest she should be spirited from his sight, as, did he refuse, might well happen.

Three days later Miriam bade farewell to her protectors, who accompanied her by hundreds to the ridge above the village. Here they stopped, and seeing that the moment of separation was at hand, Miriam's tears began to flow.

"Weep not, beloved child," said Ithiel, "for though we part with you in body, yet shall we always be with you in the spirit, now in this life, and as we think, after this life. Moreover, by night and day, we shall watch over you, and if any attempt to harm you—" here he glanced at Benoni, that brother-in-law to whom he bore but little love—"the very winds will bear us tidings, and in this way or that, help will come."

"Have no fear, Ithiel," broke in Benoni, "my bond, which you hold, is good and it will be backed by love."

"That I believe also," said Miriam; "and if it be so, grandsire, I will repay love for love." Then she turned to the Essenes and thanked them in broken words.

"Be not downhearted," said Ithiel in a thick voice, "for I hope that even in this life we shall meet again."

"May it be so," answered Miriam, and they parted, the Essenes returning sadly to their home, and Benoni taking the road through Jericho to Jerusalem.

Travelling slowly, at the evening of the second day they set their camp on open ground not far from the Damascus gate of the Holy City, but within the new north wall that had been built by Agrippa. Into the city itself Benoni would not enter, fearing lest the Roman soldiers should plunder them. At moonrise Nehushta took Miriam by the hand and led her through the resting camels to a spot a few yards from the camp.

There, standing with her back to the second wall, she pointed out to her a cliff, steep but of no great height, in which appeared little caves and ridges of rock that, looked at from this distance, gave to its face a rude resemblance to a human skull.

"See," she said solemnly. "Yonder the Lord was crucified."

Miriam heard and sank to her knees in prayer. As she knelt there the grave voice of her grandfather spoke behind her, bidding her rise.

"Child," he said, "it is true. True is it also that signs and wonders happened after the death of that false Messiah, and that for me and mine He left a curse behind Him which it may well be is not done with yet. I know your faith, and I have promised to let you follow it in peace. Yet I beseech of you, do not make prayers to your God here in public, where with malefactors He suffered as a malefactor, lest others less tolerant should see you and drag you to your father's death."

Miriam bowed her head and returned to the camp, nor at that time did any further words pass between them on this matter of her religion. Thenceforward, however, she was careful to do nothing which could bring suspicion on her grandfather.

Four days later they came to the rich and beautiful city of Tyre, and Miriam saw the sea upon which she had been born. Hitherto, she had fancied that its waters were much like those of the Dead Lake, upon whose shores she had dwelt so many years; but when she perceived the billows rushing onwards, white-crested, to break in thunder against the walls of island Tyre, she clapped her hands with joy. Indeed, from that day to the end of her life she loved the sea in all its moods, and for hours at a time would find it sufficient company. Perhaps this was because the seethe of its waves was the first sound that her ears had heard, while her first breath was salted with its spray.

From Jerusalem, Benoni had sent messengers mounted on swift horses bidding his servants make ready to receive a guest. So it came about that when she entered his palace in Tyre, Miriam found it decked as though for a bride, and wandered in amazement—she who had known nothing better than the mud-houses of the Essenes—from hall to hall of the ancient building that in bygone generations had been the home of kings and governors. Benoni followed her steps, watching her with grave eyes, till at length all was visited save the gardens belonging to him which were on the mainland.

"Are you pleased with your new home, daughter?" he asked presently.

"My grandfather, it is beautiful," she answered. "Never have I dreamed of such a place as this. Say, may I work my art in one of these great rooms?"

"Miriam," he answered, "of this house henceforth you are the mistress, as in time to come you will be its owner. Believe me, child, it was not needed that so many and such different men should demand from me sureties for your comfort and your safety. All I have is yours, whilst all you have, including your faith and your friends, of whom there seem to be many, remains your own. Yet, should it please you to give me in return some small share of your love, I who am childless and friendless shall be grateful."

"That is my desire," answered Miriam hurriedly; "only, grandsire, between you and me—"

"Speak it not," he said, with a gesture almost of despair, "or rather I will speak it—between you and me runs the river of your parents' blood. It is so, yet, Miriam, I will confess to you that I repent me of that deed. Age makes us judge more kindly. To me your faith is nothing and your God a sham, yet I know now that to worship Him is not worthy of death—at least not for that cause would I bring any to their death to-day, or even to stripes and bonds. I will go further; I will stoop even to borrow from His creed. Do not His teachings bid you to forgive those who have done you wrong?"

"They do, and that is why Christians love all mankind."

"Then bring that law into this home of ours, Miriam, and love me who sorrow for what I did in the blind rage of my zeal, and who now in my old age am haunted by its memory."

Then for the first time Miriam threw herself into the old man's arms and kissed him on the brow.

So it came about that they made their peace and were happy together.

Indeed, day by day Benoni loved her more, till at length she was everything to him, and he grew jealous of all who sought her company, and especially of Nehushta.

Chapter 12

The Ring, the Necklace and the Letter

So Miriam came to Tyre, where, for many months, her life was peaceful and happy enough. At first she had feared meeting Caleb, who she knew from her grandfather was dwelling there; but as it chanced, he had left the city upon business of his own, so for the while she was free of him. In Tyre were many Christians with whom she made friends and worshipped, Benoni pretending to know nothing of the matter. Indeed, at this time and place it was the Jews rather than the Christians who were in danger at the hands of the Syrians and Greeks, who hated them for their wealth and faith, threatening them continually with robbery and massacre. But as yet that storm did not burst, and in its brewing the Christians, who were few, humble, and of all races, escaped notice.

Thus it came about that Miriam dwelt in quiet, occupying herself much with her art of modelling and going abroad but little, since it was scarcely safe for her, the grandchild of the rich Jew merchant, to show her face in the streets. Though she was surrounded by every luxury, far more than she needed, indeed, this lack of liberty irked her who had been reared in the desert, till at times she grew melancholy and would sit for hours looking on the sea and thinking. She thought of her mother who had sat thus before her; of her father, who had perished beneath the gladiators' swords; of the kindly old men who had nurtured her, and of the sufferings of her brothers and sisters in the faith in Rome and at Jerusalem. But most of all she thought of Marcus, her Roman lover, whom, strive as she would, she could never forget—no, not for a single hour. She loved him, that was the truth of it, and between them there was a great gulf fixed, not of the sea only, which ships could sail, but of that command which the dead had laid upon her. He was a pagan and she was a Christian, and they might not wed. By now, too, it was likely that he had forgotten her, the girl who took his fancy in the desert. At Rome there were many noble and lovely women—oh! she could scarcely bear to think of it. Yet night by night she prayed for him, and morn by morn his face arose before her half-awakened eyes. Where was he? What was he doing? For aught she knew he might be dead. Nay, for then, surely, her heart would have warned her. Still, she craved for tidings, and alas! there were none.

At length tidings did come—the best of tidings. One day, wearying of the house, with the permission of her grandfather, and escorted by servants, Miriam had gone to walk in the gardens that he owned to the north of that part of the city on the mainland, which was called Palætyrus. They were lovely gardens, well watered and running down to the sea-edge, and in them grew beautiful palms and other trees, with fruitful shrubs and flowers. Here, when they had roamed a while, Miriam and Nehushta sat down upon the fallen column of some old temple and rested. Suddenly they heard a footstep, and Miriam looked up to see before her a Roman officer, clad in a cloak that showed signs of sea-travel, and, guiding him, one of Benoni's servants.

The officer, a rough but kindly looking man of middle age, bowed to her, asking in Greek if he spoke to the lady Miriam, the granddaughter of Benoni the Jew, she who had been brought up among the Essenes.

"Sir, I am she," answered Miriam.

"Then, lady, I, who am named Gallus, have an errand to perform"; and drawing from his robe a letter tied with silk and sealed, and with the letter a package, he handed them to her.

"Who sends these?" she asked, hope shining in her eyes, "and whence come they?"

"From Rome, lady, as fast as sails could waft them and me. And the sender is the noble Marcus, called the Fortunate."

"Oh!" said Miriam, blushing to her eyes, "tell me, sir, is he well?"

"Not so well but that such a look as that, lady, would better him, or any other man, could he be here to see it," answered the Roman, gazing at her with admiration.

"Did you then leave him ill? I do not understand."

"Nay, his health seemed sound, and his uncle Caius being dead his wealth can scarce be counted, or so they say, since the old man made him his heir. Perhaps that is why the divine Nero has taken such a fancy to him that he can scarce leave the palace. Therefore I cannot say that Marcus is well to-day, since sometimes Nero's friends are short-lived. Nay, be not frightened, I did but jest; your Marcus is safe enough. Read the letter, lady, and waste no time. As for me, my mission is fulfilled. Thank me not; it is reward enough to have seen that sweet face of yours. Fortunate indeed is the star of Marcus, and, though I am jealous of the man, for your sake I pray that it may lead him back to you. Lady, farewell."

"Cut the silk, Nou," said Miriam when the Captain Gallus had gone. "Quick. I have no knife."

Nehushta obeyed smiling and the letter was unrolled. It, or those parts of it which concern us, ran thus:

> "To the lady Miriam, from Marcus the Roman, her friend, by the hand of the Captain Gallus.
>
> "Dear friend and lady, greeting. Already since I came here I have written you one letter, but this day news has reached me that the ship which bore it foundered off the coast of Sicily. So, as Neptune has that letter, and with it many good men, although I write more ill than I do most things, I send you another by this occasion, hoping, I who am vain, that you have not forgotten me, and that the reading of it may even give you pleasure. Most dear Miriam, know that I accomplished my voyage to Rome in safety, visiting your grandsire on the way to pay him a debt I owed. But that story you will perhaps have heard.
>
> "From Tyre I sailed for Italy, but was cast away upon the coasts of Melita, where many of us were drowned. By the favour of some god, however—ah! what god I wonder—I escaped, and taking another ship came safely to Brundisium, whence I travelled as fast as horses would carry me to Rome. Here

I arrived but just in time, for I found my uncle Caius very will. Believing, moreover, that I had been drowned in the shipwreck at Melita, he was about to make a will bequeathing his property to the Emperor Nero, but by good fortune of this he had said nothing. Had he done so I should, I think, be as poor to-day as when I left you, dear, and perhaps poorer still, for I might have lost my head with my inheritance.

"As it was I found favour in the sight of my uncle Caius, who a week after my arrival executed a formal testament leaving to me all his land, goods, and moneys, which on his death three months later I inherited. Thus I have become rich—so rich that now, having much money to spend, by some perversity which I cannot explain, I have grown careful and spend as little as possible. After I had entered into my inheritance I made a plan to return to Judæa, for one reason and one alone—to be near to you, most sweet Miriam. At the last moment I was stayed by a very evil chance. That bust which you made of me I had managed to save from the shipwreck and bring safe to Rome—now I wish it was at the bottom of the sea, and you shall learn why.

"When I came into possession of this house in the Via Agrippa, which is large and beautiful, I set it in a place of honour in the antechamber and summoned that sculptor, Glaucus, of whom I have spoken to you, and others who follow the art, to come and pass judgment upon the work. They came, they wondered and they were silent, for each of them feared lest in praising it he should exalt some rival. When, however, I told them that it was the work of a lady in Judæa, although they did not believe me, since all of them declared that no woman had shaped that marble, knowing that they had nothing to fear from so distant an artist whoever he might be, they began to praise the work with one voice, and all that evening until the wine overcame them, talked of nothing else. Also they continued talking on the morrow, until at length the fame of the thing came to the ears of Nero, who also is an artist of music and other things. The end of it was that one day, without warning, the Emperor visited my house and demanded to see the bust, which I showed to him. For many minutes he examined it through the emerald with which he aids his sight, then asked:

"'What land had the honour to bear the genius who wrought this work?'

"I answered, 'Judæa,' a country, by the way, of which he seemed to know little, except that some fanatics dwelt there, who refused to worship him. He said that he would make that artist ruler of Judæa. I replied that the artist was a woman, whereon he answered that he cared nothing—she should still rule Judæa, or if this could not be managed he would send and bring her to Rome to make a statue of him to be set up in the Temple at Jerusalem for the Jews to worship.

"Now I saw that I had been foolish, and knowing well what would have been your fate, my Miriam, had he once set eyes on you, I sighed and answered, that alas! it was impossible, since you were dead, as I proved to him by a long story with which I will not trouble you. Moreover, now that he was sure that you were dead, I showed him the little statuette of yourself looking into water, which you gave me. Whereon he burst into tears, at the thought that such an one had departed from the earth, while it was still cursed with so many who are wicked, old and ugly.

"Still he did not go, but remained admiring the bust, till at length one of his favourites who accompanied him, whispered in my ear that I must present it to the Emperor. I refused, whereon he whispered back that if I did not, assuredly before long it would be taken, and with it all my other goods, and, perhaps, my life. So, since I must, I changed my mind and prayed him to accept it; whereon he embraced, first the marble and then me, and caused it to be borne away then and there, leaving me mad with rage.

"Now I tell you all this silly story for a reason, since it has hindered and still hinders me from leaving Rome. Thus: two days later I received an Imperial decree, in which it was stated that the incomparable work of art brought from Judæa by Marcus, the son of Emilius, had been set up in a certain temple, where those who would please their Emperor were desired to present themselves and worship it and the soul of her by whom it was fashioned. Moreover, it was commanded that I, Marcus, whose features had served as a model for the work, should be its guardian and attend twice weekly in the temple, that all might see how the genius of a great artist is able to make a thing of immortal beauty from a coarse original of flesh and blood. Oh, Miriam, I have no patience to write of this folly, yet the end of it is, that except at the cost of my fortune and the risk of my life, it is impossible for me to leave Rome. Twice every week, or by special favour, once only, must I attend in that accursed temple where my own likeness stands upon a pedestal of marble, and before it a marble altar, on which are cut the words: 'Sacrifice, O passer-by, to the spirit of the departed genius who wrought this divine work.'

"Yes, there I sit, I who am a soldier, while fools come in and gaze first at the marble and then at me, saying things for which often I long to kill them, and casting grains of incense into the little fire on the altar in sacrifice to your spirit, whereby I trust it may be benefited. Thus, Miriam, are we ruled in Rome to-day.

"Meanwhile, I am in great favour with Nero, so that men call me 'the Fortunate,' and my house the 'Fortunate House,' a title of ill-omen.

"Yet out of this evil comes some good, since because of his present affection for me, or my bust, I have now and again for your sake, Miriam, been able to do service, even to the saving of their lives, to those of your faith. Here there are many Christians whom it is an amusement to Nero to persecute, torture, and slay, sometimes by soaking them in tar and making of them living torches to illuminate his gardens, and sometimes in other fashions. The lives of sundry of these poor people he has given to me, when I begged them of him. Indeed, he has done more. Yesterday Nero came himself to the temple and suggested that certain of the Christians should be sacrificed in a very cruel fashion here as an offering to your spirit. I answered that this could give it little pleasure, seeing that in your lifetime you also were a Christian. Thereon he wrung his hands, crying out, 'Oh! what a crime have I committed,' and instantly gave orders that no more Christians should be killed. So for a little while, thanks to your handiwork, and to me who am called 'the Model,' they are safe—those who are left of them.

"I hear that there are wars and tumults in Judæa, and that Vespasian, a great general, is to be sent to quell them. If I can I will come with him, but at present—such is the madness of my master—this is too much to hope, unless, indeed, he wearies suddenly of the 'Divine Work' and its attendant 'Model.'

"Meanwhile I also cast incense upon your altar, and pray that in these troubles you may come to no harm.

"Miriam, I am most unhappy. I think of you always and yet I cannot come to you. I picture you in many dangers, and I am not there to save you. I even dare to hope that you would wish to see me again; but it is the Jew Caleb, and other men, who see you and make offerings to your sweet beauty as I make them to your spirit. I beseech you, Miriam, do not accept the offerings, lest in some day to come, when I am once more a soldier, and have ceased to be a custodian of busts, it should be the worse for those worshippers, and especially for Caleb.

"What else have I to tell you? I have sought out some of the great preachers of your faith, hoping that by the magic whereof they are said to be masters, they would be able to assure me of your welfare. But to my sorrow they gave me no magic—in which it seems they do not deal—only maxims. Also, from these I bought for a great sum certain manuscripts written by themselves containing the doctrines of your law, which I intend to study so soon as I have time. Indeed, this is a task which I wish to postpone, since did I read I might believe and turn Christian, to serve in due course as a night-light in Nero's gardens.

"I send you a present, praying that you will accept it. The emerald in the ring is cut by my friend, the sculptor Glaucus. The pearls are fine and have a history which I hope to tell you some day. Wear them always, beloved Miriam, for my sake. I do not forget your words; nay, I ponder them day and night. But at least you said you loved me, and in wearing these trinkets you break no duty to the dead. Write to me, I pray you, if you can find a messenger. Or, if you cannot write, think of me always as I do of you. Oh, that we were back together in that happy village of the Essenes, to whom, as to yourself, be all good fortune! Farewell.

"Your ever faithful friend and lover, "Marcus."

Miriam finished her letter, kissed it, and hid it in her bosom. Then she opened the packet and unlocked the ivory box within by a key that hung to it. Out of the casket she took a roll of soft leather. This she undid and uttered a little cry of joy, for there lay a necklace of the most lovely pearls that she had ever seen. Nor was this all, for threaded on the pearls was a ring, and cut upon its emerald bezel the head of Marcus, and her own head taken from the likeness she had given him.

"Look! Nou, look!" said Miriam, showing her the beauteous trinkets.

"A sight to make old eyes glisten," answered Nehushta handling them. "I know something of pearls, and these are worth a fortune. Happy maid, to whom is given such a lover."

"Unhappy maid who can never be a happy wife," sighed Miriam, her blue eyes filling with tears.

"Grieve not; that still may chance," answered Nehushta, as she fastened the pearls about Miriam's neck. "At least you have heard from him and he still loves you, which is much. Now for the ring—the marriage finger—see, how it fits."

"Nay, I have no right," murmured Miriam; still she did not draw it off again.

"Come, let us be going," said Nehushta, hiding the casket in her amble robe, "for the sun sinks, and to-night there are guests to supper."

"What guests?" asked Miriam absently.

"Plotters, every one," said Nehushta, shrugging her shoulders. "The great scheme to drive the Romans from the Holy City ripens fast, and your grandsire waters its root. I pray that we may not all of us gather bitter grapes from that vine. Have you heard that Caleb is back in Tyre?"

"Caleb!" faltered Miriam, "No."

"Well, he is. He arrived yesterday and will be among the guests to-night. He has been fighting up in the desert there, and bravely, for I am told that he was one of those who seized the fortress of Masada and put its Roman garrison to the sword."

"Then he is against the Romans?"

"Yes, because he hopes to rule the Jews, and risks much to gain more."

"I do not wish to meet him," said Miriam.

"Nay, but you must, and the sooner the better. Why do you fear the man?"

"I know not, but fear him I do, now and always."

When Miriam entered the supper chamber that night, the guests to the number of twelve were already seated on their couches, waiting for the feast to begin. By her grandfather's command she was arrayed in her richest robes fashioned and broidered after the Grecian fashion, having her hair gathered into coils upon her head and held with a golden net. Round her waist was a girdle of gold set with gems, about her throat the necklace of pearls which Marcus had sent her, and on her hand a single ring—that with his likeness and her own. As she entered the great chamber, looking most lovely, notwithstanding her lack of height, her grandfather came forward to meet her and present her to the guests, who rose in greeting. One by one they bowed to her and one by one she searched their faces with her eyes—faces for the most part stern and fierce. Now all had passed and she sighed with relief, for among them there was no Caleb. Even as she did so a curtain swung aside and Caleb entered.

It was he, of that there could be no doubt; but oh! how changed since last she had seen him two years before. Then he had been but a raw, passionate youth; now he was a tall and splendid young man, very handsome in his dark fashion, very powerful of frame also and quick of limb. His person was matched by his attire, which was that of an Eastern warrior noble, and his mien was proud and conquering. As he advanced the guests bowed to him in respect, as to a man of great and assured position who may become greater still. Yes, even Benoni showed him this respect, stepping forward to greet him. All these greetings Caleb acknowledged lightly, even haughtily, till of a sudden he saw Miriam standing somewhat in the shadow, and heedless of the other guests pushed his way towards her.

"Thus we meet again, Miriam," he said, his proud face softening as he spoke and his eyes gazing on her with a sort of rapture. "Are you pleased to see me?"

"Surely, Caleb," she answered. "Who would not be well pleased to meet the playfellow of her childhood?"

He frowned, for childhood and its play were not in his thoughts. Before he could speak again Benoni commanded the company to be seated, whereon Miriam took her accustomed place as mistress of the house.

To her surprise Caleb seated himself beside her on the couch that should have been reserved for the oldest guest, who for some moments was left a wanderer and wrathful, till Benoni, seeing what had passed, called him to his side. Then, golden vessels of scented water having been handed by slaves to each guest in turn, the feast began. As Miriam was about to dip her fingers in the water she remembered the ring upon her left hand and turned the bezel inwards. Caleb noted the action, but said nothing.

"Whence come you, Caleb?" she asked.

"From the wars, Miriam. We have thrown down the gate to Rome, and she has picked it up."

She looked at him inquiringly and asked, "Was it wise?"

"Who can tell?" he answered. "At least it is done. For my part I hesitated long, but your grandfather won me over, so now I must follow my fate."

Then he began to tell her of the taking of Masada and of the bloody struggles of the factions in Jerusalem.

After this he spoke of the Essenes, who still occupied their village, though in fear, for all about them was much fighting; and of their childish days together—talk which pleased her greatly. Whilst they spoke thus, a messenger entered the room and whispered something into the ear of Benoni, who raised his hands to Heaven as though in gratitude.

"What tidings?" asked one.

"This, my friends. Cestius Gallus the Roman has been hunted from the walls of Jerusalem and his army is destroyed in the pass of Beth- horon."

"God be praised!" said the company as though with one voice.

"God be praised," repeated Caleb, "for so great and glorious a victory! The accursed Romans are fallen indeed."

Only Miriam said nothing.

"What is in your mind?" he asked looking at her.

"That they will spring up again stronger than before," she replied, then at a signal from Benoni, rose and left the feast.

From the supper chamber Miriam passed down a passage to the portico and there seated herself, resting her arms upon the marble balustrade and listening to the waves as they lapped against the walls below.

That day had been disturbed, different, indeed, from all the peaceful days which she was wont to spend. First had come the messenger bearing her lover's gifts and letter which already she longed to read again; then hard upon his heels, like storm upon the sunshine, he who, unless she was mistaken, still wished to be her lover—Caleb. How curious was the lot of all three of them! How strangely had they been exalted! She, the orphan ward of the Essenes, was now a great and wealthy lady with everything her heart could desire—except one thing, indeed, which it desired most of all. And Marcus, the debt-saddled Roman soldier of fortune, he also, it seemed, had suddenly become great and wealthy, pomps that he held at the price of playing some fool's part in a temple to satisfy the whimsy of an Imperial madman.

Caleb, too, had found fortune, and in these tumultuous times risen suddenly to place and power. All three of them were seated upon pinnacles, but as Miriam felt, they were pinnacles of snow, which for aught she knew, might be melted by the very sun of their prosperity. She was young, she had little experience, yet as Miriam sat there watching the changeful sea, there came upon her a great sense of the instability of things, and an instinctive knowledge of their vanity. The men who were great one day, whose names sounded in the mouths of all, the next had vanished, disgraced or dead. Parties rose and parties fell, high priest succeeded high priest, general supplanted general, yet upon each and all of them, like the following waves that rolled beneath her, came dark night and oblivion. A little dancing in the sunshine, a little moaning in the shade, then death, and after death——

"What are you thinking of, Miriam?" said a rich voice at her elbow, the voice of Caleb.

She started, for here she believed herself alone, then answered:

"My thoughts matter nothing. Why are you here? You should be with your fellow—"

"Conspirators. Why do you not say the word? Well, because sometimes one wearies even of conspiracy. Just now we triumph and can take our ease. I wish to make the most of it. What ring is that you wear upon your finger?"

Miriam straightened herself and grew bold.

"One which Marcus sent me," she answered.

"I guessed as much. I have heard of him; he has become a creature of the mad Nero, the laughing-stock of Rome."

"I do not laugh at him, Caleb."

"No, you were ever faithful. But, say, do you laugh at me?"

"Indeed not; why should I, since you seem to fill a great and dangerous part with dignity?"

"Yes, Miriam, my part is both great and dangerous. I have risen high and I mean to rise higher."

"How high?"

"To the throne of Judæa."

"I think a cottage stool would be more safe, Caleb."

"Mayhap, but I do not like such seats. Listen, Miriam, I will be great or die. I have thrown in my lot with the Jews, and when we have cast out the Romans I shall rule."

"*If* you cast out the Romans, and *if* you live. Caleb, I

have no faith in the venture. We are old friends, and I pray of you to escape from it while there is yet time."

"Why, Miriam?"

"Because He Whom your people crucified and Whom I serve prophesied its end. The Romans will crush you, Caleb. His blood lies heavy upon the head of the Jews, and the hour of payment is at hand."

Caleb thought a while, and when he spoke again the note of confidence had left his voice.

"It may be so, Miriam," he said, "though I put no faith in the sayings of your prophet; but at least I have taken my part and will see the play through. Now for the second time I ask you to share its fortunes. I have not changed my mind. As I loved you in childhood and as a youth, so I love you as a man. I offer to you a great career. In the end I may fall, or I may triumph, still either the fall or the triumph will be worth your sharing. A throne, or a glorious grave—both are good; who can say which is the better? Seek them with me, Miriam."

"Caleb, I cannot."

"Why?"

"Because it is laid upon me as a birthright, or a birth-duty, that I should wed no man who is not a Christian. You know the story."

"Then if there were no such duty would you wed me, Miriam?"

"No," she answered faintly.

"Why not?"

"Because I love another man whom also I am forbid to wed, and until death I am pledged to him."

"The Roman, Marcus?"

"Aye, the Roman Marcus. See, I wear his ring," and she

lifted her hand, "and his gift is about my throat," and she touched the necklet of pearls. "Till death I am his and his alone. This I say, because it is best for all of us that you should know the truth."

Caleb ground his teeth in bitter jealousy.

"Then may death soon find him!" he said.

"It would not help you, Caleb. Oh! why cannot we be friends as we were in the old times!"

"Because I seek more than friendship, and soon or late, in this way or in that, I swear that I will have it."

As the words left his lips footsteps were heard, and Benoni appeared.

"Friend Caleb," he said, "we await you. Why, Miriam, what do you here? To your chamber, girl. Affairs are afoot in which women should have no part."

"Yet as I fear, grandfather, women will have to bear the burden," answered Miriam. Then, bowing to Caleb, she turned and left them.

Chapter 13

Woe, Woe to Jerusalem

Two more years went by, two dreadful, bloody years. In Jerusalem the factions tore each other. In Galilee let the Jewish leader Josephus, under whom Caleb was fighting, do what he would, Vespasian and his generals stormed city after city, massacring their inhabitants by thousands and tens of thousands. In the coast towns and elsewhere Syrians and Jews made war. The Jews assaulted Gadara and Gaulonitis, Sebaste and Ascalon, Anthedon and Gaza, putting many to the sword. Then came their own turn, for the Syrians and Greeks rose upon them and slaughtered them without mercy. As yet, however, there had been no blood shed in Tyre, though all knew that it must come. The Essenes, who had been driven from their home by the Dead Sea and taken refuge in Jerusalem, sent messengers to Miriam warning her to flee from Tyre, where a massacre was being planned; warning her also not to come to Jerusalem, which city they believed to be doomed, but to escape, if possible over sea. Nor was this all, for her own people, the Christians, besought her to fly for her life's sake with them to the city of Pella, where they were gathering from Jerusalem and all Judæa. To both Miriam answered that what her grandsire did, that she must do.

If he fled, she would fly; if he stayed at Tyre, she would stay; if he went to Jerusalem, she would go; for he had been good to her and she had sworn that while he lived she would not desert him. So the Essene messengers went back to Jerusalem, and the Christian elders prayed with her, and having blessed her and consigned her to the care of the Most High and His Son, their Lord, departed to Pella, where, as it was fated, through all those dreadful times not a hair of their heads was touched.

When she had parted from them, Miriam sought out her grandfather, whom she found pacing his chamber with a troubled air.

"Why do you look so sad, Miriam?" he asked. "Have some of your friends warned you that new sorrows are afoot?"

"Yes, grandfather," and she told him all.

"I do not believe them," he said passionately. "Say, do you? Where is their authority? I tell you that we shall triumph. Vespasian is now Emperor in Rome, and there will forget this little land; and the rest, those enemies who are of our own house and those without it, we will conquer and kill. The Messiah will come, the true Messiah. Many signs and wonders declare that he is at hand. Ay! I myself have had a vision concerning him. He will come, and he will conquer, and Jerusalem shall be great and free and see her desire upon her enemies. I ask—where is your authority for these croakings?"

Miriam drew a roll from her robe and read: "But when ye see Jerusalem compassed with armies, then know that her desolation is at hand. Then let them which are in Judæa flee unto the mountains; and let them which are in the midst of her depart out; and let not them that are in the country enter therein. For these are days of vengeance, that all things that are written may be fulfilled. Woe to them that are with child and to them that give suck in those days! for there shall be great distress upon the land and wrath unto this people. And they shall fall by the edge of the sword, and shall be led captive into all the nations; and Jerusalem shall be trodden down of the Gentiles until the times of the Gentiles be fulfilled."

Benoni listened patiently until she had done. Then he answered with contempt:

"So says the book of your Law, but mine tells me otherwise. Well, child, if you believe it and are afraid, begone with your friends, the Christians, and leave me to meet this storm alone."

"I do believe it," she answered quietly, "but I am not afraid."

"That is strange," he said, "since you must then believe also that you will come to a cruel death, which has terrors for the young and fair."

"Not so, grandfather, for this same writing promises that in these troubles not one of us Christians shall perish. It is for you that I fear, not for myself, who will go where you go, and bide where you bide. Therefore, once more, and for the last time, I pray you to be wise and fly—who otherwise must be slain"; and as Miriam said the words her blue eyes filled with tears.

Benoni looked at her and for a moment his courage was shaken.

"Of your book I take no account," he said, "but in the vision of your pure spirit I am tempted to believe. Perhaps the things that you foresee will happen, so, child, fly. You will not lack an escort and I can give you treasure."

She shook her head. "I have said that I will not go without you."

"Then I fear that you here must bide, for I will not leave my wealth and home, even to save my life, and still less will I desert my people in their holy war. Only, Miriam, if things fall out ill for us, remember that I entreated you to depart, and do not reproach me."

"That I shall never do," she answered, smiling, and coming to the old man kissed him tenderly.

So they abode on in Tyre, and a week later the storm burst.

For many days it had not been safe for Jews to show themselves in the streets of the city, since several who crept out about their business, or to fetch water or provisions, had been set upon and beaten to death by the mob, stirred up to the work by Roman emissaries. This time Benoni had employed in putting his house, which was part of an ancient fortress that had stood many a siege, into a state of defence, and in supplying it with an ample store of victuals. Also he sent messengers to Caleb, who was said to be in command of the Jewish force at Joppa, telling him of their peril. Because it was so strong many of the principal Jews in Tyre, to the number of over a hundred indeed, had flocked into Benoni's palace-fortress, together with their wives and children, since there was no other place in their power in the town which could be so easily defended. Lastly, in the outer courts and galleries were stationed fifty or more faithful servants and slaves who understood the use of arms.

Thus things remained, the Syrians threatening them through the gates or from the windows of high houses, and no more, till one night Miriam was awakened by a dreadful sound of screaming. She sprang from her bed and instantly Nehushta was at her side.

"What happens?" she gasped as she dressed herself hastily.

"Those Syrian dogs attack the Jews," answered Nehushta, "on the mainland and in the lower city. Come to the roof, whence we can see what passes," and hand in hand they ran to the sea-portico and up its steep steps.

The dawn was just breaking, but looking from the walled roof they had no need of its light, since everywhere in the dim city below and in Palætyrus on the mainland, houses flared like gigantic torches. In their red glare they could see the thousands of the attackers dragging out their inmates to death, or thrusting them back into the flames, while the night was made horrible with the shouts of the maddened mob, the cries of the victims and the crackling roar of burning houses.

"Oh! Christ have mercy on them," sobbed Miriam.

"Why should He?" asked Nehushta. "They slew Him and rejected Him; now they pay the price He prophesied. May He have mercy on us, His servants."

"He would not have spoken thus," said Miriam indignantly.

"Nay, but justice speaks. Those who take the sword shall perish by the sword. Even so have these Jews done to the Greeks and Syrians in many of the cities—they who are blind and mad. Now it is their hour, and mayhap ours. Come, lady, these are no sights for you, though you might do well to learn to bear them, since if you escape you may see many such. Come, and if you wish we will pray for these Jews, especially for their children, who are innocent, and for ourselves."

That day at noon, most of the poorer and least protected Jews of the city having been killed, the Syrians began their attack upon the fortified palace of Benoni. Now it was that the defenders learned that they had to deal with no mere rabble, but with savage hordes, many thousands strong, directed by officers skilled in war. Indeed these men might be seen moving among them, and from their armour and appearance it was easy to guess that they were Romans. This, in fact, was the case, since Gessius Florus, the wicked, and after him other officers, made it part of their policy to send Romans to stir up the Syrians against the Jews and to assist them in their slaughter.

First an attack was made upon the main gates, but when it was found that these were too strong to be taken easily, the assailants retreated with a loss of a score of men shot by the defenders from the wall. Then other tactics were adopted, for the Syrians, possessing themselves of the neighbouring houses, began to gall the garrison with arrows from the windows. Thus they drove them under cover, but did little more, since the palace was all of marble with cemented roofs, and could not be fired with the burning shafts they sent down upon it.

So the first day passed, and during the night no attack was made upon them. When dawn came they learned the reason, for there opposite to the gates was reared a great battering-ram; moreover, out at sea a huge galley was being rowed in as close to their walls as the depth of water would allow, that from her decks the sailors might hurl stones and siege arrows by means of catapults and thus break down their defences and destroy them.

Then it was that the real fight began. The Jews posted on the roof of the house poured arrows on the men who strove to work the ram, and killed many of them, till they were able to push the instrument so close that it could no longer be commanded. Now it got to work and with three blows of the great baulk of timber, of which the ram was fashioned, burst in the gates. Thereon the defenders, headed by old Benoni himself, rushed out and put those who served it to the sword; then before they could be overcome, retreated across the ditch to the inner wall, breaking down the wooden bridge behind them. Now, since the ram was of no further use, as it could not be dragged through the ditch, the galley, that was anchored within a hundred paces, began to hurl huge stones and arrows at them, knocking down the walls and killing several, including two women and three children.

Thus matters went on till noon, the besiegers galling them with their arrows from the land side and the galley battering them from the sea, while they could do little or nothing in return, having no engines. Benoni called a council and set out the case, which was desperate enough. It was evident, he said, that they could not hold out another day, since at nightfall the Syrians would cross the narrow protecting ditch and set up a battering-ram against the inner wall. Therefore, they must do one of two things—sally out and attempt to cut their way through and gain open country, or fight on and at the last kill the women and children and rush out, those that were left of them, to be hacked down by the besieging thousands. As the first plan gave no hope, since, cumbered as they were with helpless people, they could not expect to escape the city, in their despair they decided on the second. All must die, therefore they would perish by each other's hands. When this decision was known, a wail went up from the women and the children began to scream with fright, those of them who were old enough to understand their doom.

Nehushta caught Miriam by the arm.

"Come to the highest roof," she said; "it is safe from the stones and arrows, and thence, if need be, we can hurl ourselves into the water and die an easy death."

So they went and crouched there, praying, for their case was desperate. Suddenly Nehushta touched Miriam and pointed to the sea. She looked and saw another galley approaching fast as oars and sails could bring her.

"What of it?" she asked heavily. "It will but hasten the end."

"Nay," replied Nehushta, "this ship is Jewish; she does not fly the Eagles, or a Phœnician banner. Behold! the Syrian vessel is getting up her anchors and preparing for fight."

It was true enough, for now the oars of the Syrian shot out and she forged ahead towards the newcomer. But just then the current caught her, laying her broadside on, whereon the Jewish ship, driven by the following wind, shifted her helm and, amidst a mighty shouting from sea and shore, drove down upon her, striking her amidships with its beak so that she heeled over. Then there was more tumult, and Miriam closed her eyes to shut out the horrid sight.

When she opened them again the Syrian galley had vanished, only the water was spotted with black dots which were the heads of men.

"Gallantly done!" screamed Nehushta. "See, she anchors and puts out her boats; they will save us yet. Down to the water-gate!"

On their way they met Benoni coming to seek them, and with him won the steps which were already crowded with fugitives. The two boats of the galley drew near and in the bow of the first of them stood a tall and noble-looking figure.

"It is Caleb," said Miriam, "Caleb who has come to save us."

Caleb it was indeed. At a distance of ten paces from the steps he halted his boat and called aloud:

"Benoni, Lady Miriam and Nehushta, if you still live, stand forward."

They stood forward.

"Now wade into the sea," he cried again, and they waded out until the water reached their armpits, when they were seized one by one and dragged into the boat. Many followed them and were also dragged in, until that boat and the other were quite full, whereon they turned and were rowed to the galley. Having embarked them, the two boats went back and again were filled with fugitives, for the most part women and children.

Again they went, but as they laded for the third time, the ends of ladders appeared above the encircling walls of the steps, and Syrians could be seen rushing out upon the portico, whence they began to lower themselves with ropes. The end of that scene was dreadful. The boats were full, till the water indeed began to overflow their gunwales, but many still remained upon the steps or rushed into the water, women screaming and holding their children above their heads, and men thrusting them aside in the mad rush for life. The boats rowed off, some who could swim following them. For the rest, their end was the sword. In all, seventy souls were rescued.

Miriam flung herself downwards upon the deck of the galley and burst into tears, crying out:

"Oh! save them! Can no one save them?" while Benoni seated at her side, the water running from his blood-stained garment, moaned:

"My house sacked; my wealth taken; my people slain by the Gentiles!"

"Thank God Who has saved us," broke in old Nehushta, "God and Caleb; and as for you, master, blame yourself. Did not we Christians warn you of what was to come? Well, as it has been in the beginning, so it shall be in the end."

Just then Caleb appeared before them, proud and flushed with triumph, as he well might be who had done great things and saved Miriam from the sword. Benoni rose and, casting his arms about his neck, embraced him.

"Behold your deliverer!" he said to Miriam, and stooping down, he drew her to her feet.

"I thank you, Caleb. I can say no more," she murmured; but in her heart she knew that God had delivered her and that Caleb was but His instrument.

"I am well repaid," answered Caleb gravely. "For me this has been a fortunate day, who on it have sunk the great Syrian galley and rescued the woman—whom I love."

"Oath or no oath," broke in Benoni, bethinking him of what he had promised in the past, "the life you saved is yours, and if I have my way you shall take her and such of her heritage as remains."

"Is this a time to speak of such things?" said Miriam, looking up. "See yonder," and she pointed to the scene in progress on the seashore. "They drive our friends and servants into the sea and drown them," and once more she began to weep.

Caleb sighed. "Cease from useless tears, Miriam. We have done our best and it is the fortune of war. I dare not send out the boats again even if the mariners would listen to my command. Nehushta, lead your lady to the cabin and strip her of these wet garments lest she take cold in this bitter wind. But first, Benoni, what is your mind?"

"To go to my cousin Mathias, the high priest at Jerusalem," answered the old man, "who has promised to give me shelter if in these days any can be found."

"Nay," broke in Nehushta, "sail for Egypt."

"Where also they massacre the Jews by thousands till the streets of Alexandria run with their blood," replied Caleb with sarcasm; adding, "Well, to Egypt I cannot take you who must bring this ship to those who await her on this side of Joppa, whence I am summoned to Jerusalem."

"Whither and nowhere else I will go," said Benoni, "to share in my nation's death or triumph. If Miriam wills it, I have told her she can leave me."

"What I have said before I say again," replied Miriam, "that I will never do."

Then Nehushta took her to the cabin, and presently the oars began to beat and the great galley stood out of the harbour, till in the silence of the sea the screams of the victims and the shouts of the victors died away, and as night fell naught could be seen of Tyre but the flare from the burning houses of the slaughtered Jews.

Save for the sobs and cries of the fugitives who had lost their friends and goods the night passed in quiet, since, although it was winter, the sea was calm and none pursued their ship. At daybreak she anchored, and coming from the cabin with Nehushta, in the light of the rising sun Miriam saw before her a ridge of rocks over which the water poured, and beyond it a little bay backed by a desolate coast. Nehushta also saw and sighed.

"What is this place?" asked Miriam.

"Lady, it is the spot where you were born. On yonder flat rock lay the vessel, and there I burned her many years ago. See those blackened timbers half buried in the sand upon the beach; doubtless they are her ribs."

"It is strange that I should return hither, and thus, Nou," said Miriam sighing.

"Strange, indeed, but mayhap there is a meaning in it. Before you came in storm to grow to womanhood in peace; now, perchance, you come on a peaceful sea to pass through womanhood in storm."

"Both journeys began with death, Nou."

"As all journeys end. Blackness behind and blackness in front, and between them a space of sunshine and shadow—that is the law. Yet have no fear, for dead Anna, who had the gift of prophecy, foretold that you should live out your life, though with me, whose days are almost done, it may be otherwise."

Miriam's face grew troubled.

"I fear neither life nor death, Nou, who am willing to meet either as may chance. But to part with you—ah! that thought makes me fear."

"I think that it will not be yet awhile," said Nehushta, "for although I am old, I still have work to do before I lay me down and sleep. Come, Caleb calls us. We are to disembark while the weather holds."

So Miriam entered the boat with her grandfather and others who had escaped, for the faces of all of them were set towards Jerusalem, and was rowed to the shore over that very rock where first she drew her breath. Here they found Jews who had been watching for the coming of the galley. These men gave them a kind reception, and, what they needed even more, food, fire and some beasts of burden for their journey.

When all were gathered on the beach Caleb joined them, having handed over the galley to another Jew, who was to depart in her with those that waited on the shore, upon some secret mission of intercepting Roman cornships. When these men heard what he had done at Tyre, at first they were inclined to be angry, since they said that he had no authority to risk the vessel thus, but afterwards, seeing that he had succeeded, and with no loss of men, praised him and said that it was a very great deed.

So the galley put about and sailed away, and they, to the number of some sixty souls, began their journey to Jerusalem. A little while later they came to a village, the same where Nehushta had found the peasant and his wife, whose inhabitants, at the sight of them, fled, thinking that they were one of the companies of robbers that hunted the land in packs, like wolves, plundering or murdering all they met. When they learnt the truth, however, these people returned and heard their story in silence, for in those days such tales were common enough. As it came to an end a withered, sunburned woman advanced to Nehushta, and, laying one hand upon her arm, pointed with the other at Miriam, saying:

"Tell me, friend, is that the babe I suckled?"

Then Nehushta, knowing her to be the nurse who had travelled with them to the village of the Essenes, greeted her, and answered "Yea," whereupon the woman cast her arms about Miriam and embraced her.

"Day by day," she said, "have I thought of you, little one, and now that my eyes have seen you grown so sweet and fair, I care not—I whose husband is dead and who have no children—how soon they close upon the world." Then she blessed her, and called upon her angel to protect her yonder in Jerusalem, and found her food and an ass to ride; and so they parted, to meet no more.

As it happened, they were fortunate upon that journey, since, with the armed guard of twenty men who accompanied Caleb, they were too strong a party to be attacked by the wandering bands of thieves, and, although it was reported that Titus and his army had already reached Cæsarea from Egypt, they met no Romans. Indeed, their only enemy was the cold, which proved so bitter that when, on the second night, they camped upon the heights over against Jerusalem, having no tents and fearing to light fires, they were obliged to walk about till daylight to keep their blood astir. Then it was that they saw strange and terrible things.

In the clear sky over Jerusalem blazed a great comet, in appearance like a sword of fire. It was true that they had seen it before at Tyre, but never before had it shown so bright. Moreover, there it had not the appearance of a sword. This they thought to be an ill omen, all of them except Benoni, who said that the point of the sword stretched out over Cæsarea, presaging the destruction of the Romans by the hand of God. Towards dawn, the pale, unnatural lustre of the comet faded, and the sky grew overcast and stormy. At length the sun came up, when, to their marvelling eyes, the fiery clouds took strange shapes.

"Look, look!" said Miriam, grasping her grandfather by

the arm, “there are armies in the heavens, and they fight together.”

They looked, and, sure enough, it seemed as though two great hosts were there embattled. They could discern the legions, the wind-blown standards, the charging chariots, and the squadrons of impetuous horse. The firmament had become a battle-ground, and lo! it was red as with the blood of the fallen, while the air was full of strange and dreadful sounds, bred, perhaps, of wind and distant thunder, that came to them like the wail of the vanquished and the dull roar of triumphant armies. So terrified were they at the sight, that they crouched upon the ground and hid their faces in their hands. Only old Benoni standing up, his white beard and robes stained red by the ominous light, cried out that this celestial scene foretold the destruction of the enemies of God.

“Ay!” said Nehushta, “but which enemies?”

The tall Caleb, marching on his round of the camp, echoed:

“Yes, which enemies?”

Suddenly the light grew, all these fantastic shapes melted into a red haze, which sank down till Jerusalem before them seemed as though she floated in an ocean of blood and fire. Then a dark cloud came up and for a while the holy Hill of Zion vanished utterly away. It passed, the blue sky reappeared, and lo! the clear light streamed upon her marble palaces and clustered houses, and was reflected from the golden roofs of the Temple. So calm and peaceful did the glorious city look that none would have deemed indeed that she was already nothing but a slaughter-house, where factions fought furiously, and day by day hundreds of Jews perished beneath the knives of their own brethren.

Caleb gave the word to break their camp, and with bodies shivering in the cold and spirits terrified by fear, they marched across the rugged hills towards the Joppa gate, noting as they passed into the valley that the country had been desolated, for but little corn sprang in the fields, and that was trodden down, while of flocks and herds they saw none. Reaching the gate they found it shut, and there were challenged by soldiers, wild-looking men with ferocious faces of the army of Simon of Gerasa that held the Lower City.

"Who are you and what is your business?" these asked.

Caleb set out his rank and titles, and as these did not seem to satisfy them Benoni explained that the rest of them were fugitives from Tyre, where there had been a great slaughter of the Jews.

"Fugitives always have money; best kill them," said the captain of the gate. "Doubtless they are traitors and deserve to die."

Caleb grew angry and commanded them to open, asking by what right they dared to exclude him, a high officer who had done great service in the wars.

"By the right of the strong," they answered. "Those who let in Simon have to deal with Simon. If you are of the party of John or of Eleazer go to the Temple and knock upon its doors," and they pointed mockingly to the gleaming gates above.

"Has it come to this, then," asked Benoni, "that Jew eats Jew in Jerusalem, while the Roman wolves raven round the walls? Man, we are of no party, although, as I think, my name is known and honoured by all parties—the name of Benoni of Tyre. I demand to be led, not to

Simon, or to John, or to Eleazer, but to my cousin, Mathias, the high priest, who bids us here."

"Mathias, the high priest," said the captain; "that is another matter. Well, this Mathias let us into the city, where we have found good quarters, and good plunder; so as one turn deserves another, we may as well let in his friends. Pass, cousin of Mathias the high priest, with all your company," and he opened the gate.

They entered and marched up the narrow streets towards the Temple. It was the hour of the day when all men should be stirring and busy with their work, but lo! the place was desolate—yes, although so crowded, it still was desolate. On the pavement lay bodies of men and women slain in some midnight outrage. From behind the lattices of the windows they caught sight of the eyes of hundreds peeping at them, but none gave them a good-morrow, or said one single word. The silence of death seemed to brood upon the empty thoroughfares. Presently it was broken by a single wailing voice that reached their ears from so far away that they could not catch its meaning. Nearer and nearer it came, till at length in the dark and narrow street they caught sight of a thin, white-bearded figure, naked to the waist as though to show the hideous scars and rod-weals with which its back and breast were scored, still festering, some of them. This was the man who uttered the cries, and these were the words he spoke:

"A voice from the East! a voice from the West! a voice from the four Winds! a voice against Jerusalem and against the Temple! a voice against the bridegrooms and the brides! a voice against the whole people! Woe, woe to Jerusalem!"

Now he was upon them, yes, and marching through

them as though he saw them not, although they shrank to one side and the other of the narrow street to avoid the touch of this ominous, unclean creature who scarcely seemed to be a man.

"Fellow, what do these words mean?" cried Benoni in angry fear. But, taking no heed, his pale eyes fixed upon the heavens, the wanderer answered only, "Woe, woe to Jerusalem! Woe to you who come up to Jerusalem!"

So he passed on, still uttering those awful words, till at length they lost sight of his naked form and the sound of his crying grew faint and died away.

"What a fearful greeting is this!" said Miriam, wringing her hands.

"Ay!" answered Nehushta, "but the farewell will be worse. The place is doomed and all in it."

Only Caleb said, striving to look unconcerned:

"Have no fear, Miriam. I know the man. He is mad."

"Where does wisdom end and madness begin?" asked Nehushta.

Then they went on towards the gates of the Temple, always through the same blood-stained, empty streets.

Chapter 14

The Essenes Find Their Queen Again

They went on towards the gates of the Temple, but many a long day was destined to go by ere Miriam reached them. The entrance by which they were told they must approach if they sought speech of the high priest, was one of the two Huldah Gates on the south side of the Royal Cloister, and thither they came across the valley of Tyropæon. As they drew near to them of a sudden that gate which stood most to the east was flung wide, and out of it issued a thousand or more of armed men, like ants from a broken nest, who, shouting and waving swords, rushed towards their company. As it chanced, at the moment they were in the centre of an open space that once had been covered with houses but was now cumbered with hundreds of blackened and tottering walls, for fire had devoured them.

"It is the men of John who attack us," cried a voice, whereon, moved by a common impulse, the little band turned and fled for shelter among the ruined houses; yes, even Caleb and Benoni fled.

Before they reached them, lo! from these crumbling walls that they had thought untenanted save by wandering dogs, out rushed another body of savage warriors, the men of Simon who held the Lower City.

After this, Miriam knew little of what happened. Swords and spears flashed round her, the factions fell upon each other, slaughtering each other. She saw Caleb cut down one of the soldiers of John, to be instantly assaulted in turn by a soldier of Simon, since all desired to kill, but none cared whom they slew. She saw her grandfather rolling over and over on the ground in the grip of a man who looked like a priest; she saw women and children pierced with spears. Then Nehushta seized her by the hand, and plunging a knife into the arm of a man who would have stayed them, dragged her away. They fled, an arrow sang past her ear; something struck her on the foot. Still they fled, whither she knew not, till at length the sound of the tumult died away. But not yet would Nehushta stop, for she feared that they might be followed. So on they went, and on, meeting few and heeded by none, till at length Miriam sank to the ground, worn out with fear and flight.

"Up," said Nehushta.

"I cannot," she answered. "Something has hurt my foot. See, it bleeds!"

Nehushta looked about her, and saw that they were outside the second wall in the new city of Bezetha, not far from the old Damascus Gate, for there, to their right and a little behind them, rose the great tower of Antonia. Beneath this wall were rubbish-heaps, foul-smelling and covered over with rough grasses and some spring flowers, which grew upon the slopes of the ancient fosse. Here seemed a place where they might lie hid awhile, since there were no houses and it was unsavoury. She dragged

Miriam to her feet, and, notwithstanding her complaints and swollen ankle, forced her on, till they came to a spot where, as it is to-day, the wall was built upon foundations of living rock, roughly shaped, and lined with crevices covered by tall weeds. To one of these crevices Nehushta brought Miriam, and, seating her on a bed of grass, examined her foot, which seemed to have been bruised by a stone from a sling. Having no water with which to wash the bleeding hurt, she made a poultice of crushed herbs and tied it about the ankle with a strip of linen. Even before she had finished her task, so exhausted was Miriam that she fell fast asleep. Nehushta watched her a while, wondering what they should do next, till, in that lonely place bathed by the warm spring sun, she also began to doze.

Suddenly she awoke with a start, having dreamed that she saw a man with white face and beard peering at them from behind a rough angle of rock. She stared: there was the rock as she had dreamed of it, but no man. She looked upward. Above them, piled block upon gigantic block, rose the wall, towering and impregnable. Thither he could not have gone, since on it only a lizard could find foothold. Nor was he anywhere else, for there was no cover; so she decided that he must have been some searcher of the rubbish-heap, who, seeing them hidden in the tall grasses, had fled away. Miriam was still sound asleep, and in her weariness presently Nehushta again began to doze, till at length—it may have been one hour later, or two or three, she knew not—some sound disturbed her. Opening her eyes, once more behind that ridge of rock she saw, not one white-bearded face, but two, staring at her and Miriam. As she sat up they vanished. She remained still, pretending to sleep, and again they appeared, scanning her closely and whispering to each other in eager tones. Suddenly one of the faces turned a little so that the light fell on it. Now Nehushta knew why in her dream it had seemed familiar, and in her heart thanked God.

"Brother Ithiel," she said in a quiet voice, "why do you hide like a coney in these rocks?"

Both heads disappeared, but the sound of whispering continued. Then one of them rose again among the green grasses as a man might rise out of water. It was Ithiel's.

"It is indeed you, Nehushta?" said his well-remembered voice.

"Who else?" she asked.

"And that lady who sleeps at your side?"

"Once they called her Queen of the Essenes; now she is a hunted fugitive, waiting to be massacred by Simon, or John, or Eleazer, or Zealots, or Sicarii, or any other of the holy cut-throats who inhabit this Holy City," answered Nehushta bitterly.

Ithiel raised his hands as though in thankfulness, then said:

"Hush! hush! Here the very birds are spies. Brother, creep to that rock and look if any men are moving."

The Essene obeyed, and answered, "None; and they cannot see us from the wall."

Ithiel motioned to him to return.

"Does she sleep sound?" he asked of Nehushta, pointing to Miriam.

"Like the dead."

Then, after another whispered conference, the pair of them crept round the angle of the rock. Bidding Nehushta follow them, they lifted the sleeping Miriam, and carried her between them through a dense growth of shrubs to another rock. Here they moved some grass and pushed aside a stone, revealing a hole not much larger than a jackal would make. Into this the brother entered, heels first. Then Nehushta, by his directions, taking the feet of the senseless Miriam, with her help he bore her into the hole, that opened presently into a wide passage. Last of all Ithiel, having lifted the grasses which their feet had trodden, followed them, pulling the stone back to its place, and cutting off the light. Once more they were in darkness, but this did not seem to trouble the brethren, for again lifting Miriam, they went forward a distance of thirty or forty paces, Nehushta holding on to Ithiel's robe. Now, at length, the cold air of this cave, or perhaps its deep gloom and the motion, awoke Miriam from her swoon-like sleep. She struggled in their hands, and would have cried out, had not Nehushta bade her to be silent.

"Where am I?" she said. "Is this the hall of death?"

"Nay, lady. Wait a while, all shall be explained."

While she spoke and Miriam clung to her affrighted, Ithiel struck iron and flint together. Catching the spark upon tinder he blew it to a flame and lighted a taper which burnt up slowly, causing his white beard and face to appear by degrees out of the darkness, like that of a ghost rising from the tomb.

"Oh! surely I am dead," said Miriam, "for before me stands the spirit of my uncle Ithiel."

"Not the spirit, Miriam, but the flesh," answered the old man in a voice that trembled with joy. Then, since he could restrain himself no longer, he gave the taper to the brother, and, taking her in his arms, kissed her again and again.

"Welcome, most dear child," he said; "yes, even to this darksome den, welcome, thrice welcome, and blessed be the eternal God Who led our feet forth to find you. Nay, do not stop to talk, we are still too near the wall. Give me your hand and come."

Miriam glanced up as she obeyed, and by the feeble light of the taper saw a vast rocky roof arching above them. On either side of her also were walls of rough-hewn rock down which dripped water, and piled upon the floor or still hanging half-cut from the roof, boulders large enough to fashion a temple column.

"What awful place is this, my uncle?" she asked.

"The cavern whence Solomon, the great king, drew stone for the building of the Temple. Look, here are his mason's marks upon the wall. Here he fashioned the blocks and thus it happened that no sound of saw or hammer was heard within the building. Doubtless also other kings before and since his day have used this quarry, as no man knows its age."

While he spoke thus he was leading her onwards over the rough, stone- hewn floor, where the damp gathered in little pools. Following the windings of the cave they turned once, then again and yet again, so that soon Miriam was utterly bewildered and could not have found her way back to the entrance for her life's sake. Moreover, the air had become so hot and stifling that she could scarcely breathe.

"It will be better presently," said Ithiel, noticing her distress, as he drew her limping after him into what seemed to be a natural crevice of rock hardly large enough to allow the passage of his body. Along this crevice they scrambled for eight or ten paces, to find themselves suddenly in a tunnel lined with masonry, and so large that they could stand upright.

"Once it was a watercourse," explained Ithiel, "that filled the great tank, but now it has been dry for centuries."

Down this darksome shaft hobbled Miriam, till presently it ended in a wall, or what seemed to be a wall—for when Ithiel pressed upon a stone it turned. Beyond it the tunnel continued for twenty or thirty paces, leading them at length into a vast chamber with arched roof and cemented sides and bottom, which in some bygone age had been a water- tank. Here lights were burning, and even a charcoal fire, at which a brother was engaged in cooking. Also the air was pure and sweet, doubtless because of the winding water-channels that ran upwards. Nor did the place lack inhabitants, for there, seated in groups round the tapers, or watching the cooking over the charcoal fire, were forty or fifty men, still clad, for the most part, in the robes of the Essenes.

"Brethren," cried Ithiel, in answer to the challenge of one who was set to watch the entry, "I bring back to you her whom we lost a while ago, the lady Miriam."

They heard, and seizing the tapers, ran forward.

"It is she!" they cried, "our queen and none other, and with her Nehushta the Libyan! Welcome, welcome, a thousand times, dear lady!"

Miriam greeted them one and all, and before these greetings were finished they brought her food to eat, rough but wholesome, also good wine and sweet water. Then while she ate she heard all their story. It seemed that more than a year ago the Romans, marching on Jericho, had fallen upon their village and put a number of them to death, seizing others as slaves. Thereon the remnant fled to Jerusalem, where many more perished, for, being peaceable folk, all the factions robbed and slew them. Seeing, at last, that to live at large in the city would be to doom themselves to extinction, and yet not daring to leave it, they sought a refuge in this underground place, of which, as it chanced, one of their brethren had the secret. This he had inherited from his father, so that it was known to no other living man.

Here by degrees they laid up a great store of provisions of all sorts, of charcoal for burning, and other necessaries, carrying into the place also clothes, bedding, cooking utensils and even some rough furniture. These preparations being made, the fifty of them who remained removed themselves to the vaults where now they had already dwelt three months, and here, so far as was possible, continued to practise the rules of their order. Miriam asked how they kept their health in this darkness, to which they replied that sometimes they went out by that path which she had just followed, and mingled with the people in the city, returning to their hole at night. Ithiel and his companion were on such a journey when they found her. Also they had another passage to the upper air which they would show her later.

When Miriam had finished eating, dressed her hurt, and rested a while, they took her to explore the wonders of the place. Beyond this great cistern, that was their common room, lay more to the number of six or seven, one of the smallest of which was given to Nehushta and herself to dwell in. Others were filled with stores enough to last them all for months. Last of all was a cave, not very large, but deep, which always held sweet water. Doubtless there was a spring at the bottom of it, which, when the other rain-fed tanks grew dry, still kept it supplied. From this cistern that had been used for generations after the others were abandoned, a little stair ran upwards, worn smooth by the feet of folk long dead, who had come hither to draw water.

"Where does it lead?" asked Miriam.

"To the ruined tower above," answered Ithiel. "Nay, another time I will show you. Now your place is made ready for you, go, let Nehushta bathe your foot, and sleep, for you must need it sorely."

So Miriam went and laid herself down to rest in the little cemented vault which was to be her home for four long months; and being worn out, notwithstanding the sufferings she had passed and her fears for her grandfather, slept there as soundly as ever she had done in her wind-swept chamber at the palace of Tyre, or in her house at the village of the Essenes.

When she awoke and saw the darkness all about her, she thought that it must be night; then remembering that in this place it was always night, called to Nehushta, who uncovered the little lamp that burned in a corner of the vault, and went out, to return presently with the news that according to the Essenes, it was day. So she rose and put on her robes, and they passed together into the great chamber. Here they found the Essenes at prayer and making their reverences to the sun which they could not see, after which they ate their morning meal. Now Miriam spoke to Ithiel, telling him of her trouble about her grandfather, who, if he himself still lived, would think that she was dead.

"One thing is certain," replied her great-uncle: "that

you shall not go out to seek him, nor must you tell him of your hiding-place, since soon or late this might mean that all of us would be destroyed, if only for the sake of the food which we have hoarded."

Miriam asked if she could not send a message. He answered:

"No, since none would dare to take it." In the end, however, after she had pleaded with him long and earnestly, it was agreed that she should write the words, "I am safe and well, but in a place that I must not tell you of," and sign her name upon a piece of parchment. This letter Ithiel, who purposed to creep out into the city that evening disguised as a beggar, to seek for tidings, said he would take, and, if might be, bribe some soldier to deliver it to Benoni at the house of the high priest, if he were there.

So Miriam wrote the letter, and at nightfall Ithiel and another brother departed, taking it with them.

On the following morning they returned, safe, but with a dreadful tale of the slaughters in the city and in the Temple courts, where the mad factions still fought furiously.

"Your tidings, my uncle?" said Miriam, rising to meet him. "Does he still live?"

"Be of good comfort," he answered. "Benoni reached the house of Mathias in safety, and Caleb also, and now they are sheltering within the Temple walls. This much I had from one of the high priest's guards, who, for the price of a piece of gold I gave him, swore that he would deliver the letter without fail. But, child, I will take no more, for that soldier eyed me curiously and said it was scarcely safe for beggars to carry gold."

Miriam thanked him for his goodness and his news, saying that they lifted a weight from her heart.

"I have other tidings that may perhaps make it lighter still," went on the old man, looking at her sideways. "Titus with a mighty host draws near to Jerusalem from Cæsarea."

"There is no joy in that tale," replied Miriam, "for it means that the Holy City will be besieged and taken."

"Nay, but among that host is one who, if all the stories are true," and again he glanced at her face, "would rather take you than the city."

"Who?" she said, pressing her hands against her heart and turning redder than the lamplight.

"One of Titus' prefects of horse, the noble Roman, Marcus, whom in byegone days you knew by the banks of Jordan."

Now the red blood fled back to Miriam's heart, and she turned so faint that had not the wall been near at hand she would have fallen.

"Marcus?" she said. "Well, he swore that he would come, yet it will bring him little nearer me;" and she turned and sought her chamber.

So Marcus had come. Since he sent the letter and the ring that was upon her hand, and the pearls which were about her throat, she had heard no more of him. Twice she had written and forwarded the writings by the most trusty messenger whom she could find, but whether they reached him she did not know. For more than two years the silence between them had been that of death, till, indeed, at times she thought that he must be dead. And now he was come back, a commander in the army of Titus, who marched to punish the rebellious Jews. Would she ever see him again? Miriam could not tell. Yet she knelt and prayed from her pure heart that if it were once only, she might speak with him face to face. Indeed, it was this hope of meeting that, more than any other, supported her through all those dreadful days.

A week went by, and although the hurt to her foot had healed, like some flower in the dark Miriam drooped and languished in those gloomy vaults. Twice she prayed her uncle to be allowed to creep to the mouth of the hole behind the ridge of rock, there to breathe the fresh air and see the blessed sky. But this he would not suffer. The thing was too dangerous, he said; for although none knew the secret of their hiding-place, already two or three fugitives had found their way into the quarries by other entrances, and these it was very difficult to pass unseen.

"So be it," answered Miriam, and crept back to her cell.

Nehushta looked after her anxiously, then said:

"If she cannot have air I think that she will soon die. Is there no way?"

"One," answered Ithiel, "but I fear to take it. The staircase from the spring leads to an ancient tower that, I am told, once was a palace of the kings, but now for these many years has been deserted, for its entrance is bricked up lest thieves should make it their home. None can come into that tower, nor is it used for purposes of war, not standing upon any wall, and there she might sit at peace and see the sun; yet I fear to let her do so."

"It must be risked," answered Nehushta. "Take me to visit this place."

So Ithiel led her to the cistern, and from the cistern up a flight of steps to a little vaulted chamber, into which they entered through a stone trap-door, made of the same substance as the paving of the chamber, so that, when it was closed, none would guess that there was a passage beneath. From this old store-room, for such it doubtless was, ran more steps, ending, to all appearance, in a blank wall. Coming to it, Ithiel thrust a piece of flat iron, a foot or more in length, into a crack in this wall, lifted some stone latch within, and pushed, whereon a block of masonry of something more than the height and width of a man, and quite a yard in thickness, swung outwards. Nehushta passed through the aperture, followed by Ithiel.

"See," he said, loosing his hold of the stone, which without noise instantly closed, so that behind them there appeared to be nothing but a wall, "it is well hung, is it not? and to come hither without this iron would be dangerous. Here is the crack where it must be set to lift the latch within."

"Whoever lived here guarded their food and water well," answered Nehushta.

Then Ithiel showed her the place. It was a massive tower of a square of about forty feet, whereof the only doorway, as he told her, had been bricked up many years before to keep the thieves and vagabonds from sheltering there. In height it must have measured nearly a hundred feet, and its roof had long ago rotted away. The staircase, which was of stone, still remained, however, leading to four galleries, also of stone. Perhaps once there were floors as well, but if so these had vanished, only the stone galleries and their balustrades remaining. Ithiel led Nehushta up the stair, which, though narrow, was safe and easy. Resting at each story, at length they came to that gallery which projected from its sides within ten feet of the top of the tower, and saw Jerusalem and the country round spread like a map beneath. Then, as it was sunset, they returned. At the foot of the stair Ithiel gave Nehushta the piece of iron and showed her how to lift the secret latch and pull upon the block of hewn stone that was a door, so that it opened to swing to again behind them.

Next morning, before it was dawn in the world above, Miriam aroused Nehushta. She had been promised that this day she should be taken up the Old Tower, and so great was her longing for the scent of the free air and the sight of the blue sky that she had scarcely closed her eyes this night.

"Have patience, lady," said Nehushta, "have patience. We cannot start until the Essenes have finished their prayers to the sun, which, down in this black hole, they worship more earnestly than ever."

So Miriam waited, though she would eat nothing, till at length Ithiel came and led them past the cistern up the stairs to the store or treasure chamber, where the trap-door stood wide, since, except in case of some danger, they had no need to shut it. Next, they reached the door of solid stone which Ithiel showed her how to open, and entered the base of the massive building. There, far above her, Miriam saw the sky again, red from the lights of morning, and at the sight of it clapped her hands and called aloud.

"Hush!" said Ithiel. "These walls are thick, yet it is not safe to raise a voice of joy in Jerusalem, that home of a thousand miseries, lest, perchance, some should hear it through a cleft in the masonry, and cause search to be made for the singer. Now, if you will, follow me."

So they went up and up, till at last they reached the topmost gallery, where the wall was pierced with loopholes and overhanging platforms, whence stones and other missiles could be hurled upon an attacking force. Miriam looked out eagerly, walking round the gallery from aperture to aperture.

To the south lay the marble courts and glittering buildings of the Temple, whence, although men fought daily in them, the smoke of sacrifice still curled up to heaven. Behind these were the Upper and the Lower City, crowded with thousands of houses, packed, every one of them, with human beings who had fled hither for refuge, or, notwithstanding the dangers of the time, to celebrate the Passover. To the east was the rugged valley of Jehoshaphat, and beyond it the Mount of Olives, green with trees soon to be laid low by the Romans. To the north the new city of Bezetha, bordered by the third wall and the rocky lands beyond. Not far away, also, but somewhat in front of them and to the left, rose the mighty tower of Antonia, now one of the strongholds of John of Gischala and the Zealots, while also to the west, across the width of the city, were the towers of Hippicus, Phasæl and Mariamne, backed by the splendid palace of Herod. Besides these were walls, fortresses, gates and palaces without number, so intricate and many that the eye could scarcely follow or count them, and, between, the numberless narrow streets of Jerusalem. These and many other things Ithiel pointed out to Miriam, who listened eagerly till he wearied of the task. Then they looked downwards through the overhanging platforms of stone to the large market-place beneath and to the front, and upon the roofs of the houses, mostly of the humbler sort, that were built behind almost up to the walls of the Old Tower, whereon many people were gathered as though for safety, eating their morning meal, talking anxiously together, and even praying.

Whilst they were thus engaged, Nehushta touched Miriam and pointed to the road which ran from the Valley of Thorns on the northeast. She looked, and saw a great cloud of dust that advanced swiftly, and presently, through the dust, the sheen of spears and armour.

"The Romans!" said Nehushta quietly.

She was not the only one who had caught sight of them, for suddenly the battlement of every wall and tower, the roof of every lofty house, the upper courts of the Temple, and all high places became crowded with thousands and tens of thousands of heads, each of them staring towards that advancing dust. In silence they stared as though their multitudes were stricken dumb, till presently, from far below out of the maze of winding streets, floated the wail of a single voice.

"Woe, woe to Jerusalem!" said the voice. "Woe, woe to the City and the Temple!"

They shuddered, and as it seemed to them, all the listening thousands within reach of that mournful cry shuddered also.

"Aye!" repeated Ithiel, "woe to Jerusalem, for yonder comes her doom."

Now on the more rocky ground the dust grew thinner, and through it they could distinguish the divisions of the mighty army of destroyers. First came thousands of Syrian allies and clouds of scouts and archers, who searched the country far and wide. Next appeared the road-makers and the camp-setters, the beasts of burden with the general's baggage and its great escort, followed by Titus himself, his bodyguard and officers, by pikemen and by horsemen. Then were seen strange and terrible-looking engines of war beyond count, and with them the tribunes, and the captains of cohorts and their guards who preceded the engines, and that “abomination of desolation,” the Roman Eagles, surrounded by bands of trumpeters, who from time to time uttered their loud, defiant note. After them marched the vast army in ranks six deep, divided into legions and followed by their camp- bearers and squadrons of horse. Lastly were seen the packs of baggage, and mercenaries by thousands and tens of thousands. On the Hill of Saul the great host halted and began to encamp. An hour later a band of horsemen five or six hundred strong emerged out of this camp and marched along the straight road to Jerusalem.

“It is Titus himself,” said Ithiel. “See, the Imperial Standard goes before him.”

On they came till, from their lofty perch, Miriam, who was keen- sighted, could see their separate armour and tell the colour of their horses. Eagerly she searched them with her eyes, for well she guessed that Marcus would be one of those who accompanied his general upon this service. That plumed warrior might be he, or that with the purple cloak, or that who galloped out from near by the Standard on an errand. He was there; she was sure he was there, and yet they were as far apart as when the great sea rolled between them.

Now, as they reconnoitred and were passing the Tower of Women, of a sudden the gate opened, and from alleys and houses where they had lain in ambush were poured out thousands of Jews. Right through the thin line of horsemen they pierced, uttering savage cries, then doubled back upon the severed ends. Many were cut down; Miriam could see them falling from their horses.

The Imperial Standard sank, then rose and sank again to rise once more. Now dust hid the combat, and she thought that all the Romans must be slain. But no, for presently they began to appear beyond the dust, riding back by the way they had come, though fewer than they were. They had charged through the multitude of Jews and escaped. But who had escaped and who were left behind? Ah! that she could not tell; and it was with a sick and anxious heart that Miriam descended the steps of the tower into the darkness of the caves.

Chapter 15

What Passed in the Tower

Nearly four months had gone by. Perhaps, during the whole history of the world there never has been and never will be more cruel suffering than was endured by the inhabitants of Jerusalem during that period, or rather by the survivors of the nation of the Jews who were crowded together within its walls. Forgetting their internecine quarrels in the face of overwhelming danger, too late the factions united and fought against the common foe with a ferocity that has been seldom equalled. They left nothing undone which desperate men could do. Again and again they sallied forth against the Romans, slaughtering thousands of them. They captured their battering-rams and catapults. They undermined the great wooden towers which Titus erected against their walls, and burnt them. With varying success they made sally upon sally. Titus took the third wall and the new city of Bezetha. He took the second wall and pulled it down. Then he sent Josephus, the historian, to persuade the Jews to surrender, but his countrymen cursed and stoned him, and the war went on.

At length, as it seemed to be impossible to carry the place by assault, Titus adopted a surer and more terrible plan. Enclosing the first unconquered wall, the Temple, and the fortress by another wall of his own making, he sat down and waited for starvation to do its work. Then came the famine. At the beginning, before the maddened, devil-inspired factions began to destroy each other and to prey upon the peaceful people, Jerusalem was amply provisioned. But each party squandered the stores that were within its reach, and, whenever they could do so, burnt those of their rivals, so that the food which might have supplied the whole city for months, vanished quickly in orgies of wanton waste and destruction. Now all, or almost all, was gone, and by tens and hundreds of thousands the people starved.

Those who are curious about such matters, those who desire to know how much human beings can endure, and of what savagery they can be capable when hunger drives them, may find these details set out in the pages of Josephus, the renegade Jewish historian. It serves no good purpose and will not help our story to repeat them; indeed for the most part they are too terrible to be repeated. History does not record, and the mind of man cannot invent a cruelty which was not practised by the famished Jews upon other Jews suspected of the crime of having hidden food to feed themselves or their families. Now the fearful prophecy was fulfilled, and it came about that mothers devoured their own infants, and children snatched the last morsel of bread from the lips of their dying parents. If these things were done between those who were of one blood, what dreadful torment was there that was not practised by stranger upon stranger? The city went mad beneath the weight of its abominable and obscene misery. Thousands perished every day, and every night thousands more escaped, or attempted to escape, to the Romans, who caught the poor wretches and crucified them beneath the walls, till there was no more wood of which to make the crosses, and no more ground whereon to stand them.

All these things and many others Miriam saw from her place of outlook in the gallery of the deserted tower. She saw the people lying dead by hundreds in the streets beneath. She saw the robbers hale them from their houses and torture them to discover the hiding-place of the food which they were supposed to have hidden, and when they failed, put them to the sword. She saw the Valley of the Kidron and the lower slopes of the Mount of Olives covered with captive Jews writhing on their crosses, there to die as the Messiah whom they had rejected, died. She saw the furious attacks, the yet more furious sallies and the dreadful daily slaughter, till at length her heart grew so sick within her, that although she still took refuge in the ruined tower to escape the gloom beneath, Miriam would spend whole hours lying on her face, her fingers thrust into her ears, that she might shut out the sights and sounds of this unutterable woe.

Meanwhile, the Essenes, who still had stores of food, ventured forth but rarely, lest the good condition of their bodies, although their faces were white as death from dwelling in the darkness, should tempt the starving hordes to seize and torture them in the hope of discovering the hiding-places of their nutriment. Indeed, to several of the brethren this happened; but in obedience to their oaths, as will be seen in the instance of the past President Theophilus—who went out and was no more heard of—they endured all and died without a murmur, having betrayed nothing. Still, notwithstanding the danger, driven to it by utter weariness of their confinement in the dark and by the desire of obtaining news, from time to time one of them would creep forth at night to return again before daybreak. From these men Miriam heard that after the murder of the high priest Mathias and his sons, together with sixteen of the Sanhedrim, on a charge of correspondence with the Romans, her grandfather, Benoni, had been elected to that body, in which he exercised much influence and caused many to be put to death who were accused of treason or of favouring the Roman cause. Caleb also was in the Temple and foremost in every fight. He was said to have sworn an oath that he would slay the Prefect of Horse, Marcus, with whom he had an ancient quarrel, or be slain himself. It was told, indeed, that they had met once already and struck some blows at each other, before they were separated by an accident of war.

The beginning of August came at length, and the wretched city, in addition to its other miseries, panted in the heat of a scorching summer sun and was poisoned by the stench from the dead bodies that filled the streets and were hurled in thousands from the walls. Now the Romans had set up their battering engines at the very gates of the Temple, and slowly but surely were winning their way into its outer courts.

On a certain night, about an hour before the dawn, Miriam woke Nehushta, telling her that she was stifling there in those vaults and must ascend the tower. Nehushta said that it was folly, whereon Miriam answered that she would go alone. This she would not suffer her to do, so together they passed up the stairs according to custom, and, having gained the base of the tower through the swinging door of stone, climbed the steps that ran in the thickness of the wall till they reached the topmost gallery. Here they sat, fanned by the faint night wind, and watched the fires of the Romans stretched far and wide around the walls and even among the ruins of the houses almost beneath them, since that part of the city was taken.

Presently the dawn broke, a splendid, fearful dawn. It was as though the angel of the daybreak had dipped his wing into a sea of blood and dashed it against the brow of Night, still crowned with her fading stars. Of a sudden the heavens were filled with blots and threads of flaming colour latticed against the pale background of the twilight sky. Miriam watched it with a kind of rapture, letting its glory and its peace sink into her troubled soul, while from below arose the sound of awakening camps making ready for the daily battle. Soon a ray of burning light, cast like a spear from the crest of the Mount of Olives across the Valley of Jehoshaphat, struck full upon the gold- roofed Temple and its courts. At its coming, as though at a signal, the northern gates were thrown wide, and through them poured a flood of gaunt and savage warriors. They came on in thousands, uttering fierce war-cries. Some pickets of Romans tried to stay their rush; in a minute they were overcome and destroyed. Now they were surging round the feet of a great wooden tower filled with archers. Here the fight was desperate, for the soldiers of Titus rushed up by companies to defend their engine. But they could not drive back that onset, and presently the tower was on fire, and in a last mad effort to save their lives its defenders were casting themselves headlong from the lofty platform. With shouts of triumph the Jews rushed through the breaches in the second wall, and leaving what remained of the castle of Antonia on the left, poured down into the maze of streets and ruined houses that lay immediately behind the Old Tower whence Miriam watched.

In front of this building, which the Romans had never attempted to enter, since for military purposes it was useless to them, lay the open space, once, no doubt, part of its garden, but of late years used as a cattle market and a place where young men exercised themselves in arms. Bordering the waste on its further side were strong fortifications, the camping ground of the twelfth and fifteenth legions. Across this open space those who remained of the Romans fled back towards their outer line, followed by swarms of furious Jews. They gained them, such as were not overtaken, but the Jews who pursued were met with so fierce a charge, delivered by the fresh troops behind the defences, that they were in turn swept back and took refuge among the ruined houses. Suddenly Miriam's attention became concentrated upon the mounted officer who led this charge, a gallant-looking man clad in splendid armour, whose clear, ringing voice, as he uttered the words of command, had caught her ear even through the tumult and the shouting. The Roman onslaught having reached its limit, began to fall back again like the water from an exhausted wave upon a slope of sand. At the moment the Jews were in no condition to press the enemy's retreat, so that the mounted officer who withdrew last of all, had time to turn his horse, and heedless of the arrows that sang about him, to study the ground now strewn with the wounded and the dead. Presently he looked up at the deserted tower as though wondering whether he could make use of it, and Miriam saw his face. It was Marcus, grown older, more thoughtful also, and altered somewhat by a short curling beard, but still Marcus and no other.

"Look! look!" she said.

Nehushta nodded. "Yes, it is he; I thought so from the first. And now, having seen him, lady, shall we be going?"

"Going?" said Miriam, "wherefore?"

"Because one army or the other may chance to think that this building would be useful to them, and break open the walled-up door. Also they might explore this staircase, and then—"

"And then," answered Miriam quietly, "we should be taken. What of it? If the Jews find us we are of their party; if the Romans—well, I do not greatly fear the Romans."

"You mean you do not fear one Roman. But who knows, but that he may presently lie dead—"

"Oh! say it not," answered Miriam, pressing her hand upon her heart. "Nay, safe or unsafe, I will see this fight out. Look, yonder is Caleb—yes, Caleb himself, shouting to the Jews. How fierce is his face, like that of a hyena in a snare. Nay, now I will not go—go you and leave me in peace to watch the end."

"Since you are too heavy and strong for my old arms to carry down those steep steps, so be it," answered Nehushta calmly. "After all, we have food with us, and our angels can guard us as well on the top of a tower as in those dirty cisterns. Also this fray is worth the watching."

As she spoke, the Romans having re-formed, led by the Prefect Marcus and other officers, advanced from their entrenchment, to be met half- way by the Jews, now reinforced from the Temple, among whom was Caleb. There, in the open space, they fought hand to hand, for neither force would yield an inch. Miriam, watching through the stone bars from above, had eyes for only two of all that multitude of men—Marcus, whom she loved, and Caleb, whom she feared. Marcus was attacked by a Jew, who stabbed his horse, to be instantly stabbed himself by a Roman who came to the rescue of his commander. After this he fought on foot. Caleb killed first one soldier than another. Watching him, Miriam grew aware that he was cutting his way towards some point, and that the point was Marcus. This Marcus seemed to know; at least, he also strove to cut his way towards Caleb. Nearer and nearer they came, till at length they met and began to rain blows upon each other; but not for long, for just then a charge of some Roman horsemen separated them. After this both parties retired to their lines, taking their wounded with them.

Thus, with pauses, sometimes of two or three hours, the fight went on from morning to noon, and from noon to sunset. During the latter part of the time the Romans made no more attacks, but were contented with defending themselves while they awaited reinforcements from without the city, or perhaps the results of some counter-attack in another part.

Thus the advantage rested, or seemed to rest, with the Jews, who held all the ruined houses and swept the open space with their arrows. Now it was that Nehushta's fears were justified, for having a little leisure the Jews took a beam of wood and battered in the walled-up doorway of the tower.

"Look!" said Nehushta, pointing down.

"Oh, Nou!" Miriam answered, "I was wrong. I have run you into danger. But indeed I could not go. What shall we do now?"

"Sit quiet until they come to take us," said Nehushta grimly, "and then, if they give us time, explain as best we may."

As it chanced, however, the Jews did not come, since they feared that if they mounted the stair some sudden rush of Romans might trap such of them as were within before they had time to descend again. Only they made use of the base of the tower to shelter those of their wounded whose hurts were so desperate that they dared not move them.

Now the fighting having ceased for a while, the soldiers of both sides amused themselves with shouting taunts and insults at each other, or challenges to single combat. Presently Caleb stepped forward from the shelter of a wall and called out that if the Prefect Marcus would meet him alone in the open space he had something to say which he would be glad to hear. Thereupon Marcus, stepping out from his defences, where several of his officers seemed to be striving to detain him, answered:

"I will come," and walked to the centre of the market, where he was met by Caleb.

Here the two of them spoke together alone, but of what they said Miriam and Nehushta, watching them from above, could catch no word.

"Oh! will they fight?" said Miriam.

"It seems likely, since each of them has sworn to slay the other," answered Nehushta.

While she spoke Marcus, shaking his head as though to decline some proposal, and pointing to the men of his command, who stood up watching him, turned to walk back to his own lines, followed by Caleb, who shouted out that he was a coward and did not dare to stand alone before him. At this insult Marcus winced, then went on again, doubtless because he thought it his duty to rejoin his company, whereon Caleb, drawing his sword, struck him with the flat of it across the back. Now the Jews laughed, while the Romans uttered a shout of rage at the intolerable affront offered to their commander. As for Marcus, he wheeled round, sword in hand, and flew straight at Caleb's throat.

But it was for this that the Jew had been waiting, since he knew that no Roman, and least of all Marcus, would submit to the indignity of such a blow. As his adversary came on, made almost blind with fury, he leapt to one side lightly as a lion leaps, and with all the force of his long sinewy arm brought down his heavy sword upon the head of Marcus. The helm was good, or the skull beneath must have been split in two by that blow, which, as it was, shore through it and bit deeply into the bone. Beneath the shock Marcus staggered, threw his arms wide, and let fall his sword. With a shout Caleb sprang at him to make an end of him, but before he could strike the Roman seemed to recover himself, and, knowing that his weapon was gone, did the only thing he could, rushed straight at his foe. Caleb's sword fell on his shoulder, but the tempered mail withstood it, and next instant Marcus had gripped him in his arms. Down they came together to the earth, rolling over each other, the Jew trying to stab the Roman, the Roman to choke the Jew with his bare hand. Then from the Roman lines rose a cry of "Rescue!" and from the Jews a cry of "Take him."

Out poured the combatants from either side of the market-place by hundreds and by thousands, and there in its centre, round the struggling forms of Caleb and of Marcus, began the fiercest fight of all that day. Where men stood, there they fell, for none would give back, since the Romans, outnumbered though they were, preferred to die rather than leave a wounded and beloved captain a prisoner in the hands of cruel enemies, while the Jews knew too well the value of such a prize to let it escape them easily. So great was the slaughter that presently Marcus and Caleb were hidden beneath the bodies of the fallen. More and more Jews rushed into the fray, but still the Romans pushed onwards with steady valour, fighting shoulder to shoulder and shield to shield.

Then of a sudden, with a savage yell a fresh body of Jews, three or four hundred strong, appeared at the west end of the market-place, and charged upon the Romans, taking them in flank. The officer in command saw his danger, and knowing that it was better that his captain should die than that the whole company should be destroyed and the arms of Cæsar suffer a grave defeat, gave orders for a retirement. Steadily, as though they were on parade, and dragging with them those of their wounded comrades who could not walk, the legionaries fell back, heedless of the storm of spears and arrows, reaching their own lines before the outflanking body of Jews could get among them. Then seeing that there was nothing more to be gained, since to attempt to storm the Roman works was hopeless, the victorious Jews also retreated, this time not to the houses behind the tower, but only to the old market wall thirty or forty paces in front of it, which they proceeded to hold and strengthen in the fading light. Seeing that they were lost, such of the wounded Romans as remained upon the field committed suicide, preferring to fall upon their own spears than into the hands of the Jews to be tortured and crucified. Also for this deed they had another reason, since it was the decree of Titus that any soldier who was taken living should be publicly disgraced by name and expelled from the ranks of the legion, and, if recaptured, in addition suffer death or banishment.

Gladly would Marcus have followed their example and thereby—though he knew it not—save himself much misery and shame in the future, but he had neither time nor weapon; moreover, so weak was he with struggling and the loss of blood, that even as he and Caleb were dragged by savage hands from among the fallen, he fainted. At first they thought that he was dead, but one of the Jews, who chanced to be a physician by trade, declared that this was not so, and that if he were left quiet for a while, he would come to himself again. Therefore, as they desired to preserve this Prefect alive, either to be held as an hostage or to be executed in sight of the army of Titus, they brought him into the Old Tower, clearing it of their own wounded, except such of them as had already breathed their last. Here they set a guard over him, though of this there seemed to be little need, and went under the command of the victorious Caleb to assist in strengthening the market-wall.

All of these things Miriam watched from above in such an agony of fear and doubt, that at times she thought that she would die. She saw her lover and Caleb fall locked in each other's arms; she saw the hideous fray that raged around them. She saw them dragged from the heap of slain, and at the end of it all, by the last light of day, saw Marcus, living or dead, she knew not which, borne into the tower, and there laid upon the ground.

"Take comfort," whispered Nehushta, pitying her dreadful grief. "The lord Marcus lives. If he were dead they would have stripped him and left his body with the others. He lives, and they purpose to hold him captive, else they would have suffered Caleb to put his sword through him, as you noted he wished to do so soon as he found his feet."

"Captive," answered Miriam. "That means that he will be crucified like the others whom we saw yesterday upon the Temple wall."

Nehushta shrugged her shoulders.

"It may be so," she said, "unless he finds means to destroy himself or—is saved."

"Saved! How can he be saved?" Then in her woe the poor girl fell upon her knees clasping her hands and murmuring: "Oh! Jesus Christ whom I serve, teach me how to save Marcus. Oh! Jesus, I love him, although he is not a Christian; love him also because I love him, and teach me how to save him. Or if one must die, take my life for his, oh! take my life for his."

"Cease," said Nehushta, "for I think I hear an answer to your prayer. Look now, he is laid just where the stair starts and not six feet from the stone door that leads down into the cistern. Except for some dead men the tower is empty; also the two sentries stand outside the breach in the brickwork with which it was walled up, because there they find more light, and their prisoner is unarmed and helpless, and cannot attempt escape. Now, if the Roman lives and can stand, why should we not open that door and thrust him through it?"

"But the Jews might see us and discover the secret of the hiding-place of the Essenes, whom they would kill because they have hidden food."

"Once we were the other side of the door, they could never come at them, even if they have time to try," answered Nehushta. "Before ever they could burst the door the stone trap beneath can be closed and the roof of the stair that leads to it let down by knocking away the props and flooded in such a fashion that a week of labour would not clear it out again. Oh! have no fear, the Essenes know and have guarded against this danger."

Miriam threw her arms about the neck of Nehushta and kissed her.

"We will try, Nou, we will try," she whispered, "and if we fail, why then we can die with him."

"To you that prospect may be pleasing, but I have no desire to die with the lord Marcus," answered Nehushta drily. "Indeed, although I like him well, were it not for your sake I should leave him to his chance. Nay, do not answer or give way to too much hope. Remember, perhaps he is dead, as he seems to be."

"Yes, yes," said Miriam wildly, "we must find out. Shall we go now?"

"Aye, while there is still a little light, for these steps are breakneck in the dark. No, do you follow me."

So on they glided down the ancient, darksome stairway, where owls hooted and bats flittered in their faces. Now they were at the last flight, which descended to a little recess set at right angles to the steps and flush with the floor of the basement, for once the door of the stairway had opened here. Thus a person standing on the last stair could not be seen by any in the tower. They reached the step and halted. Then very stealthily Nehushta went on to her hands and knees and thrust her head forward so that she could look into the base of the tower. It was dark as the grave, only a faint gleam of starlight reflected from his armour showed where Marcus lay, so close that she could touch him with her hand. Also almost opposite to her the gloom was relieved by a patch of faint grey light. Here it was that the wall had been broken in, for Nehushta could see the shadows of the sentries crossing and recrossing before the ragged opening.

She leant yet lower towards Marcus and listened. He was not dead, for he breathed. More, she heard him stir his hand and thought that she could see it move upwards towards his wounded head. Then she drew back.

"Lady," she whispered, "he lives, and I think he is awake. Now you must do the rest as your wit may teach you how, for if I speak to him he will be frightened, but your voice he may remember if he has his senses."

At these words all her doubts and fears seemed to vanish from Miriam's heart, her hand grew steady and her brain clear, for Nature told her that if she wished to save her lover she would need both clear brain and steady hand. The timid, love-racked girl was transformed into a woman of iron will and purpose. In her turn she kneeled and crept a little forward from the stair, so that her face hung over the face of Marcus. Then she spoke in a soft whisper.

"Marcus, awake and listen, Marcus; but I pray of you do not stir or make a noise. I am Miriam, whom once you knew."

At this name the dim form beneath her seemed to quiver, and the lips muttered, "Now I know that I am dead. Well, it is better than I hoped for. Speak on, sweet shade of Miriam."

"Nay, Marcus, you are not dead, you are only wounded and I am not a spirit, I am a woman, that woman whom once you knew down by the banks of Jordan. I have come to save you, I and Nehushta. If you will obey what I tell you, and if you have the strength to stand, we can guide you into a secret place where the Essenes are hidden, who for my sake will take care of you until you are able to return to the Romans. If you do not escape I fear that the Jews will crucify you."

"By Bacchus, so do I," said the whisper beneath, "and that will be worse than being beaten by Caleb. But this is a dream, I know it is a dream. If it were Miriam I should see her, or be able to touch her. It is but a dream of Miriam. Let me dream on," and he turned his head.

Miriam thought for a moment. Time was short and it was necessary to make him understand. Well, it was not difficult. Slowly she bent a little lower and pressed her lips upon his.

"Marcus," she went on, "I kiss you now to show you that I am no dream and how needful it is that you should be awakened. Had I light I could prove to you that I am Miriam by your ring which is upon my fingers and your pearls which are about my neck."

"Cease," he answered, "most beloved, I was weak and wandering, now I know that this is not a dream, and I thank Caleb who has brought us together again, against his wish, I think. Say, what must I do?"

"Can you stand?" asked Miriam.

"Perhaps. I am not sure. I will try."

"Nay, wait. Nehushta, come hither; you are stronger than I. Now, while I unlatch the secret door, do you lift him up. Be swift, I hear the guard stirring without."

Nehushta glided forward and knelt by the wounded man, placing her arms beneath him.

"Ready," she said. "Here is the iron."

Miriam took it, and stepping to the wall, felt with her

fingers for the crack, which in that darkness it took time to find. At length she had it, and inserting the thin hooked iron, lifted the hidden latch and pulled. The stone door was very heavy and she needed all her strength to move it. At last it began to swing.

"Now," she said to Nehushta, who straightened herself and dragged the wounded Marcus to his feet.

"Quick, quick!" said Miriam, "the guards enter."

Supported by Nehushta, Marcus took three tottering steps and reached the open door. Here, on its very threshold indeed, his strength failed him, for he was wounded in the knee as well as in the head. Groaning, "I cannot," he fell to the ground, dragging the old Libyan with him, his breastplate clattering loud against the stone threshold. The sentry without heard the sound and called to a companion to give him the lantern. In an instant Nehushta was up again, and seizing Marcus by his right arm, began to drag him through the opening, while Miriam, setting her back against the swinging stone to keep it from closing, pushed against his feet.

The lantern appeared round the angle of the broken masonry.

"For your life's sake!" said Miriam, and Nehushta dragged her hardest at the heavy, helpless body of the fallen man. He moved slowly. It was too late; if that light fell on him all was lost. In an instant Miriam took her resolve. With an effort she swung the door wide, then as Nehushta dragged again she sprang forward, keeping in the shadow of the wall. The Jew who held the lantern, alarmed by the sounds within, entered hastily and, catching his foot against the body of a dead man who lay there, stumbled so that he fell upon his knee. In her hand Miriam held the key, and as the guard regained his feet, but not before its light fell upon her, she struck with it at the lamp, breaking and extinguishing it.

Then she turned to fly, for, as she knew well, the stone would now be swinging on its pivot.

Alas! her chance had gone, for the man, stretching out his arm, caught her about the middle and held her fast, shouting loudly for help. Miriam struggled, she battered him with the iron and dragged at him with her left hand, but in vain, for in that grip she was helpless as a child who fights against its nurse. While she fought thus she heard the dull thud of the closing stone, and even in her despair rejoiced, knowing that until Marcus was beyond its threshold it could not be shut. Ceasing from her useless struggle she gathered the forces of her mind. Marcus was safe; the door was shut and could not be opened from the further side until another iron was procured; the guard had seen nothing. But her escape was impossible. Her part was played, only one thing remained for her to do—keep silence and his secret.

Men bearing lights were rushing into the tower. Her right hand, which held the iron, was free, and lest it should tell a tale she cast the instrument from her towards that side of the deserted place which she knew was buried deep in fallen stones, fragments of rotted timber and dirt from the nests of birds. Then she stood still. Now they were upon her, Caleb at the head of them.

"What is it?" he cried.

"I know not," answered the guard. "I heard a sound as of clanking armour and ran in, when some one struck the lantern from my hand, a strong rascal with whom I have struggled sorely, notwithstanding the blows that he rained upon me with his sword. See, I hold him fast."

They held up their lights and saw a beautiful, dishevelled maid, small and frail of stature, whereon they laughed out loud.

"A strong thief, truly," said one. "Why, it is a girl! Do you summon the watch every time a girl catches hold of you?"

Before the words died upon the speaker's lips, another man called out, "The Roman! The Prefect has gone! Where is the prisoner?" and with a roar of wrath they began to search the place, as a cat searches for the mouse that escapes her. Only Caleb stood still and stared at the girl.

"Miriam!" he said.

"Yes, Caleb," she answered quietly. "This is a strange meeting, is it not? Why do you break in thus upon my hiding-place?"

"Woman," he shouted, mad with anger, "where have you hidden the Prefect Marcus?"

"Marcus?" she answered; "is he here? I did not know it. Well, I saw a man run from the tower, perhaps that was he. Be swift and you may catch him."

"No man left the tower," answered the other sentry. "Seize that woman, she has hidden the Roman in some secret place. Seize her and search."

So they caught Miriam, bound her and began running round and round the wall. "Here is a staircase," called a man, "doubtless he has gone up it. Come, friends."

Then taking lights with them, they mounted the stairs to the very top, but found no one. Even as they came down again a trumpet blew and from without rose the sound of a mighty shouting.

"What happens now?" said one.

As he spoke an officer appeared in the opening of the tower.

"Begone," he cried. "Back to the Temple, taking your prisoner with you. Titus himself is upon us at the head of two fresh legions, mad at the loss of his Prefect and so many of his soldiers. Why! where is the wounded Roman, Marcus?"

"He has vanished," answered Caleb sullenly. "Vanished"—here he glanced at Miriam with jealous and vindictive hate—"and in his place has left to us this woman, the grand-daughter of Benoni, Miriam, who strangely enough was once his love."

"Is it so?" said the officer. "Girl, tell us what you have done with the Roman, or die. Come, we have no time to lose."

"I have done nothing. I saw a man walk past the sentries, that is all."

"She lies," said the officer contemptuously. "Here, kill this traitress."

A man advanced lifting his sword, and Miriam, thinking that all was over, hid her eyes while she waited for the blow. Before it fell, however, Caleb whispered something to the officer which caused him to change his mind.

"So be it," he said. "Hold your hand and take this woman with you to the Temple, there to be tried by her grandfather, Benoni, and the other judges of the Sanhedrim. They have means to cause the most obstinate to speak, whereas death seals the lips forever. Swift, now, swift, for already they are fighting on the market-place."

So they seized Miriam and dragged her away from the Old Tower, which an hour later was taken possession of by the Romans, who destroyed it with the other buildings.

Chapter 16

The Sanhedrim

The Jewish soldiers haled Miriam roughly through dark and tortuous streets, bordered by burnt-out houses, and up steep stone slopes deep with the débris of the siege. Indeed, they had need to hasten, for, lit with the lamp of flaming dwellings, behind them flowed the tide of war. The Romans, driven back from this part of the city by that day's furious sally, under cover of the night were re-occupying in overwhelming strength the ground that they had lost, forcing the Jews before them and striving to cut them off from their stronghold in the Temple and that part of the Upper City which they still held.

The party of Jews who had Miriam in their charge were returning to the Temple enclosure, which they could not reach from the north or east because the outer courts and cloisters of the Holy House were already in possession of the Romans. So it happened that they were obliged to make their way round by the Upper City, a long and tedious journey. Once during that night they were driven to cover until a great company of Romans had marched past. Caleb wished to attack them, but the other captains said that they were too few and weary, so they lay hid for nearly three hours, then went on again. After this there were other delays at gates still in the hands of their own people, which one by one were unbolted to them. Thus it was not far from daylight when at length they passed over a narrow bridge that spanned some ravine and through massive doors into a vast dim place which, as Miriam gathered from the talk of her captors, was the inner enclosure of the Temple. Here, at the command of that captain who had ordered her to be slain, she was thrust into a small cell in one of the cloisters. Then the men in charge of her locked the door and went away.

Sinking exhausted to the floor, Miriam tried to sleep, but could not, for her brain seemed to be on fire. Whenever she shut her eyes there sprang up before them visions of some dreadful scene which she had witnessed, while in her ears echoed now the shouts of the victors, now the pitiful cry of the dying, and now again the voice of the wounded Marcus calling her "Most Beloved." Was this indeed so, she wondered? Was it possible that he had not forgotten her during those years of separation when there must have been so many lovely ladies striving to win him, the rich, high-placed Roman lord, to be their lover or their husband? She did not know, she could not tell: perhaps, in such a plight, he would have called any woman who came to save him his Most Beloved, yes, even old Nehushta, and even then and there she smiled a little at the thought. Yet his voice rang true, and he had sent her the ring, the pearls and the letter, that letter which, although she knew every word of it, she still carried hidden in the bosom of her robe. Oh! she believed that he did love her, and, believing, rejoiced with all her heart that it had pleased God to allow her to save his life, even at the cost of her own. She had forgotten. There was his wound—he might die of it. Nay, surely he would not die. For her sake, the Essenes who knew him would treat him well, and they were skilful healers; also, what better nurse than Nehushta could be found? Ah! poor Nou, how she would grieve over her. What sorrow must have taken hold of her when she heard the rock door shut and found that her nursling was cut off and captured by the Jews.

Happy, indeed, was it for Miriam that she could not witness what had chanced at the further side of that block of stone; that she could not see Nehushta beating at it with her hands and striving to thrust her thin fingers to the latch which she had no instrument to lift, until the bones were stripped of skin and flesh. That she could not hear Marcus, come to himself again, but unable to rise from off his knees, cursing and raving with agony at her loss, and because she, the tender lady whom he loved, for his sake had fallen into the hands of the relentless Jews. Yes, that she could not hear him cursing and raving in his utter helplessness, till at length the brain gave in his shattered head, and he fell into a fevered madness, that for many weeks was unpierced by any light of reason or of memory. All this, at least, was spared to her.

Well, the deed was done and she must pay the price, for without a doubt they would kill her, as they had a right to do, who had saved a Roman general from their clutches. Or if they did not, Caleb would, Caleb whose bitter jealousy, as her instinct told her, had turned his love to hate. Never would he let her live to fall, perchance, as his share of the Temple spoil, into the hands of the Roman rival who had escaped him.

It was not too great a price. Because of the birth doom laid upon her, even if he sought it, and fortune brought them back together again, she could never be a wife to Marcus. And for the rest she was weary, sick with the sight and sound of slaughter and with the misery that in these latter days, as her Lord had prophesied, was come upon the city that rejected him and the people who had slain Him, their Messiah. Miriam wished to die, to pass to that home of perfect and eternal peace in which she believed; where, mayhap, it might be given to her in reward of her sufferings, to watch from afar over the soul of Marcus, and to make ready an abode for it to dwell in through all the ages of infinity. The thought pleased her, and lifting his ring, she pressed it to her lips which that very night had been pressed upon his lips, then drew it off and hid it in her hair. She wished to keep that ring until the end, if so she might. As for the pearls, she could not hide them, and though she loved them as his gift—well, they must go to the hand of the spoiler, and to the necks of other women, who would never know their tale.

This done Miriam rose to her knees and began to pray with the vivid, simple faith that was given to the first children of the Church. She prayed for Marcus, that he might recover and not forget her, and that the light of truth might shine upon him; for Nehushta, that her sorrow might be soothed; for herself, that her end might be merciful and her awakening happy; for Caleb, that his heart might be turned; for the dead and dying, that their sins might be forgiven; for the little children, that the Lord of Pity would have pity on their sufferings; for the people of the Jews, that He would lift the rod of His wrath from off them; yes, and even for the Romans, though for these, poor maid, she knew not what petition to put up.

Her prayer finished, once more Miriam strove to sleep

and dozed a little, to be aroused by a curious sound of feeble sighing, which seemed to come from the further side of the cell. By now the dawn was streaming through the stone lattice work above the doorway, and in its faint light Miriam saw the outlines of a figure with snowy hair and beard, wrapped in a filthy robe that had once been white. At first she thought that this figure must be a corpse thrust here out of the way of the living, it was so stirless. But corpses do not sigh as this man seemed to do. Who could he be, she wondered? A prisoner like herself, left to die, as, perhaps, she would be left to die? The light grew a little. Surely there was something familiar about the shape of that white head. She crept nearer, thinking that she might be able to help this old man who was so sick and suffering. Now she could see his face and the hand that lay upon his breast. They were those of a living skeleton, for the bones stood out, and over them the yellow skin was drawn like shrivelled parchment; only the deep sunk eyes still shone round and bright. Oh! she knew the face. It was that of Theophilus the Essene, a past president of the order indeed, who had been her friend from earliest childhood and the master who taught her languages in those far-off happy years which she spent in the village by the Dead Sea. This Theophilus she had found dwelling with the Essenes in their cavern home, and none of them had welcomed her more warmly. Some ten days ago, against the advice of Ithiel and others, he had insisted on creeping out to take the air and gather news in the city. Then he was a stout and hale old man, although pale-faced from dwelling in the darkness. From that journey he had not returned. Some said that he had fled to the country, others that he had gone over to the Romans, and yet others that he had been slain by some of Simon's men. Now she found him thus!

Miriam came and bent over him.

"Master," she said, "what ails you? How came you here?"

He turned his hollow, vacant eyes upon her face.

"Who is it that speaks to me thus gently?" he asked in a feeble voice.

"I, your ward, Miriam."

"Miriam! Miriam! What does Miriam in this torture-den?"

"Master, I am a prisoner. But speak of yourself."

"There is little to say, Miriam. They caught me, those devils, and seeing that I was still well-fed and strong, although sunk in years, demanded to know whence I had my food in this city of starvation. To tell them would have been to give up our secret and to bring doom upon the brethren, and upon you, our guest and lady. I refused to answer, so, having tortured me without avail, they cast me in here to starve, thinking that hunger would make me speak. But I have not spoken. How could I, who have taken the oath of the Essenes, and been their ruler? Now at length I die."

"Oh! say not so," said Miriam, wringing her hands.

"I do say it and I am thankful. Have you any food?"

"Yes, a piece of dried meat and barley bread, which chanced to be in my robe when I was captured. Take them and eat."

"Nay, Miriam, that desire has gone from me, nor do I wish to live, whose days are done. But save the food, for doubtless they will starve you also. And, look, there is water in that jar, they gave it me to make me live the longer. Drink, drink while you can, who to-morrow may be thirsty."

For a time there was silence, while the tears that gathered in Miriam's eyes fell upon the old man's face.

"Weep not for me," he said presently, "who go to my rest. How came you here?"

She told him as briefly as she might.

"You are a brave woman," he said when she had finished, "and that Roman owes you much. Now I, Theophilus, who am about to die, call down the blessing of God upon you, and upon him also for your sake, for your sake. The shield of God be over you in the slaughter and the sorrow."

Then he shut his eyes and either could not or would not speak again.

Miriam drank of the pitcher of water, for her thirst was great. Crouched at the side of the old Essene, she watched him till at length the door opened, and two gaunt, savage-looking men entered, who went to where Theophilus lay and kicked him brutally.

"What would you now?" he said, opening his eyes.

"Wake up, old man," cried one of them. "See, here is flesh," and he thrust a lump of some filthy carrion to his lips. "Smell it, taste it," he went on, "ah! is it not good? Well, tell us where is that store of food which made you so fat who now are so thin, and you shall have it all, yes, all, all."

Theophilus shook his head.

"Bethink you," cried the man, "if you do not eat, by sunrise to-morrow you will be dead. Speak then and eat, obstinate dog, it is your last chance."

"I eat not and I tell not," answered the aged martyr in a voice like a hollow groan. "By to-morrow's sunrise I shall be dead, and soon you and all this people will be dead, and God will have judged each of us according to his works. Repent you, for the hour is at hand."

Then they cursed him and smote him because of his words of ill-omen, and so went away, taking no notice of Miriam in the corner. When they had gone she came forward and looked. His jaw had fallen. Theophilus the Essene was at peace.

Another hour went by. Once more the door was opened and there appeared that captain who had ordered her to be killed. With him were two Jews.

"Come, woman," he said, "to take your trial."

"Who is to try me?" Miriam asked.

"The Sanhedrim, or as much as is left of it," he answered. "Stir now, we have no time for talking."

So Miriam rose and accompanied them across the corner of the vast court, in the centre of which the Temple rose in all its glittering majesty. As she walked she noticed that the pavement was dotted with corpses, and that from the cloisters without went up flames and smoke. They seemed to be fighting there, for the air was full of the sound of shouting, above which echoed the dull, continuous thud of battering rams striking against the massive walls.

They took her into a great chamber supported by pillars of white marble, where many starving folk, some of them women who carried or led hollow-cheeked children, sat silent on the floor, or wandered to and fro, their eyes fixed upon the ground as though in aimless search for they knew not what. On a daïs at the end of the chamber twelve or fourteen men sat in carved chairs; other chairs stretched to the right and left of them, but these were empty. The men were clad in magnificent robes, which seemed to hang ill upon their gaunt forms, and, like those of the people in the hall, their eyes looked scared and their faces were white and shrunken. These were all who were left of the Sanhedrim of the Jews.

As Miriam entered one of their number was delivering judgment upon a wretched starving man. Miriam looked at the judge. It was her grandfather, Benoni, but oh! how changed. He who had been tall and upright was now drawn almost double, his teeth showed yellow between his lips, his long white beard was ragged and had come out in patches, his hand shook, his gorgeous head-dress was awry. Nothing was the same about him except his eyes, which still shone bright, but with a fiercer fire than of old. They looked like the eyes of a famished wolf.

"Man, have you aught to say?" he was asking of the prisoner.

"Only this," the prisoner answered. "I had hidden some food, my own food, which I bought with all that remained of my fortune. Your hyæna- men caught my wife, and tormented her until she showed it them. They fell upon it, and, with their comrades, ate it nearly all. My wife died of starvation and her wounds, my children died of starvation, all except one, a child of six, whom I fed with what remained. Then she began to die also, and I bargained with the Roman, giving him jewels and promising to show him the weak place in the wall if he would convey the child to his camp and feed her. I showed him the place, and he fed her in my presence, and took her away, whither I know not. But, as you know, I was caught, and the wall was built up, so that no harm came of my treason. I would do it again to save the life of my child, twenty times over, if needful. You murdered my wife and my other children; murder me also if you will. I care nothing."

"Wretch," said Benoni, "what are your miserable wife and children compared to the safety of this holy place, which we defend against the enemies of Jehovah? Lead him away, and let him be slain upon the wall, in the sight of his friends, the Romans."

"I go," said the victim, rising and stretching out his hands to the guards, "but may you also all be slain in the sight of the Romans, you mad murderers, who, in your lust for power, have brought doom and agony upon the people of the Jews."

Then they dragged him out, and a voice called—"Bring in the next traitor."

Now Miriam was brought forward. Benoni looked up and knew her.

"Miriam?" he gasped, rising, to fall back again in his seat, "Miriam, you here?"

"It seems so, grandfather," she answered quietly.

"There is some mistake," said Benoni. "This girl can have harmed none. Let her be dismissed."

The other judges looked up.

"Best hear the charge against her first?" said one suspiciously, while another added, "Is not this the woman who dwelt with you at Tyre, and who is said to be a Christian?"

"We do not sit to try questions of faith, at least not now," answered Benoni evasively.

"Woman, is it true that you are a Christian?" queried one of the judges.

"Sir, I am," replied Miriam, and at her words the faces of the Sanhedrim grew hard as stones, while someone watching in the crowd hurled a fragment of marble at her.

"Let it be for this time," said the judge, "as the Rabbi Benoni says, we are trying questions of treason, not of faith. Who accuses this woman, and of what?"

A man stepped forward, that captain who had wished to put Miriam to death, and she saw that behind him were Caleb, who looked ill at ease, and the Jew who had guarded Marcus.

"I accuse her," he said, "of having released the Roman Prefect, Marcus, whom Caleb here wounded and took prisoner in the fighting yesterday, and brought into the Old Tower, where he was laid till we knew whether he would live or die."

"The Roman Prefect, Marcus?" said one. "Why, he is the friend of Titus, and would have been worth more to us than a hundred common men. Also, throughout this war, none has done us greater mischief. Woman, if, indeed, you let him go, no death can repay your wickedness. Did you let him go?"

"That is for you to discover," answered Miriam, for now that Marcus was safe she would tell no more lies.

"This renegade is insolent, like all her accursed sect," said the judge, spitting on the ground. "Captain, tell your story, and be brief."

He obeyed. After him that soldier was examined from whose hand Miriam had struck the lantern. Then Caleb was called and asked what he knew of the matter.

"Nothing," he answered, "except that I took the Roman and saw him laid in the tower, for he was senseless. When I returned the Roman had gone, and this lady Miriam was there, who said that he had escaped by the doorway. I did not see them together, and know no more."

"That is a lie," said one of the judges roughly. "You told

the captain that Marcus had been her lover. Why did you say this?"

"Because years ago by Jordan she, who is a sculptor, graved a likeness of him in stone," answered Caleb.

"Are artists always the lovers of those whom they picture, Caleb?" asked Benoni, speaking for the first time.

Caleb made no answer, but one of the Sanhedrim, a sharp-faced man, named Simeon, the friend of Simon, the son of Gioras, the Zealot, who sat next to him, cried, "Cease this foolishness; the daughter of Satan is beautiful; doubtless Caleb desires her for himself; but what has that to do with us?" though he added vindictively, "it should be remembered against him that he is striving to hide the truth."

"There is no evidence against this woman, let her be set free," exclaimed Benoni.

"So we might expect her grandfather to think," said Simeon, with sarcasm. "Little wonder that we are smitten with the Sword of God when Rabbis shelter Christians because they chance to be of their house, and when warriors bear false witness concerning them because they chance to be fair. For my part I say that she is guilty, and has hidden the man away in some secret place. Otherwise why did she dash the light from the soldier's hand?"

"Mayhap to hide herself lest she should be attacked," answered another, "though how she came in the tower, I cannot guess."

"I lived there," said Miriam. "It was bricked up until yesterday and safe from robbers."

"So!" commented that judge, "you lived alone in a deserted tower like a bat or an owl, and without food or water. Then these must have been brought to you from without the walls, perhaps by some secret passage that was known to none, down which you loosed the Prefect, but had no time to follow him. Woman, you are a Roman spy, as a Christian well might be. I say that she is worthy of death."

Then Benoni rose and rent his robes.

"Does not enough blood run through these holy courts?" he asked, "that you must seek that of the innocent also? What is your oath? To do justice and to convict only upon clear, unshaken testimony. Where is this testimony? What is there to show that the girl Miriam had any dealings with this Marcus, whom she had not seen for years? In the Holy Name I protest against this iniquity."

"It is natural that you should protest," said one of his brethren.

Then they fell into discussion, for the question perplexed them sorely, who, although they were savage, still wished to be honest.

Suddenly Simeon looked up, for a thought struck him.

"Search her," he said, "she is in good case, she may have food, or the secret of food, about her, or," he added—"other things."

Now two hungry-looking officers of the court seized Miriam and rent her robe open at the breast with their rough hands, since they would not be at the pains of loosening it.

"See," cried one of them, "here are pearls, fit wear for so fine a lady. Shall we take them?"

"Fool, let the trinkets be," answered Simeon angrily. "Are we common thieves?"

"Here is something else," said the officer, drawing the roll of Marcus's cherished letter from her breast.

"Not that, not that," the poor girl gasped.

"Give it here," said Simeon, stretching out his lean hand.

Then he undid the silk case and, opening the letter, read its first lines aloud. "'To the lady Miriam, from Marcus the Roman, by the hand of the Captain Gallus.' What do you say to that, Benoni and brethren? Why, there are pages of it, but here is the end: 'Farewell, your ever faithful friend and lover, Marcus.' So, let those read it who have the time; for my part I am satisfied. This woman is a traitress; I give my vote for death."

"It was written from Rome two years ago," pleaded Miriam; but no one seemed to heed her, for all were talking at once.

"I demand that the whole letter be read," shouted Benoni.

"We have no time, we have no time," answered Simeon. "Other prisoners await their trial, the Romans are battering our gates. Can we waste more precious minutes over this Nazarene spy? Away with her."

"Away with her," said Simon the son of Gioras, and the others nodded their heads in assent.

Then they gathered together discussing the manner of her end, while Benoni stormed at them in vain. Not quite in vain, however, for they yielded something to his pleading.

"So be it," said their spokesman, Simon the Zealot. "This is our sentence on the traitress—that she suffer the common fate of traitors and be taken to the upper gate, called the Gate Nicanor, that divides the Court of Israel from the Court of Women, and bound with the chain to the central column that is over the gate, where she may be seen both of her friends the Romans and of the people of Israel whom she has striven to betray, there to perish of hunger and of thirst, or in such fashion as God may appoint, for so shall we be clean of a woman's blood. Yet, because of the prayer of Benoni, our brother, of whose race she is, we decree that this sentence shall not be carried out before the set of sun, and that if in the meanwhile the traitress elects to give information that shall lead to the recapture of the Roman prefect, Marcus, she shall be set at liberty without the gates of the Temple. The case is finished. Guards, take her to the prison whence she came."

So they seized Miriam and led her thence through the crowd of onlookers, who paused from their wanderings and weary searching of the ground to spit at or curse her, and thrust her back into her cell and to the company of the cold corpse of Theophilus the Essene.

Here Miriam sat down, and partly to pass the time, partly because she needed it, ate the bread and dried flesh which she had left hidden in the cell. After this sleep came to her, who was tired out and the worst being at hand, had nothing more to fear. For four or five hours she rested sweetly, dreaming that she was a child again, gathering flowers on the banks of Jordan in the spring season, till, at length, a sound caused her to awake. She looked up to see Benoni standing before her.

"What is it, grandfather?" she asked.

"Oh! my daughter," groaned the wretched old man, "I am come here at some risk, for because of you and for other reasons they suspect me, those wolf-hearted men, to bid you farewell and to ask your pardon."

"Why should you ask my pardon, grandfather? Seeing things as they see them, the sentence is just enough. I am a Christian, and—if you would know it—I did, as I hope, save the life of Marcus, for which deed my own is forfeit."

"How?" he asked.

"That, grandfather, I will not tell you."

"Tell me, and save yourself. There is little chance that they will take him, since the Jews have been driven from the Old Tower."

"The Jews might re-capture the tower, and I will not tell you. Also, the lives of others are at stake, of my friends who have sheltered me, and who, as I trust, will now shelter him."

"Then you must die, and by this death of shame, for I am powerless to save you. Yes, you must die tied to a pinnacle of the gateway, a mockery to friend and foe. Why, if it had not been that I still have some authority among them, and that you are of my blood, girl though you be, they would have crucified you upon the wall, serving you as the Romans serve our people."

"If it pleases God that I should die, I shall die. What is one life among so many tens of thousands? Let us talk of other things while we have time."

"What is there to talk of, Miriam, save misery, misery, misery?" and again he groaned. "You were right, and I have been wrong. That Messiah of yours whom I rejected, yes, and still reject, had at least the gift of prophecy, for the words that you read me yonder in Tyre will be fulfilled upon this people and city, aye, to the last letter. The Romans hold even the outer courts of the Temple; there is no food left. In the upper town the inhabitants devour each other and die, and die till none can bury the dead. In a day or two, or ten—what does it matter?—we who are left must perish also by hunger and the sword. The nation of the Jews is trodden out, the smoke of their sacrifices goes up no more, and the Holy House that they have builded will be pulled stone from stone, or serve as a temple for the worship of heathen gods."

"Will Titus show no mercy? Can you not surrender?" asked Miriam.

"Surrender? To be sold as slaves or dragged a spectacle at the wheels of Cæsar's triumphal car, through the shouting streets of Rome? No, girl, best to fight it out. We will seek mercy of Jehovah and not of Titus. Oh! I would that it were done with, for my heart is broken, and this judgment is fallen on me—that I, who, of my own will, brought my daughter to her death, must bring her daughter to death against my will. If I had hearkened to you, you would have been in Pella, or in Egypt. I lost you, and, thinking you dead, what I have suffered no man can know. Now I find you, and because of the office that was thrust upon me, I, even I, from whom your life has sprung, must bring you to your doom."

"Grandfather," Miriam broke in, wringing her hands, for the grief of this old man was awful to witness, "cease, I beseech you, cease. Perhaps, after all, I shall not die."

He looked up eagerly. "Have you hope of escape?" he asked. "Perchance Caleb—"

"Nay, I know naught of Caleb, except that there is still good in his heart, since at the last he tried to save me—for which I thank him. Still, I had sooner perish here alone, who do not fear death in my spirit, whatever my flesh may fear, than escape hence in his company."

"What then, Miriam? Why should you think——?" and he paused.

"I do not think, I only trust in God and—hope. One of

our faith, now long departed, who foretold that I should be born, foretold also that I should live out my life. It may be so—for that woman was holy, and a prophetess."

As she spoke there came a rolling sound like that of distant thunder, and a voice without called:

"Rabbi Benoni, the wall is down. Tarry not, Rabbi Benoni, for they seek you."

"Alas! I must begone," he said, "for some new horror is fallen upon us, and they summon me to the council. Farewell, most beloved Miriam, may my God and your God protect you, for I cannot. Farewell, and if, by any chance, you live, forgive me, and try to forget the evil that, in my blindness and my pride, I have brought upon yours and you, but oh! most of all upon myself."

Then he embraced her passionately and was gone, leaving Miriam weeping.

Chapter 17

The Gate of Nicanor

Another two hours went by, and the lengthening shadows cast through the stonework of the lattice told Miriam that the day was drawing to its end. Suddenly the bolts were shot and the door opened.

"The time is at hand," she said to herself, and at the thought her heart beat fast and her knees trembled, while a mist came before her eyes, so that she could not see. When it passed she looked up, and there before her, very handsome and stately, though worn with war and hunger, stood Caleb, sword in hand and clad in a breast plate dinted with many blows. At the sight, Miriam's courage came back to her; at least before him she would show no fear.

"Are you sent to carry out my sentence?" she asked.

He bowed his head. "Yes, a while hence, when the sun sinks," he answered bitterly. "That judge, Simeon, who ordered you to be searched, is a man with a savage heart. He thought that I tried to save you from the wrath of the Sanhedrim; he thought that I—"

"Let be what he thought," interrupted Miriam, "and, friend Caleb, do your office. When we were children together often you tied my hands and feet with flowers, do you remember? Well, tie them now with cords, and make an end."

"You are cruel," he said, wincing.

"Indeed! some might have thought that you are cruel. If, for instance, they had heard your words in that tower last night when you gave up my name to the Jews and linked it with another's."

"Oh! Miriam," he broke in in a pleading voice, "if I did this—and in truth I scarcely know what I did—it was because love and jealousy maddened me."

"Love? The love of the lion for the lamb! Jealousy? Why were you jealous? Because, having striven to murder Marcus—oh! I saw the fight and it was little better, for you smote him unawares, being fully prepared when he was not—you feared lest I might have saved him from your fangs. Well, thanks be to God! I did save him, as I hope. And now, officer of the most merciful and learned Sanhedrim, do your duty."

"At least, Miriam," Caleb went on, humbly, for her bitter words, unjust as they were in part, seemed to crush him, "at least, I strove my best for you to-day—after I found time to think."

"Yes," she answered, "to think that other lions would get the lamb which you chance to desire for yourself."

"More," he continued, taking no note. "I have made a plan."

"A plan to do what?"

"To escape. If I give the signal on your way to the gate where I must lead you, you will be rescued by certain friends of mine who will hide you in a place of safety, while I, the officer, shall seem to be cut down. Afterwards I can join you and under cover of the night, by a way of which I know, we will fly together."

"Fly? Where to?"

"To the Romans, who will spare you because of what you did yesterday—and me also."

"Because of what *you* did yesterday?"

"No—because you will say that I am your husband. It will not be true, but what of that?"

"What of it, indeed?" asked Miriam, "since it can always become true. But how is it that you, being one of the first of the Jewish warriors, are prepared to fly and ask the mercy of your foes? Is it because—"

"Spare to insult me, Miriam. You know well why it is. You know well that I am no traitor, and that I do not fly for fear."

"Yes," she answered, in a changed tone, for his manly words touched her, "I know that."

"It is for you that I fly, for your sake I will eat this dirt and crown myself with shame. I fly that for the second time I may save you."

"And in return you demand—what?"

"Yourself."

"That I will not give, Caleb. I reject your offer."

"I feared it," he answered huskily, "who am accustomed to such denials. Then I demand this, for know that if once you pass your word I may trust it: that you will not marry the Roman Marcus."

"I cannot marry the Roman Marcus any more than I can marry you, because neither of you are Christians, and as you know well it is laid upon me as a birth duty that I may take no man to husband who is not a Christian."

"For your sake, Miriam," he answered slowly, "I am prepared to be baptised into your faith. Let this show you how much I love you."

"It does not show that you love the faith, Caleb, nor if you did love it could I love you. Jew or Christian, I cannot be your wife."

He turned his face to the wall and for a while was silent. Then he spoke again.

"Miriam, so be it. I will still save you. Go, and marry Marcus, if you can, only, if I live, I will kill him if I can, but that you need scarcely fear, for I do not think that I shall live."

She shook her head. "I will not go, who am weary of flights and hidings. Let God deal with me and Marcus and you as He pleases. Yet I thank you, and am sorry for the unkind words I spoke. Oh! Caleb, cannot you put me out of your mind? Are there not many fairer women who would be glad to love you? Why do you waste your life upon me? Take your path and suffer me to take mine. Yet all this talk is foolishness, for both are likely to be short."

"Yours, and that of Marcus the Roman, and my own are all one path, Miriam, and I seek no other. As a lad, I swore that I would never take you, except by your own wish, and to that oath I hold. Also, I swore that if I could I would kill my rival, and to that oath I hold. If he kills me, you may wed him. If I kill him, you need not wed me unless you so desire. But this fight is to the death, yes, whether you live or die, it is still to the death as between me and him. Do you understand?"

"Your words are very plain, Caleb, but this is a strange hour to choose to speak them, seeing that, for aught I know, Marcus is already dead, and that within some short time I shall be dead, and that death threatens you and all within this Temple."

"Yet we live, Miriam, and I believe that for none of the three of us is the end at hand. Well, you will not fly, either with me or without me?"

"No, I will not fly."

"Then the time is here, and, having no choice, I must do my duty, leaving the rest to fate. If, perchance, I can rescue you afterwards, I will, but do not hope for such a thing."

"Caleb, I neither hope nor fear. Henceforth I struggle no more. I am in other hands than yours, or those of the Jews, and as They fashion the clay so shall it be shaped. Now, will you bind me?"

"I have no such command. Come forth if it pleases you, the officers wait without. Had you wished to be rescued, I should have taken the path on which my friends await us. Now we must go another."

"So be it," said Miriam, "but first give me that jar of water, for my throat is parched."

He lifted it to her lips and she drank deeply. Then they went. Outside the cloister four men were waiting, two of them those doorkeepers who had searched her in the morning, the others soldiers.

"You have been a long while with the pretty maid, master," said one of them to Caleb. "Have you been receiving confession of her sins?"

"I have been trying to receive confession of the hiding-place of the Roman, but the witch is obstinate," he answered, glaring angrily at Miriam.

"She will soon change her tune on the gateway, master, where the nights are cold and the day is hot for those who have neither cloaks for their backs nor water for their stomachs. Come on, Blue Eyes, but first give me that necklet of pearls, which may serve to buy a bit of bread or a drink of wine," and he thrust his filthy hand into her breast.

Next instant a sword flashed in the red light of the evening to fall full on the ruffian's skull, and down he went dead or dying.

"Brute," said Caleb with an angry snarl, "go to seek bread and wine in Gehenna. The maid is doomed to death, not to be plundered by such as you. Come forward."

The companions of the fallen man stared at him. Then one laughed, for death was too common a sight to excite pity or surprise, and said:

"He was ever a greedy fellow. Let us hope that he has gone where there is more to eat."

Then, preceded by Caleb, they marched through the long cloisters, passed an inner door, turned down more cloisters on the right, and, following the base of the great wall, came to its beautiful centre gate, Nicanor, that was adorned with gold and silver, and stood between the Court of Women and the Court of Israel. Over this gateway was a square building, fifty feet or more in height, containing store chambers and places where the priests kept their instruments of music. On its roof, which was flat, were three columns of marble, terminated by gilded spikes. By the gate one of the Sanhedrim was waiting for them, that same relentless judge, Simeon, who had ordered Miriam to be searched.

"Has the woman confessed where she hid the Roman?" he asked of Caleb.

"No," he answered, "she says that she knows nothing of any Roman."

"Is it so, woman?"

"It is so, Rabbi."

"Bring her up," he went on sternly, and they passed through some stone chambers to a place where there was a staircase with a door of cedar- wood. The judge unlocked it, locking it again behind them, and they climbed the stairs till they came to another little door of stone, which, being opened, Miriam found herself on the roof of the gateway. They led her to the centre pillar, to which was fastened an iron chain about ten feet in length. Here Simeon commanded that her hands should be bound behind her, which was done. Then he brought out of his robe a scroll written in large letters, and tied it on to her breast. This was the writing on the scroll:

> "Miriam, Nazarene and Traitress, is doomed here to die as God shall appoint, before the face of her friends, the Romans."

Then followed several signatures of members of the Sanhedrim, including that of her grandfather, Benoni, who had thus been forced to show the triumph of patriotism over kinship.

This done the end of the chain was made fast round her middle and riveted with a hammer in such fashion that she could not possibly escape its grip. Then all being finished the men prepared to leave. First, however, Simeon addressed her:

"Stay here, accursed traitress, till your bones fall piecemeal from that chain," he said, "stay, through storm and shine, through light and darkness, while Roman and Jew alike make merry of your sufferings, which, if my voice had been listened to, would have been shorter, but more cruel. Daughter of Satan, go back to Satan and let the Son of the carpenter save you if he can."

"Spare to revile the maid," broke in Caleb furiously, "for curses are spears that fall on the heads of those that throw them."

"Had I my will," answered the Rabbi, "a spear should fall upon your head, insolent, who dare to rebuke your elders. Begone before me, and be sure of this, that if you strive to return here it shall be for the last time. More is known about you, Caleb, then you think, and perhaps you also would make friends among the Romans."

Caleb made no answer, for he knew the venom and power of this Zealot Simeon, who was the chosen friend and instrument of the savage John of Gischala. Only he looked at Miriam with sad eyes, and, muttering "You would have it so, I can do no more. Farewell," left her to her fate.

So there in the red light of the sunset, with her hands bound, a placard setting out her shame upon her breast, and chained like a wild beast to the column of marble, Miriam was left alone. Walking as near to the little battlement as the length of her chain would allow, she looked down into the Court of Israel, where many of the Zealots had gathered to catch sight of her. So soon as they saw her they yelled and hooted and cast a shower of stones, one of which struck her on the shoulder. With a little cry of pain she ran back as far as she could reach on the further side of the pillar. Hence she could see the great Court of Women, whence the Gate Nicanor was approached by fifteen steps forming the half of a circle and fashioned of white marble. This court now was nothing but a camp, for the outer Court of the Gentiles having been taken by the

Romans, their battering rams were working at its walls.

Then the night fell, but brought no peace with it, for the rams smote continually, and since they were not strong enough to break through the huge stones of the mighty wall, the Romans renewed their attempt to take them by storm in the hours of darkness. But, indeed, it was no darkness, for the Jews lit fires upon the top of the wall, and by their light drove off the attacking Romans. Again and again, from her lofty perch, Miriam could see the scaling ladders appear above the crest of the wall. Then up them would come long lines of men, each holding a shield above his head. As the foremost of these scrambled on to the wall, the waiting Jews rushed at them and cut them down with savage shouts, while other Jews seizing the rungs of the ladder, thrust it from the coping to fall with its living load back into the ditch beneath. Once there were great cries of joy, for two standard- bearers had come up the ladders carrying their ensigns with them. The men were overpowered and the ensigns captured to be waved derisively at the Romans beneath, who answered the insult with sullen roars of rage.

So things went on till at length the legionaries, wearing of this desperate fighting, took another counsel. Hitherto Titus had desired to preserve all the Temple, even to the outer courts and cloisters, but now he commanded that the gates, built of great beams of cedar and overlaid with silver plates, should be fired. Through a storm of spears and arrows soldiers rushed up to them and thrust lighted brands into every joint and hinge. They caught, and presently the silver plates ran down their blazing surface in molten streams of metal. Nor was this all, for from the gates the fire spread to the cloisters on either side, nor did the outworn Jews attempt to stay its ravages. They drew back sullenly, and seated in groups upon the paving of the Court of Women, watching the circle of devouring flame creep slowly on. At length the sun rose. Now the Romans were labouring to extinguish the fire at the gateway, and to make a road over the ruins by which they might advance. When it was done at last, with shouts of triumph the legionaries, commanded by Titus himself and accompanied by a body of horsemen, advanced into the Court of Women. Back before them fled the Jews, pouring up the steps of the Gate Nicanor, on the roof of which Miriam was chained to her pinnacle. But of her they took no note, none had time to think, or even to look at a single girl bound there on high in punishment for some offence, of which the most of them knew nothing. Only they manned the walls to right and left, and held the gateway, but to the roof where Miriam was they did not climb, because its parapet was too low to shelter them from the arrows of their assailants.

The Romans saw her, however, for she perceived that some of his officers were pointing her out to a man on horseback, clad in splendid armour, over which fell a purple cloak, whom she took to be Titus himself. Also one of the soldiers shot an arrow at her which struck upon the spiked column above her head and, rebounding, fell at her feet. Titus noted this, for she saw the man brought before him, and by his gestures gathered that the general was speaking to him angrily. After this no more arrows were shot at her, and she understood that their curiosity being stirred by the sight of a woman chained upon a gateway, they did not wish to do her mischief.

Now the August sun shone out from a cloudless sky till

the hot air danced above the roofs of the Temple and the pavings of the courts, and the thousands shut within their walls were glad to crowd into the shadow to shelter from its fiery beams. But Miriam could not escape them thus. In the morning and again in the afternoon she was able indeed, by creeping round it, to take refuge in the narrow line of shade thrown by the marble column to which she was made fast. At mid- day, however, it flung no shadow, so for all those dreadful hours she must pant in the burning heat without a drop of water to allay her thirst. Still she bore it till at length came evening and its cool.

That day the Romans made no attack, nor did the Jews attempt a sally. Only some of the lighter of the engines were brought into the Court of Women, whence they hurled their great stones and heavy darts into the Court of Israel beyond. Miriam watched these missiles as they rushed by her, once or twice so close that the wind they made stirred her hair. The sight fascinated her and took her mind from her own sufferings. She could see the soldiers working at the levers and pulleys till the strings of the catapult or the boards of the balista were drawn to their places. Then the darts or the stones were set in the groove prepared to receive it, a cord was pulled and the missile sped upon its way, making an angry humming noise as it clove the air. At first it looked small; then approaching it grew large, to become small again to her following sight as its journey was accomplished. Sometimes, the stones, which did more damage than the darts, fell upon the paving and bounded along it, marking their course by fragments of shattered marble and a cloud of dust. At others, directed by an evil fate, they crashed into groups of Jews, destroying all they touched. Wandering to and fro among these people was that crazed man Jesus, the son of Annas, who had met them with his wild prophetic cry as they entered into Jerusalem, and whose ill-omened voice Miriam had heard again before Marcus was taken at the fight in the Old Tower. To and fro he went, none hindering him, though many thrust their fingers in their ears and looked aside as he passed, wailing forth: "Woe, woe to Jerusalem! Woe to the city and the Temple!" Of a sudden, as Miriam watched, he was still for a moment, then throwing up his arms, cried in a piercing voice, "Woe, woe to myself!" Before the echo of his words had died against the Temple walls, a great stone cast from the Court of Women rushed upon him through the air and felled him to the earth. On it went with vast bounds, but Jesus, the son of Annas, lay still. Now, in the hour of the accomplishment of his prophecy, his pilgrimage was ended.

All the day the cloisters that surrounded the Court of Women burned fiercely, but the Jews, whose heart was out of them, did not sally forth, and the Romans made no attack upon the inner Court of Israel. At length the last rays of the setting sun struck upon the slopes of the Mount of Olives, the white tents of the Roman camps, and the hundreds of crosses, each bearing its ghastly burden, that filled the Valley of Jehoshaphat and climbed up the mountain sides wherever space could be found for them to stand. Then over the tortured, famished city down fell the welcome night. To none was it more welcome than to Miriam, for with it came a copious dew which seemed to condense upon the gilded spike of her marble pillar, whence it trickled so continually, that by licking a little channel in the marble, she was enabled, before it ceased, to allay the worst pangs of her thirst. This dew gathered upon her hair, bared neck and garments, so that through them also she seemed to take in moisture and renew her life. After this she slept a while, expecting always to be awakened by some fresh conflict. But on that night none took place, the fight was for the morrow. Meanwhile there was peace.

Miriam dreamed in her uneasy sleep, and in this dream many visions came to her. She saw this sacred hill of Moriah, whereon the Temple stood, as it had been in the beginning, a rugged spot clothed with ungrafted carob trees and olives, and inhabited, not of men, but by wild boars and the hyænas that preyed upon their young. Almost in its centre lay a huge black stone. To this stone came a man clad in the garb of the Arabs of the desert, and with him a little lad whom he bound upon the stone as though to offer him in sacrifice. Then, as he was about to plunge a knife into his heart, a glory shone round the place, and a voice cried to him to hold his hand. That was a vision of the offering of Isaac. It passed, and there came another vision.

Again she saw the sacred height of Moriah, and lo! a Temple stood upon it, a splendid building, but not that which she knew, and in front of this Temple the same black rock. On the rock, where once the lad had been bound, was an altar, and before the altar a glorious man clad in priestly robes, who offered sacrifice of lambs and oxen and in a sonorous voice gave praise to Jehovah in the presence of a countless host of people. This she knew was the vision of Solomon the King.

It passed, and lo! by this same black rock stood another man, pale and eager-faced, with piercing eyes, who reproached the worshippers in the Temple because of the wickedness of their hearts, and drove them from before him with a scourge of cords. This she knew was a vision of Jesus, the Son of Mary, that Messiah Whom she worshipped, for as He drove out the people He prophesied the desolation that should fall upon them, and as they fled they mocked Him.

The picture passed, and again she saw the black rock, but now it lay beneath a gilded dome and light fell upon it through painted windows. About it moved many priests whose worship was strange to her, and so they seemed to move for ages. At length the doors of that dome were burst open, and upon the priests rushed fair-faced, stately-looking men, clad in white mail and bearing upon their shields and breastplates the symbol of the Cross. They slaughtered the votaries of the strange worship, and once more the rock was red with blood. Now they were gone in turn and other priests moved beneath the dome, but the Cross had vanished thence, and its pinnacles were crowned with crescents.

That vision passed, and there came another of dim, undistinguishable hordes that tore down the crescents and slaughtered the ministers of the strange faith, and gave the domed temple to the flames.

That vision passed, and once more the summit of Mount Moriah was as it had been in the beginning: the wild olive and the wild fig flourished among its desolate terraces, the wild boar roamed beneath their shade, and there were none to hunt him. Only the sunlight and the moonlight still beat upon the ancient Rock of Sacrifice.

That vision passed, and lo! around the rock, filling the Valley of Jehoshaphat and the valleys beyond, and the Mount of Olives and the mountains above, yes, and the empty air between earth and sky, further than the eye could reach, stood, rank upon rank, all the countless million millions of mankind, all the millions that had been and were yet to be, gazing, every one of them, anxiously and in utter silence upon the scarred and naked Rock of Sacrifice. Now upon the rock there grew a glory so bright that at the sight of it all the million of millions abased their eyes. And from the glory pealed forth a voice of a trumpet, that seemed to say:

"This is the end and the beginning, all things are accomplished in their order, now is the day of Decision."

Then, in her dream, the sun turned red as blood and the stars seemed to fall and winds shook the world, and darkness covered it, and in the winds and the darkness were voices, and standing upon the rock, its arms stretched east and west, a cross of fire, and filling the heavens above the cross, company upon company of angels. This last vision of judgment passed also and Miriam awoke again from her haunted, horror- begotten sleep, to see the watch-fires of the Romans burning in the Court of Women before her, and from the Court of Israel behind her, where they were herded like cattle in the slaughterer's yard, to hear the groans of the starving Jews who to-morrow were destined to the sword.

Chapter 18

The Death-Struggle of Israel

Now the light began to grow, but that morning no sun rose upon the sight of the thousands who waited for its coming. The whole heaven was dark with a gray mist that seemed to drift up in billows from the sea, bringing with it a salt dampness. For this mist Miriam was thankful, since had the sun shone hotly she knew not how she would have lived through another day. Already she grew very weak, who had suffered so much and eaten so little, and whose only drink had been the dew, but she felt that while the mist hid the sun her life would bide with her.

To others also this mist was welcome. Under cover of it Caleb approached the gateway, and although he could not ascend it, as the doors were locked and guarded, he cast on to its roof so cleverly, that it fell almost at Miriam's feet, a linen bag in which was a leathern bottle containing wine and water, and with it a mouldy crust of bread, doubtless all that he could find, or buy, or steal. Kneeling down, Miriam loosed the string of the bag with her teeth and devoured the crust of bread, again returning thanks that Caleb had been moved to this thought. But from the bottle she could not drink, for her hands being bound behind her, she was able neither to lift it nor to untie the thong that made fast its neck. Therefore, as, notwithstanding the dew which she had lapped, she needed drink sorely and longed also for the use of her hands to protect herself from the tormenting attacks of stinging gnats and carrion flies, she set herself to try to free them.

Now the gilt spike that crowned her pillar was made fast with angle- irons let into the marble and the edge of one of these irons projected somewhat and was rough. Looking at it the thought came into Miriam's mind that it might serve to rub through the cord with which her hands were bound. So standing with her back to the pillar she began her task, to find that it must be done little by little, since the awkward movement wearied her, moreover, her swollen arms chafing against the marble of the column became intolerably sore. Yet, although the pain made her weep, from time to time she persevered. But night fell before the frayed cord parted.

In the mist also the Romans came near to the gate, notwithstanding the risk, for they were very curious about her, and called to her asking why she was bound there. She replied in the Latin language, which was understood by very few of the Jews, that it was because she had rescued a Roman from death. Before they could speak again those who questioned her were driven back by a shower of arrows discharged from the wall, but in the distance she thought that she saw one of them make report to an officer, who on receipt of it seemed to give some orders.

Meanwhile, also under cover of the mist, the Jews were preparing themselves for battle. To the number of over four thousand men they gathered silently in the Court of Israel. Then of a sudden the gates were thrown open, and among them that of Nicanor. The trumpets blew a signal and out they poured into the Court of Women, driving in the Roman guards and outposts as sticks and straws are driven by a sudden flood. But the legionaries beyond were warned, and locking their shields together stood firm, so that the Jews fell back from their iron line as such a flood falls from an opposing rock. Yet they would not retreat, but fought furiously, killing many of the Romans, until at length Titus charged on them at the head of a squadron of horse and drove them back headlong through the gates. Then the Romans came on and put those whom they had captured to the sword, but as yet they did not attempt the storming of the gates. Only officers advanced as near to the wall as they dared and called to the Jews to surrender, saying that Titus desired to preserve their Temple and to spare their lives. But the Jews answered them with insults, taunts, and mockery, and Miriam, listening, wondered what spirit had entered into these people and made them mad, so that they chose death and destruction rather than peace and mercy. Then she remembered her strange visions of the night, and in them seemed to find an answer.

Having repulsed this desperate sally the Roman officers set thousands of men to work to attempt to extinguish the flaming cloisters, since, notwithstanding the answer of the Jews, Titus still desired to save the Temple. As for its defenders, beyond guarding the walls of the Court of Israel, they did no more. Gathering in such places as were most protected from the darts and stones thrown by the engines, they crouched upon the ground, some in sullen silence, some beating their breasts and rending their robes, while the women and children wailed in their misery and hunger, throwing dust upon their heads. The Gate of Nicanor, however, was still held by a strong guard, who suffered none to approach it, nor did any attempt to ascend to its roof. That Caleb still lived Miriam knew, for she had seen him, covered with dust and blood, driven back by the charge of Roman horse up the steps of the gateway. This, indeed, he was one of the last to pass before it was closed and barred to keep out the pursuing Romans. After that she saw no more of him for many a month.

So that day also, the last of the long siege, wore away. At nightfall the thick mist cleared, and for the last time the rich rays of sunset shone upon the gleaming roof and burning pinnacles of the Temple and were reflected from the dazzling whiteness of its walls. Never had it looked more beautiful than it did in that twilight as it towered, still perfect, above the black ruins of the desolated city. The clamour and shouting had died away, even the mourners had ceased their pitiful cries; except the guards, the Romans had withdrawn and were eating their evening meal, while those who worked the terrible engines ceased from their destroying toil. Peace, an ominous peace, brooded on the place, and everywhere, save for the flames that crackled among the cedar-wood beams in the roofs of the cloisters, was deep silence, such as in tropic lands precedes the bursting of a cyclone. To Miriam who watched, it seemed as though in the midst of this unnatural quiet Jehovah was withdrawing Himself from the house where His Spirit dwelt and from the people who worshipped Him with their lips, but rejected Him in their hearts. Her tormented nerves shuddered with a fear that was not of the body, as she stared upwards at the immense arch of the azure evening sky, half expecting that her mortal eyes would catch some vision of the departing wings of the

Angel of the Lord. But there she could see nothing except the shapes of hundreds of high-poised eagles. "Where the carcase is there shall the eagles be gathered together," she muttered to herself, and remembering that these four birds were come to feast upon the bones of the whole people of the Jews and upon her own, she shut her eyes and groaned.

Then the light died on the Temple towers and faded from the pale slopes of the mountains, and in place of the wheeling carrion birds bright stars shone out one by one upon the black mantle of the night.

Once again, setting her teeth because of the agony that the touch of the marble gave to her raw and swollen flesh, Miriam began to fret the cords which bound her wrists against the rough edge of the angle-iron. She was sure that it was nearly worn through, but oh! how could she endure the agony until it parted? Still she did endure, for at her feet lay the bottle, and burning thirst drove her to the deed. Suddenly her reward came, and she felt that her arms were free; yes, numbed, swollen and bleeding, they fell against her sides, wrenching the stiffened muscles of her shoulders back to their place in such a fashion that she well-nigh fainted with the pain. Still they were free, and presently she was able to lift them, and with the help of her teeth to loose the ends of the cord, so that the blood could run once more through her blackened wrists and hands. Again she waited till some feeling had come back into her fingers, which were numb and like to mortify. Then she knelt down, and drawing the leather bottle to her, held it between her palms, while, with her teeth, she undid its thong. The task was hard, for it was well tied, but at length the knots gave, and Miriam drank. So fearful was her thirst that she could have emptied the bottle at a draught, but this she, who had lived in the desert, was too wise to do, for she knew that it might kill her. Also when that was gone there was no more. So she drank half of it in slow sips, then tied the string as well as she was able and set it down again.

Now the wine, although it was mixed with water, took hold of her who for so long had eaten nothing save a mouldy crust, so that strange sounds drummed in her ears, and sinking down against the column she became senseless for a while. She awoke again, feeling somewhat refreshed and, though her head seemed as though it did not belong to her, well able to think. Her arms also were better and her fingers had recovered their feeling. If only she could loose that galling chain, she thought to herself, she might escape, for now death, however strong her faith, was very near and unlovely; also she suffered in many ways. To die and pass quick to Heaven—that would be well, but to perish by inches of starvation, heat, cold, and cramped limbs, with pains within and without and a swimming sickness of the head, ah! it was hard to bear. She knew that even were she free she could not hope to descend the gateway by its staircase, since the doors were locked and barred, and if she passed them it would be but to find herself among the Jews in the vaulted chambers beneath. But, so she thought, perhaps she could drop from the roof, which was not so very high, on to the paving in front of the first stair, and then, if she was unhurt, run or crawl to the Romans, who might give her shelter.

So Miriam tried to undo the chain, only to find that as well might she hope to pull down the Gate Nicanor with her helpless hands. At this discovery she wept, for now she grew weak. Well for Miriam was it that she could not have her wish, for certainly had she attempted to drop down from the gateway to the marble paving, or even on to the battlements of the walls which ran up to it on either side, her bones would have been shattered like the shell of an egg and she must have perished miserably.

While she grieved thus, Miriam heard a stir in the Court of Israel, and by the dim starlight saw that men were gathering, to do what she knew not. Presently, as she wondered, the great gates were opened very softly and out poured the Jews upon their last sally. Miriam was witnessing the death-struggle of the nation of Israel. At the foot of the marble steps they divided, one-half of them rushing towards the cloister on the right, and the other to that upon the left. Their object, as it seemed to her, was to slay those Roman soldiers, who, by the command of Titus, were still engaged in fighting the flames that devoured these beautiful buildings, and then to surprise the camp beyond. The scheme was such as a madman might have made, seeing that the Romans, warned by the sortie of the morning, had thrown up a wall across the lower part of the Court of Women, and beyond that were protected by every safeguard known to the science of ancient war. Also the moment that the first Jew set his foot upon the staircase, watching sentries cried out in warning and trumpets gave their call to arms.

Still, they reached the cloisters and killed a few Romans who had not time to get away. Following those who fled, they came to the wall and began to try to force it, when suddenly on its crest and to the rear appeared thousands of those men whom they had hoped to destroy, every one of them wakeful, armed and marshalled. The Jews hesitated, and, like a living stream of steel, the Roman ranks poured over the wall. Then, of a sudden, terror seized those unhappy men, and, with a melancholy cry of utter despair, they turned to flee back to the Court of Israel. But this time the Romans were not content with driving them away, they came on with them; some of them even reached the gate before them. Up the marble steps poured friend and foe together; together they passed the open gate, in their mad rush sweeping away those who had stayed to guard it, and burst into the Court of Israel. Then leaving some to hold the gate and reinforced continually by fresh companies from the camps within and without the Temple courts, the Romans ran on towards the doors of the Holy House, cutting down the fugitives as they went. Now none attempted to stand; there was no fight made; even the bravest of the Jewish warriors, feeling that their hour was come and that Jehovah had deserted His people, flung down their weapons and fled, some to escape to the Upper City, more to perish on the Roman spears.

A few attempted to take refuge in the Holy House itself, and after these followed some Romans bearing torches in their hands. Miriam, watching terrified from the roof of the Gate Nicanor, saw them go, the torches floating on the dusky air like points of wind-tossed fire. Then suddenly from a certain window on the north side of the Temple sprang out a flame so bright that from where she stood upon the gate, Miriam could see every detail of the golden tracery. A soldier mounted on the shoulders of another and not knowing in his madness that he was a destroying angel, had cast a torch into and fired the window. Up ran the bright, devouring flame spreading outwards like a fan, so that within some few minutes all that side of the Temple was but a roaring furnace. Meanwhile the Romans were pressing through the Gate Nicanor in an unending stream, till presently there was a cry of "Make way! Make way!"

Miriam looked down to see a man, bare-headed and with close-cropped hair, white-robed also and unarmoured, as though he had risen from his couch, riding on a great war-horse, an ivory wand in his hand and preceded by an officer who bore the standard of the Roman Eagles. It was Titus itself, who as he came shouted to the centurions to beat back the legionaries and extinguish the fire. But who now could beat them back? As well might he have attempted to restrain the hosts of Gehenna burst to the upper earth. They were mad with the lust of blood and the lust of plunder, and even to the voice of their dread lord they paid no heed.

New flames sprang up in other parts of the vast Temple. It was doomed. The golden doors were burst open and, attended by his officers, Titus passed through them to view for the first and last time the home of Jehovah, God of the Jews. From chamber to chamber he passed, yes, even into the Holy of Holies itself, whence by his command were brought out the golden candlesticks and the golden table of shrewbread, nor, since God had deserted His habitation, did any harm come to him for that deed.

Now the Temple which for one thousand one hundred and thirty years had stood upon the sacred summit of Mount Moriah, went upwards in a sheet of flame, itself the greatest of the sacrifices that had ever been offered there; while soldiers stripped it of its gold and ornaments, tossing the sacred vessels to each other and tearing down the silken curtains of the shrine. Nor were victims lacking to that sacrifice, for in their blind fury the Romans fell upon the people who were crowded in the Court of Israel, and slew them to the number of more than ten thousand, warrior and priest, citizen and woman and child together, till the court swarm with blood and the Rock of Offering was black with the dead who had taken refuge there. Yet these did not perish quite unavenged, for many of the Romans, their arms filled with priceless spoils of gold and silver, the treasures of immemorial time, sank down overcome by the heat, and where they fell they died.

From the Court of Israel went up one mighty wail of those who sank beneath the sword. From the thousands of the Romans went up a savage shout of triumph, the shout of those who put them to the sword. From the multitude of the Jews who watched this ruin from the Upper City went up a ceaseless scream of utter agony, and dominating all, like the accompaniment of some fearful music, rose the fierce, triumphant roar of fire. In straight lines and jagged pinnacles the flames soared hundreds of feet into the still air, leaping higher and ever higher as the white walls and gilded roofs fell in, till all the Temple was but one gigantic furnace, near which none could bide save the dead, whose very garments took fire as they lay upon the ground. Never, was such a sight seen before; never, perhaps, will such a sight be seen again—one so awesome, yet so majestic.

Now every living being whom they could find was slain, and the Romans drew back, bearing their spoil with them. But the remainder of the Jews, to the number of some thousands, escaped by the bridges, which they broke down behind them, across the valley into the Upper

City, whence that piercing, sobbing wail echoed without cease. Miriam watched till she could bear the sight no longer. The glare blinded her, the heat of the incandescent furnace shrivelled her up, her white dress scorched and turned brown. She crouched behind the shelter of her pinnacle gasping for breath. She prayed that she might die, and could not. Now she remembered the drink that remained in the leathern bottle, and swallowed it to the last drop. Then she crouched down again against the pillar, and lying thus her senses left her.

When they came back it was daylight, and from the heap of ashes that had been the Temple of Herod and the most glorious building in the whole world, rose a thick cloud of black smoke, pierced here and there by little angry tongues of fire. The Court of Israel was strewn so thick with dead that in places the soldiers walked on them as on a carpet, or to be rid of them, hurled them into the smouldering ruins. Upon the altar that stood on the Rock of Sacrifice a strange sight was to be seen, for set up there was an object like the shaft of a lance wreathed with what seemed to be twining snakes and surmounted by a globe on which she stood a golden eagle with outspread wings. Gathered in front of it were a vast number of legionaries who did obeisance to this object. They were offering worship to the Roman standards upon the ancient altar of the God of Israel! Presently a figure rode before them attended by a glittering staff of officers, to be greeted with a mighty shout of "Titus *Imperator!* Titus *Imperator!*" Here on the sense of his triumph his victorious legions named their general Cæsar.

Nor was the fighting altogether ended, for on the roofs of some of the burning cloisters were gathered a few of the most desperate of the survivors of the Jews, who, as the cloisters crumbled beneath them, retreated slowly towards the Gate Nicanor, which still stood unharmed. The Romans, weary with slaughter, called to them to come down and surrender, but they would not, and Miriam watching them, to her horror saw that one of these men was none other than her grandfather, Benoni. As they would not yield, the Romans shot at them with arrows, so that presently every one of them was down except Benoni, whom no dart seemed to touch.

"Cease shooting," cried a voice, "and bring a ladder. That man is brave and one of the Sanhedrim. Let him be taken alive."

A ladder was brought and reared against the wall near the Gate Nicanor and up it came Romans. Benoni retreated before them till he stood upon the edge of the gulf of advancing fire. Then he turned round and faced them. As he turned he caught sight of Miriam huddled at the base of her column upon the roof of the gate, and thinking that she was dead, wrung his hands and tore his beard. She guessed his grief, but so weak and parched was she, that she could call no word of comfort to him, or do more than watch the end with fascinated eyes.

The soldiers came on along the top of the wall till they feared to approach nearer to the fire, lest they should fall through the burning rafters.

"Yield!" they cried. "Yield, fool, before you perish! Titus gives you your life."

"That he may drag me, an elder of Israel, in chains through the streets of Rome," answered the old Jew scornfully. "Nay, I will not yield, and I pray God that the same end which you have brought upon this city and its children, may fall upon your city and its children at the hands of men even more cruel than yourselves."

Then stooping down he lifted a spear which lay upon the wall and hurled it at them so fiercely, that it transfixed the buckler of one of the soldiers and the arm behind the buckler.

"Would that it had been your heart, heathen, and the heart of all your race!" he screamed, and lifting his hands as though in invocation, suddenly plunged headlong into the flames beneath.

Thus, fierce and brave to the last, died Benoni the Jew.

Again Miriam fainted, again to be awakened. The door that led from the gate chambers to its roof burst open and through it sped a figure bare-headed and dishevelled, his torn raiment black with blood and smoke. Staring at him, Miriam knew the man who Simeon—yes, Simeon, her cruel judge, who had doomed her to this dreadful end. After him, gripping his robe indeed, came a Roman officer, a stout man of middle age, with a weather-beaten kindly face, which in some dim way seemed to be familiar to her, and after him again, six soldiers.

"Hold him!" he panted. "We must have one of them to show if only that the people may know what a live Jew is like," and the officer tugged so fiercely at the robe that in his struggles to be free, for he also hoped to die by casting himself from the gateway tower, Simeon fell down.

Next instant the soldiers were on him and held him fast. Then it was for the first time that the captain caught sight of Miriam crouched at the foot of her pillar.

"Why," he said, "I had forgotten. That is the girl whom we saw yesterday from the Court of Women and whom we have orders to save. Is the poor thing dead?"

Miriam lifted her wan face and looked at him.

"By Bacchus!" he said, "I have seen that face before; it is not one that a man would forget. Ah! I have it now." Then he stooped and eagerly read the writing that was tied upon her breast:

> "Miriam, Nazarene and traitress, is doomed here to die as God shall appoint before the face of her friends, the Romans."

"Miriam," he said, then started and checked himself.

"Look!" cried one of the soldiers, "the girl wears pearls, and good ones. Is it your pleasure that I should cut them off?"

"Nay, let them be," he answered. "Neither she nor her pearls are for any of us. Loosen her chain, not her necklet."

So with much trouble they broke the rivets of the chain.

"Can you stand, lady?" said the captain to Miriam.

She shook her head.

"Then I needs must carry you," and stooping down he lifted her in his strong arms as though she had been but a child, and, bidding the soldiers bring the Jew Simeon with them, slowly and with great care descended the staircase up which Miriam had been taken more than sixty hours before.

Passing through the outer doors into the archway where the great gate by which the Romans had gained access to the Temple stood wide, the captain turned into the Court of Israel, where some soldiers who were engaged in dividing spoil looked up laughing and asked him whose baby he had captured. Paying no heed to them he walked across the court, picking his way through the heaps of dead to a range of the southern cloisters which were still standing, where officers might be seen coming and going. Under one of these cloisters, seated on a stool and employed in examining the vessels and other treasures of the Temple, which were brought before him one by one, was Titus. Looking up he saw this strange procession and commanded that they should be brought before him.

"Who is it that you carry in your arms, captain?" he asked.

"That girl, Cæsar," he answered, "who was bound upon the gateway and whom you have orders should not be shot at."

"Does she still live?"

"She lives—no more. Thirst and heat have withered her."

"How came she there?"

"This writing tells you, Cæsar."

Titus read. "Ah!" he said, "Nazarene. An evil sect, worse even than these Jews, or so thought the late divine Nero. Traitress also. Why, the girl must have deserved her fate. But what is this? 'Is doomed to die as God shall appoint before the face of her friends, the Romans.' How are the Romans her friends, I wonder? Girl, if you can speak, tell me who condemned you."

Miriam lifted her dark head from the shoulder of the captain on which it lay and pointed with her finger at the Jew, Simeon.

"Is that so, man?" asked Cæsar. "Now tell the truth, for I shall learn it, and if you lie you die."

"She was condemned by the Sanhedrim, among whom was her own grandfather, Benoni; there is his signature with the rest upon the scroll," Simeon answered sullenly.

"For what crime?"

"Because she suffered a Roman prisoner to escape, for which deed," he added furiously, "may her soul burn in Gehenna for ever and aye!"

"What was the name of the prisoner?" asked Titus.

"I do not remember," answered Simeon.

"Well," said Cæsar, "it does not greatly matter, for either he is safe or he is dead. Your robes, what are left of them, show that you also are one of the Sanhedrim. Is it not so?"

"Yes. I am Simeon, a name that you have heard."

"Ah! Simeon, here it is, written on this scroll first of all. Well, Simeon, you doomed a high-born lady to a cruel death because she saved, or tried to save, a Roman soldier, and it is but just that you should drink of your own wine. Take him and fasten him to the column on the gateway and leave him there to perish. Your Holy House is destroyed, Simeon, and being a faithful priest, you would not wish to survive your worship."

"There you are right, Roman," he answered, "though I should have been better pleased with a quicker end, such as I trust may overtake you."

Then they led him off, and presently Simeon appeared upon the gateway with Miriam's chain about his middle and Miriam's rope knotted afresh about his wrists.

"Now for this poor girl," went on Titus Cæsar. "It seems that she is a Nazarene, a sect of which all men speak ill, for they try to subvert authority and preach doctrines that would bring the world to ruin. Also she was false to her own people, which is a crime, though one in this instance whereof we Romans cannot complain. Therefore, if only for the sake of example it would be wrong to set her free; indeed, to do so, would be to give her to death. My command is, then, that she shall be taken good care of, and if she recovers, be sent to Rome to adorn my Triumph, should the gods grant me such a thing, and afterwards be sold as a slave for the benefit of the wounded soldiers and the poor. Meanwhile, who will take charge of her?"

"I," said that officer who had freed Miriam. "There is an old woman who tends my tent, who can nurse her in her sickness."

"Understand, friend," answered Titus, "that no harm is to be done to this girl, who is my property."

"I understand, O Cæsar," said the officer. "She shall be treated as though she were my daughter."

"Good. You who are present, remember his words and my decree. In Rome, if we live to reach it, you shall give account to me of the captive lady, Miriam. Now take her away, for there are greater matters to be dealt with than the fortunes of this girl."

Chapter 19

Pearl-Maiden

Many days had gone by, but still the fighting was not ended, for the Jews continued to hold the Upper City. As it chanced, however, in one of the assaults upon it that officer who had rescued Miriam was badly hurt by a spear-thrust in the leg, so that he could be of no more service in this war. Therefore, because he was a man whom Titus trusted, he was ordered to sail with others of the sick for Rome, taking in his charge much of the treasure that had been captured, and for this purpose travelled down to Tyre, whence his vessel was to put to sea. In obedience to the command of Cæsar he had carried the captive Miriam to the camp of his legion upon the Mount of Olives, and there placed her in a tent, where an old slave-woman tended her. For a while it was not certain whether she should live or die, for her sufferings and all that she had seen brought her so near to death that it was hard to keep her from passing its half-opened gates. Still, with good food and care, the strength came back to her body. But in mind Miriam remained sick, since during all these weeks she wandered in her talk, so that no word of reason passed her lips.

Now, many would have wearied of her and thrust her

out to take her chance with hundreds of other poor creatures who roamed about the land until they perished or were enslaved of Arabs. But this Roman did not act thus; in truth, as he had promised it should be, had she been his daughter, Miriam would not have been better tended. Whenever his duties gave him time he would sit with her, trying to beguile her madness, and after he himself was wounded, from morning to night they were together, till at length the poor girl grew to love him in a crazy fashion, and would throw her arms about his neck and call him "uncle," as in the old days she had named the Essenes. Moreover, she learned to know the soldiers of that legion, who became fond of her and would bring her offerings of fruit and winter flowers, or of aught else that they thought would please her. So when the captain received his orders to proceed to Tyre with the treasure and take ship there, he and his guard took Miriam with them, and journeying easily, reached the city on the eighth day.

As it chanced their ship was not ready, so they camped on the outskirts of Paleotyrus, and by a strange accident in that very garden which had been the property of Benoni. This place they reached after sunset one evening and set up their tents, that of Miriam and the old slave-woman being placed on the seashore next to the tent of her protector. This night she slept well, and being awakened at the dawn by the murmur of the sea among the rocks, went to the door of the tent and looked out. All the camp was sleeping, for here they had no enemy to fear, and a great calm lay upon the sea and land. Presently the mist lifted and the rays of the rising sun poured across the blue ocean and its gray, bordering coast.

With that returning light, as it happened, the light returned also into Miriam's darkened mind. She became aware that this scene was familiar; she recognised the outlines of the proud and ancient island town. More, she remembered that garden; yes, there assuredly was the palm-tree beneath which she had often sat, and there the rock, under whose shadow grew white lilies, where she had rested with Nehushta when the Roman captain brought her the letter and the gifts from Marcus. Instinctively Miriam put her hand to her neck. About it still hung the collar of pearls, and on the pearls the ring which the slave- woman had found in her hair and tied there for safety. She took off the ring and placed it back upon her finger. Then she walked to the rock, sat down and tried to think. But for this, as yet her mind was not strong enough, for there rose up in it vision after vision of blood and fire, which crushed and overwhelmed her. All that went before the siege was clear, the rest one red confusion.

While she sat thus the Roman captain hobbled from his pavilion, resting on a crutch, for his leg was still lame and shrivelled. First he went to Miriam's tent to inquire after her of the old woman, as was his custom at the daybreak, then, learning that she had gone out of it, looked round for her. Presently he perceived her sitting in the shade of the rock gazing at the sea, and followed to join her.

"Good morning to you, daughter," he said. "How have you slept after your long journey?" and paused, expecting to be answered with some babbling, gentle nonsense such as flowed from Miriam's lips in her illness. But instead of this she rose and stood before him looking confused. Then she replied:

"Sir, I thank you, I have slept well; but tell me, is not yonder town Tyre, and is not this the garden of my grandfather, Benoni, where I used to wander? Nay, how can it be? So long has passed since I walked in this garden, and so many things have happened—terrible, terrible things which I cannot remember," and she hid her eyes in her hand and moaned.

"Don't try to remember them," he said cheerfully. "There is so much in life that it is better to forget. Yes, this is Tyre, sure enough. You could not recognise it last night because it was too dark, and this garden, I am told, did belong to Benoni. Who it belongs to now I do not know. To you, I suppose, and through you to Cæsar."

Now while he spoke thus somewhat at random, for he was watching her all the while, Miriam kept her eyes fixed upon his face, as though she searched there for something which she could but half recall. Suddenly an inspiration entered into them and she said:

"Now I have it! You are the Roman captain, Gallus, who brought me the letter from—" and she paused, thrusting her hand into the bosom of her robe, then went on with something like a sob: "Oh! it is gone. How did it go? Let me think."

"Don't think," said Gallus; "there are so many things in the world which it is better not to think about. Yes, as it happens, I am that man, and some years ago I did bring you the letter from Marcus, called The Fortunate. Also, as it chanced, I never forgot your sweet face and knew it again at a time when it was well that you should find a friend. No, we won't talk about it now. Look, the old slave calls you. It is time that you should break your fast, and I also must eat and have my wound dressed. Afterwards we will talk."

All that morning Miriam saw nothing more of Gallus. Indeed, he did not mean that she should, since he was sure that her new-found sense ought not to be overstrained at first, lest it should break down again, never to recover. So she went out and sat alone by the garden beach, for the soldiers had orders to respect her privacy, and gazed at the sea.

As she sat thus in quiet, event by event the terrible past came back to her. She remembered it all now—their flight from Tyre; the march into Jerusalem; the sojourn in the dark with the Essenes; the Old Tower and what befell there; the escape of Marcus; her trial before the Sanhedrim; the execution of her sentence upon the gateway; and then that fearful night when the flames of the burning Temple scorched to her very brain, and the sights and sounds of slaughter withered her heart. After this she could recall but one more thing—the vision of the majestic figure of Benoni standing against a background of black smoke upon the lofty cloister-roof and defying the Romans before he plunged headlong in the flames beneath. Of her rescue on the roof of the Gate Nicanor, of her being carried before Titus Cæsar in the arms of Gallus, and of his judgment concerning her she recollected nothing. Nor, indeed, did she ever attain to a clear memory of those events, while the time between them and the recovery of her reason by the seashore in the garden at Tyre always remained a blank. That troubled fragment of her life was sunk in a black sea of oblivion.

At length the old woman came to summon Miriam to her midday meal, and led her, not to her own tent, but to that which was pitched to serve as an eating-place for the captain, Gallus. As she went she saw knots of soldiers gathered across her path as though to intercept her, and turned to fly, for the sight of them brought back the terrors of the siege.

"Have no fear of them," said the old woman, smiling. "Ill would it go here with him who dared to lift a finger against their Pearl-Maiden."

"Pearl-Maiden! Why?" asked Miriam.

"That is what they call you, because of the necklace that was upon your breast when you were captured, which you wear still. As for why—well, I suppose because they love you, the poor sick thing they nursed. They have heard that you are better and gather to give you joy of it; that is all."

Sure enough, the words were true, for, as Miriam approached, these rough legionaries cheered and clapped their hands, while one of them an evil-looking fellow with a broken nose, who was said to have committed great cruelties during the siege, came forward bowing and presented her with a handful of wild-flowers, which he must have collected with some trouble, since, at this season of the year they were not common. She took them, and being still weak, burst into tears.

"Why should you treat me thus," she asked, "who am, as I understand, but a poor captive?"

"Nay, nay," answered a sergeant, with an uncouth oath. "It is we who are your captives, Pearl-Maiden, and we are glad, because your mind has come to you, though, seeing how sweet you were without it, we do not know that it can better you very much."

"Oh! friends, friends," began Miriam, then once more broke down.

Meanwhile, hearing the disturbance Gallus had come from his tent and was hobbling towards them, when suddenly he caught sight of the tears upon Miriam's face and broke out into such language as could only be used by a Roman officer of experience.

"What have you been doing to her, you cowardly hounds?" he shouted. "By Cæsar and the Standards, if one of you has even said a word that she should not hear, he shall be flogged until the bones break through his skin," and his very beard bristling with wrath, Gallus uttered a series of the most fearful maledictions upon the head of that supposed offender, his female ancestry, and his descendants.

"Your pardon, captain," said the sergeant, "but *you* are uttering many words that no maiden should hear."

"Do you dare to argue with me, you foul-tongued camp scavenger?" shouted Gallus. "Here, guard, lash him to that tree! Fear not, daughter; the insult shall be avenged; we shall teach his dirty tongue to sing another tune," and again he cursed him, naming him by new names.

"Oh! sir, sir," broke in Miriam, "what are you about to do? This man offered me no insult, none of them offered me anything except kind words and flowers."

"Then how is it that you weep?" asked Gallus suspiciously.

"I wept, being still weak, because they who are conquerors were so kind to one who is a slave and an outcast."

"Oh!" said Gallus. "Well, guard, you need not tie him up this time, but after all I take back nothing that I have said, seeing that in this way or in that they did make you weep. What business had they to insult you with their kindness? Men, henceforth you will be so good as to remember that this maiden is the property of Titus Cæsar, and after Cæsar, of myself, in whose charge he placed her.

If you have any offerings to make to her, and I do not dissuade you from that practice, they must be made through me. Meanwhile, there is a cask of wine, that good old stuff from the Lebanon which I had bought for the voyage. If you should wish to drink the health of our—our captive, it is at your service."

Then taking Miriam by the hand he led her into the eating-tent, still grumbling at the soldiers, who for their part laughed and sent for the wine. They knew their captain's temper, who had served with them through many a fight, and knew also that this crazed Pearl-Maiden whom he saved had twined herself into his heart, as was her fortune with most men of those among whom from time to time fate drove her to seek shelter.

In the tent Miriam found two places set, one for herself and one for the captain Gallus.

"Don't talk to me," he said, "but sit down and eat, for little enough you have swallowed all the time you were sick, and we sail to-morrow evening at the latest, after which, unless you differ from most women, little enough will you swallow on these winter seas until it pleases whatever god we worship to bring us to the coasts of Italy. Now here are oysters brought by runner from Sidon, and I command that you eat six of them before you say a word."

So Miriam ate the oysters obediently, and after the oysters, fish, and after the fish the breast of a woodcock. But from the autumn lamb, roasted whole, which followed, she was forced to turn.

"Send it out to the soldiers," she suggested, and it was sent as her gift.

"Now, my captive," said Gallus, drawing his stool near to her, "I want you to tell me what you can remember of your story. Ah! you don't know that for many days past we have dined together and that it had been your fashion to sit with your arm round my old neck and call me your uncle. Nay, child, you need not blush, for I am more than old enough to be your father, let alone your uncle, and nothing but a father shall I ever be to you."

"Why are you so good to me?" asked Miriam.

"Why? Oh! for several reasons. First, you were the friend of a comrade of mine who often talked of you, but who now is dead. Secondly, you were a sick and helpless thing whom I chanced to rescue in the great slaughter, and who ever since has been my companion; and thirdly—yes, I will say it, though I do not love to talk of that matter, I had a daughter, who died, and who, had she lived, would have been of about your age. Your eyes remind me of hers—there, is that not enough?

"But now for the story. Stay. I will tell you what I know of it. Marcus, he whom they called The Fortunate, but whose fortune has deserted him, was in love with you—like the rest of us. Often he talked to me of you in Rome, where we were friends after a fashion, though he was set far above me, and by me sent to you that letter which I delivered here in this garden, and the trinket that you wear about your neck, and if I remember right, with it a ring—yes, it is upon your finger. Well, I took note of you at the time and went my way to the war, and when I chanced to find you lately upon the top of the Gate Nicanor, although you were more like a half-burnt cinder than a fair maiden, I knew you again and carried you off to Cæsar, who named you his slave and bade me take charge of you and deliver you to him in Rome. Now I want to know how you came to be upon that gateway."

So Miriam began and told him all her tale, while he listened patiently. When she had done he rose and, limping round the little table, bent over and kissed her solemnly upon the brow.

"By all the gods of the Romans, Greeks, Christians, Jews, and barbarian nations, you are a noble-hearted woman," he said, "and that kiss is my tribute to you. Little wonder that puppy, Marcus, is called The Fortunate, since, even when he deserved to die who suffered himself to be taken alive, you appeared to save him—to save him, by Venus, at the cost of your own sweet self. Well, most noble traitress, what now?"

"I ask that question of you, Gallus. What now? Marcus, whom you should call no ill name, and who was overwhelmed through no fault of his own, fighting like a hero, has vanished—"

"Across the Styx, I fear me. Indeed that would be best for him, since no Roman must be taken prisoner and live."

"Nay, I think not, or at the least I hope he lives. My servant, Nehushta, would nurse him for my sake, and for my sake the Essenes, among whom I dwelt, would guard him, even to the loss of their own lives. Unless his wound killed him I believe that Marcus is alive to-day."

"And if that is so you wish to communicate with him?"

"What else, Gallus? Say, what fate will befall me when I reach Rome?"

"You will be kept safe till Titus comes. Then, according to his command, you must walk in his Triumph, and after that, unless he changes his mind, which is not likely, since he prides himself upon never having reversed a decree, however hastily it was made, or even added to or taken from a judgment, you must, alas! be set up in the Forum and sold as a slave to the highest bidder."

"Sold as a slave to the highest bidder!" repeated Miriam faintly. "That is a poor fate for a woman, is it not? Had it been that daughter of yours who died, for instance, you would have thought it a poor fate for her, would you not?"

"Do not speak of it, do not speak of it," muttered Gallus into his beard. "Well, in this, as in other things, let us hope that fortune will favour you."

"I should like Marcus to learn that I am to march in the Triumph, and afterwards to be set up in the Forum and sold as a slave to the highest bidder," said Miriam.

"I should like Marcus to learn—but, in the name of the gods—how is he to learn, if he still lives? Look you, we sail to-morrow night. What do you wish me to do?"

"I wish you to send a messenger to Marcus bearing a token from me to him."

"A messenger! What messenger? Who can find him? I can despatch a soldier, but your Marcus is with the Essenes, who for their own sakes will keep him fast enough as a hostage, if they have cured him. Also the Essenes live, according to your story, in some hyæna-burrow, opening out of an underground quarry in Jerusalem, that is, if they have not been discovered and killed long ago. How, then, will any soldier find their hiding-place?"

"I do not think that such a man would find it," answered Miriam, "but I have friends in this city, and if I could come at them I might discover one who would meet with better fortune. You know that I am a Christian who was brought up among the Essenes, both of them persecuted people that have their secrets. If I find a Christian or an Essene he would take my message and—unless he was killed—deliver it."

Now Gallus thought for a while, then he said, "If I were to go out in Tyre asking for Christians or Essenes, none would appear. As well might a stork go out and call upon a frog. But that old slave-woman, who has tended on me and you, she is cunning in her way, and if I promised to set her at liberty should she succeed, well, perhaps she might succeed. Stay, I will summon her," and he left the tent.

Some minutes later he returned, bringing the slave with him.

"I have explained the matter to this woman, Miriam," he said, "and I think that she understands, and can prove to any who are willing to visit you, that they will have a free pass in to and out of the camp, and need fear no harm. Tell her, then, where she is to go and whom she must seek."

So Miriam told the woman, saying, "Tell any Essene whom you can find that she who is called their Queen, bids his presence, and if he asks more, give him this word—'The sun rises.' Tell any Christian whom you can find that Miriam, their sister, seeks his aid, and if he asks more, give him this word—'The dawn comes.' Do you understand?"

"I understand," answered the woman.

"Then go," said Gallus, "and be back by nightfall, remembering that if you fail, in place of liberty you travel to Rome, whence you will return no more."

"My lord, I go," answered the woman, beating her forehead with her hand and bowing herself from their presence.

By nightfall she was back again with the tidings that no Christians seemed to be left in Tyre; all had fled to Pella, or elsewhere. Of the Essenes, however, she had found one, a minor brother of the name of Samuel, who, on hearing that Miriam was the captive, and receiving the watchword, said that he would visit the camp after dark, although he greatly feared that this might be some snare set to catch him.

After dark he came accordingly, and was led by the old woman, who waited outside to meet him, to the tent where Miriam sat with Gallus. This Samuel proved to be a brother of the lowest order of the Essenes, whom, although he knew of her, Miriam had never seen. He had been absent from the village by the Jordan at the time of the flight of the sect, having come to Tyre by leave of the Court to bid farewell to his mother, who was on her deathbed. Hearing that the brethren had fled, and his mother being still alive, he had remained in Tyre instead of seeking to rejoin them at Jerusalem, thus escaping the terrors of the siege. That was all his story. Now, having buried his mother, he desired to rejoin the brotherhood, if any of them were left alive.

After Gallus had left the tent, since it was not lawful that she should speak of their secrets in the presence of any man who was not of the order, Miriam, having first satisfied herself that he was in truth a brother, told this Samuel all she knew of the hiding-place of the Essenes beyond the ancient quarry, and asked him if he was willing to try to seek it out. He said yes, for he desired to find them; also he was bound to give her what help he could, since should the brethren discover that he had refused it, he would be expelled from their order. Then, having pledged him to be faithful to her trust, not by oath, which the Essenes held unlawful, but in accordance with their secret custom which was known to her, she took from her hand the ring that Marcus had sent her, bidding him find out the Essenes, and, if their Roman prisoner was yet alive, and among them, to deliver it to him with a message telling him of her fate and whither she had gone. If he was dead, or not to be found anywhere, then he was to deliver the ring to the Libyan woman named Nehushta, with the same message. If he could not find her either, then to her uncle Ithiel, or, failing him, to whoever was president of the Essenes, with the same message, praying any or all of them to succour her in her troubles, should that be possible. At the least they were to let her have tidings at the house of Gallus, the captain, in Rome, where he proposed to place her in charge of his wife until the time came for her to be handed over to Titus and to walk in the Triumph. Moreover, in case the brother should forget, she wrote a letter that he might deliver to any of those for whom she gave the message. In this letter Miriam set out briefly all that had befallen her since that night of parting in the Old Tower, and by the help of Gallus, whom she now recalled to the tent, the particulars of her rescue and of the judgment of Cæsar upon her person, ending it with these words:

> "If it be the will of God and your will, O you who may read this letter, haste, haste to help me, that I may escape the shame more sore than death which awaits me yonder in Rome."

This letter she signed, "Miriam, of the house of Benoni," but she did not write upon it the names of those to whom it was addressed, fearing lest it should fall into other hands and bring trouble upon them.

Then Gallus asked the man Samuel what money he needed for his journey and as a reward for his service. He answered that it was against his rule to take any money, who was bound to help those under the protection of the order without reward or fee, whereat Gallus stared and said that there were stranger folk in this land than in any others that he knew, and they were many.

So Samuel, having bowed before Miriam and pressed her hand in a certain fashion in token of brotherhood and fidelity, was led out of the camp again, nor did she ever see him more. Yet, as it proved, he was a faithful messenger, and she did well to trust him.

Next day, at the prayer of Miriam, Gallus also wrote a letter, which gave him much trouble, to a friend of his, who was a brother officer with the army at Jerusalem, enclosing one to be handed to Marcus if, perchance, he should have rejoined the Standards.

"Now daughter," he said, "we have done all that can be done, and must leave the rest to fate."

"Yes," she answered with a sigh, "we must leave the rest to fate, as you Romans call God."

In the evening they set sail for Italy, and with them much of the captured treasure, many sick and wounded men and a guard of soldiers. As it chanced, having taken the sea after the autumn gales and before those of mid-winter began, they had a swift and prosperous voyage, enduring no hardships save once from want of water. Within thirty days they came to Rhegium, whence they marched overland to Rome, being received everywhere very gladly by people who were eager for tidings of the war.

Chapter 20

The Merchant Demetrius

When on that fateful night in the Old Tower Miriam sprang forward to strike the lantern from the hand of the Jew, Nehushta, who was bending over the fallen Marcus and dragging at his body, did not even see that she had left the door.

With an effort, the slope of the rocky passage beyond favouring her, she half-drew, half-lifted the Roman through the entrance. Then it was, as she straightened herself a little to take breath, that she heard the thud of the rock door closing behind her. Still, as it was dark, she did not guess that Miriam was parted from them, for she said:

"Ah! into what troubles do not these men lead us poor women. Well, just in time, and I think that none of them saw us."

There was no answer. Sound could not pierce that wall and the place was silent as a tomb.

"Lady! In the Name of Christ, where are you, lady?" asked Nehushta in a piercing whisper, and the echoes of the gallery answered—"Where are you, lady?"

Just then Marcus awoke.

"What has chanced? What place is this, Miriam?" he asked.

"This has chanced," answered Nehushta in the same awful voice. "We are in the passage leading to the vaults; Miriam is in the hands of the Jews in the Old Tower, and the door is shut between us. Accursed Roman! to save your life she has sacrificed herself. Without doubt she sprang from the door to dash the lantern from the hand of the Jew, and before she could return again it had swung home. Now they will crucify her because she rescued you—a Roman."

"Don't talk, woman," broke in Marcus savagely, "open the door. I am still a man, I can still fight, or," he added with a groan, remembering that he had no sword, "at the least I can die for her."

"I cannot," gasped Nehushta. "She had the iron that lifts the secret latch. If you had kept your sword, Roman, it might perhaps have served, but that has gone also."

"Break it down," said Marcus. "Come, I will help."

"Yes, yes, Roman, you will help to break down three feet of solid stone."

Then began that hideous scene whereof something has been said. Nehushta strove to reach the latch with her fingers. Marcus, standing upon one foot, strove to shake the stone with his shoulder, the black, silent stone that never so much as stirred. Yet they worked madly, their breath coming in great gasps, knowing that the work was in vain, and that even if they could open the door, by now it would be to find Miriam gone, or at the best to be taken themselves. Suddenly Marcus ceased from his labour.

"Lost!" he moaned, "and for my sake. O ye gods! for my sake." Then down he fell, his harness clattering on the rocky step, and lay there, muttering and laughing foolishly.

Nehushta ceased also, gasping: "The Lord help you, Miriam, for I cannot. Oh! after all these years to lose you thus, and because of that man!" and she glared through the darkness towards the fallen Marcus, thinking in her heart that she would kill him.

"Nay," she said to herself, "she loved him, and did she know it might pain her. Better kill myself; yes, and if I were sure that she is dead this, sin or no sin, I would do."

As she sat thus, helpless, hopeless, she saw a light coming up the stair towards them. It was borne by Ithiel. Nehushta rose and faced him.

"Praise be to God! there you are at length," he said. "Thrice have I been up this stair wondering why Miriam did not come."

"Brother Ithiel," answered Nehushta, "Miriam will come no more; she is gone, leaving us in exchange this man Marcus, the Roman prefect of Horse."

"What do you mean? What do you mean?" he gasped. "Where is Miriam?"

"In the hands of the Jews," she answered. Then she told him all that story.

"There is nothing to be done," he moaned when she had finished. "To open the door now would be but to reveal the secret of our hiding- place to the Jews or to the Romans, either of whom would put us to the sword, the Jews for food, the Romans because we are Jews. We can only leave her to God and protect ourselves."

"Had I my will," answered Nehushta, "I would leave myself to God and still strive to protect her. Yet you are right, seeing that many lives cannot be risked for the sake of one girl. But what of this man?"

"We will do our best for him," answered Ithiel, "for so she who sacrificed herself for his sake would have wished. Also years ago he was our guest and befriended us. Stay here a while and I will bring men to carry him to the vault."

So Ithiel went away to return with sundry of the brethren, who lifted Marcus and bore him down the stairs and passages to that darksome chamber where Miriam had slept, while other brethren shut the trap- door, and loosened the roof of the passage, blocking it with stone so that without great labour none could pass that path for ever.

Here in this silent, sunless vault for many, many days Marcus lay sick with a brain fever, of which, had it not been for the skilful nursing of Nehushta and of the leeches among the Essenes, he must certainly have died. But these leeches, who were very clever, doctored the deep sword-cut in his head, removing with little iron hooks the fragments of bone which pressed upon his brain, and dressing that wound and another in his knee with salves.

Meanwhile, they learned by their spies that both the Temple and Mount Sion had fallen. Also they heard of the trial of Miriam and of her exposure on the Gate Nicanor, but of what happened to her afterwards they could gather nothing. So they mourned her as dead.

Now, their food being at length exhausted and the watch of the Romans having relaxed, they determined, those who were left of them, for some had died and Ithiel himself was very ill, to attempt to escape from the hateful vaults that had sheltered them for all these months. A question arose as to what was to be done with Marcus, now but a shadow of a man, who still wandered somewhat in his mind, but who had passed the worst of his sickness and seemed like to live. Some were for abandoning him; some for sending him back to the Romans; but Nehushta showed that it would be wise to keep him as a hostage, so that if they were attacked they might produce him and in return for their care, perhaps buy their lives. In the end they agreed upon this course, not so much for what they might gain by it, but because they knew that it would have pleased the lost maid whom they called their Queen, who had perished to save this man.

So it came about that upon a certain night of rain and storm, when none were stirring, a number of men with faces white as lepers, of the hue, indeed, of roots that have pushed in the dark, might have been seen travelling down the cavern quarries, now tenanted only by the corpses of those who had perished there from starvation, and so through the hole beneath the wall into the free air. With them went litters bearing their sick, and among the sick, Ithiel and Marcus. None hindered their flight, for the Romans had deserted this part of the ruined city and were encamped around the towers in the neighbourhood of Mount Sion, where some few Jews still held out.

Thus it happened that by morning they were well on the road to Jericho, which, always a desert country, was now quite devoid of life. On they went, living on roots and such little food as still remained to them, to Jericho itself, where they found nothing but a ruin haunted by a few starving wretches. Thence they travelled to their own village, to discover that, for the most part, this also had been burnt. But certain caverns in the hillside behind, which they used as store-houses, remained, and undiscovered in them a secret stock of corn and wine that gave them food.

Here, then, they camped and set to work to sow the fields which no Romans or robbers had been able to destroy, and so lived hardly, but unmolested, till at length the first harvest came and with it plenty.

In this dry and wholesome air Marcus recovered rapidly, who by nature was very strong. When first his wits returned to him he recognised Nehushta, and asked her what had chanced. She told him all she knew, and that she believed Miriam to be dead, tidings which caused him to fall into a deep melancholy. Meanwhile, the Essenes treated him with kindness, but let him understand that he was their prisoner. Nor if he had wished it, and they had given him leave to go, could he have left them at that time, seeing that the slightest of his hurts proved to be the worst, since the spear or sword-cut having penetrated to the joint and let out the oil, the wound in his knee would heal only by very slow degrees, and for many weeks left him so lame that he could not walk without a crutch. So here he sat by the banks of the Jordan, mourning the past and well-nigh hopeless for the future.

Thus in solitude, tended by Nehushta, who now had grown very grim and old, and by the poor remnant of the Essenes, Marcus passed four or five miserable months. As he grew stronger he would limp down to the village where his hosts were engaged in rebuilding some of their dwellings, and sit in the garden of the house that was once occupied by Miriam. Now it was but an overgrown place, yet among the pomegranate bushes still stood that shed which she had used as a workshop, and in it, lying here and there as they had fallen, some of her unfinished marbles, among them one of himself which she began and cast aside before she executed that bust which Nero had named divine and set him to guard in the Temple at Rome. To Marcus it was a sad place, haunted by a thousand memories, yet he loved it because those memories were all of Miriam.

Titus, said rumour, having accomplished the utter destruction of Jerusalem, had moved his army to Cæsarea or Berytus, where he passed the winter season in celebrating games in the amphitheatres. These he made splendid by the slaughter of vast numbers of Jewish prisoners, who were forced to fight against each other, or, after the cruel Roman fashion, exposed to the attacks of ravenous wild beasts. But although he thought of doing so, Marcus had no means of communicating with Titus, and was still too lame to attempt escape. Could he have found any, indeed, to make use of them might have brought destruction upon the Essenes, who had treated him kindly and saved his life. Also among the Romans it was a disgrace for a soldier, and especially for an officer of high rank, to be made prisoner, and he was loth to expose his own shame. As Gallus had told Miriam, no Roman should be taken alive. So Marcus attempted to do nothing, but waited, sick at heart, for whatever fate fortune might send him. Indeed, had he been quite sure that Miriam was dead, he, who was disgraced and a captive, would have slain himself and followed her. But although none doubted her death—except Nehushta—his spirit did not tell him that this was so. Thus it came about that Marcus lived on among the Essenes till his health and strength came back to him, as it was appointed that he should do until the time came for him to act. At length that time came.

When Samuel, the Essene, left Tyre, bearing the letter and the ring of Miriam, he journeyed to Jerusalem to find the Holy City but a heap of ruins, haunted by hyænas and birds of prey that feasted on the innumerable dead. Still, faithful to his trust, he strove to discover that entrance to the caverns of which Miriam had told him, and to this end hovered day by day upon the north side of the city near to the old Damascus Gate. The hole he could not find, for there were thousands of stones behind which jackals had burrowed, and how was he to know which of these openings led to caverns, nor were there any left to direct him. Still, Samuel searched and waited in the hope that one day an Essene might appear who would guide him to the hiding-place of the brethren. But no Essene appeared, for the good reason that they had fled already. In the end he was seized by a patrol of Roman soldiers who had observed him hovering about the place and questioned him very strictly as to his business. He replied that it was to gather herbs for food, whereon their officer said that they would find him food and with it some useful work. So they took him and pressed him into a gang of captives who were engaged in pulling down the walls, that Jerusalem might nevermore become a fortified city. In this gang he was forced to labour for over four months, receiving only his daily bread in payment, and with it many blows and hard words, until at last he found an opportunity to make his escape.

Now among his fellow-slaves was a man whose brother belonged to the Order of the Essenes, and from him he learned that they had gone back to Jordan. So thither Samuel started, having Miriam's ring still hidden safely about his person. Reaching the place without further accident he declared himself to the Essenes, who received him with joy, which was not to be wondered at, since he was able to tell them that Miriam, whom they named their Queen and believed to be dead, was still alive. He asked them if they had a Roman prisoner called Marcus hidden away among them, and when they answered that this was so, said that he had a message from Miriam which he was charged to deliver to him. Then they led him to the garden where her workshop had been, telling him that there he would find the Roman.

Marcus was seated in the garden, basking in the sunshine, and with him Nehushta. They were talking of Miriam—indeed, they spoke of little else.

"Alas! although I seem to know her yet alive, I fear that she must be dead," Marcus was saying. "It is not possible that she could have lived through that night of the burning of the Temple."

"It does not seem possible," answered Nehushta, "yet I believe that she did live—as in your heart you believe also. I do not think it was fated that any Christian should perish in that war, since it has been prophesied otherwise."

"Prove it to me, woman, and I should be inclined to become a Christian, but of prophecies and such vague talk I am weary."

"You will become a Christian when your heart is touched and not before," answered Nehushta sharply. "That light is from within."

As she spoke the bushes parted and they saw the Essene, Samuel, standing in front of them.

"Whom do you seek, man?" asked Nehushta, who did not know him.

"I seek the noble Roman, Marcus," he answered, "for whom I have a message. Is that he?"

"I am he," said Marcus, "and now, who sent you and what is your message?"

"The Queen of the Essenes, whose name is Miriam, sent me," replied the man.

Now both of them sprang to their feet.

"What token do you bear?" asked Marcus in a slow, restrained voice, "for know, we thought that lady dead."

"This," he answered, and drawing the ring from his robe he handed it to him, adding, "Do you acknowledge the token?"

"I acknowledge it. There is no such other ring. Have you aught else?"

"I had a letter, but it is lost. The Roman soldiers robbed me of my robe in which it was sewn, and I never saw it more. But the ring I saved by hiding it in my mouth while they searched me."

Marcus groaned, but Nehushta said quickly:

"Did she give you no message? Tell us your story and be swift."

So he told them all.

"How long was this ago?" asked Nehushta.

"Nearly five months. For a hundred and twenty days I was kept as a slave at Jerusalem, labouring at the levelling of the walls."

"Five months," said Marcus. "Tell me, do you know whether Titus has sailed?"

"I heard that he had departed from Alexandria on his road to Rome."

"Miriam will walk in his Triumph, and afterwards be sold as a slave! Woman, there is no time to lose," said Marcus.

"None," answered Nehushta; "still, there is time to thank this faithful messenger."

"Ay," said Marcus. "Man, what reward do you seek? Whatever it be it shall be paid to you who have endured so much. Yes, it shall be paid, though here and now I have no money."

"I seek no reward," replied the Essene, "who have but fulfilled my promise and done my duty."

"Yet Heaven shall reward you," said Nehushta. "And now let us hence to Ithiel."

Back they went swiftly to the caves that were occupied by the Essenes during the rebuilding of their houses. In a little cabin that was open to the air lay Ithiel. The old man was on his death-bed, for age, hardship, and anxiety had done their work with him, so that now he was unable to stand, but reclined upon a pallet awaiting his release. To him they told their story.

"God is merciful," he said, when he had heard it. "I feared that she might be dead, for in the presence of so much desolation, my faith grows weak."

"It may be so," answered Marcus, "but your merciful God will allow this maiden to be set up in the Forum at Rome and sold to the highest bidder. It would have been better that she perished on the gate Nicanor."

"Perhaps this same God," answered Ithiel with a faint smile, "will deliver her from that fate, as He has delivered her from many others. Now what do you seek, my lord Marcus?"

"I seek liberty, which hitherto you have refused to me, Ithiel. I must travel to Rome as fast as ships and horses can carry me. I desire to be present at that auction of the captives. At least, I am rich and can purchase Miriam—unless I am too late."

"Purchase her to be your slave?"

"Nay, to be my wife."

"She will not marry you; you are not a Christian."

"Then, if she asks it, to set her free. Man, would it not be better that she should fall into my hands than into those of the first passer-by who chances to take a fancy to her face?"

"Yes, I think it is better," answered Ithiel, "though who am I that I should judge? Let the Court be summoned and at once. This matter must be laid before them. If you should purchase her and she desires it, do you promise that you will set her free?"

"I promise it."

Ithiel looked at him strangely and said: "Good, but in the hour of temptation, if it should come, see that you do not forget your word."

So the Court was called together, not the full hundred that used to sit in the great hall, but a bare score of the survivors of the Essenes, and to them the brother, Samuel, repeated his tale. To them also Marcus made his petition for freedom, that he might journey to Rome with Nehushta, and if it were possible, deliver Miriam from her bonds. Now, some of the more timid of the Essenes spoke against the release of so valuable a hostage upon the chance of his being able to aid Miriam, but Ithiel cried from his litter:

"What! Would you allow our own advantage to prevail against the hope that this maiden, who is loved by everyone of us, may be saved? Shame upon the thought. Let the Roman go upon his errand, since we cannot."

So in the end they agreed to let him go, and, as he

had none, even provided money for his faring out of their scanty, secret store, trusting that he might find opportunity to repay it in time to come.

That night Marcus and Nehushta bade farewell to Ithiel.

"I am dying," said the old Essene. "Before ever you can set foot in Rome the breath will be out of my body, and beneath the desert sand I shall lie at peace—who desire peace. Yet, say to Miriam, my niece, that my spirit will watch over her spirit, awaiting its coming in a land where there are no more wars and tribulations, and that, meanwhile, I who love her bid her to be of good cheer and to fear nothing."

So they parted from Ithiel and travelled upon horses to Joppa, Marcus disguising his name and rank lest some officer among the Romans should detain him. Here by good fortune they found a ship sailing for Alexandria, and in the port of Alexandria a merchant vessel bound for Rhegium, in which they took passage, none asking them who they might be.

Upon the night of the burning of the Temple, Caleb, escaping the slaughter, was driven with Simon the Zealot across the bridge into the Upper City, which bridge they broke down behind them. Once he tried to return, in the mad hope that during the confusion he might reach the gate Nicanor and, if she still lived, rescue Miriam. But already the Romans held the head of the bridge, and already the Jews were hacking at its timbers, so in that endeavour he failed and in his heart made sure that Miriam had perished. So bitterly did Caleb mourn, who, fierce and wayward as he was by nature, still loved her more than all the world besides, that for six days or more he sought death in every desperate adventure which came to his hand, and they were many. But death fled him, and on the seventh day he had tidings.

A man who was hidden among the ruins of the cloisters managed to escape to the Upper City. From him Caleb learned that the woman, who was said to have been found upon the roof of the gate Nicanor, had been brought before Titus, who gave her over to the charge of a Roman captain, by whom she had been taken without the walls. He knew no more. The story was slight enough, yet it sufficed for Caleb, who was certain that this woman must be Miriam. From that moment he determined to abandon the cause of the Jews, which, indeed, was now hopeless, and to seek out Miriam, wherever she might be. Yet, search as he would, another fifteen days went by before he could find his opportunity.

At length Caleb was placed in charge of a watch upon the wall, and, the other members of his company falling asleep from faintness and fatigue, contrived in the dark to let himself down by a rope which he had secreted, dropping from the end of it into the ditch. In this ditch he found many dead bodies, and from one of them, that of a peasant who had died but recently, took the clothes and a long winter cloak of sheepskins, which he exchanged for his own garments. Then, keeping only his sword, which he hid beneath the cloak, he passed the Roman pickets in the gloom and fled into the country. When daylight came Caleb cut off his beard and trimmed his long hair short. After this, meeting a countryman with a load of vegetables which he had licence to sell in the Roman camp Caleb bought his store from him for a piece of gold, for he was well furnished with money, promising the simple man that if he said a word of it he would find him out and kill him. Then counterfeiting the speech and actions of a peasant, which he, who had been brought up among them down by the banks of Jordan, well could do, Caleb marched boldly to the nearest Roman camp and offered his wares for sale.

Now this camp was situated outside the gate of Gennat, not far from the tower Hippicus. Therefore, it is not strange that although in the course of his bargaining he made diligent inquiry as to the fate of the girl who had been taken to the gate Nicanor, Caleb could hear nothing of her, seeing that she was in a camp situated on the Mount of Olives, upon the other side of Jerusalem. Baffled for that day, Caleb continued his inquiries on the next, taking a fresh supply of vegetables, which he purchased from the same peasant, to another body of soldiers camping in the Valley of Himnon. So he went on from day to day searching the troops which surrounded the city, and working from the Valley of Himnon northwards along the Valley of the Kedron, till on the tenth day he came to a little hospital camp pitched on the slope of the hill opposite to the ruin which once had been the Golden Gate. Here, while proffering his vegetables, he fell into talk with the cook who was sent to chaffer with him.

"Ah!" said the cook handling the basket with satisfaction, "it is a pity, friend, that you did not bring this stuff here a while ago when we wanted it sorely and found it hard to come by in this barren, sword-wasted land."

"Why?" asked Caleb carelessly.

"Oh! because of a prisoner we had here, a girl whose sufferings had made her sick in mind and body, and whose appetite I never knew how to tempt, for she turned from meat, and ever asked for fish, of which, of course, we had none, or failing that, for green food and fruits."

"What were her name and story?" asked Caleb.

"As for her name I know it not. We called her Pearl-Maiden because of a collar of pearls she wore and because also she was white and beautiful as a pearl. Oh! beautiful indeed, and so gentle and sweet, even in her sickness, that the roughest brute of a legionary with a broken head could not choose but to love her. Much more then, that old bear, Gallus, who watched her as though she were his own cub."

"Indeed? And where is this beautiful lady now? I should like to sell her something."

"Gone, gone, and left us all mourning."

"Not dead?" said Caleb in a new voice of eager dismay, "Oh! not dead?"

The fat cook looked at him calmly.

"You take a strange interest in our Pearl-Maiden, Cabbage seller," he said. "And, now that I come to think of it, you are a strange-looking man for a peasant."

With an effort Caleb recovered his self-command.

"Once I was better off than I am now, friend," he answered. "As you know, in this country the wheel of fortune has turned rather quick of late."

"Yes, yes, and left many crushed flat behind it."

"The reason why I am interested," went on Caleb, taking no heed, "is that I may have lost a fine market for my goods."

"Well, and so you have, friend. Some days ago the Pearl-Maiden departed to Tyre in charge of the captain, Gallus, on her way to Rome. Perhaps you would wish to follow and sell her your onions there."

"Perhaps I should," answered Caleb. "When you Romans have gone this seems likely to become a bad country for gardeners, since owls and jackals do not buy fruit, and you will leave no other living thing behind you."

"True," answered the cook. "Cæsar knows how to handle a broom and he has made a very clean sweep," and he pointed complacently to the heaped-up ruins of the Temple before them. "But how much for the whole basket full?"

"Take them, friend," said Caleb, "and sell them to your mess for the best price that you can get. You need not mention that you paid nothing."

"Oh! no, I won't mention it. Good morning, Mr. Cabbage-grower, good morning."

Then he stood still watching as Caleb vanished quickly among the great boles of the olive trees. "What can stir a Jew so much," he reflected to himself, "as to make him give something for nothing, and especially to a Roman? Perhaps he is Pearl-Maiden's brother. No, that can't be from his eyes—her lover more likely. Well, it is no affair of mine, and although he never grew them, the vegetables are good and fresh."

That evening when Caleb, still disguised as a peasant, was travelling through the growing twilight across the hills that bordered the road to Tyre, he heard a mighty wailing rise from Jerusalem and knew that it was the death-cry of his people. Now, everywhere above such portions of the beleaguered city as remained standing, shot up tall spires and wreaths of flame. Titus had forced the walls, and thousands upon thousands of Jews were perishing beneath the swords of his soldiers, or in the fires of their burning homes. Still, some ninety thousand were left alive, to be driven like cattle into the Court of Women.

Here more than ten thousand died of starvation, while some were set aside to grace the Triumph, some to be slaughtered in the amphitheatres at Cæsarea and Berytus, but the most were transported to Egypt, there, until they died, to labour in the desert mines. Thus was the last desolation accomplished and the prophecy fulfilled: "And the Lord shall bring thee into Egypt again with ships . . . and there ye shall sell yourselves unto your enemies for bondmen and for bondwomen, and no man shall buy you." Thus did "Ephraim return to Egypt," whence he came forth to sojourn in the Promised Land until the cup of his sin was full. Now once more that land was a desert without inhabitants; all its pleasant places were waste; all its fenced cities destroyed, and over their ruins and the bones of their children flew Cæsar's eagles. The war was ended, there was peace in Judæa. *Solitudinem faciunt pacem appellant!*

When Caleb reached Tyre, by the last light of the setting sun he saw a white-sailed galley beating her way out to sea. Entering the city, he inquired who went in the galley and was told Gallus, a Roman captain, in charge of a number of sick and wounded men, many of the treasures of the Temple, and a beautiful girl, who was said to be the grand- daughter of Benoni of that town.

Then knowing that he was too late, Caleb groaned in bitterness of spirit. Presently, however, he took thought. Now, Caleb was wise in his generation, for at the beginning of this long war he had sold all his land and houses for gold and jewels, which, to a very great value, he had left hidden in Tyre in the house of a man he trusted, an old servant of his father's. To this store he had added from time to time out of the proceeds of plunder, of trading, and of the ransom of a rich Roman knight who was his captive, so that now his wealth was great. Going to the man's house, Caleb claimed and packed this treasure in bales of Syrian carpets to resemble merchandise.

Then the peasant who had travelled into Tyre upon business about a mule, was seen no more, but in place of him appeared Demetrius, the Egyptian merchant, who bought largely, though always at night, of the merchandise of Tyre, and sailed with it by the first ship to Alexandria. Here this merchant bought much more goods, such as would find a ready sale in the Roman market, enough to fill the half of a galley, indeed, which lay in the harbour near the Pharos lading for Syracuse and Rhegium.

At length the galley sailed, meaning to make Crete, but was caught by a winter storm and driven to Paphos in Cyprus, where, being afraid to attempt the seas again, let the merchant, Demetrius, do what he would to urge them forward, the captain and crew of the galley determined to winter. So they beached her in the harbour and went up to the great temple, rejoicing to pay their vows and offer gifts to Venus, who had delivered them from the fury of the seas, that they might swell the number of her votaries.

But although he accompanied them, since otherwise they might have suspected that he was a Jew, Demetrius, who sought another goddess, cursed Venus in his heart, knowing that had it not been for her delights the sailors would have risked the weather. Still, there was no help for it and no other ship by which he could sail, so here he abode for more than three months, spending his time in Curium, Amathos and Salamis, trading among the rich natives of Cyprus, out of whom he made a large profit, and adding wine, and copper from Tamasus to his other merchandise, as much as there was room for on the ship.

In the end after the great spring festival, for the captain said that it would not be fortunate to leave until this had been celebrated, they set sail and came by way of Rhodes to the Island of Crete, and thence touching at Cythera to Syracuse in Sicily, and so at last to Rhegium. Here the merchant, Demetrius, transhipped his goods into a vessel that was sailing to the port of Centum Cellæ, and having reached that place hired transport to convey them to Rome, nearly forty miles away.

Chapter 21

The Cæsars and Prince Domitian

When the captain Gallus reached the outskirts of Rome he halted, for he did not desire that Miriam should be led through the streets in the daytime, and thus cause questions to be asked concerning her. Also he sent on a messenger bidding the man find out his wife, Julia, if she were still alive, since of this Gallus, who had not seen her for several years, could tell nothing, and inform her that he would be with her shortly, bringing with him a maiden who had been placed in his charge by Titus. Before nightfall, the messenger returned, and with him Julia herself, a woman past middle-age, but, although grey- haired, still handsome and stately.

Miriam saw their meeting, which was a touching sight, since this childless couple who had been married for almost thirty years, had now been separated for a long time. Moreover, a rumour had reached Julia that her husband was not only wounded, but dead, wherefore her joy and thankfulness at his coming were even greater than they would otherwise have been. One thing, however, Miriam noted, that whereas her friend and benefactor, Gallus, held up his hands and thanked the gods that he found his wife living and well, Julia on her part said:

"Aye, I thank God," touching her breast with her fingers as she spoke the words.

Presently the matron seemed to notice her, and, looking at her with a doubtful eye, asked:

"How comes it, husband, that you are in charge of this captive Jewess, if Jewess she be who is so fair?"

"By the orders of Titus Cæsar, wife," he answered, "to whom she must be delivered on his arrival. She was condemned to perish on the gate Nicanor as a traitress to the Jews and a Nazarene."

Julia started and looked at the girl over her shoulder.

"Are you of that faith, daughter?" she asked in a changed voice, crossing her hands upon her breast as though by chance.

"I am, mother," answered Miriam, repeating the sign.

"Well, well, husband," said Julia, "the maid's tale can wait. Whether she was a traitress to the Jews, or a follower of Christus, is not our affair. At least she is in your charge, and therefore welcome to me," and stepping to where Miriam stood with bowed head she kissed her on the forehead, saying aloud:

"I greet you, daughter, who are so sweet to see and in misfortune," adding beneath her breath, "in the Name you know."

Then Miriam was sure that she had fallen into the hands of a woman who was a Christian, and was thankful in her heart, for while the Cæsars sat upon the Roman throne the Christians of every clime, rank and race were one great family.

That evening, so soon as the darkness fell, they entered

Rome by the Appian Gate. Here they separated, Gallus leading his soldiers to convoy the treasure to the safe keeping of that officer who was appointed to receive it, and afterwards to the camp prepared for them, while Julia, with Miriam and an escort of two men only, departed to her own home, a small dwelling in a clean but narrow and crowded street that overhung the Tiber between the Pons Ælius and the Porta Flamina. At the door of the house Julia dismissed the soldiers, saying:

"Go without fear, and take witness that I am bond for the safety of this captive."

So the men went gladly enough, for they desired to rest after the toils of their long journey, and the door of the house having been opened by a servant and locked again behind them, Julia led Miriam across a little court to the sitting-room that lay beyond. Hanging lamps of bronze burned in the room, and by their light Miriam saw that it was very clean and well, though not richly, furnished.

"This is my own house, daughter," she explained, "which my father left me, where I have dwelt during all these weary years that my husband has been absent in the wars of the East. It is a humble place, but you will find peace and safety in it, and, I trust, comfort. Poor child," she added in a gentle voice, "I who am also a Christian, though as yet of this my husband knows nothing, welcome you in the Name of the Lord."

"In the Name of our Lord, I thank you," answered Miriam, "who am but a friendless slave."

"Such find friends," said Julia, "and if you will suffer it I think that I shall be one of them." Then at a sign from the elder woman they knelt down, and in silence each of them put up her prayer of thanksgiving, the wife because her husband had come back to her safe, the maiden because she had been led to a house ruled by a woman of her own faith.

After this they ate, a plain meal but well cooked and served. When it was done Julia conducted Miriam to the little whitewashed chamber which had been prepared for her. It was lighted from the court by a lattice set high in the wall, and, like all the house, very clean and sweet, with a floor of white marble.

"Once another maid slept here," said Julia with a sigh, glancing at the white bed in the corner.

"Yes," said Miriam, "she was named Flavia, was she not, your only child? Nay, do not be astonished. I have heard so much of her that I seem to have known her well, who can be known no more—here."

"Did Gallus tell you?" asked Julia. "He used rarely to speak of her."

Miriam nodded. "Gallus told me. You see he was very good to me and we became friends. For all that he has done, may Heaven bless him, who, although he seems rough, has so kind a heart."

"Yes, may Heaven bless all of us, living and dead," answered Julia. Then she kissed Miriam and left her to her rest.

When Miriam came out of her bedchamber on the following morning, she found Gallus clad in his body armour, now new cleaned, though dinted with many a blow, standing in the court and watching the water which squirted from a leaden pipe to fall into a little basin.

"Greeting, daughter," he said, looking up. "I trust that you have rested well beneath my roof who have sojourned so long in tents."

"Very well," she answered, adding, "If I might ask it, why do you wear your mail here in peaceful Rome?"

"Because I am summoned to have an audience of Cæsar, now within an hour."

"Is Titus come, then?" she asked hurriedly.

"Nay, nay, not Titus Cæsar, but Vespasian Cæsar, his father, to whom I must make report of all that was passing in Judæa when we left, of the treasure that I brought with me and—of yourself."

"Oh! Gallus," said Miriam, "will he take me away from your charge?"

"I know not. I hope not. But who can say? It is as his fancy may move him. But if he listens to me I swear that you shall stay here for ever; be sure of that."

Then he went, leaning on a spear shaft, for the wound in his leg had caused it to shrink so much that he could never hope to be sound again.

Three hours later he returned to find the two women waiting for him anxiously enough. Julia glanced at his face as he came through the door of the street wall into the vestibulum or courtyard where they were waiting.

"Have no fear," she said. "When Gallus looks so solemn he brings good tidings, for if they are bad he smiles and makes light of them," and advancing she took him by the hand and led him past the porter's room into the atrium.

"What news, husband?" she asked when the door was shut behind them so that none might overhear their talk.

"Well," he answered, "first, my fighting days are over, since I am discharged the army, the physicians declaring that my leg will never be well again. Wife, why do you not weep?"

"Because I rejoice," answered Julia calmly. "Thirty

years of war and bloodshed are enough for any man. You have done your work. It is time that you should rest who have been spared so long, and at least I have saved while you were away, and there will be food to fill our mouths."

"Yes, yes, wife, and as it happens, more than you think, since Vespasian, being gracious and pleased with my report, has granted me half-pay for all my life, to say nothing of a gratuity and a share of the spoil, whatever that may bring. Still I grieve, who can never hope to lift spear more."

"Grieve not, for thus I would have had it, Gallus. But what of this maid?"

"Well, I made my report about her, as I was bound to do, and at first Domitian, Cæsar's son, being curious to see her, prompted Vespasian to order that she should be brought to the palace. Almost Cæsar spoke the word, then a thought seemed to strike him and he was silent, whereon I said that she had been very sick and still needed care and nursing, and that if it was his will, my wife could tend her until such time as Titus Cæsar, whose spoil she was, might arrive. Again Domitian interrupted, but Vespasian answered, 'The Jewish maid is not your slave, Domitian, or my slave. She is the slave of your brother, Titus. Let her bide with this worthy officer until Titus comes, he being answerable in his person and his goods that she shall then be produced before him, she or proof of her death.' Then, waving his hand to show that the matter was done with, he went on to speak of other things, demanding details of the capture of the Temple and comparing my list of the vessels and other gear with that which was furnished by the treasurer, into whose charge I handed them yesternight. So, Maid Miriam, till Titus comes you are safe."

"Yes," answered Miriam with a sigh, "till Titus comes. But after that—what?"

"The gods alone know," he said impatiently. "Meanwhile, since my head is on it, I must ask your word of you that you will attempt no flight."

"I give it, Gallus," she answered smiling, "who would die rather than bring evil on you or yours. Also, whither should I fly?"

"I know not. But you Christians find many friends: the rats themselves have fewer hiding-places. Still, I trust you, and henceforth you are free, till Titus comes."

"Aye," repeated Miriam, "—till Titus comes."

So for hard upon six months, till midsummer, indeed, Miriam dwelt in the house of Gallus and his wife, Julia. She was not happy, although to them she became as a daughter. Who could be happy even in the sunshine of a peaceful present, that walked her world between two such banks of shadow? Behind was the shadow of the terrible past; in front, black and forbidding, rose the shadow of the future, which might be yet more terrible, the future when she would be the slave of some man unknown. Sometimes walking with Julia, humbly dressed and mingling with the crowd, her head-dress arranged to hide her face as much as might be, she saw the rich lords of Rome go by in chariots, on horseback, in litters, all sorts and conditions of them, fat, proud men with bold eyes; hard-faced statesmen or lawyers; war-worn, cruel- looking captains; dissolute youths with foppish dress and perfumed hair, and shuddering, wondered whether she was appointed to any one of these. Or was it, perhaps, to that rich and greasy tradesman, or to yon low-born freedman with a cunning leer? She knew not, God alone knew, and in Him must be her trust.

Once as Miriam was walking thus, gorgeously clad slaves armed with rods of office appeared, bursting a way through the crowded streets to an accompaniment of oaths and blows. After these came lictors bearing the fasces on their shoulders; then a splendid chariot drawn by white horses, and driven by a curled and scented charioteer. In it, that he might be the better seen, stood a young man, tall, ruddy-faced, and clad in royal attire, who looked downward as though from bashfulness, but all the while scanned the crowd out of the corners of his dim blue eyes shaded by lids devoid of lashes. For a moment Miriam felt those eyes rest upon her, and knew that she was the subject of some jest which their owner addressed to the exquisite charioteer, causing him to laugh. Then a horror of that man took hold of her, and when he had gone by, bowing in answer to the shouts of the people, who, as it seemed to her, cheered from fear and not with joy, she asked Julia who he might be.

"Who but Domitian," she answered, "the son of one Cæsar and the brother of another, who hates both and would like to wear their crown. He is an evil man, and if he should chance to cross your path, beware of him, Miriam."

Miriam shuddered and said:

"As well, mother, might you bid the mouse that is caught abroad to beware of the cat it meets at night."

"Some mice find holes that cats cannot pass," answered Julia with meaning as they turned their faces homeward.

During all this time, although Gallus made diligent inquiry among the soldiers who arrived from Judæa, Miriam could hear nothing of Marcus, so that at last she came to believe that he must be dead, and with him the beloved and faithful Nehushta, and to hope that if this were so she also might be taken. Still amongst all this trouble she had one great comfort. Under the mild rule of Vespasian, although their meeting-places were known, the Christians had peace for a while. Therefore, in company with Julia and many others of the brotherhood, she was able to visit the catacombs on the Appian Way by night, and there in those dismal, endless tombs to offer prayer and receive the ministrations of the Church. The great Apostles, St. Peter and St. Paul, had suffered martyrdom, indeed, but they had left many teachers behind them, and the chief of these soon grew to know and love the poor Jewish captive who was doomed to slavery. Therefore here also she found friends and consolation of spirit.

In time Gallus came to learn that his wife was also of the Faith, and for a while this knowledge seemed to cast him down. In the end, however, he shrugged his shoulders and said that she was certainly of an age to judge for herself and that he trusted no harm might come of it. Indeed, when the principles of the Christian hope were explained to him, he listened to them eagerly enough, who had lost his only child, and until now had never heard this strange story of resurrection and eternal life. Still, although he listened, and even from time to time was present when the brethren prayed, he would not be baptised, who said that he was too sunk in years to throw incense on a new altar.

At length Titus came, the Senate, which long before his arrival had decreed him a Triumph, meeting him outside the walls, and there, after some ancient formalities communicating to him their decision. Moreover, it was arranged that Vespasian, his father, should share in this Triumph, because of the great deeds which he had done in Egypt, so that it was said everywhere that this would be the most splendid ceremony which Rome had ever seen. After this Titus passed to his palace and there lived privately for several weeks, resting while the preparations for the great event went forward.

One morning early Gallus was summoned to the palace, whence he returned rubbing his hands and trying to look pleased, with him, as Julia had said, a sure sign of evil tidings.

"What is it, husband?" she asked.

"Oh! nothing, nothing," he answered, "except that our Pearl-Maiden here must accompany me after the mid-day meal into the august presences of Vespasian and Titus. The Cæsars wish to see her, that they may decide where she is to walk in the procession. If she is held to be beautiful enough, they will grant to her a place of honour, by herself. Do you hear that, wife—by herself, not far in front of the very chariot of Titus? As for the dress that she will wear," he went on nervously, since neither of his auditors seemed delighted with this news, "it is to be splendid, quite splendid, all of the purest white silk with little discs of silver sewn about it, and a representation of the Gate Nicanor worked in gold thread upon the breast of the robe."

At this tidings Miriam broke down and began to weep.

"Dry your tears, girl," he said roughly, although the thickness of his voice suggested that water and his own eyes were not far apart. "What must be, must be, and now is the time for that God you worship to show you some mark of favour. Surely, He should do so, seeing how long and how often you pray to Him in burrows that a jackal would turn from."

"I think He will," answered Miriam, ceasing her sobs with a bold up- lifting of her soul towards the light of perfect faith.

"I am sure He will," added Julia, gently stroking Miriam's dark and curling hair.

"Then," broke in Gallus, driving the point to its logical conclusion, "what have you to fear? A long, hot walk through the shouting populace, who will do no harm to one so lovely, and after that, whatever good fate your God may choose for you. Come, let us eat, that you may look your best when you appear before the Cæsars."

"I would rather look my worst," said Miriam, bethinking her of Domitian and his bleared eyes. Still, to please Gallus, she tried to eat, and afterwards, accompanied by him and by Julia, was carried in a closed litter to the palace.

Too soon she was there, arriving a little before them, and was helped from the litter by slaves wearing the Imperial livery. Now she found herself alone in a great marble court filled with officers and nobles awaiting audience.

"That is the Pearl-Maiden," said one of them, whereon they all crowded around her, criticising her aloud in their idle curiosity.

"Too short," said one. "Too thin," said another. "Too small in the foot for her ankle," said a third. "Fools," broke in a fourth, a young man with a fine figure and dark rings round his eyes, "what is the use of trying to cheapen this piece of goods thus in the eyes of the experienced? I say that this Pearl-Maiden is as perfect as those pearls about her own neck; on a small scale, perhaps, but quite perfect, and you will admit that I ought to know."

"Lucius says that she is perfect," remarked one of them in a tone of acquiescence, as though that verdict settled the matter.

"Yes," went on the critical Lucius, "now, to take one thing only, a point so often overlooked. Observe how fresh and firm her flesh is. When I press it thus," and he suited the action to the word, "as I thought, my finger leaves scarcely any mark."

"But my arm does," said a gruff voice beside him, and next moment this scented judge of human beings received the point of the elbow of Gallus between the eyes just where the nose is set into the forehead. With such force and skill was the blow directed that next instant the critic was sprawling on his back upon the pavement, the blood gushing from his nostrils. Now most of them laughed, but some murmured, while Gallus said:

"Way there, friends, way there! I am charged to deliver this lady to the Cæsars and to certify that while she was in my care no man has so much as laid a finger on her. Way there, I pray you! And as for that whimpering puppy on his back, if he wishes it, he knows where to find Gallus. My sword will mark him worse than my elbow, if he wants blood- letting, that I swear."

Now with jests and excuses they fell back one and all. There were few of them who did not know that, lame as he might be now, old Gallus was still the fiercest and most dreaded swordsman of his legion. Indeed he was commonly reported to have slain eighteen men in single combat, and when young even to have faced the most celebrated gladiator of the day for sport, or to win a private bet, and given him life as he lay at his mercy.

So they passed on through long halls guarded by soldiers, till at length they came to a wide passage closed with splendid curtains, where the officer on duty asked them their business. Gallus told him and he vanished through the curtains, whence he returned presently, beckoning them to advance. They followed him down a corridor set with busts of departed emperors and empresses, to find themselves in a round marble chamber, very cool and lighted from above. In this chamber sat and stood three men: Vespasian, whom they knew by his strong, quiet face and grizzled hair; Titus, his son, "the darling of mankind," thin, active, and æsthetic-looking, with eyes that were not unkindly, a sarcastic smile playing about the corners of his mouth; and Domitian, his brother, who has already been described, a man taller than either of them by half a head, and more gorgeously attired. In front of the august three was a master of ceremonies clad in a dark-coloured robe, who was showing them drawings of various sections of the triumphal procession, and taking their orders as to such alterations as they wished.

Also there were present, a treasurer, some officers and two or three of the intimate friends of Titus.

Vespasian looked up.

"Greeting, worthy Gallus," he said in the friendly, open voice of one who has spent his life in camps, "and to your wife, Julia, greeting also. So that is the Pearl-Maiden of whom we have heard so much talk. Well, I do not pretend to be a judge of beauty, still I say that this Jewish captive does not belie her name. Titus, do you recognise her?"

"In truth, no, father. When last I saw her she was a sooty, withered little thing whom Gallus yonder carried in his great arms, as a child might carry a large doll that he had rescued from the fire. Yes, I agree that she is beautiful and worthy of a very good place in the procession. Also she should fetch a large price afterwards, for that necklace of pearls goes with her—make a note of this, Scribe—and the reversion to considerable property in Tyre and elsewhere. This, by special favour, she will be allowed to inherit from her grandfather, the old rabbi, Benoni, one of the Sanhedrim, who perished in the burning of the Temple."

"How can a slave inherit property, son?" asked Vespasian, raising his eyebrows.

"I don't know," answered Titus with a laugh. "Perhaps Domitian can tell you. He says that he has studied law. But so I have decreed."

"A slave," interrupted Domitian wisely, "has no rights and can hold no property, but the Cæsar of the East"—here he sneered—"can declare that certain lands and goods will pass to the highest bidder with the person of the slave, and this, Vespasian Cæsar, my father, is what I understand Titus Cæsar, my brother, has thought it good to do in the present instance."

"Yes," said Titus in a quiet voice, though his face flushed, "that, Domitian, is what I have thought it good to do. In such a matter is not my will enough?"

"Conqueror of the East," replied Domitian, "Thrower-down of the mountain stronghold called Jerusalem, to which the topless towers of Ilium were as nothing, and Exterminator of a large number of misguided fanatics, in what matter is not your will enough? Yet a boon, O Cæsar. As you are great, be generous," and with a mocking gesture he bowed the knee to Titus.

"What boon do you seek of me, brother, who know that all I have is, or," he added slowly, "will be—yours?"

"One that is already granted by your precious words, Titus. Of all you have, which is much, I seek only this Pearl-Maiden, who has taken my fancy. The girl only, not her property in Tyre, wherever that may be, which you can keep for yourself."

Vespasian looked up, but before he could speak, Titus answered quickly:

"I said, Domitian, 'all I have.' This maid I have not, therefore the words do not apply. I have decreed that the proceeds of the sale of these captives is to be divided equally between the wounded soldiers and the poor of Rome. Therefore she is their property, not mine. I will not rob them."

"Virtuous man! No wonder that the legions love him who cannot withdraw one lot from a sale of thousands, even to please an only brother," soliloquised Domitian.

"If you wish for the maid," went on Titus, taking no heed of the insult, "the markets are open—buy her. It is my last word."

Suddenly Domitian grew angry, the false modesty left his face, his tall form straightened itself, and he stared round with his blear, evil-looking eyes.

"I appeal," he shouted, "I appeal from Cæsar the Small to Cæsar the Great, from the murderer of a brave barbarian tribe to the conqueror of the world. O Cæsar, Titus here declared that all he has is mine. Yet when I ask him for the gift of one captive girl he refuses me. Command, I pray you, that he should keep his word."

Now the officers and the secretaries looked up, for of a sudden this small matter had become very important.

For long the quarrel between Titus and his jealous brother had smouldered, now over the petty question of a captive it had broken into flame.

The face of Titus grew hard and stern as that of some statue of the offended Jove.

"Command, I pray you, father," he said, "that my brother should cease to offer insult to me. Command also that he should cease to question my will and my authority in matters great or small that are within my rule. Since you are appealed to as Cæsar, as Cæsar judge, not of this thing only but of all, for there is much between him and me that needs to be made plain."

Vespasian looked round him uneasily, but seeing no escape and that beneath the quarrel lay issues which were deep and wide, he spoke out in his brave, simple-minded fashion.

"Sons," he said, "seeing that there are but two of you who together, or one after the other, must inherit the world, it is an evil-omened thing that you should quarrel thus, since on the chances of your enmity may hang your own fates and the fates of peoples. Be reconciled, I pray you. Is there not enough for both? As for the matter in hand—this is my judgment. With all the spoils of Judæa, this fair maid is the property of Titus. Titus, whose boast it is that he does not go back upon his word, has decreed that she shall be sold and her price divided between the sick soldiers and the poor. Therefore she is no longer his to give away, even to his brother. With Titus I say—if you desire the girl, Domitian, bid your agent buy her in the market."

"Aye, I will buy her," snarled Domitian, "but this I swear, that soon or late Titus shall pay the price and one that he will be loth to give." Then followed by his secretary and an officer, he turned and left the audience hall.

"What does he mean?" asked Vespasian, looking after him with anxious eyes.

"He means that—" and Titus checked himself. "Well, time and my destiny will show the world what he means. So be it. As for you, Pearl-Maiden, who, though you know it not, have cost Cæsar so dear, well, you are fairer than I thought, and shall have the best of places in the pageant. Yet, for your sake, I pray that one may be found who, when you come to the market-place, may outbid Domitian," and he waved his hand to show that the audience was at an end.

Chapter 22

The Triumph

Another week went by and the eve of the Triumph was at hand. On the afternoon before the great day sewing-women had come to the house of Gallus, bringing with them the robe that Miriam must wear. As had been promised, it was splendid, of white silk covered with silver discs and having the picture of the gate Nicanor fashioned on the breast, but cut so low that it shamed Miriam to put it on.

"It is naught, it is naught," said Julia. "The designer has made it thus that the multitude may see those pearls from which you take your name." But to herself she thought: "Oh! monstrous age, and monstrous men, whose eyes can delight in the disgrace of a poor unfriended maiden. Surely the cup of iniquity of my people is full, and they shall drink it to the dregs!"

That same afternoon also came an assistant of the officer, who was called the Marshal, with orders to Gallus as to when and where he was to deliver over his charge upon the morrow. With him he brought a packet, which, when opened, proved to contain a splendid golden girdle, fashioned to the likeness of a fetter. The clasp was an amethyst, and round it were cut these words: "The gift of Domitian to her who to-morrow shall be his."

Miriam threw the thing from her as though it were a snake.

"I will not wear it," she said. "I say that I will not wear it; at least to-day I am my own," while Julia groaned and Gallus cursed beneath his breath.

Knowing her sore plight, that evening there came to visit her one of the elders of the Christian Church in Rome, a bishop named Cyril, who had been the friend and disciple of the Apostle Peter. To him the poor girl poured out all the agony of her heart.

"Oh! my father, my father in Christ," she said, "I swear to you that were I not of our holy faith, rather than endure this shame I would slay myself to-night! Other dangers have I passed, but they have been of the body alone, whereas this——. Pity me and tell me, you in whose ear God speaks, tell me, what must I do?"

"Daughter," answered the grave and gentle man, "you must trust in God. Did He not save you in the house at Tyre? Did He not save you in the streets of Jerusalem? Did He not save you on the gate Nicanor?"

"He did," answered Miriam.

"Aye, daughter, and so shall He save you in the slave-market of Rome. I have a message for your ear, and it is that no shame shall come near to you. Tread your path, drink your cup, and fear nothing, for the Lord shall send His angel to protect you until such time as it pleases Him to take you to Himself."

Miriam looked at him, and as she looked peace fell upon her soul and shone in her soft eyes.

"I hear the word of the Lord spoken through the mouth

of His messenger," she said, "and henceforth I will strive to fear nothing, no, not even Domitian."

"Least of all Domitian, daughter, that son of Satan, whom Satan shall pay in his own coin."

Then going to the door he summoned Julia, and while Gallus watched without, the two of them prayed long and earnestly with Miriam. When their prayer was finished the bishop rose, blessed her, and bade her farewell.

"I leave you, daughter," he said, "but though you see him not, another takes my place. Do you believe?"

"I have said that I believe," murmured Miriam.

Indeed, in those days when men still lived who had seen the Christ and His voice still echoed through the world, to the strong faith of His followers, it was not hard to credit that His angel did descend to earth to protect and save at their Master's bidding.

So Cyril, the bishop, went, and that night from many a catacomb prayers rose up to Heaven for Miriam in her peril. That night also she slept peacefully.

Two hours before the dawn, Julia awoke her and arrayed her in the glittering, hateful garments. When all was ready, with tears she bade her farewell.

"Child, child," she said, "you have become to me as my own daughter was, and now I know not how and when we shall meet again."

"Perhaps sooner than you think," Miriam answered. "But if not, if, indeed, I speak to you for the last time, why, then, my blessings on you who have played a mother's part to a helpless maid that was no kin of yours. Yes, and on you Gallus also, who have kept me safe through so many dangers."

"And who hopes, dear one, to keep you safe through

many more. Since I may not swear by the gods before you, I swear it by the Eagles that Domitian will do well to have a care how he deals by you. To him I owe no fealty and, as has been proved before to-day, the sword of vengeance can reach the heart of princes."

"Aye, Gallus," said Miriam gently, "but let it not be your sword, nor, I trust, shall you need to think of vengeance."

Then the litter was brought into the courtyard, with the guards that were sent to accompany it, and they started for the gathering-place beyond the Triumphal Way. Dark though it still was, all Rome was astir. On every side shone torches, from every house and street rose the murmur of voices, for the mighty city made herself ready to celebrate the greatest festival which her inhabitants had seen. Even now at times the press was so dense that the soldiers were obliged to force a way through the crowd, which poured outwards to find good places along the line of the Triumph, or to take up their station on stands of timber, and in houses they had hired, whose roofs, balconies and windows commanded the path of the pageant.

They crossed the Tiber. This Miriam knew by the roar of the water beneath, and because the crush upon the narrow bridge was so great. Thence she was borne along through country comparatively open, to the gateways of some large building, where she was ordered to dismount from the litter. Here officers were waiting who took charge of her, giving to Gallus a written receipt for her person. Then, either because he would not trust himself to bid her farewell, or because he did not think it wise to do so in the presence of the officers, Gallus turned and left her without a word.

"Come on, girl," said a man, but a secretary, looking up from his tablets, called to him:

"Gently there with that lot, or you will hear about it. She is Pearl- Maiden, the captive who made the quarrel between the Cæsars and Domitian, of which all Rome is talking. Gently, I tell you, gently, for many free princesses are worth less to-day."

Hearing this, the man bowed to Miriam, almost with reverence, and begged her to follow him to a place that had been set apart for her. She obeyed, passing through a great number of people, of whom all she could see in the gloom of the breaking dawn was that, like herself, they were captives, to a little chamber where she was left alone watching the light grow through the lattice, and listening to the hum of voices that rose without, mingled now and again with sobs and wails of grief. Presently the door opened and a servant entered with bread on a platter and milk in an earthenware vessel. These she took thankfully, knowing that she would need food to support her during the long day, but scarcely had she begun to eat when a slave appeared clad in the imperial livery, and bearing a tray of luxurious meats served in silver vessels.

"Pearl-Maiden," he said, "my master, Domitian, sends you greeting and this present. The vessels are your own, and will be kept for you, but he bids me add, that to-night you shall sup off dishes of gold."

Miriam made no answer, though one rose to her lips; but after the man had departed, with her foot she overset the tray so that the silver vases fell clattering to the floor, where the savory meats were spilled. Then she went on eating the bread and milk till her hunger was satisfied.

Scarcely had she finished her meal, when an officer entered the cell and led her out into a great square, where she was marshalled amongst many other prisoners. By now the sun was up and she saw before her a splendid building, and gathered below the building all the Senate of Rome in their robes, and many knights on horses, and nobles, and princes from every country with their retinues—a very wonderful and gallant sight. In front of the building were cloisters, before which were set two ivory chairs, while to right and left of these chairs, as far as the eye could reach, were drawn up thousand upon thousands of soldiers; the Senate, the Knights and the Princes, as she could see from the rising ground whereon she stood, being in front of them and of the chairs. Presently from the cloisters, clad in garments of silk and wearing crowns of laurel, appeared the Cæsars, Vespasian and Titus, attended by Domitian and their staffs. As they came the soldiers saw them and set up a mighty triumphant shout which sounded like the roar of the sea, that endured while the Cæsars sat themselves upon their thrones. Up and up went the sound of the continual shouting, till at length Vespasian rose and lifted his hand.

Then silence fell and, covering his head with his cloak, he seemed to make some prayer, after which Titus also covered his head with his cloak and offered a prayer. This done, Vespasian addressed the soldiers, thanking them for their bravery and promising them rewards, whereon they shouted again until they were marched off to the feast that had been made ready. Now the Cæsars vanished and the officers began to order the great procession, of which Miriam could see neither the beginning nor the end. All she knew was that before her in lines eight wide were marshalled two thousand or more Jewish prisoners bound together with ropes, among whom, immediately in front of her, were a few women. Next she came, walking by herself, and behind her, also walking by himself, a dark, sullen-looking man, clad in a white robe and a purple cloak, with a gilded chain about his neck.

Looking at him she wondered where she had seen his face, which seemed familiar to her. Then there rose before her mind a vision of the Court of the Sanhedrim sitting in the cloisters of the Temple, and of herself standing there before them. She remembered that this man was seated next to that Simeon who had been so bitter against her and pronounced upon her the cruel sentence of death, also that some one in the crowd had addressed him as Simon, the son of Gioras, none other than the savage general whom the Jews had admitted into the city to make way upon the Zealot, John of Gischala. From that day to this she had heard nothing of him till now they met again, the judge and the victim, caught in a common net. Presently, in the confusion they were brought together and he knew her.

"Are you Miriam, the grand-daughter of Benoni?" he asked.

"I am Miriam," she answered, "whom you, Simon, and your fellows doomed to a cruel death, but who have been preserved—"

"——To walk in a Roman Triumph. Better that you had died, maiden, at the hands of your own people."

"Better that you had died, Simon, at your own hands, or at those of the Romans."

"That I am about to do," he replied bitterly. "Fear not, woman, you will be avenged."

"I ask no vengeance," she answered. "Nay, cruel as you

are I grieve that you, a great captain, should have come to this."

"I grieve also, maiden. Your grandsire, old Benoni, chose the better part."

Then the soldiers separated them and they spoke no more.

An hour passed and the procession began its march along the Triumphal Way. Of it Miriam could see little. All she knew was that in front there were ranks of fettered prisoners, while behind men carried upon trays and tables the golden vessels of the Temple, the seven-branched candlestick and the ancient sacred book of the Jewish law. They were followed by other men, who bore aloft images of victory in ivory and gold. Then, although these did not join them till they reached the Porta Triumphalis, or the Gate of Pomp, attended, each of them, by lictors having their fasces wreathed with laurel, came the Cæsars. First went Vespasian Cæsar, the father. He rode in a splendid golden chariot, to which were harnessed four white horses led by Libyan soldiers. Behind him stood a slave clad in a dull robe, set there to avert the influence of the evil eye and of the envious gods, who held a crown above the head of the Imperator, and now and again whispered in his ear the ominous words, *Respice post te, hominem memento te* ("Look back at me and remember thy mortality.")

After Vespasian Cæsar, the father, came Titus Cæsar, the son, but his chariot was of silver, and graved upon its front was a picture of the Holy House of the Jews melting in the flames. Like his father he was attired in the *toga picta* and *tunica palmata,* the gold-embroidered over-robe and the tunic laced with silver leaves, while in his right hand he held a laurel bough, and in his left a sceptre. He also was attended by a slave who whispered in his ear the message of mortality.

Next to the chariot of Titus, alongside of it indeed, and as little behind as custom would allow, rode Domitian, gloriously arrayed and mounted on a splendid steed. Then came the tribunes and the knights on horseback, and after them the legionaries to the number of five thousand, every man of them having his spear wreathed in laurel.

Now the great procession was across the Tiber, and, following its appointed path down broad streets and past palaces and temples, drew slowly towards its object, the shrine of Jupiter Capitolinus, that stood at the head of the Sacred Way beyond the Forum. Everywhere the side paths, the windows of houses, the great scaffoldings of timber, and the steps of temples were crowded with spectators. Never before did Miriam understand how many people could inhabit a single city. They passed them by thousands and by tens of thousands, and still, far as the eye could reach, stretched the white sea of faces. Ahead that sea would be quiet, then, as the procession pierced it, it began to murmur. Presently the murmur grew to a shout, the shout to a roar, and when the Cæsars appeared in their glittering chariots, the roar to a triumphant peal which shook the street like thunder. And so on for miles and miles, till Miriam's eyes were dim with the glare and glitter, and her head swam at the ceaseless sound of shouting.

Often the procession would halt for a while, either because of a check to one of the pageants in front, or in order that some of its members might refresh themselves with drink which was brought to them. Then the crowd, ceasing from its cheers, would make jokes, and criticise whatever person or thing they chanced to be near. Greatly did they criticise Miriam in this fashion, or at the least she thought so, who must listen to it all. Most of them, she found, knew her by her name of Pearl-Maiden, and pointed out to each other the necklace about her throat. Many, too, had heard something of her story, and looked eagerly at the picture of the gate Nicanor blazoned upon her breast. But the greater part concerned themselves only with her delicate beauty, passing from mouth to mouth the gossip concerning Domitian, his quarrel with the Cæsars, and the intention which he had announced of buying this captive at the public sale. Always it was the same talk; sometimes more brutal and open than others—that was the only difference.

Once they halted thus in the street of palaces through which they passed near to the Baths of Agrippa. Here the endless comments began again, but Miriam tried to shut her ears to it and looked about her. To her left was a noble-looking house built of white marble, but she noticed that its shutters were closed, also that it was undecorated with garlands, and idly wondered why. Others wondered too, for when they had wearied of discussing her points, she heard one plebeian ask another whose house that was and why it had been shut up upon this festal day. His fellow answered that he could not remember the owner's name, but he was a rich noble who had fallen in the Jewish wars, and that the palace was closed because it was not yet certain who was his heir.

At that moment her attention was distracted by a sound of groans and laughter coming from behind. She looked round to see that the wretched Jewish general, Simon, had sunk fainting to the ground, overcome by the heat, or the terrors of his mind, or by the sufferings which he was forced to endure at the hands of his cruel guards, who flogged him as he walked, for the pleasure of the people. Now they were beating him to life again with their rods; hence the laughter of the audience and the groans of the victim. Sick at heart, Miriam turned away from this horrid sight, to hear a tall man, whose back was towards her, but who was clad in the rich robes of an Eastern merchant, asking one of the marshals of the Triumph, in a foreign accent, whether it was true that the captive Pearl-Maiden was to be sold that evening in the auction-mart of the Forum. The marshal answered yes, such were the orders as regarded her and the other women, since there was no convenient place to house them, and it was thought best to be rid of them and let their masters take them home at once.

"Does she please you, sir? Are you going to bid?" he added. "If so, you will find yourself in high company."

"Perhaps, perhaps," answered the man with a shrug of his shoulders.

Then he vanished into the crowd.

Now, for the first time that day, Miriam's spirit seemed to fail her. The weariness of her body, the foul talk, the fouler cruelty, the cold discussion of the sale of human beings to the first-comer as though they were sheep or swine, the fear of her fate that night, pressed upon and overcame her mind, so that she felt inclined, like Simon, the son of Gioras, to sink fainting to the pavement and lie there till the cruel rods beat her to her feet again. Hope sank low and faith grew dim, while in her heart she wondered vaguely what was the meaning of it all, and why poor men and women were made to suffer thus for the pleasure of other men and women; wondered also what escape there could be for her.

While she mused thus, like a ray of light through the clouds, a sense of consolation, sweet as it was sudden, seemed to pierce the darkness of her bitter thoughts. She knew not whence it came, nor what it might portend, yet it existed, and the source of it seemed near to her. She scanned the faces of the crowd, finding pity in a few, curiosity in more, but in most gross admiration if they were men, or scorn of her misfortune and jealousy of her loveliness if they were women. Not from among these did that consolation flow. She looked up to the sky, half expecting to see there that angel of the Lord into whose keeping the bishop, Cyril, had delivered her. But the skies were empty and brazen as the faces of the Roman crowd; not a cloud could be seen in them, much less an angel.

As her eyes sank earthwards their glance fell upon one of the windows of the marble house to her left. If she remembered right some few minutes before the shutters of that window had been closed, now they were open, revealing two heavy curtains of blue embroidered silk. Miriam thought this strange, and, without seeming to do so, kept her eyes fixed upon the curtains. Presently, for her sight was good, she saw fingers between them—long, dark-coloured fingers. Then very slowly the curtains were parted, and in the opening thus made appeared a face, the face of an old woman, dark and noble looking and crowned with snow-white hair. Even at that distance Miriam knew it in an instant.

Oh, Heaven! it was the face of Nehushta, Nehushta whom she thought dead, or at least for ever lost. For a moment Miriam was paralysed, wondering whether this was not some vision born of the turmoil and excitement of that dreadful day. Nay, surely it was no vision, surely it was Nehushta herself who looked at her with loving eyes, for see! she made the sign of the cross in the air before her, the symbol of Christian hope and greeting, then laid her finger upon her lips in token of secrecy and silence. The curtain closed and she was gone, who not five seconds before had so mysteriously appeared.

Miriam's knees gave way beneath her, and while the marshals shouted to the procession to set forward, she felt that she must sink to the ground. Indeed, she would have fallen had not some woman in the crowd stepped forward and thrust a goblet of wine into her hands, saying:

"Drink that, Pearl-Maiden, it will make your pale cheeks even prettier than they are."

The words were coarse, but Miriam, looking at the woman, knew her for one of the Christian community with whom she had worshipped in the catacombs. So she took the cup, fearing nothing, and drank it off. Then new strength came to her, and she went forward with the others on that toilsome, endless march.

At length, however, it did end, an hour or so before sunset. They had passed miles of streets; they had trodden the Sacred Way bordered by fanes innumerable and adorned with statues set on columns; and now marched up the steep slope that was crowned by the glorious temple of Jupiter Capitolinus. As they began to climb it guards broke into their lines, and seizing the chain that hung about the neck of Simon, dragged him away.

"Whither do they take you?" asked Miriam as he passed her.

"To what I desire—death," he answered, and was gone.

Now the Cæsars, dismounting from their chariots, took up their stations by altars at the head of the steps, while beneath them, rank upon rank, gathered all those who had shared their Triumph, each company in its allotted place. Then followed a long pause, the multitude waiting for Miriam knew not what. Presently men were seen running from the Forum up a path that had been left open, one of them carrying in his hand some object wrapped in a napkin. Arriving in face of the Cæsars he threw aside the cloth and held up before them and in sight of all the people the grizzly head of Simon, the son of Gioras. By this public murder of a brave captain of their foes was consummated the Triumph of the Romans, and at the sight of its red proof trumpets blew, banners waved, and from half a million throats went up a shout of victory that seemed to rend the very skies, for the multitude was drunk with the glory of its brutal vengeance.

Then silence was called, and there before the Temple of Jove the beasts were slain, and the Cæsars offered sacrifice to the gods that had given them victory.

Thus ended the Triumph of Vespasian and Titus, and with it the record of the struggle of the Jews against the iron beak and claws of the Roman Eagle.

Chapter 23

The Slave-Ring

Had Miriam chanced to look out of her litter as she passed the Temple of Isis, escorted by Gallus and the guards before dawn broke upon that great day of the Triumph, and had there been light to enable her to see, she might have beheld two figures galloping into Rome as fast as their weary horses would carry them. Both rode after the fashion of men, but one of them, wrapped in an Eastern garment that hid the face, was in fact a woman.

"Fortune favours us, Nehushta," said the man in a strained voice. "At least, we are in time for the Triumph, who might so easily have been too late. Look, yonder they gather already by Octavian's Walks," and he pointed to the companies of soldiers who hurried past them to the meeting-place.

"Yes, yes, my lord Marcus, we are in time. There go the eagles and here comes their prey," and in her turn Nehushta pointed to a guarded litter—had they but known it, the very one that carried the beloved woman whom they sought. "But whither now? Would you also march in the train of Titus?"

"Nay, woman, it is too late. Also I know not what would be my welcome."

"Your welcome? Why, you were his friend, and Titus is faithful to his friends."

"Aye, but perhaps not to those who have been taken prisoner by the enemy. Towards the commencement of the siege that happened to a man I knew. He was captured with a companion. The companion the Jews slew, but as he was about to be beheaded upon the wall, this man slipped from the hands of the executioner, and leaping from it escaped with little hurt. Titus gave him his life, but dismissed him from his legion. Why should I fare better?"

"That you were taken was no fault of yours, who were struck senseless and overwhelmed."

"Maybe, but would that avail me? The rule, a good rule, is that no Roman soldier should yield to an enemy. If he is captured while insensible, then on finding his wits he must slay himself, as I should have striven to do, had I awakened to find myself in the hands of the Jews. But things fell out otherwise. Still, I tell you, Nehushta, that had it not been for Miriam, I should not have turned my face to Rome, at any rate until I had received pardon and permission from Titus."

"What then are your plans, lord Marcus?"

"To go to my own house near the Baths of Agrippa. The Triumph must pass there, and if Miriam is among the captives we shall see her. If not, then either she is dead or already sold, or perchance given as a present to some friend of Cæsar's."

Now they ceased talking, for the people were so many that they could only force their way through the press riding one after the other. Thus, Nehushta following Marcus, they crossed the Tiber and passed through many streets, decorated, most of them, for the coming pageant, till at length Marcus drew rein in front of a marble mansion in the Via Agrippa.

"A strange home-coming," he muttered. "Follow me," and he rode round the house to a side-entrance.

Here he dismounted and knocked at the small door for some time without avail. At length it was opened a little way, and a thin, querulous voice, speaking through the crack, said:

"Begone, whoever you are. No one lives here. This is the house of Marcus, who is dead in the Jewish war. Who are you that disturb me?"

"The heir of Marcus."

"Marcus has no heir, unless it be Cæsar, who doubtless will take his property."

"Open, Stephanus," said Marcus, in a tone of command, at the same time pushing the door wide and entering. "Fool," he added, "what kind of a steward are you that you do not know your master's voice?"

Now he who had kept the door, a withered little man in a scribe's brown robe, peered at this visitor with his sharp eyes, then threw up his hands and staggered back, saying:

"By the spear of Mars! it is Marcus himself, Marcus returned from the dead! Welcome, my lord, welcome."

Marcus led his horse through the deep archway, and when Nehushta had followed him into the courtyard beyond, returned, closed and locked the door.

"Why did you think me dead, friend?" he asked.

"Oh! my lord," answered the steward, "because all who have come home from the war declared that you had vanished away during the siege of the city of the Jews, and that you must either be dead or taken prisoner. Now I knew well that you would never disgrace your ancient house, or your own noble name, or the Eagles which you serve, by falling alive into the hands of the enemy. Therefore, I was sure that you were dead."

Marcus laughed bitterly, then turning to Nehushta, said:

"You hear, woman, you hear. If such is the judgment of my steward and freedman, what will be that of Cæsar and my peers?" Then he added, "Now, Stephanus, that what you thought impossible—what I myself should have thought impossible—has happened. I was taken prisoner by the Jews, though through no fault of mine."

"Oh! if so," said the old steward, "hide it, my lord, hide it. Why, two such unhappy men who had surrendered to save their lives and were found in some Jewish dungeon, have been condemned to walk in the Triumph this day. Their hands are to be tied behind them; in place of their swords they must wear a distaff, and on their breasts a placard with the words written: 'I am a Roman who preferred dishonour to death.' You would not wish their company, my lord."

The face of Marcus went first red, then white.

"Man," he said, "cease your ill-omened talk, lest I should fall upon my sword here before your eyes. Bid the slaves make ready the bath and food, for we need both."

"Slaves, my lord? There are none here, save one old woman, who attends to me and the house."

"Where are they then?" asked Marcus angrily.

"The most part of them I have sent into the country, thinking it better that they should work upon your estates rather than live here idle, and others who were not needed I have sold."

"You were ever careful, Stephanus." Then he added by an afterthought, "Have you any money in the house?"

The old steward looked towards Nehushta suspiciously and seeing that she was engaged with the horses out of earshot, answered in a whisper: "Money? I have so much of it that I know not what to do. The strong place you know if is almost full of gold and still it comes. There are the rents and profits of your great estates for three years; the proceeds of the sale of slaves and certain properties, together with the large outstanding amount that was due to my late master, the Lord Caius, which I have at length collected. Oh! at least you will not lack for money."

"There are other things that I could spare less readily," said Marcus, with a sigh; "still, it may be needed. Now tie up those horses by the fountain, and give us food, what you have, for we have ridden these thirty hours without rest. Afterwards you can talk."

It was mid-day. Marcus, bathed, anointed, and clad in the robes of his order, was standing in one of the splendid apartments of his marble house, looking through an opening in the shutters at the passing of the Triumph. Presently old Nehushta joined him. She also was clad in clean, white robes which the slave woman had found for her.

"Have you any news?" asked Marcus impatiently.

"Some, lord, which I have pieced together from what is known by the slave-woman, and by your steward, Stephanus. A beautiful Jewish captive is to walk in the Triumph and afterwards to be sold with other captives in the Forum. They heard of her because it is said that there has been a quarrel between Titus and his brother Domitian, and Vespasian also, on account of this woman."

"A quarrel? What quarrel?"

"I, or rather your servants, know little of it, but they have heard that Domitian demanded the girl as a gift, whereon Titus told him that if he wished for her, he might buy her. Then the matter was referred to Vespasian Cæsar, who upheld the decree of Titus. As for Domitian, he went away in a rage, declaring that he would purchase the girl and remember the affront which had been put upon him."

"Surely the gods are against me," said Marcus, "if they have given me Domitian for a rival."

"Why so, lord? Your money is as good as his, and perhaps you will pay more."

"I will pay to my last piece, but will that free me from the rage and hate of Domitian?"

"Why need he knew that you were the rival bidder?"

"Why? Oh! in Rome everything is known—even the truth sometimes."

"Time enough to trouble when trouble comes. First let us wait and see whether this maid be Miriam."

"Aye," he answered, "let us wait—since we must."

So they waited and with anxious eyes watched the great show roll by them. They saw the cars painted with scenes of the taking of Jerusalem and the statues of the gods fashioned in ivory and gold. They saw the purple hangings of the Babylonian broidered pictures, the wild beasts, and the ships mounted upon wheels. They saw the treasures of the temple and the images of victory, and many other things, for that pageant seemed to be endless, and still the captives and the Emperors did not come.

One sight there was also that caused Marcus to shrink as though fire had burned him, for yonder, set in the midst of a company of jugglers and buffoons that gibed and mocked at them, were the two unhappy men who had been taken prisoners by the Jews. On they tramped, their hands bound behind them, clad in full armour, but wearing a woman's distaff where the sword should have been, and round their necks the placards which proclaimed their shame. The brutal Roman mob hooted them also, that mob which ever loved spectacles of cruelty and degradation, calling them cowards. One of the men, a bull-necked, black-haired fellow, suffered it patiently, remembering that at even he must be set free to vanish where he would. The other, who was blue-eyed and finer- featured, having gentle blood in his veins, seemed to be maddened by their talk, for he glared about him, gnashing his teeth like a wild beast in a cage. Opposite to the house of Marcus came the climax.

"Cur," yelled a woman in the mob, casting a pebble that struck him on the cheek. "Cur! Coward!"

The blue-eyed man stopped, and, wheeling round, shouted in answer:

"I am no coward, I who have slain ten men with my own hand, five of them in single combat. You are the cowards who taunt me. I was overwhelmed, that is all, and afterwards in the prison I thought of my wife and children and lived on. Now I die and my blood be on you."

Behind him, drawn by eight white oxen, was the model of a ship with the crew standing on its deck. Avoiding his guard, the man ran down the line of oxen and suddenly cast himself upon the ground before the wooden-wheeled car, which passed over his neck, crushing the life out of him.

"Well done! Well done!" shouted the crowd, rejoicing at this unexpected sight. "Well done! He was brave after all."

Then the body was carried away and the procession moved forward. But Marcus, who watched, hid his face in his hands, and Nehushta, lifting hers, uttered a prayer for the passing soul of the victim.

Now the prisoners began to go past, marching eight by eight, hundreds upon hundreds of them, and once more the mob shouted and rejoiced over these unfortunates, whose crime was that they had fought for their country to the end. The last files passed, then at a little distance from them, tramping forward wearily, appeared the slight figure of a girl dressed in a robe of white silk blazoned at its breast with gold. Her bowed head, from which the curling tresses fell almost to her waist, was bared to the fierce rays of the sun, and on her naked bosom lay a necklace of great pearls.

"Pearl-Maiden, Pearl-Maiden!" shouted the crowd.

"Look!" said Nehushta, gripping the shoulder of Marcus with her hand.

He looked, and after long years once more beheld Miriam, for though he had heard her voice in the Old Tower at Jerusalem, then her face was hidden from him by the darkness. There was the maid from whom he had parted in the desert village by Jordan, the same, and yet changed. Then she had been a lovely girl, now she was a woman on whom sorrow and suffering had left their stamp. The features were finer, the deep, patient eyes were frightened and reproachful; her beauty was such as we see in dreams, not altogether that of earth.

"Oh! my darling, my darling," murmured Nehushta, stretching out her arms towards her. "Christ be thanked, that I have found you, my darling." Then she turned to Marcus, who was devouring Miriam with his eyes, and said in a fierce voice:

"Roman, now that you see her again, do you still love her as much as of old time?"

He took no note and she repeated the question. Then he answered:

"Why do you trouble me with such idle words. Once she was a woman to be won, now she is a spirit to be worshipped."

"Woman or spirit, or woman and spirit, beware how you deal with her, Roman," snarled Nehushta still more fiercely, "or—" and she left her hand fall upon the knife that was hidden in her robe.

"Peace, peace!" said Marcus, and as he spoke the procession came to a halt before his windows. "How weary she is, and sad," he went on speaking to himself. "Her heart seems crushed. Oh! that I must stay here and see her thus, who dare not show myself! If she could but know! If she could but know!"

Nehushta thrust him aside and took his place. Fixing her eyes upon Miriam she made some effort of the will, so fierce and concentrated that beneath the strain her body shook and quivered. See! Her thought reached the captive, for she looked up.

"Stand to one side," she whispered to Marcus, then unlatched the shutters and slowly pushed them open. Now between her and the air was nothing but the silken curtains. Very gently she parted these with her hands, for some few seconds suffering her face to be seen between them. Then laying her fingers on her lips she drew back and they closed again.

"It is well," she said, "she knows."

"Let her see me also," said Marcus.

"Nay, she can bear no more. Look, look, she faints."

Groaning in bitterness of spirit they watched Miriam, who seemed about to fall. Now a woman gave her the cup of wine, and drinking she recovered herself.

"Note that woman," muttered Marcus, "that I may reward her."

"It is needless," answered Nehushta, "she seeks no reward."

"She is more than a Roman, she is a Christian. As she passed it she made a sign of the cross with the cup."

The waggons creaked; the officers shouted; the procession moved forward. From behind the curtain the pair kept their eyes fixed upon Miriam until she vanished in the dust and crowd. When she had gone they seemed to see little else; even the sight of the glorious Cæsars could not hold their eyes.

Marcus summoned the steward, Stephanus.

"Go forth," he said, "and discover when and where the captive Pearl- Maiden is to be sold. Then return to me swiftly. Be secret and silent, and let none suspect whence you come or what you seek. Your life hangs upon it. Go."

The sun was sinking fast, staining the marble temples and colonnades of the Forum blood-red with its level beams. For the most part the glorious place was deserted now, since, the Triumph over at length, the hundreds of thousands of the Roman populace, wearied out with pleasure and excitement, had gone home to spend the night in feasting. About one of the public slave-markets, however, a round of marble enclosed with a rope and set in front of a small building, where the slaves were sheltered until the moment of their sale, a mixed crowd was gathered, some of them bidders, some idlers drawn thither by curiosity.

Others were in the house behind examining the wares before they came to the hammer. Presently an old woman, meanly clad with her face veiled to the eyes, and bearing on her back a heavy basket such as was used to carry fruit to market, presented herself at the door of the house.

"What do you want?" asked the gatekeeper.

"To inspect the slaves," she answered in Greek.

"Go away," he said roughly, "you are not a buyer."

"I may be if the stuff is good enough," she replied, slipping a gold coin into his hand.

"Pass in, old lady, pass in," and in another second the door had closed behind her, and Nehushta found herself among the slaves.

In this building the light was already so low that torches were burning for the convenience of visitors. By the flare of them Nehushta saw the unfortunate captives—there were but fifteen—seated upon marble benches, while slave women moved from the one to the other, washing their hands and feet and faces in scented water, brushing and tying their hair and removing the dust of the procession from their robes, so that they might look more comely to the eyes of the purchasers. Also there were present a fair number of bidders, twenty or thirty of them, who strolled from girl to girl discussing the points of each and at times asking them to stand up, or turn round, or show their arms and ankles, that they might judge of them better. At the moment when Nehushta entered one of these, a fat man with greasy curls who looked like an Eastern, was endeavouring to persuade a dark and splendid Jewess to let him see her foot. Pretending not to understand she sat still and sullen, till at length he stooped down and lifted her robe. Then in an instant the girl dealt him such a kick in the face that amidst the laughter of the spectators he rolled backwards on the floor, whence he rose with a cut and bloody forehead.

"Very good, my beauty, very good," he muttered in a savage voice, "before twelve hours are over you shall pay for that."

But again the girl sat sullen and motionless, pretending not to understand.

Most of the public, however, were gathered about Miriam, who sat upon a chair by herself, her hands folded, her head bent down, a very picture of pitiful, outraged modesty. One by one as their turns came and the attendant suffered them to approach, the men advanced and examined her closely, though Nehushta noted that none of them were allowed to touch her with their hands. Placing herself at the end of the line she watched with all her eyes and listened with all her ears. Soon she had her reward. A tall man, dressed like a merchant of Egypt, went up to Miriam and bent over her.

"Silence!" said the attendant. "I am ordered to suffer none to speak to the slave who is called Pearl-Maiden. Move on, sir, move on."

The man lifted his head, and although in that gloom she could not see his face, Nehushta knew its shape. Still she was not sure, till presently he moved his right hand so that it came between her and the flame of one of the torches, and she perceived that the top joint of the first finger was missing.

"Caleb," she thought to herself, "Caleb, escaped and in Rome! So Domitian has another rival." Then she went back to the door-keeper and asked him the name of the man.

"A merchant of Alexandria named Demetrius," he said.

Nehushta returned to her place. In front of her two men, agents who bought slaves and other things for wealthy clients, were talking.

"More fit for a sale of dogs," said one, "after sunset when everybody is tired out, than for that of one of the fairest women who ever stood upon the block."

"Pshaw," answered the other, "the whole thing is a farce. Domitian is in a hurry, that's all, so the auction must be held to-night."

"He means to buy her?"

"Of course. I am told that his factor, Saturius, has orders to go up to a thousand sestertia if need be," and he nodded towards a quiet man dressed in a robe of some rich, dark stuff, who stood in a corner of the place watching the company.

"A thousand sestertia! For one slave girl! Ye gods! a thousand sestertia!"

"The necklace goes with her, that is worth something, and there is property at Tyre."

"Property in Tyre," said the other, "property in the moon. Come on, let us look at something a little less expensive. As I wish to keep my head on my shoulders, I am not going to bid against the prince in any case."

"No, nor anyone else either. I expect he will get his fancy pretty cheap after all."

Then the two men moved away, and a minute afterwards Nehushta found that it was her turn to approach Miriam.

"Here comes a curious sort of buyer," said one of the attendants.

"Don't judge the taste of the fruit by the look of the rind, young man," answered Nehushta, and at the sound of that voice for the first time Pearl-Maiden lifted her head, then dropped it quickly.

"She is well enough," Nehushta said aloud, "but there used to be prettier women when I was young; in fact, though dark, I was myself," a statement at which those within hearing, noting her gaunt and aged form bent beneath the heavy basket, tittered aloud. "Come, lift up your head, my dear," she went on, trying to entice the captive to consent by encouraging waves of her hand.

They were fruitless; still, had any thought of it there was meaning in them. On Nehushta's finger, as it chanced, shone a ring which Miriam ought to know, seeing that for some years she had worn it on her own.

It would seem that she did know it, at any rate her bosom and neck grew red and a spasm passed across her face which even the falling hair did not suffice to hide.

The ring told Miriam that Marcus lived and that Nehushta was his messenger. This suspense at least was ended.

Now the door-keeper called a warning and the buyers flocked from the building. Outside, the auctioneer, a smooth-faced, glib-tongued man, was already mounting the rostrum. Calling for silence he began his speech. On this evening of festival, he said, he would be brief. The lots he had to offer to the select body of connoisseurs he saw before him, were the property of the Imperator Titus, and the proceeds of the sale, it was his duty to tell them, would not go into Cæsar's pocket, but were to be equally divided between the poor of Rome and deserving soldiers who had been wounded or had lost their health in the war, a fact which must cause every patriotic citizen to bid more briskly. These lots, he might say, were unique, being nothing else than the fifteen most beautiful girls, believed all of them to be of noble blood, among the many thousands who had been captured at the sack of Jerusalem, the city of the Jews, especially selected to adorn the great conqueror's Triumph. No true judge, who desired a charming memento of the victory of his country's arms, would wish to neglect such an opportunity, especially as he was informed that the Jewish women were affectionate, docile, well instructed in many arts, and very hard-working. He had only one more thing to say, or rather two things. He regretted that this important sale should be held at so unusual an hour. The reason was that there was really no place where these slaves could be comfortably kept without risk of their maltreatment or escape, so it was held to be best that they should be removed at once to the seclusion of their new homes, a decision, he was sure, that would meet the wishes of buyers. The second point was that among them was one lot of surpassing interest; namely, the girl who had come to be generally spoken of as Pearl-Maiden.

This young woman, who could not be more than three or four-and-twenty years of age, was the last representative of a princely family of the Jews. She had been found exposed upon one of the gates of the holy house of that people, where it would seem she was sentenced to perish for some offence against their barbarous laws. As the clamours of the populace that day had testified, she was of the most delicate and distinguished beauty, and the collar of great pearls which she wore about her neck gave evidence of her rank. If he knew anything of the tastes of his countrymen the price which would be paid for her must prove a record even in that ring. He was aware that among the vulgar a great, almost a divine name had been coupled with that of this captive. Well, he knew nothing, except this, that he was certain that if there was any truth in the matter the owner of the name, as became a noble and a generous nature, would wish to obtain his prize fairly and openly. The bidding was as free to the humblest there—provided, of course, that he could pay, and he might remark that not an hour's credit would be given except to those who were known to him—as to Cæsar himself. Now, as the light was failing, he would order the torches to be lit and commence the sale. The beauteous Pearl-Maiden, he might add, was Lot No. 7.

So the torches were lit, and presently the first victim was led out and placed upon a stand of marble in the centre of the flaring ring. She was a dark-haired child of about sixteen years of age, who stared round her with a frightened gaze.

The bidding began at five sestertia and ran up to fifteen, or about £120 of our money, at which price she was knocked down to a Greek, who led her back into the receiving house, paid the gold to a clerk who was in attendance, and took her away, sobbing as she went. Then followed four others, who were sold at somewhat better prices. No. 6 was the dark and splendid Jewess who had kicked the greasy-curled Eastern in the face. As soon as she appeared upon the block, this brute stepped forward and bid twenty sestertia for her. An old grey- bearded fellow answered with a bid of twenty-five. Then some one bid thirty, which the Eastern capped with a bid of forty. So it went on till the large total of sixty sestertia was offered, whereon the Eastern advanced two more, at which price, amidst the laughter of the audience, she was knocked down to him.

"You know me and that the money is safe," he said to the auctioneer. "It shall be paid to you to-morrow; I have enough to carry without lading myself up with so much gold. Come on, girl, to your new home, where I have a little score to settle with you," and grasping her by the left wrist he pulled her from the block and led her unresisting through the crowd and to the shadows beyond.

Already No. 7 had been summoned to the block and the auctioneer was taking up his tale, when from out of these shadows rose the sound of a dreadful yell. Some of the audience snatched torches from their stands and ran to the spot whence it came. There, on the marble pavement lay the Eastern dead or dying, while over him stood the Jewess, a red dagger, his own, which she had snatched from its scabbard, in her hand, and on her stately face a look of vengeful triumph.

"Seize her! Seize the murdering witch! Beat her to death with rods," they cried, and at the command of the auctioneer slaves ran up to take her.

She waited till they were near, then, without a word or a sound, lifted her strong, white arm and drove the knife deep into her own heart. For a moment she stood still, till suddenly she stretched her hands wide and fell face downwards dead upon the body of the brute who had bought her.

The crowd gasped and was silent. Then one of them, a sickly looking patrician, called out:

"Oh! I did well to come. What a sight! What a sight! Blessings on you, brave girl, you have given Julius a new pleasure."

After this there was tumult and confusion while the attendants carried away the bodies. A few minutes later the auctioneer climbed back into his rostrum and alluded in moving terms to the "unfortunate accident" which had just happened.

"Who would think," he said, "that one so beautiful could also be so violent? I weep when I consider that this noble purchaser, whose name I forget at the moment, but whose estate, by the way, is liable for the money, should have thus suddenly been transferred from the arms of Venus to that of Pluto, although it must be admitted that he gave the woman some provocation. Well, gentlemen, grief will not bring him to life again, and we who still stand beneath the stars have business to attend. Bear me witness, all of you, that I am blameless in this affair, and, slaves, bring out that priceless gem, the Pearl-Maiden."

Chapter 24

Master and Slave

Now a hush of expectancy fell upon the crowd, till presently two attendants appeared, each of them holding in his hand a flaming torch, and between them the captive Pearl-Maiden. So beautiful did she look as she advanced thus with bowed head, the red light of the torches falling upon her white robe and breast and reflected in a faint, shimmering line from the collar of pearls about her neck, that even that jaded company clapped as she came. In another moment she had mounted the two steps and was standing on the block of marble. The crowd pressed closer, among them the merchant of Egypt, Demetrius, and the veiled woman with the basket, who was now attended by a little man dressed as a slave and bearing on his back another basket, the weight of which he seemed to find irksome, since from time to time he groaned and twisted his shoulders. Also the chamberlain, Saturius, secure in the authority of his master, stepped over the rope and against the rule began to walk round and round the captive, examining her critically.

"Look at her!" said the auctioneer. "Look for yourselves. I have nothing to say, words fail me—unless it is this. For more than twenty years I have stood in this rostrum, and during that time I suppose that fifteen or sixteen thousand young women have been knocked down to my hammer. They have come out of every part of the world; from the farthest East, from the Grecian mountains, from Egypt and Cyprus, from the Spanish plains, from Gaul, from the people of the Teutons, from the island of the Britons, and other barbarous places that lie still further north. Among them were many beautiful women, of every style and variety of loveliness, yet I tell you honestly, my patrons, I do not remember one who came so near perfection as this maiden whom I have the honour to sell to-night. I say again—look at her, look at her, and tell me with what you can find fault.

"What do you say? Oh! yes, I am informed that her teeth are quite sound, there is no blemish to conceal, none at all, and the hair is all her own. That gentleman says that she is rather small. Well, she is not built upon a large scale, and to my mind that is one of her attractions. Little and good, you know, little and good. Only consider the proportions. Why, the greatest sculptors, ancient or modern, would rejoice to have her as model, and I hope that in the interests of the art-loving public"—here he glanced at the Chamberlain, Saturius—"that the fortunate person into whose hands she passes will not be so selfish as to deny them this satisfaction.

"Now I have said enough and must but add this, that by the special decree of her captor, the Imperator Titus, the beautiful necklace of pearls worn by the maiden goes with her. I asked a jeweller friend of mine to look at it just now, and judging as well as he could without removing it from her neck, which was not allowed, he values it at least at a hundred sestertia. Also, there goes with this lot considerable property, situated in Tyre and neighbouring places, to which, had she been a free woman, she would have succeeded by inheritance. You may think that Tyre is a long way off and that it will be difficult to take possession of this estate, and, of course, there is something in the objection. Still, the title to it is secure enough, for here I have a deed signed by Titus Cæsar himself, commanding all officials, officers and others concerned, to hand over without waste or deduction all property, real or personal, belonging to the estate of the late Benoni, the Jewish merchant of Tyre, and a member of the Sanhedrim—the lot's grandfather, I am informed, gentleman—to her purchaser, who has only to fill in his own name in the blank space, or any representatives whom he may appoint, which deed is especially declared to be indefeasible. Any one wish to see it? No? Then we will take it as read. I know that in such a matter, my patrons, my word is enough for you.

"Now I am about to come to business, with the remark that the more liberal your bidding the better will our glorious general, Titus Cæsar, be pleased; the better will the poor and the invalided soldiers, who deserve so well at your hands, be pleased; the better will the girl herself be pleased, who I am sure will know how to reward a generous appreciation of her worth; and the better shall I, your humble friend and servant, be pleased, because, as I may inform you in strict secrecy, I am paid, not by a fixed salary, but by commission.

"Now, gentlemen, what may I say? A thousand sestertia to begin with? Oh! don't laugh, I expect more than that. What! Fifty? You are joking, my friend. However, the acorn grows into the oak, doesn't it? and I am told that you can stop the sources of the Tiber with your hat; so

I'll start with fifty. Fifty—a hundred. Come, bid up, gentlemen, or we shall never get home to supper. Two hundred—three, four, five, six, seven, eight—ah! that's better. What are you stopping for?" and he addressed a hatchet-faced man who had thrust himself forward over the rope of the ring.

The man shook his head with a sigh. "I'm done," he said. "Such goods are for my betters," a sentiment that seemed to be shared by his rivals, since they also stopped bidding.

"Well, friend Saturius," said the auctioneer, "have you gone to sleep, or have you anything to say? Only in hundreds, now, gentlemen, mind, only in hundreds, unless I give the word. Thank you, I have nine hundred," and he looked round rather carelessly, expecting at heart that this bid would be the last.

Then the merchant from Alexandria stepped forward and held up his finger.

"A thousand, by the Gods!"

Saturius looked at the man indignantly. Who was this that dared to bid against Domitian, the third dignitary in all the Roman empire, Cæsar's son, Cæsar's brother, who might himself be Cæsar? Still he answered with another bid of eleven hundred.

Once more the finger of Domitian went up.

"Twelve. Twelve hundred!" said the auctioneer, in a voice of suppressed excitement, while the audience gasped, for such prices had not been heard of.

"Thirteen," said the Chamberlain.

Again the finger went up.

"Fourteen hundred. I have fourteen hundred. Against you, worthy Saturius. Come, come, I must knock the lot down, which perhaps would not please some whom I could mention. Don't be stingy, friend, you have a large purse to draw on, and it is called the Roman Empire. Now. Thank you, I have fifteen hundred. Well, my friend yonder. What! Have you had enough?" and he pointed to the Alexandrian merchant, who, with a groan, had turned aside and hidden his face in his hands.

"Knocked out, knocked out, it seems," said the auctioneer, "and though it is little enough under all the circumstances for this lot, who is as lovely as she is historical, I suppose that I can scarcely expect—" and he looked around despondently.

Suddenly the old woman with the basket glanced up and, speaking in a quiet matter-of-fact voice but with a foreign accent, said:

"Two thousand."

A titter of laughter went around the room.

"My dear madam?" queried the auctioneer, looking at her dubiously, "might I ask if you mean sester*tii* or sester*tia?*[1] Your pardon, but it has occurred to me that you might be confounding the two sums."

"Two thousand sester*tia,*" repeated the matter-of-fact voice with the foreign accent.

"Well, well," said the auctioneer, "I suppose that I must accept the bid. Friend Saturius, I have two thousand sestertia, and it is against you."

"Against me it must remain, then," replied the little man in a fury. "Do all the kings in the world want this girl? Already I have exceeded my limit by five hundred sestertia. I dare do no more. Let her go."

---

1. A *sestertius* was worth less than 2d., a *sestertium* was a sum of money of the value of about £8.

"Don't vex yourself, Saturius," said the auctioneer, "bidding is one thing, paying another. At present I have a bona-fide bid of fifteen hundred from you. Unless this liberal but unknown lady is prepared with the cash I shall close on that. Do you understand, madam?"

"Perfectly," answered the veiled old woman. "Being a stranger to Rome I thought it well to bring the gold with me, since strangers cannot expect credit."

"To bring the gold with you!" gasped the auctioneer. "To bring two thousand sestertia with you! Where is it then?"

"Where? Oh! in my servant's and my own baskets, and something more as well. Come, good sir, I have made my bid. Does the worthy gentleman advance?"

"No," shouted Saturius. "You are being fooled, she has not got the money."

"If he does not advance and no other worthy gentleman wishes to bid, then will you knock the lot down?" said the old woman. "Pardon me if I press you, noble seller of slaves, but I must ride far from Rome to-night, to Centum Cellæ, indeed, where my ship waits; therefore, I have no time to lose."

Now the auctioneer saw that there was no choice, since under the rules of the public mart he must accept the offer of the highest bidder.

"Two thousand sestertia are bid for this lot No. 7, the Jewish captive known as Pearl-Maiden, sold by order of Titus Imperator, together with her collar of pearls and the property to which, as a free woman, she would have been entitled. Any advance on two thousand sestertia?" and he looked at Saturius, who shook his head. "No? Then—going—going—gone! I declare the lot sold, to be delivered on payment of the cash to the person named—by the way, madam, what is your name?"

"Mulier."

At this the company burst into a loud laugh.

"Mulier?" repeated the auctioneer, "M u l i e r—Woman?"

"Yes, am I not a woman, and what better name can I have than is given to all my sex?"

"In truth, you are so wrapped up that I must take your word for it," replied the auctioneer. "But come, let us put an end to this farce. If you have the money, follow me into the receiving house—for I must see to the matter myself—and pay it down."

"With pleasure, sir, but be so good as to bring my property with you. She is too valuable to be left here unprotected amongst these distinguished but disappointed gentlemen."

Accordingly Miriam was led from the marble stand into an office annexed to the receiving-house, whither she was followed by the auctioneer and by Nehushta and her servant, whose backs, it was now observed, bent beneath the weight of the baskets that were strapped upon them. Here the door was locked, and with the help of her attendant Nehushta loosened her basket, letting it fall upon the table with a sigh of relief.

"Take it and count, he said to the auctioneer, untying the lid.

He lifted it and there met his eye a layer of lettuces neatly packed.

"By Venus!" he began in a fury.

"Softly, friend, softly," said Nehushta, "these lettuces are of a kind which only grow in yellow soil. Look," and lifting the vegetables she revealed beneath row upon row of gold coin. "Examine it before you count," she said.

He did so by biting pieces at hazard with his teeth and causing them to ring upon the marble table.

"It is good," he said.

"Quite so. Then count."

So he and the clerk counted, even to the bottom of the basket, which was found to contain gold to the value of over eleven hundred sestertia.

"So far well," he said, "but that is not enough."

The buyer beckoned to the man with her who stood in the corner, his face hidden by the shadow, and he dragged forward the second basket, which he had already unstrapped from his shoulders. Here also were lettuces, and beneath the lettuces gold. When the full two thousand sestertia were counted, that is, over fifteen thousand pounds of our money, this second basket still remained more than a third full.

"I ought to have run you up, madam," said the auctioneer, surveying the shining gold with greedy eyes.

"Yes," she replied calmly, "if you had guessed the truth you might have done so. But who knows the truth, except myself?"

"Are you a sorceress?" he asked.

"Perhaps. What does it matter? At least, the gold will not melt. And, by the way, it is troublesome carrying so much of the stuff back again. Would you like a couple of handfuls for yourself, and say ten pieces for your clerk? Yes? Well, please first fill in that deed with the name that I shall give you and with your own as witness? Here it is—'Miriam, daughter of Demas and Rachel, born in the year of the death of Herod Agrippa.' Thank you. You have signed, and the clerk also, I think. Now I will take that roll.

"One thing more, there is another door to this Receiving-house? With your leave I should prefer to go out that way, as my newly acquired property seems tired, and for one day has had enough of public notice. You will, I understand, give us a few minutes to depart before you return to the rostrum, and your clerk will be so courteous as to escort us out of the Forum. Now help yourself. Man, can't you make your hand larger than that? Well, it will suffice to pay for a summer holiday. I see a cloak there which may serve to protect this slave from the chill air of the night. In case it should be claimed, perhaps these five pieces will pay for it. Most noble and courteous sir, again I thank you. Young woman, throw this over your bare shoulders and your head; that necklace might tempt the dishonest.

"Now, if our guide is ready we will be going. Slave, bring the basket, at the weight of which you need no longer groan, and you, young woman, strap on this other basket; it is as well that you should begin to be instructed in your domestic duties, for I tell you at once that having heard much of the skill of the Jews in those matters, I have bought you to be my cook and to attend to the dressing of my hair. Farewell, sir, farewell; may we never meet again."

"Farewell," replied the astonished auctioneer, "farewell, my lady Mulier, who can afford to give two thousand sestertia for a cook! Good luck to you, and if you are always as liberal as this, may we meet once a month, say I. Yet have no fear," he added meaningly, "I know when I have been well treated and shall not seek you out—even to please Cæsar himself."

Three minutes later, under the guidance of the clerk,

who was as discreet as his master, they had passed, quite undisturbed, through various dark colonnades and up a flight of marble stairs.

"Now you are out of the Forum, so go your ways," he said.

They went, and the clerk stood watching them until they were round a corner, for he was young and curious, and to him this seemed the strangest comedy of the slave-market of which he had ever even heard.

As he turned to go he found himself face to face with a tall man, in whom he recognized that merchant of Egypt who had bid for Pearl-Maiden up to the enormous total of fourteen hundred sestertia.

"Friend," said Demetrius, "which way did your companions go?"

"I don't know," answered the clerk.

"Come, try to remember. Did they walk straight on, or turn to the left, or turn to the right? Fix your attention on these, it may help you," and once more that fortunate clerk found five gold pieces thrust into his hand.

"I don't know that they help me," he said, for he wished to be faithful to his hire.

"Fool," said Demetrius in a changed voice, "remember quickly, or here is something that will—" and he showed him a dagger glinting in his hand. "Now then, do you wish to go the same road as they carried the Jewish girl and the Eastern?"

"They turned to the right," said the clerk sulkily. "It is the truth, but may that road you speak of be yours who draw knives on honest folk."

With a bound Demetrius left his side, and for the second time the clerk stood still, watching him go.

"A strange business," he said to himself, "but, perhaps my master was right and that old woman is a sorceress, or, perhaps, the young one is the sorceress, since all men seem ready to pay a tribe's tribute to get hold of her; or, perhaps, they are both sorceresses. A strange story, of which I should like to know the meaning, and so, I fancy, would the Prince Domitian when he comes to hear of it. Saturius, the chamberlain, has a fat place, but I would not take it to-night, no, not if it were given to me."

Then that young man returned to the mart in time to hear his master knock down Lot thirteen, a very sweet-looking girl, to Saturius himself, who proposed, though with a doubtful heart, to take her to Domitian as a substitute.

Meanwhile, Nehushta, Miriam and the steward Stephanus, disguised as a slave, went on as swiftly as they dared towards the palace of Marcus in the Via Agrippa. The two women held each other by the hand but said nothing; their hearts seemed too full for speech. Only the old steward kept muttering—"Two thousand sestertia! The savings of years! Two thousand sestertia for that bit of a girl! Surely the gods have smitten him mad."

"Hold your peace, fool," said Nehushta at length. "At least, I am not mad; the property that went with her is worth more than the money."

"Yes, yes," replied the aggrieved Stephanus, "but how will that benefit my master? You put it in her name. Well, it is no affair of mine, and at least this accursed basket is much lighter."

Now they were at the side door of the house, which Stephanus was unlocking with his key.

"Quick," said Nehushta, "I hear footsteps."

The door opened and they passed in, but at that moment one went by them, pausing to look until the door closed again.

"Who was that?" asked Stephanus nervously.

"He whom they called Demetrius, the merchant of Alexandria, but whom once I knew by another name," answered Nehushta in a slow voice while Stephanus barred the door.

They walked through the archway into an antechamber lit by a single lamp, leaving Stephanus still occupied with his bolts and chains. Here with a sudden motion Nehushta threw off her cloak and tore the veil from her brow. In another instant, uttering a low, crooning cry, she flung her long arms about Miriam and began to kiss her again and again on the face.

"My darling," she moaned, "my darling."

"Tell me what it all means, Nou," said the poor girl faintly.

"It means that God has heard my prayers and suffered my old feet to overtake you in time, and provided the wealth to preserve you from a dreadful fate."

"Whose wealth? Where am I?" asked Miriam.

Nehushta made no answer, only she unstrapped the basket from Miriam's back and unclasped the cloak from about her shoulders. Then, taking her by the hand, she led her into a lighted passage and thence through a door into a great and splendid room spread with rich carpets and adorned with costly furniture and marble images. At the end of this room was a table lighted by two lamps, and on the further side of this table sat a man as though he were asleep, for his face was hidden upon his arms. Miriam saw him and clung to Nehushta trembling.

"Hush!" whispered her guide, and they stood still in the shadow.

The man lifted his head so that the light fell full upon it, and Miriam saw that it was Marcus. Marcus grown older and with a patch of grey hair upon his temple where the sword of Caleb had struck him, very worn and tired-looking also, but still Marcus and no other. He was speaking to himself.

"I can bear it no longer," he said. "Thrice have I been to the gate and still no sign. Doubtless the plan has miscarried and by now she is in the palace of Domitian. I will go forth and learn the worst," and he rose from the table.

"Speak to him," whispered Nehushta, pushing Miriam forward.

She advanced into the circle of the lamplight, but as yet Marcus did not see her, for he had gone to the window-place to find a cloak that lay there. Then he turned and saw her. Before him in her robe of white, the soft light shining on her gentle loveliness, stood Miriam. He stared at her bewildered.

"Do I dream?" he said.

"Nay, Marcus," she answered in her sweet voice, "you do not dream. I am Miriam."

In an instant he was at her side and held her in his arms, nor did she resist him, for after so many fears and sufferings they seemed to her a home.

"Loose me, I pray you," she said at length, "I am faint, I can bear no more."

At her entreaty he suffered her to sink upon the cushions of a couch that was at hand.

"Tell me, tell me everything," he said.

"Ask it of Nehushta," she answered, leaning back. "I am spent."

Nehushta ran to her side and began to chafe her hands. "Let be with your questions," she said. "I bought her, that's enough. Ask that old huckster, Stephanus, the price. But first in the name of charity give her food. Those who have walked through a Triumph to end the day on the slave block need victuals."

"It is here, it is here," Marcus said confusedly, "such as there is." Taking a lamp he led the way to a table that was placed in the shadow, where stood some meat and fruit with flagons of rich coloured wine and pure water and shallow silver cups to drink from.

Putting her arm about Miriam's waist, Nehushta supported her to the table and sat her down upon one of the couches. Then she poured out wine and put it to her lips, and cut meat and made her swallow it till Miriam would touch no more. Now the colour came back to her face, and her eyes grew bright again, and resting there upon the couch, she listened while Nehushta told Marcus all the story of the slave sale.

"Well done," he said, laughing in his old merry fashion, "well done, indeed! Oh! what favouring god put it into the head of that honest old miser, Stephanus, from year to year to hoard up all that sum of gold against an hour of sudden need which none could foresee!"

"My God and hers," answered Nehushta solemnly, "to Whom if He give you space, you should be thankful, which, by the way, is more than Stephanus is, who has seen so much of your savings squandered in an hour."

"Your savings?" said Miriam, looking up. "Did you buy me, Marcus?"

"I suppose so, beloved," he answered.

"Then, then, I am your slave?"

"Not so, Miriam," he replied nervously. "As you know well, it is I who am yours. All I ask of you is that you should become my wife."

"That cannot be, Marcus," she answered in a kind of cry. "You know that it cannot be."

His face turned pale.

"After all that has come and gone between us, Miriam, do you still say so?"

"I still say so."

"You could give your life for me, and yet you will not give your life to me?"

"Yes, Marcus."

"Why? Why?"

"For the reasons that I gave you yonder by the banks of Jordan; because those who begat me laid on me the charge that I should marry none who is not a Christian. How then can I marry you?"

Marcus thought a moment.

"Does the book of your law forbid it?" he asked.

She shook her head. "No, but the dead forbid it, and rather will I join them than break their command."

Again Marcus thought and spoke.

"Well, then, since I must, I will become a Christian."

She looked at him sadly and answered:

"It is not enough. Do you remember what I told you far away in the village of the Essenes, that this is no matter of casting incense on an altar, but rather one of a changed spirit. When you can say those words from your heart as well as with your lips, then, Marcus, I will listen to you, but unless God calls you this you can never do."

"What then do you propose?" he asked.

"I? I have not had time to think. To go away, I suppose."

"To Domitian?" he queried. "Nay, forgive me, but a sore heart makes bitter lips."

"I am glad you asked forgiveness for those words, Marcus," she said quivering. "What need is there to insult a slave?"

The word seemed to suggest a new train of thought to Marcus.

"Yes," he said, "a slave—my slave whom I have bought at a great price. Well, why should I let you go? I am minded to keep you."

"Marcus, you can keep me if you will, but then your sin against your own honour will be greater even than your sin against me."

"Sin!" he said, passionately. "What sin? You say you cannot marry me, not because you do not wish it, if I understand you right, but for other reasons which have weight, at any rate with you. But the dead give no command as to whom you should love."

"No, my love is my own, but if it is not lawful it can be denied."

"Why should it be denied?" he asked softly and coming towards her. "Is there not much between you and me? Did not you, brave and blessed woman that you are, risk your life for my sake in the Old Tower at Jerusalem? Did you not for my sake stand there upon the gate Nicanor to perish miserably? And I, though it be little, have I not done something for you? Have I not so soon as your message reached me, journeyed here to Rome, at the cost, perhaps, of what I value more than life—my honour?"

"Your honour?" she asked. "Why your honour?"

"Because those who have been taken prisoner by the enemy and escaped are held to be cowards among the Romans," he answered bitterly, "and it may be that such a lot awaits me."

"Coward! You a coward, Marcus?"

"Aye. When it is known that I live, that is what my enemies will call me who lived on for your sake, Miriam—for the sake of a woman who denies me."

"Oh!" she said, "this is bitter. Now I remember and understand what Gallus meant."

"Then will you still deny me? Must I suffer thus in vain? Think, had it not been for you I could have stayed afar until the thing was forgotten, that is, if I still chose to live; but now, because of you, things are thus, and yet, Miriam—you deny me," and he put his arms about her and drew her to his breast.

She did not struggle, she had no strength, only she wrung her hands and sobbed, saying:

"What shall I do? Woe is me, what shall I do?"

"Do?" said the voice of Nehushta, speaking clear as a clarion from the shadows. "Do your duty, girl, and leave the rest to Heaven."

"Silence, accursed woman!" gasped Marcus, turning pale with anger.

"Nay," she answered, "I will not be silent. Listen, Roman; I like you well, as you have reason to know, seeing that it was I who nursed you back to life, when for one hour's want of care you must have died. I like you well, and above everything on earth I wish that ere my eyes shut for the last time they may see your hand in her hand, and her hand in your hand, man and wife before the face of all men. Yet I tell you that now indeed you are a coward in a deeper fashion than that the Romans dream of; you are a coward who try to work upon the weakness of this poor girl's loving heart, who try in the hour of her sore distress to draw her from the spirit, if not from the letter, of her duty. So great a coward are you that you remind her even that she is your slave and threaten to deal with her as you heathen deal with slaves. You put a gloss upon the truth; you try to filch the fruit you may not pluck; you say 'you may not marry me, but you are my property, and therefore if you give way to your master it is no sin.' I tell you it is a sin, doubly a sin, since you would bind the weight of it on her back as well as on your own, and a sin that in this way or in that would bring its reward to both of you."

"Have you finished?" asked Marcus coldly, but suffering Miriam to slip from his arms back upon the couch.

"No, I have not finished; I spoke of the fruits of evil; now as my heart prompts me I speak of the promise of good. Let this woman go free as you have the power to do; strike the chains off her neck and take back the price that you have paid for her, since she has property which will discharge it to the last farthing, which property to-day stands in her name and can be conveyed to you. Then, go search the Scriptures and see if you can find no message in them. If you find it, well and good, then take her with a clean heart and be happy. If you find it not, well and good, then leave her with a clean heart and be sorrowful, for so it is decreed. Only in this matter do not dare to be double-minded, lest the last evil overtake you and her, and your children and hers. Now I have done, and, my lord Marcus, be so good as to signify your pleasure to your slave, Pearl-Maiden, and your servant, Nehushta the Libyan."

Marcus began to walk up and down the room, out of the light into the shadow, out of the shadow into the light. Presently he halted, and the two women watching saw that his face was drawn and ashen, like the face of an old man.

"My pleasure," he said vacantly, "—that is a strange word on my lips to-night, is it not? Well, Nehushta, you have the best of the argument. All you say is quite true, if a little over-coloured. Of course, Miriam is quite right not to marry me if she has scruples, and, of course, I should be quite wrong to take advantage of the accident of my being able to purchase her in the slave-ring. I think that is all I have to say. Miriam, I free you, as indeed I remember I promised the Essenes that I would do. Since no one knows you belong to me, I suppose that no formal ceremony will be necessary. It is a manumission 'inter amicos,' as the lawyers say, but quite valid. As to the title to the Tyre property, I accept it in payment of the debt, but I beg that you will keep it a while on my behalf, for, at present, there might be trouble about transferring it into my name. Now, good- night. Nehushta will take you to her room, Miriam, and to-morrow you can depart whither you will. I wish you all fortune, and—why do you not thank me? Under the circumstances, it would be kind."

But Miriam only burst into a flood of tears.

"What will you do, Marcus? Oh! what will you do?" she sobbed.

"In all probability, things which I would rather you did not know of," he answered bitterly, "or I may take it into my head to accept the suggestion of our friend, Nehushta, and begin to search those Scriptures of which I have heard so much; that seem, by the way, specially designed to prevent the happiness of men and women." Then he added fiercely, "Go, girl, go at once, for if you stand there weeping before me any longer, I tell you that I shall change my mind, and as Nehushta says, imperil the safety of your soul, and of my own—which does not matter."

So Miriam stumbled from the room and through the curtained doorway. As Nehushta followed her Marcus caught her by the arm.

"I have half a mind to murder you," he said, quietly.

The old Libyan only laughed.

"All I have said is true and for your own good, Marcus," she answered, "and you will live to know it."

"Where will you take her?"

"I don't know yet, but Christians always have friends."

"You will let me hear of her."

"Surely, if it is safe."

"And if she needs help you will tell me?"

"Surely, and if you need her help, and it can be done, I will bring her to you."

"Then may I need help soon," he said. "Begone."

Chapter 25

The Reward of Saturius

Meanwhile, in one of the palaces of the Cæsars not far from the Capitol, was being enacted another and more stormy scene. It was the palace of Domitian, whither, the bewildering pomp of the Triumph finished at last, the prince had withdrawn himself in no happy mood. That day many things had happened to vex him. First and foremost, as had been brought home to his mind from minute to minute throughout the long hours, its glory belonged not to himself, not even to his father, Vespasian, but to his brother, the conqueror of the Jews. Titus he had always hated, Titus, who was as beloved of mankind for his virtues, such as virtues were in that age, as he, Domitian, was execrated for his vices. Now Titus had returned after a brilliant and successful campaign to be crowned as Cæsar, to be accepted as the sharer of his father's government, and to receive the ovations of the populace, while his brother Domitian must ride almost unnoted behind his chariot. The plaudits of the roaring mob, the congratulations of the Senate, the homage of the knights and subject princes, the offerings of foreign kings, all laid at the feet of Titus, filled him with a jealousy that went nigh to madness. Soothsayers had told him, it was true, that his hour would come, that he would live and reign after Vespasian and Titus had gone down, both of them, to Hades. But even if they spoke the truth this hour seemed a long way off.

Also there were other things. At the great sacrifice before the temple of Jupiter, his place had been set too far back where the people could not see him; at the feast which followed the master of the ceremonies had neglected, or had forgotten, to pour a libation in his honour.

Further, the beautiful captive, Pearl-Maiden, had appeared in the procession unadorned by the costly girdle which he had sent her; while, last of all, the different wines that he had drunk had disagreed with him, so that because of them, or of the heat of the sun, he suffered from the headache and sickness to which he was liable. Pleading this indisposition as an excuse, Domitian left the banquet very early, and attended by his slaves and musicians retired to his own palace.

Here his spirits revived somewhat, since he knew that before long his chamberlain, Saturius, would appear with the lovely Jewish maiden upon whom he had set his fancy. This at least was certain, for he had arranged that the auction should be held that evening and instructed him to buy her at all costs, even for a thousand sestertia. Indeed, who would dare to bid for a slave that the Prince Domitian desired?

Learning that Saturius had not yet arrived, he went to his private chambers, and to pass away the time commanded his most beautiful slaves to dance before him, where he inflamed himself by drinking more wine of a vintage that he loved. As the fumes of the strong liquor mounted to his brain the pains in his head ceased, at any rate for a while. Very soon he became half-drunk, and as was his nature when in drink, savage. One of the dancing slaves stumbled and growing nervous stepped out of time, whereon he ordered the poor half-naked girl to be scourged before him by the hands of her own companions. Happily for her, however, before the punishment began a slave arrived with the intelligence that Saturius waited without.

"What, alone?" said the prince, springing to his feet.

"Nay, lord," said the slave, "there is a woman with him."

At this news instantly his ill-temper was forgotten.

"Let that girl go," he said, "and bid her be more careful another time. Away, all the lot of you, I wish to be private. Now, slave, bid the worthy Saturius enter with his charge."

Presently the curtains were drawn apart and through them came Saturius rubbing his hands and smiling somewhat nervously, followed by a woman wrapped in a long cloak and veiled. He began to offer the customary salutations, but Domitian cut him short.

"Rise, man," he said. "That sort of thing is very well in public, but I don't want it here. So you have got her," he added, eyeing the draped form in the background.

"Yes," replied Saturius doubtfully.

"Good, your services shall be remembered. You were ever a discreet and faithful agent. Did the bidding run high?"

"Oh! my lord, enormous, ee—normous. I never heard such bidding," and he stretched out his hands.

"Impertinence! Who dared to compete with me?" remarked Domitian. "Well, what did you have to give?"

"Fifty sestertia, my lord."

"Fifty sestertia?" answered Domitian with an air of relief. "Well, of course it is enough, but I have known beautiful maidens fetch more. By the way, dear one," he went on, addressing the veiled woman, "you must, I fear, be tired after all that weary, foolish show."

The "dear one" making no audible reply, Domitian went on:

"Modesty is pleasing in a maid, but now I pray you, forget it for awhile. Unveil yourself, most beautiful, that I may behold that loveliness for which my heart has ached these many days. Nay, that task shall be my own," and he advanced somewhat unsteadily towards his prize.

Saturius thought that he saw his chance. Domitian was so intoxicated that it would be useless to attempt to explain matters that night. Clearly he should retire as soon as possible.

"Most noble prince and patron," he began, "my duty is done, with your leave I will withdraw."

"By no means, by no means," hiccupped Domitian, "I know that you are an excellent judge of beauty, most discriminating Saturius, and I should like to talk over the points of this lady with you. You know, dear Saturius, that I am not selfish, and to tell the truth, which you won't mind between friends—who could be jealous of a wizened, last year's walnut of a man like you? Not I, Saturius, not I, whom everybody acknowledges to be the most beautiful person in Rome, much better looking than Titus is, although he does call himself Cæsar. Now for it. Where's the fastening? Saturius, find the fastening. Why do you tie up the poor girl like an Egyptian corpse and prevent her lord and master from looking at her?"

As he spoke the slave did something to the back of her

head and the veil fell to the ground, revealing a girl of very pleasing shape and countenance, but who, as might be expected, looked most weary and frightened. Domitian stared at her with his bleared and wicked eyes, while a puzzled expression grew upon his face.

"Very odd!" he said, "but she seems to have changed! I thought her eyes were blue, and that she had curling black hair. Now they are dark and she has straight hair. Where's the necklace, too? Where's the necklace? Pearl-Maiden, what have you done with your necklace? Yes, and why didn't you wear the girdle I sent you to-day?"

"Sir," answered the Jewess, "I never had a necklace—"

"My lord Domitian," began Saturius with a nervous laugh, "there is a mistake—I must explain. This girl is not Pearl-Maiden. Pearl-Maiden fetched so great a price that it was impossible that I should buy her, even for you—"

He stopped, for suddenly Domitian's face had become terrible. All the drunkenness had left it, to be replaced by a mask of savage cruelty through which glared the pale and glittering eyes. The man appeared as he was, half satyr and half fiend.

"A mistake—" he said. "Oh! a mistake? And I have been counting on her all these weeks, and now some other man has taken her from me—the prince Domitian. And you—you dare to come to me with this tale, and to bring this slut with you instead of my Pearl-Maiden—" and at the thought he fairly sobbed in his drunken, disappointed rage. Then he stepped back and began to clap his hands and call aloud.

Instantly slaves and guards rushed into the chamber, thinking that their lord was threatened with some evil.

"Men," he said, "take that woman and kill her. No, it

might make a stir, as she was one of Titus's captives. Don't kill her, thrust her into the street."

The girl was seized by the arms and dragged away.

"Oh! my lord," began Saturius.

"Silence, man, I am coming to you. Seize him, and strip him. Oh! I know you are a freedman and a citizen of Rome. Well, soon you shall be a citizen of Hades, I promise you. Now, bring the heavy rods and beat him till he dies."

The dreadful order was obeyed, and for a while nothing was heard save the sound of heavy blows and the smothered moans of the miserable Saturius.

"Wretches," yelled the Imperial brute, "you are playing, you do not hit hard enough. I will teach you how to hit," and snatching a rod from one of the slaves he rushed at his prostrate chamberlain, the others drawing back to allow their master to show his skill in flogging.

Saturius saw Domitian come, and knew that unless he could change his purpose in another minute the life would be battered out of him. He struggled to his knees.

"Prince," he cried, "hearken ere you strike. You can kill me if you will who are justly angered, and to die at your hands is an honour that I do not merit. Yet, dread lord, remember that if you slay me then you will never find that Pearl-Maiden whom you desire."

Domitian paused, for even in his fury he was cunning. "Doubtless," he thought, "the knave knows where the girl is. Perhaps even he has hidden her away for himself."

"Ah!" he said aloud, quoting the vulgar proverb, "'the rod is the mother of reason.' Well, can you find her?"

"Surely, if I have time. The man who can afford to pay two thousand sestertia for a single slave cannot easily be hidden."

"Two thousand sestertia!" exclaimed Domitian astonished. "Tell me that story. Slaves, give Saturius his robe and fall back—no, not too far, he may be treacherous."

The chamberlain threw the garment over his bleeding shoulders and fastened it with a trembling hand. Then he told his tale, adding:

"Oh! my lord, what could I do? You have not enough money at hand to pay so huge a sum."

"Do, fool? Why you should have bought her on credit and left me to settle the price afterwards. Oh! never mind Titus, I could have outwitted him. But the mischief is done; now for the remedy, so far as it can be remedied," he added, grinding his teeth.

"That I must seek to-morrow, lord."

"To-morrow? And what will you do to-morrow?"

"To-morrow I will find where the girl's gone, or try to, and then—why he who has bought her might die and—the rest will be easy."

"Die he surely shall be who has dared to rob Domitian of his darling," answered the prince with an oath. "Well, hearken, Saturius, for this night you are spared, but be sure that if you fail for the second time you also shall die, and after a worse fashion than I promised you. Now go, and to-morrow we will take counsel. Oh! ye gods, why do you deal so hardly with Domitian? My soul is bruised and must be comforted with poesy. Rouse that Greek from his bed and send him to me. He shall read to me of the wrath of Achilles when they robbed him of his Briseis, for the hero's lot is mine."

So this new Achilles departed, now that his rage had left him, weeping maudlin tears of disappointed passion, to comfort his "bruised soul" with the immortal lines of

Homer, for when he was not merely a brute Domitian fancied himself a poet. It was perhaps as well for his peace of mind that he could not see the face of Saturius, as the chamberlain comforted his bruised shoulders with some serviceable ointment, or hear the oath which that useful and industrious officer uttered as he sought his rest, face downwards, since for many days thereafter he was unable to lie upon his back. It was a very ugly oath, sworn by every god who had an altar in Rome, with the divinities of the Jews and the Christians thrown in, that in a day to come he would avenge Domitian's rods with daggers. Had the prince been able to do so, there might have risen in his mind some prescience of a certain scene, in which he must play a part on a far-off but destined night. He might have beheld a vision of himself, bald, corpulent and thin-legged, but wearing the imperial robes of Cæsar, rolling in a frantic struggle for life upon the floor of his bed-chamber, at death grips with one Stephanus, while an old chamberlain named Saturius drove a dagger again and again into his back, crying at each stroke:

"Oho! That for thy rods, Cæsar! Oho! Dost remember the Pearl-Maiden? That for thy rods, Cæsar, and that—and that—and *that*——!"

But Domitian, weeping himself to sleep over the tale of the wrongs of the god-like Achilles, which did but foreshadow those of his divine self, as yet thought nothing of the rich reward that time should bring him.

On the morrow of the great day of the Triumph the merchant Demetrius of Alexandria, whom for many years we have known as Caleb, sat in the office of the storehouse which he had hired for the bestowal of his goods in one of the busiest thoroughfares of Rome. Handsome, indeed, noble-looking as he was, and must always be, his countenance presented a sorry sight. From hour to hour during the previous day he had fought a path through the dense crowds that lined the streets of Rome, to keep as near as might be to Miriam while she trudged her long route of splendid shame.

Then came the evening, when, with the other women slaves, she was put up to auction in the Forum. To prepare for this sale Caleb had turned almost all his merchandise into money, for he knew that Domitian was a purchaser, and guessed that the price of the beautiful Pearl-Maiden, of whom all the city was talking, would rule high. The climax we know. He bid to the last coin that he possessed or could raise, only to find that others with still greater resources were in the market. Even the agent of the prince had been left behind, and Miriam was at last knocked down to some mysterious stranger woman dressed like a peasant. The woman was veiled and disguised; she spoke with a feigned voice and in a strange tongue, but from the beginning Caleb knew her. Incredible as it might seem, that she should be here in Rome, he was certain that she was Nehushta, and no other.

That Nehushta should buy Miriam was well, but how came she by so vast a sum of money, here in a far-off land? In short, for whom was she buying? Indeed, for whom would she buy? He could think of one only—Marcus. But he had made inquiries and Marcus was not in Rome. Indeed he had every reason to believe that his rival was long dead, that his bones were scattered among the tens of thousands which whitened the tumbled ruins of the Holy City in Judæa. How could it be otherwise? He had last seen him wounded, as he thought to death—and he should know, for the stroke fell from his own hand—lying senseless in the Old Tower in Jerusalem. Then he vanished away, and where Marcus had been Miriam was found. Whither did he vanish, and if it was true that she succeeded in hiding him in some secret hole, what chance was there that he could have lived on without food and unsuccoured? Also if he lived, why had he not appeared long before? Why was not so wealthy a Patrician and distinguished a soldier riding in the triumphant train of Titus?

With black despair raging in his breast, he, Caleb, had seen Miriam knocked down to the mysterious basket-laden stranger whom none could recognise. He had seen her depart together with the auctioneer and a servant, also basket-laden, to the office of the receiving house, whither he had attempted to follow upon some pretext, only to be stopped by the watchman. After this he hung about the door until he saw the auctioneer appear alone, when it occurred to him that the purchaser and the purchased must have departed by some other exit, perhaps in order to avoid further observation. He ran round the building to find himself confronted only by the empty, star-lit spaces of the Forum. Searching them with his eyes, for one instant it seemed to him that far away he caught sight of a little knot of figures climbing a black marble stair in the dark shadow of some temple. He sped across the open space, he ran up the great stair, to find at the head of it a young man in whom he recognised the auctioneer's clerk, gazing along a wide street as empty as was the stair.

The rest is known to us. He followed, and twice perceived the little group of dark-robed figures hurrying round distant corners. Once he lost them altogether, but a passer-by on his road to some feast told him courteously enough which way they had gone. On he ran almost at hazard, to be rewarded in the end by the sight of them vanishing through a narrow doorway in the wall. He came to the door and saw that it was very massive. He tried it even, it was locked. Then he thought of knocking, only to remember that to state his business would probably be to meet his death. At such a place and hour those who purchased beautiful slaves might have a sword waiting for the heart of an unsuccessful rival who dared to follow them to their haunts.

Caleb walked round the house, to find that it was a palace which seemed to be deserted, although he thought that he saw light shining through one of the shuttered windows. Now he knew the place again. It was here that the procession had halted and one of the Roman soldiers who had committed the crime of being taken captive escaped the taunts of the crowd by hurling himself beneath the wheel of a great pageant car. Yes, there was no doubt of it, for his blood still stained the dusty stones and by it lay a piece of the broken distaff with which, in their mockery, they had girded the poor man. They were gentle folk, these Romans! Why, measured by this standard, some such doom would have fallen upon his rival, Marcus, for Marcus also was taken prisoner—by himself. The thought made Caleb smile, since well he knew that no braver soldier lived. Then came other thoughts that pressed him closer. Somewhere in that great dead-looking house was Miriam, as far off from him as though she were still in Judæa. There was Miriam—and who was with her? The new-found lord who had spent two thousand sestertia on her purchase? The thought of it almost turned his brain.

Heretofore, the life of Caleb had been ruled by two passions—ambition and the love of Miriam. He had aspired to be ruler of the Jews, perhaps their king, and to this end had plotted and fought for the expulsion of the Romans from Judæa. He had taken part in a hundred desperate battles. Again and again he had risked his life; again and again he had escaped. For one so young he had reached high rank, till he was numbered among the first of their captains.

Then came the end, the last hideous struggle and the downfall. Once more his life was left in him. Where men perished by the hundred thousand he escaped, winning safety, not through the desire of it, but because of the love of Miriam which drove him on to follow her. Happily for himself he had hidden money, which, after the gift of his race, he was able to turn to good account, so that now he, who had been a leader in war and council, walked the world as a merchant in Eastern goods. All that glittering past had gone from him; he might become wealthy, but, Jew as he was, he could never be great nor fill his soul with the glory that it craved. There remained to him, then, nothing but this passion for one woman among the millions who dwelt beneath the sun, the girl who had been his playmate, whom he loved from the beginning, although she had never loved him, and whom he would love until the end.

Why had she not loved him? Because of his rival, that accursed Roman, Marcus, the man whom time upon time he had tried to kill, but who had always slipped like water from his hands. Well, if she was lost to him she was lost to Marcus also, and from that thought he would take such comfort as he might. Indeed he had no other, for during those dreadful hours the fires of all Gehenna raged in his soul. He had lost—but who had found her?

Throughout the long night Caleb tramped round the cold, empty-looking palace, suffering perhaps as he had never suffered before, a thing to be pitied of gods and men. At length the dawn broke and the light crept down the splendid street, showing here and there groups of weary and half-drunken revellers staggering homewards from the feast, flushed men and dishevelled women. Others appeared also, humble and industrious citizens going to their daily toil. Among them were people whose business it was to clean the roads, abroad early this morning, for after the great procession they thought that they might find articles of value let fall by those who walked in it, or by the spectators. Two of these scavengers began sweeping near the place where Caleb stood, and lightened their toil by laughing at him, asking him if he had spent his night in the gutter and whether he knew his way home. He replied that he waited for the doors of the house to be opened.

"Which house?" they asked. "The 'Fortunate House?'" and they pointed to the marble palace of Marcus, which, as Caleb now saw for the first time, had these words blazoned in gold letters on its portico.

He nodded.

"Well," said one of them, "you will wait for some time, for that house is no longer fortunate. Its owner is dead, killed in the wars, and no one knows who his heir may be."

"What was his name?" he asked.

"Marcus, the favourite of Nero, also called the Fortunate."

Then, with a bitter curse upon his lips Caleb turned and walked away.

Chapter 26

The Judgment of Domitian

Two hours had gone by and Caleb, with fury in his heart, sat brooding in the office attached to the warehouse that he had hired. At that moment he had but one desire—to kill his successful rival, Marcus. Marcus had escaped and returned to Rome; of that there could be no doubt. He, one of the wealthiest of its patricians, had furnished the vast sum which enabled old Nehushta to buy the coveted Pearl-Maiden in the slave-ring. Then his newly acquired property had been taken to this house, where he awaited her. This then was the end of their long rivalry; for this he, Caleb, had fought, toiled, schemed and suffered. Oh! rather than such a thing should be, in that dark hour of his soul, he would have seen her cast to the foul Domitian, for Domitian, at least, she would have hated, whereas Marcus, he knew, she loved.

Now there remained nothing but revenge. Revenged he must be, but how? He might dog Marcus and murder him, only then his own life would be hazarded, since he knew well the fate that awaited the foreigner, and most of all the Jew, who dared to lift his hand against a Roman noble, and if he hired others to do the work they might bear evidence against him. Now Caleb did not wish to die;

life seemed the only good that he had left. Also, while he lived he might still win Miriam—after his rival had ceased to live. Doubtless, then she would be sold with his other slaves, and he could buy her at the rate such tarnished goods command. No, he would do nothing to run himself into danger. He would wait, wait and watch his opportunity.

It was near at hand, for of old as to-day the king of evil was ever ready to aid those who called upon him with sufficient earnestness. Indeed, even as Caleb sat there in his office, there came a knock upon the door.

"Open!" he cried savagely, and through it entered a small man with close-cropped hair and a keen, hard face which seemed familiar to him. Just now, however, that face was somewhat damaged, for one of the eyes had been blackened and a wound upon the temple was strapped with plaster. Also its owner walked lame and continually twitched his shoulders as though they gave him uneasiness. The stranger opened his lips to speak, and Caleb knew him at once. He was the chamberlain of Domitian who had been outbid by Nehushta in the slave ring.

"Greeting, noble Saturius," he said. "Be seated, I pray, for it seems to pain you to stand."

"Yes, yes," answered the chamberlain, "still I had rather stand. I met with an accident last night, a most unpleasant accident," and he coughed as though to cover up some word that leapt to his lips. "You also, worthy Demetrius—that is your name, is it not?" he added, eyeing him keenly—"look as though you had not slept well."

"No," answered Caleb, "I also met with an accident—oh! nothing that you can see—a slight internal injury which is, I fear, likely to prove troublesome. Well, noble

Saturius, how can I—serve you? Anything in the way of Eastern shawls, for instance?"

"I thank you, friend, no. I come to speak of shoulders, not shawls," and he twitched his own—"women's shoulders, I mean. A remarkably fine pair for their size had that Jewish captive, by the way, in whom you seemed to take an interest last night—to the considerable extent indeed of fourteen hundred sestertia."

"Yes," said Caleb, "they were well shaped."

Then followed a pause.

"Perhaps as I am a busy man," suggested Caleb presently, "you would not mind coming to the point."

"Certainly, I was but waiting for your leave. As you may have heard, I represent a very noble person—"

"Who, I think, took an interest in the captive to the extent of fifteen hundred sestertia," suggested Caleb.

"Quite so—and whose interest unfortunately remains unabated, or rather, I should say, that it is transferred."

"To the gentleman whose deep feeling induced him to provide five hundred more?" queried Caleb.

"Precisely. What intuition you have! It is a gift with which the East endows her sons."

"Suppose you put the matter plainly, worthy Saturius."

"I will, excellent Demetrius. The great person to whom I have alluded was so moved when he heard of his loss that he actually burst into tears, and even reproached me, whom he loves more dearly than his brother—"

"He might easily do that, if all reports are true," said Caleb, drily, adding, "Was it then that you met with your accident?"

"It was. Overcome at the sight of my royal master's grief, I fell down."

"Into a well, I suppose, since you managed to injure your eye, your back, and your leg all at once. There—I understand—these things will happen—in the households of the Great where the floors are so slippery that the most wary feet may slide. But that does not console the sufferer whose hurt remains, does it?"

"No," answered Saturius with a snarl, "but until he is in a position to relay the floors, he must find chalk for his sandals and ointment for his back. I want the purchaser's name, and thought perhaps that you might have it, for the old woman has vanished, and that fool of an auctioneer knows absolutely nothing."

"Why do you want his name?"

"Because Domitian wants his head. An unnatural desire indeed that devours him; still one which, to be frank, I find it important to satisfy."

Of a sudden a great light seemed to shine in Caleb's mind, it was as though a candle had been lit in a dark room.

"Ah!" he said. "And supposing I can show him how to get this head, even how to get it without any scandal, do you think that in return he would leave me the lady's hand? You see I knew her in her youth and take a brotherly interest in her."

"Quite so, just like Domitian and the two thousand sestertia man and, indeed, half the male population of Rome, who, when they saw her yesterday were moved by the same family feeling. Well, I don't see why he shouldn't. You see my master never cared for pearls that were not perfectly white, or admired ladies upon whom report cast the slightest breath of scandal. But he is of a curiously jealous disposition, and it is, I think, the head that he requires, not the hand."

"Had you not better make yourself clear upon the point before we go any further?" asked Caleb. "Otherwise I do not feel inclined to undertake a very difficult and dangerous business."

"With pleasure. Now would you let me have your demands, in writing, perhaps. Oh! of course, I understand—to be answered in writing."

Caleb took parchment and pen and wrote:

> "A free pardon, with full liberty to travel, live and trade throughout the Roman empire, signed by the proper authorities, to be granted to one Caleb, the son of Hilliel, for the part he took in the Jewish war.
>
> "A written promise, signed by the person concerned, that if the head he desires is put within his reach the Jewish slave named Pearl-Maiden shall be handed over at once to Demetrius, the merchant of Alexandria, whose property she shall become absolutely and without question."

"That's all," he said, giving the paper to Saturius. "The Caleb spoken of is a Jewish friend of mine to whom I am anxious to do a good turn, without whose help and evidence I should be quite unable to perform my share of the bargain. Being very shy and timid—his nerves were much shattered during the siege of Jerusalem—he will not stir without this authority, which, by the way, will require the signature of Titus Cæsar, duly witnessed. Well, that is merely an offering to friendship; of course *my* fee is the reversion to the lady, whom I desire to restore to her relations, who mourn her loss in Judæa."

"Precisely—quite so," replied Saturius. "Pray do not trouble to explain further. I have always found those of Alexandria most excellent merchants. Well, I hope to be back within two hours."

"Mind you come alone. As I have told you, everything depends upon this Caleb, and if he is in any way alarmed there is an end of the affair. He only has a possible key to the mystery. Should it be lost your patron will never get his head, and I shall never get my hand."

"Oh! bid the timid Caleb have no fear. Who would wish to harm a dirty Jewish deserter from his cause and people? Let him come out of his sewer and look upon the sun. The Cæsars do not war with carrion rats. Most worthy Demetrius, I go swiftly, as I hope to return again with all you need."

"Good, most noble Saturius, and for both our sakes—remember that the palace floor is slippery, and do not get another fall, for it might finish you."

"I am in deep waters, but I think that I can swim well," reflected Caleb as the door closed behind his visitor. "At any rate it gives me a chance who have no other, and that prince is playing for revenge, not love. What can Miriam be to him beyond the fancy of an hour, of which a thief has robbed him? Doubtless he wishes to kill the thief, but kings do not care for faded roses, which are only good enough to weave the chaplet of a merchant of Alexandria. So I cast for the last time, let the dice fall as it is fated."

Very shortly afterwards in the palace of Domitian the dice began to fall. Humbly, most humbly, did that faithful chamberlain, Saturius, lay the results of his mission before his august master, Domitian, who suffering from a severe bilious attack that had turned his ruddy complexion to a dingy yellow, and made the aspect of his pale eyes more unpleasant than usual, was propped up among cushions, sniffing attar of roses and dabbing vinegar water upon his forehead.

He listened indifferently to the tale of his jackal, until the full meaning of the terms asked by the mysterious Eastern merchant penetrated his sodden brain.

"Why," he said, "the man wants Pearl-Maiden; that's his share, while mine is the life of the fellow who bought her, whoever he may be. Are you still mad, man, that you should dare to lay such a proposal before me? Don't you understand that I need both the woman and the blood of him who dared to cheat me out of her?"

"Most divine prince, I understand perfectly, but this fish is only biting; he must be tempted or he will tell nothing."

"Why not bring him here and torture him?"

"I have thought of that, but those Jews are so obstinate. While you were twisting the truth out of him the other man would escape with the girl. Much better promise everything he asks and then—"

"And then—what?"

"And then forget your promises. What can be simpler?"

"But he needs them in writing."

"Let him have them in writing, my writing, which your divine self can repudiate. Only the pardon to Caleb, who I suppose is this Demetrius himself, can be signed by Titus. It will not affect you whether a Jew more or less has the right to trade in the Empire, if thereby you can win his services in an important matter. Then, when the time comes, you can net both your unknown rival and the lady, leaving our friend Demetrius to report the facts to her relatives in

Judæa, for whom, as he states, he is alone concerned."

"Saturius," said Domitian, growing interested, "you are not so foolish as I thought you were. Decidedly that trouble last night has quickened your wits. Be so good as to stop wriggling your shoulders, will you, it makes me nervous, and I wish that you would have that eye of yours painted. You know that I cannot bear the sight of black; it reminds me, who am by nature joyous and light-hearted as a child, of melancholy things. Now forge a letter for my, or rather for your signature, promising the reversion of Pearl-Maiden to this Demetrius. Then bear my greetings to Titus, begging his signature to an order granting the desired privileges to one Caleb, a Jew who fought against him at Jerusalem—with less success than I could have wished—whom I desire to favour."

Three hours later Saturius presented himself for the second time in the office of the Alexandrian merchant.

"Most worthy Demetrius," he said, "I congratulate you. Everything has been arranged as you wish. Here is the order, signed by Titus and duly witnessed, granting to you—I mean to your friend, Caleb—pardon for whatever he may have done in Judæa, and permission to live and trade anywhere that he may wish within the bounds of the Empire. I may tell you that it was obtained with great difficulty, since Titus, worn out with toil and glory, leaves this very day for his villa by the sea, where he is ordered by his physicians to rest three months, taking no part whatever in affairs. Does the document satisfy you?"

Caleb examined the signatures and seals.

"It seems to be in order," he said.

"It is in order, excellent Demetrius. Caleb can now appear in the Forum, if it pleases him, and lecture upon the fall of Jerusalem for the benefit of the vulgar. Well, here also is a letter from the divine—or rather the half divine—Domitian to yourself, Demetrius of Alexandria, also witnessed by myself and sealed. It promises to you that if you give evidence enabling him to arrest that miscreant who dared to bid against him—no, do not be alarmed, the lady was not knocked down to you—you shall be allowed to take possession of her or to buy her at a reasonable valuation, not to exceed fifteen sestertia. That is as much as she will fetch now in the open market. Are you satisfied with this document?"

Caleb read and scrutinised the letter.

"The signatures of Domitian and of yourself as witness seem much alike," he remarked suspiciously.

"Somewhat," replied Saturius, with an airy gesture. "In royal houses it is customary for chamberlains to imitate the handwriting of their imperial masters."

"And their morals—no, they have none—their manners also," commented Caleb.

"At the least," went on Saturius, "you will acknowledge the seals—"

"Which might be borrowed. Well, I will take the risk, for if there is anything wrong about these papers I am sure that the prince Domitian would not like to see them exhibited in a court of law."

"Good," answered Saturius, with a relief which he could not altogether conceal. "And now for the culprit's name."

"The culprit's name," said Caleb, leaning forward and speaking slowly, "is Marcus, who served as one of Titus Cæsar's prefects of horse in the campaign of Judæa. He bought the lady Miriam, commonly known as Pearl-

Maiden, by the agency of Nehushta, an old Libyan woman, who conveyed her to his house in the Via Agrippa, which is known as the 'Fortunate House,' where doubtless, she now is."

"Marcus," said Saturius. "Why, he was reported dead, and the matter of the succession to his great estates is now being debated, for he was the heir of his uncle, Caius, the pro-consul, who amassed a vast fortune in Spain. Also after the death of the said Caius, this Marcus was a favourite of the late divine Nero, who constituted him guardian of some bust of which he was enamoured. In short, he is a great man, if, as you say, he still lives, whom even Domitian will find it hard to meddle with. But how do you know all this?"

"Through my friend Caleb. Caleb followed the black hag, Nehushta, and the beautiful Pearl-Maiden to the very house of Marcus, which he saw them enter. Marcus who was her lover, yonder in Judæa—"

"Oh! never mind the rest of the story, I understand it all. But you have not yet shown that Marcus was in the house, and if he was, bad taste as it may have been to bid against the prince Domitian, well, at a public auction it is lawful."

"Ye—es, but if Marcus has committed a crime, could he not be punished for that crime?"

"Without doubt. But what crime has Marcus committed?"

"The crime of being taken prisoner by the Jews and escaping from them with his life, for which, by an edict of Titus, whose laws are those of the Medes and Persians, the punishment is death, or at the least, banishment and degradation."

"Well, and who can prove all this?"

"Caleb can, because he took him prisoner."

"And where," asked Saturius in exasperation, "where is this thrice accursed cur, Caleb?"

"Here," answered Demetrius. "I am Caleb, O thrice blessed chamberlain, Saturius."

"Indeed," said Saturius. "Well, that makes things more simple. And now, friend Demetrius—you prefer that name, do you not—what do you propose?"

"I propose that the necessary documents should be procured, which, to your master, will not be difficult; that Marcus should be arrested in his house, put upon his trial and condemned under the edict of Titus, and that the girl, Pearl-Maiden, should be handed over to me, who will at once remove her from Rome."

"Good," said Saturius. "Titus having gone, leaving Domitian in charge of military affairs, the thing, as it chances, is easy, though any sentence that may be passed must be confirmed by Cæsar himself. And now, again farewell. If our man is in Rome, he shall be taken to-night, and to-morrow your evidence may be wanted."

"Will the girl be handed over to me then?"

"I think so," replied Saturius, "but of course I cannot say for certain, as there may be legal difficulties in the way which would hinder her immediate re-sale. However, you may rely upon me to do the best I can for you."

"It will be to your advantage," answered Caleb significantly. "Shall we say—fifty sestertia on receipt of the slave?"

"Oh! if you wish it, if you wish it, for gifts cement the hearts of friends. On account? Well, to a man with many expenses, five sestertia always come in useful. You know what it is in these palaces, so little pay and so much to keep up. Thank you, dear Demetrius, I will give you and the lady a supper out of the money—when you get her," he added to himself as he left the office.

When early on the following morning Caleb came to his warehouse from the dwelling where he slept, he found waiting for him two men dressed in the livery of Domitian, who demanded that he would accompany them to the palace of the prince.

"What for?"

"To give evidence in a trial," they said.

Then he knew that he had made no mistake, that his rival was caught, and in the rage of his burning jealousy, such jealousy as only an Eastern can feel, his heart bounded with joy. Still, as he trudged onward through streets glittering in the morning sunlight, Caleb's conscience told him that not thus should this rival be overcome, that he who went to accuse the brave Marcus of cowardice was himself a coward, and that from the lie which he was about to act if not to speak, could spring no fruit of peace or happiness. But he was mad and blind. He could think only of Miriam—the woman whom he loved with all his passionate nature and whose life he had preserved at the risk of his own—fallen at last into the arms of his rival. He would wrench her thence, yes, even at the price of his own honour and of her life- long agony, and, if it might be, leave those arms cold in death, as often already he had striven to do. When Marcus was dead perhaps she would forgive him. At the least he would occupy his place. She would be his slave, to whom, notwithstanding all that had been, he would give the place of wife. Then, after a little while, seeing how good and tender he was to her, surely she must forget this Roman who had taken her girlish fancy and learn to love him.

Now they were passing the door of the palace. In the outer hall Saturius met them and motioned to the slaves to stand back.

"So you have them," said Caleb, eagerly.

"Yes, or to be exact, one of them. The lady has vanished."

Caleb staggered back a pace.

"Vanished! Where?"

"I wish that I could tell you. I thought that perhaps you knew. At least we found Marcus alone in his house, which he was about to leave, apparently to follow Titus. But come, the court awaits you."

"If she has gone, why should I come?" said Caleb, hanging back.

"I really don't know, but you must. Here, slaves, escort this witness."

Then seeing that it was too late to change his mind, Caleb waved them back and followed Saturius. Presently they entered an inner hall, lofty, but not large. At the head of it, clad in the purple robes of his royal house, sat Domitian in a chair, while to his right and left were narrow tables, at which were gathered five or six Roman officers, those of Domitian's own bodyguard, bare-headed, but arrayed in their mail. Also there were two scribes with their tablets, a man dressed in a lawyer's robe, who seemed to fill the office of prosecutor, and some soldiers on guard.

When Caleb entered, Domitian, who, notwithstanding his youthful, ruddy countenance, looked in a very evil mood, was engaged in talking earnestly to the lawyer. Glancing up, he saw him and asked:

"Is that the Jew who gives evidence, Saturius?"

"My lord, it is the man," answered the chamberlain; "also the other witness waits without."

"Good. Then bring in the accused."

There was a pause, till presently Caleb heard footsteps behind him and looked round to see Marcus advancing up the hall with a proud and martial air. Their eyes met, and for an instant Marcus stopped.

"Oh!" he said aloud, "the Jew Caleb. Now I understand." Then he marched forward and gave the military salute to the prince.

Domitian stared at him with hate in his pale eyes, and said carelessly:

"Is this the accused? What is the charge?"

"The charge is," said the lawyer, "that the accused Marcus, a prefect of horse serving with Titus Cæsar in Judæa, suffered himself to be taken prisoner by the Jews when in command of a large body of Roman troops, contrary to the custom of the army and to the edict issued by Titus Cæsar at the commencement of the siege of Jerusalem. This edict commanded that no soldier should be taken alive, and that any soldier who was taken alive and subsequently rescued, or who made good his escape, should be deemed worthy of death, or at the least of degradation from his rank and banishment. My lord Marcus, do you plead guilty to the charge?"

"First, I ask," said Marcus, "what court is this before which I am put upon my trial? If I am to be tried I demand that it shall be by my general, Titus."

"Then," said the prosecutor, "you should have reported yourself to Titus upon your arrival in Rome. Now he has gone to where he may not be troubled, leaving the charge of military matters in the hands of his Imperial brother, the Prince Domitian, who, with these officers, is therefore your lawful judge."

"Perhaps," broke in Domitian with bitter malice, "the lord Marcus was too much occupied with other pursuits on his arrival in Rome to find time to explain his conduct to the Cæsar Titus."

"I was about to follow him to do so when I was seized," said Marcus.

"Then you put the matter off a little too long. Now you can explain it here," answered Domitian.

Then the prosecutor took up the tale, saying that it had been ascertained on inquiry that the accused, accompanied by an old woman, arrived in Rome upon horseback early on the morning of the Triumph; that he went straight to his house, which was called "The House Fortunate," where he lay hid all day; that in the evening he sent out the old woman and a slave carrying on their backs a great sum of gold in baskets, with which gold he purchased a certain fair Jewish captive, known as Pearl-Maiden, at a public auction in the Forum. This Pearl-Maiden, it would seem, was taken to his house, but when he was arrested on the morrow neither she nor the old woman were found there. The accused, he might add, was arrested just as he was about to leave the house, as he stated, in order to report himself to Titus Cæsar, who had already departed from Rome. This was the case in brief, and to prove it he called a certain Jew named Caleb, who was now living in Rome, having received an amnesty given by the hand of Titus. This Jew was now a merchant who traded under the name of Demetrius.

Then Caleb stood forward and told his tale. In answer

to questions that were put to him, he related how he was in command of a body of the Jews which fought an action with the Roman troops at a place called the Old Tower, a few days before the capture of the Temple. In the course of this action he parleyed with a captain of the Romans, the Prefect Marcus, who now stood before him, and at the end of the parley challenged him to single combat. As Marcus refused the encounter and tried to run away, he struck him on the back with the back of his sword. Thereon a fight ensued in which he, the witness, had the advantage. Being wounded, the accused let fall his sword, sank to his knees and asked for mercy. The fray having now become general he, Caleb, dragged his prisoner into the Old Tower and returned to the battle.

When he went back to the Tower it was to find that the captive had vanished, leaving in his place a lady who was known to the Romans as Pearl-Maiden, and who was afterwards taken by them and exposed for sale in the Forum, where she was purchased by an old woman whom he recognised as her nurse. He followed the maiden, having bid for her and being curious as to her destination, to a house in the Via Agrippa, which he afterwards learned was the palace of the accused Marcus. That was all he knew of the matter.

Then the prosecutor called a soldier, who stated that he had been under the command of Marcus on the day in question. There he saw the Jew leader, whom he identified with Caleb, at the conclusion of a parley strike the accused, Marcus, on the back with the flat of his sword. After this ensued a fight, in which the Romans were repulsed. At the end of it, he saw their captain, Marcus, being led away prisoner. His sword had gone and blood was running from the side of his head.

The evidence being concluded, Marcus was asked if he had anything to say in defence.

"Much," he answered proudly, "when I am given a fair trial. I desire to call the men of my legion who were with me, none of whom I see here to-day except that man who has given evidence against me, a rogue whom, I remember, I caused to be scourged for theft, and dismissed his company. But they are in Egypt, so how can I summon them? As for the Jew, he is an old enemy of mine, who was guilty of murder in his youth, and whom once I overcame in a duel in Judæa, sparing his life. It is true that when my back was turned he struck me with his sword, and as I flew at him smote me a blow upon the head, from the effects of which I became senseless. In this state I was taken prisoner and lay for weeks sick in a vault, in the care of some people of the Jews, who nursed me. From them I escaped to Rome, desiring to report myself to Titus Cæsar, my master. I appeal to Titus Cæsar."

"He is absent and I represent him," said Domitian.

"Then," answered Marcus, "I appeal to Vespasian Cæsar, to whom I will tell all. I am a Roman noble of no mean rank, and I have a right to be tried by Cæsar, not by a packed court, whose president has a grudge against me for private matters."

"Insolent!" shouted Domitian. "Your appeal shall be laid before Cæsar, as it must—that is, if he will hear it. Tell us now, where is that woman whom you bought in the Forum, for we desire her testimony?"

"Prince, I do not know," answered Marcus. "It is true that she came to my house, but then and there I gave her freedom and she departed from it with her nurse, nor can

I tell whither she went."

"I thought that you were only a coward, but it seems that you are a liar as well," sneered Domitian. Then he consulted with the officers and added, "We judge the case to be proved against you, and for having disgraced the Roman arms, when, rather than be taken prisoner, many a meaner man died by his own hand, you are worthy of whatever punishment it pleases Cæsar to inflict. Meanwhile, till his pleasure is known, I command that you shall be confined in the private rooms of the military prison near the Temple of Mars, and that if you attempt to escape thence you shall be put to death. You have liberty to draw up your case in writing, that it may be transmitted to Cæsar, my father, together with a transcript of the evidence against you."

"Now," replied Marcus bitterly, "I am tempted to do what you say I should have done before, die by my own hand, rather than endure such shameful words and this indignity. But that my honour will not suffer. When Cæsar has heard my case and when Titus, my general, also gives his verdict against me, I will die, but not before. You, Prince, and you, Captains, who have never drawn sword outside the streets of Rome, you call me coward, me, who have served with honour through five campaigns, who, from my youth till now have been in arms, and this upon the evidence of a renegade Jew who, for years, has been my private enemy, and of a soldier whom I scourged as a thief. Look now upon this breast and say if it is that of a coward!" and rending his robes asunder, Marcus exposed his bosom, scarred with four white wounds. "Call my comrades, those with whom I have fought in Gaul, in Sicily, in Egypt and in Judæa, and ask them if Marcus is a coward?

Ask that Jew even, to whom I gave his life, whether Marcus is a coward?"

"Have done with your boasting," said Domitian, "and hide those scratches. You were taken prisoner by the Jews—it is enough. You have your prayer, your case shall go to Cæsar. If the tale you tell is true you would produce that woman who is said to have rescued you from the Jews and whom you purchased as a slave. When you do this we will take her evidence. Till then to your prison with you. Guards, remove the man Marcus, called the Fortunate, once a Prefect of Horse in the army of Judæa."

Chapter 27

The Bishop Cyril

On the morning following the day of the Triumph Julia, the wife of Gallus, was seated in her bed-chamber looking out at the yellow waters of the Tiber that ran almost beneath its window. She had risen at dawn and attended to the affairs of her household, and now retired to rest and pray. Mingled with the Roman crowd on the yesterday she had seen Miriam, whom she loved, marching wearily through the streets of Rome. Then, able to bear no more, she went home, leaving Gallus to follow the last acts of the drama. About nine o'clock that night he joined her and told her the story of the sale of Miriam for a vast sum of money, since, standing in the shadow beyond the light of the torches, he had been a witness of the scene at the slave-market. Domitian had been outbid, and their Pearl-Maiden was knocked down to an old woman with a basket on her back who looked like a witch, after which she vanished with her purchaser. That was all he knew for certain. Julia thought it little enough, and reproached her husband for his stupidity in not learning more. Still, although she seemed to be vexed, at heart she rejoiced. Into whoever's hand the maid had fallen, for a while at least she had escaped the vile Domitian.

Now, as she sat and prayed, Gallus being abroad to gather more tidings if he could, she heard the courtyard door open, but took no notice of it, thinking that it was but the servant who returned from market. Presently, however, as she knelt, a shadow fell upon her and Julia looked up to see Miriam, none other than Miriam, and with her a dark- skinned, aged woman, whom she did not know.

"How come you here?" she gasped.

"Oh! mother," answered the girl in a low and thrilling voice, "mother, by the mercy of God and by the help of this Nehushta, of whom I have often told you, and—of another, I am escaped from Domitian, and return to you free and unharmed."

"Tell me that story," said Julia, "for I do not understand. The thing sounds incredible."

So Miriam told her tale. When it was done, Julia said:

"Heathen though he is, this Marcus must be a noble-hearted man, whom may Heaven reward."

"Yes," answered Miriam with a sigh, "may Heaven reward him, as I wish I might."

"As you would have done had I not stayed you," put in Nehushta. Her voice was severe, but as she spoke something that Julia took to be a smile was seen for an instant on her grim features.

"Well, friend, well," said Julia, "we have all of us fallen into temptation from time to time."

"Pardon me, lady," answered Nehushta, "but speak for yourself. I never fell into any temptation—from a man. I know too much of men."

"Then, friend," replied Julia, "return thanks for the good armour of your wisdom. For my part, I say that, like the lord Marcus, this maid has acted well, and my prayer is that she also may not lose her reward."

"Mine is," commented Nehushta, "that Marcus may escape the payment which he will doubtless receive from the hand of Domitian if he can hunt him out," a remark at which the face of Miriam grew very troubled.

Just then Gallus returned, and to him the whole history had to be told anew.

"It is wonderful," he said, "wonderful! I never heard the like of it. Two people who love each other and who, when their hour comes, separate over some question of faith, or rather in obedience to a command laid upon one of them by a lady who died years and years ago. Wonderful—and I hope wise, though had I been the man concerned I should have taken another counsel."

"What counsel, husband?" asked Julia.

"Well—to get away from Rome with the lady as far as possible, and without more delay than was necessary. It seems to me that under the circumstances it would have been best for her to consider her scruples in another land. You see Domitian is not a Christian any more than Marcus is, and our maid here does not like Domitian and does like Marcus. No, it is no good arguing the thing is done, but I think that you Christians might very well add two new saints to your calendar. And now to breakfast, which we all need after so much night duty."

So they went and ate, but during that meal Gallus was very silent, as was his custom when he set his brain to work. Presently he asked:

"Tell me, Miriam, did any see you or your companion enter here?"

"No, I think not," she answered, "for as it chanced the door of the courtyard was ajar and the servant has not yet returned."

"Good," he said. "When she does return I will meet her and send her out on a long errand."

"Why?" asked his wife.

"Because it is as well that none should know what guests we have till they are gone again."

"Until they are gone again!" repeated Julia, astonished. "Surely you would not drive this maid, who has become to us as our daughter, from your door?"

"Yes, I would, wife, for that dear maid's sake," and he took Miriam's little hand in his great palm and pressed it. "Listen now," he went on, "Miriam, the Jewish captive, has dwelt in our care these many months, has she not, as is known to all, is it not? Well, if any one wants to find her, where will they begin by looking?"

"Aye! where?" echoed Nehushta.

"Why should any one wish to find her?" asked Julia. "She was bought in the slave-market for a great price by the lord Marcus, who, of his own will, has set her at liberty. Now, therefore, she is a free woman whom none can touch."

"A free woman!" answered Gallus with scorn. "Is any woman free in Rome upon whom Domitian has set his mind? Surely, you Christians are too innocent for this world. Peace now, for there is no time to lose. Julia, do you cloak yourself and go seek that high-priest of yours, Cyril, who also loves this maid. Tell the tale to him, and say that if he would save her from great dangers he had best find some secret hiding-place among the Christians, for her and her companion, until means can be found to ship them far from Rome. What think you of that plan, my Libyan friend?"

"I think that it is good, but not good enough," answered Nehushta. "I think that we had best depart with the lady, your wife, this very hour, for who can tell how soon the dogs will be laid upon our slot?"

"And what say you, maid Miriam?" asked Gallus.

"I? Oh! I thank you for your thought, and I say—let us hide in any place you will, even a drain or a stable, if it will save me from Domitian."

Two hours later, in a humble and densely peopled quarter of the city, such as in our own day we should call a slum, where folk were employed making those articles which ministered to the comfort or the luxury of the more fortunate, a certain master-carpenter known as Septimus was seated at his mid-day meal in a little chamber above his workshop. His hands were rough with toil, and the dust of his trade was upon his garments and even powdered over his long gray beard, so that at first sight it would not have been easy to recognise in him that Cyril who was a bishop among the Christians. Yet it was he, one of the foremost of the Faith in Rome.

A woman entered the room and spoke with him in a low voice.

"The dame Julia, the wife of Gallus, and two others with her?" he said. "Well, we need fear none whom she brings; lead them hither."

Presently the door opened and Julia appeared, followed by two veiled figures. He raised his hands to bless her, then checked himself.

"Daughter, who are these?" he said.

"Declare yourselves," said Julia, and at her bidding Miriam and Nehushta unveiled.

At the sight of Miriam's face the bishop started, then turned to study that of her companion.

"Who vouches for this woman?" he asked.

"I vouch for myself," answered Nehushta, "seeing that I am a Christian who received baptism a generation since at the hands of the holy John, and who stood to pay the price of faith in the arena at Cæsarea."

"Is this so?" asked the bishop of Miriam.

"It is so," she answered. "This Libyan was the servant of my grandmother. She nursed both my mother and myself, and many a time has saved my life. Have no fear, she is faithful."

"Your pardon," said the bishop with a grave smile and addressing Nehushta, "but you who are old will know that the Christian who entertains strangers sometimes entertains a devil." Then he lifted up his hands and blessed them, greeting them in the name of their Master.

"So, maid Miriam," he said, still smiling, "it would seem that I was no false prophet, and though you walked in the Triumph and were sold in the slave-ring—for this much I have heard—still the Angel of the Lord went with you."

"Father, he went with me," she answered, "and he leads me here."

Then they told him all the tale, and how Miriam sought a refuge from Domitian. He looked at her, stroking his long beard.

"Is there anything you can do?" he asked. "Anything useful, I mean? But perhaps that is a foolish question, seeing that women—especially those who are well-favoured—do not learn a trade."

"I have learnt a trade," answered Miriam, flushing a little. "Once I was held of some account as a sculptor; indeed I have heard that your Emperor Nero decreed divine honours to a bust from my hand."

The bishop laughed outright. "The Emperor Nero! Well, the poor madman has gone to his own place, so let us say no more of him. But I heard of that bust; indeed I saw it; it was a likeness of Marcus Fortunatus, was it not, and in its fashion a great work? But our people do not make such things; we are artisans, not artists."

"The artisan should be an artist," said Miriam, setting her mouth.

"Perhaps, but as a rule he isn't. Do you think that you could mould lamps?"

"There is nothing I should like better, that is if I am not forced to copy one pattern," she added as an afterthought.

"Then," said the bishop, "I think, daughter, that I can show you how to earn a living, where none are likely to seek for you."

Not a hundred paces away from the carpenter's shop where the master craftsman, Septimus, worked, was another manufactory, in which vases, basins, lamps, and all such articles were designed, moulded and baked. The customers who frequented the place, wholesale merchants for the most part, noted from and after the day of this interview a new workwoman, who, so far as her rough blouse permitted them to judge, seemed to be young and pretty, seated in a corner apart, beneath a window by the light of which she laboured. Later on they observed also, those of them who had any taste, that among the lamps produced by the factory appeared some of singular and charming design, so good, indeed, that although the makers reaped little extra benefit, the middlemen found no difficulty in disposing of these pieces at a high price. All day long Miriam sat fashioning them, while old Nehushta, who had learnt something of the task years ago by Jordan, prepared and tempered the clay and carried the finished work to the furnace.

Now, though none would have guessed it, in this workshop all the labourers were Christians, and the product of their toil was cast into a common treasury on the proceeds of which they lived, taking, each of them, such share as their elders might decree, and giving the surplus to brethren who had need, or to the sick. Connected with these shops were lodging houses, mean enough to look at, but clean within. At the top of one of them, up three flights of narrow stairs, Miriam and Nehushta dwelt in a large attic that was very hot when the sun shone on the roof, and very cold in the bitter winds and rains of winter. In other respects, however, the room was not unpleasant, since being so high there were few smells and little noise; also the air that blew in at the windows was fresh and odorous of the open lands beyond the city.

So there they dwelt in peace, for none came to search for the costly and beautiful Pearl-Maiden in those squalid courts, occupied by working folk of the meaner sort. By day they laboured, and at night they rested, ministering and ministered to in the community of Christian brotherhood, and, notwithstanding their fears and anxieties for themselves and another, were happier than they had been for years. So the weeks went by.

Very soon tidings came to them, for these Christians knew of all that passed in the great city; also, when they met in the catacombs at night, as was their custom, especially upon the Lord's Day, Julia gave them news. From her they learned that they had done wisely to flee her house.

Within three hours of their departure, indeed before Julia had returned there, officers arrived to inquire whether they had seen anything of the Jewish captive named Pearl-Maiden, who had been sold in the Forum on the previous night, and, as they said, escaped from her purchaser, on whose behalf they searched. Gallus received them, and, not being a Christian, lied boldly, vowing that he had seen nothing of the girl since he gave her over into the charge of the servants of Cæsar upon the morning of the Triumph. So suspecting no guile they departed and troubled his household no more.

From the palace of Domitian Marcus was taken to his prison near the Temple of Mars. Here, because of his wealth and rank, because also he made appeal to Cæsar and was therefore as yet uncondemned of any crime, he found himself well treated. Two good rooms were given him to live in, and his own steward, Stephanus, was allowed to attend him and provide him with food and all he needed. Also upon giving his word that he would attempt no escape, he was allowed to walk in the gardens between the prison and the Temple, and to receive his friends at any hour of the day. His first visitor was the chamberlain, Saturius, who began by condoling with him over his misfortune and most undeserved position. Marcus cut him short.

"Why am I here?" he asked.

"Because, most noble Marcus, you have been so unlucky as to incur the displeasure of a very powerful man."

"Why does Domitian persecute me?" he asked again.

"How innocent are you soldiers!" said the chamberlain. "I will answer your question by another. Why do you buy beautiful captives upon whom royalty chances to have set its heart?"

Marcus thought a moment, then said, "Is there any way out of this trouble?"

"My lord Marcus, I came to show you one. Nobody really believes that you of all men failed in your duty out there in Jerusalem. Why, the thing is absurd, as even those carpet-captains before whom you were tried knew well. Still, your position is most awkward. There is evidence against you—of a sort. Vespasian will not interfere, for he is aware that this is some private matter of Domitian's, and having had one quarrel with his son over the captive, Pearl-Maiden, he does not wish for another over the man who bought her. No, he will say—this prefect was one of the friends and officers of Titus, let Titus settle the affair as it may please him when he returns."

"At least Titus will do me justice," said Marcus.

"Yes, without doubt, but what will that justice be? Titus issued an edict. Have you ever known him to go back upon his edicts, even to save a friend? Titus declared throughout his own camps those Romans who were taken prisoner by the Jews to be worthy of death or disgrace, and two of them, common men and cowards, have been publicly disgraced in the eyes of Rome. You were taken prisoner by the Jews and have returned alive, unfortunately for yourself, to incur the dislike of Domitian, who has raked up a matter that otherwise never would have been mooted."

"Now," he says to Titus—"Show justice and no favour, as you showed in the case of the captive Pearl-Maiden, whom you refused to the prayer of your only brother, saying that she must be sold according to your decree. Even if he loves you dearly, as I believe he does, what, my lord Marcus, can Titus answer to that argument, especially as he also seeks no further quarrel with Domitian?"

"You said you came to show me a way to safety—yet you tell me that my feet are set in the path of disgrace and death. Must this way of yours, then, be paved with gold?"

"No," answered Saturius drily, "with pearls. Oh! I will be plain. Give up that necklace—and its wearer. What do you answer?"

Now Marcus understood, and a saying that he heard on the lips of Miriam arose in his mind, though he knew not whence it came.

"I answer," he said with set face and flashing eyes, "that I will not cast pearls before swine."

"A pretty message from a prisoner to his judge," replied the chamberlain with a curious smile. "But have no fear, noble Marcus, it shall not be delivered. I am not paid to tell my royal master the truth. Think again."

"I have thought," answered Marcus. "I do not know where the maiden is and therefore cannot deliver her to Domitian, nor would I if I could. Rather will I be disgraced and perish."

"I suppose," mused Saturius, "that this is what they call true love, and to speak plainly," he added with a burst of candour, "I find it admirable and worthy of a noble Roman. My lord Marcus, my mission has failed, yet I pray that the Fates may order your deliverance from your enemies, and, in reward for these persecutions, bring back to you unharmed that maiden whom you desire, but whom I go to seek. Farewell."

Two days later Stephanus, the steward of Marcus who waited upon him in his prison, announced that a man who said his name was Septimus wished speech with him, but would say nothing of his business.

"Admit him," said Marcus, "for I grow weary of my own company," and letting his head fall upon his hand he stared through the bars of his prison window.

Presently he heard a sound behind him, and looked round to see an old man clad in the robe of a master-workman, whose pure and noble face seemed in a strange contrast to his rough garments and toil-scarred hands.

"Be seated and tell me your business," said Marcus courteously, and with a bow his visitor obeyed.

"My business, my lord Marcus," he said in an educated and refined voice, "is to minister to those who are in trouble."

"Then, sir, your feet have led you aright," answered Marcus with a sad laugh, "for this is the house of trouble and you see I am its inhabitant."

"I know, and I know the cause."

Marcus looked at him curiously. "Are you a Christian, sir?" he asked. "Nay, do not fear to answer; I have friends who are Christians," and he sighed, "nor could I harm you if I would, who wish to harm none, least of all a Christian."

"My lord Marcus, I fear hurt at no man's hand; also the days of Nero have gone by and Vespasian reigns, who molests us not. I am Cyril, a bishop of the Christians in Rome, and if you will hear me I am come to preach to you my faith, which, I trust, may yet be yours."

Marcus stared at the man; it was to him a matter of amazement that this priest should take so much trouble for a stranger. Then a thought struck him and he asked:

"What fee do you charge for these lessons in a new religion?"

The bishop's pale face flushed.

"Sir," he answered, "if you wish to reject my message, do it without insult. I do not sell the grace of God for lucre."

Again Marcus was impressed.

"Your pardon," he said, "yet I have known priests take money, though it is true they were never of your faith. Who told you about me?"

"One, my lord Marcus, to whom you have behaved well," answered Cyril gravely.

Marcus sprang from his seat.

"Do you mean—do you mean—?" he began and paused, looking round him fearfully.

"Yes," replied the bishop in a whisper, "I mean Miriam. Fear not, she and her companions are in my charge, and for the present, safe. Seek to know no more, lest perchance their secret should be wrung from you. I and her brethren in the Lord will protect her to the last."

Marcus began to pour out his thanks.

"Thank me not," interrupted Cyril, "for what is at once my duty and my joy."

"Friend Cyril," said Marcus, "the maid is in great danger. I have just learned that Domitian's spies hunt through Rome to find her, who, when she is found, will be spirited to his palace and a fate that you can guess. She must escape from Rome. Let her fly to Tyre, where she has friends and property. There, if she lies hid a while, she will be molested by none."

The bishop shook his head.

"I have thought of it," he said, "but it is scarcely possible. The officers at every port have orders to search all ships that sail with passengers, and detain any woman on them who answers to the description of her who was called Pearl-Maiden. This I know for certain, for I also have my officers, more faithful perhaps than those of Cæsar," and he smiled.

"Is there then no means to get her out of Rome and across the sea?"

"I can think of only one, which would cost more money than we poor Christians can command. It is that a ship be bought in the name of some merchant and manned with sailors who can be trusted, such as I know how to find. Then she could be taken aboard at night, for on such a vessel there would be no right of search nor any to betray."

"Find the ship and trusty men and I will find the money," said Marcus, "for I still have gold at hand and the means of raising more."

"I will make inquiries," answered Cyril, "and speak with you further on the matter. Indeed it is not necessary that you should give this money, since such a ship and her cargo, if she comes there safely, should sell at a great profit in the Eastern ports. Meanwhile have no fear; in the protection of God and her brethren the maid is safe."

"I hope so," said Marcus devoutly. "Now, if you have the time to spare, tell me of this God of whom you Christians speak so much but who seems so far away from man."

"But who, in the words of the great apostle, my master, in truth is not far from any one of us," answered Cyril. "Now hearken, and may your heart be opened."

Then he began his labour of conversion, reasoning till the sun sank and it was time for the prison gates to close.

"Come to me again," said Marcus as they parted, "I would hear more."

"Of Miriam or of my message?" asked Cyril with a smile.

"Of both," answered Marcus.

Four days went by before Cyril returned. They were heavy days for Marcus, since on the morrow of the bishop's visit he had learned that as Saturius had foretold, Vespasian refused to consider his case, saying that it must abide the decision of Titus when he came back to Rome. Meanwhile, he commanded that the accused officer should remain in prison, but that no judgment should issue against him. Here, then, Marcus was doomed to lie, fretting out his heart like a lion in a cage.

From Cyril Marcus learned that Miriam was well and sent him her greetings, since she dared neither visit him nor write. The bishop told him also that he had found a certain Grecian mariner, Hector by name, a Roman citizen, who was a Christian and faithful. This man desired to sail for the coasts of Syria and was competent to steer a vessel thither. Also he thought that he could collect a crew of Christians and Jews who might be trusted. Lastly, he knew of several small galleys that were for sale, one of which, named the *Luna,* was a very good ship and almost new. Cyril told him, moreover, that he had seen Gallus and his wife Julia, and that these good people, having no more ties in Rome, partly because they desired to leave the city, and partly for love of Miriam, though more the second reason than the first, were willing to sell their house and goods and to sail with her to Syria.

Marcus asked how much money would be needed, and when Cyril named the sum, sent for Stephanus and commanded him to raise it and to pay it over to the craftsman Septimus, taking his receipt in discharge. This Septimus promised to do readily enough by a certain day, believing that the gold was needed for his master's ransom. Then having settled all as well as might be, Cyril took up his tale and preached to Marcus of the Saviour of the world with great earnestness and power.

Thus the days went on, and twice or thrice in every week Cyril visited Marcus, giving him tidings and instructing him in the Faith. Now the ship *Luna* was bought and the most of her crew hired; also a cargo of such goods as would be salable in Syria was being laid into her hold at Ostia, the Greek, Hector, giving it out that this was a private venture of his own and some other merchants. As the man was well known for a bold trader who had bought and sold in many lands his tale caused neither wonder nor suspicion, none knowing that the capital was furnished by the steward of the prisoner Marcus through him who passed as the master craftsman and contractor Septimus. Indeed, until the after days Miriam did not know this herself, for it was kept from her by the special command of Marcus, and if Nehushta guessed the truth she held her tongue.

Two full months had gone by. Marcus still languished in prison, for Titus had not yet returned to Rome, but as he learned from Cyril, Domitian wearied somewhat of his fruitless search for Miriam, although he still vowed vengeance against the rival who had robbed him. The ship *Luna* was laden and ready for sea; indeed, if the wind and weather were favourable, she was to sail within a week. Gallus and Julia, having wound up their affairs, had removed to Ostia, whither Miriam was to be brought secretly on the night of the sailing of the *Luna*. Marcus was now at heart a Christian, but as yet had refused to accept baptism. Thus matters stood when Cyril visited the prison bringing with him Miriam's farewell message to her lover. It was very short.

"Tell Marcus," she said, "that I go because he bids me, and that I know not whether we shall meet again. Say that perhaps it is best that we should not meet, since for reasons which he knows, even if he should still wish it, we may not marry. Say that in life or death I am his, and his only, and that until my last hour my thought and prayer will be for him. May he be delivered from all those troubles which, as I fear, I have brought upon him, through no will of mine. May he forgive me for them and let my love and gratitude make some amends for all that I have done amiss."

To this Marcus answered: "Tell Miriam that from my heart I thank her for her message, and that my desire is that she should be gone from Rome so soon as may be, since here danger dogs her steps. Tell her that although it is true that mine has brought me shame and sorrow, still I give her love for love, and that if I come living from my prison I will follow her to Tyre and speak further of these matters. If I die, I pray that good fortune may attend her and that from time to time she will make the offering of an hour's thought to the spirit which once was Marcus."

Chapter 28

The Lamp

If Domitian at length slackened in his fruitless search for Miriam, Caleb, whose whole heart was in the hunt, proved more diligent. Still, he could find no trace of her. At first he made sure that if she was in Rome she would return to visit her friends and protectors, Gallus and his wife, and in the hope of thus discovering her, Caleb caused a constant watch to be kept on their abode. But Miriam never came there, nor, although their footsteps were dogged from day to day, did they lead him to her, since in truth Julia and Miriam met only in the catacombs, where he and his spies dared not venture. Soon, however, Gallus discovered that his home was kept under observation and its inmates tracked from place to place. It was this knowledge indeed which, more than any other circumstance, brought him to make up his mind to depart from Rome and dwell in Syria, since he said that he would no longer live in a city where night by night he and his were hunted like jackals. But when he left for Ostia, to wait there till the ship *Luna* was ready, Caleb followed him, and in that small town soon found out all his plans, learning that he meant to sail with his wife in the vessel. Then, as he could hear nothing of Miriam, he returned to Rome.

After all it was by chance that he discovered her and not through his own cleverness. Needing a lamp for his chamber he entered a shop where such things were sold, and examined those that the merchant offered to him. Presently he perceived one of the strange design of two palms with intertwining trunks and feathery heads nodding apart, having a lamp hanging by a little chain from the topmost frond of each of them. The shape of the trees struck him as familiar, and he let his eye run down their stems until it reached the base, which, to support so tall a piece, was large. Yes, the palms grew upon a little bank, and there beneath the water rippled, while between bank and water was a long, smooth stone, pointed at one end. Then in a flash Caleb recognised the place, as well he might, seeing that on many and many an evening had he and Miriam sat side by side upon that stone, angling for fish in the muddy stream of Jordan. There was no doubt about it, and, look! half hidden in the shadow of the stone lay a great fish, the biggest that ever he had caught—he could swear to it, for its back fin was split.

A mist came before Caleb's eyes and in it across the years he saw himself a boy again. There he stood, his rod of reed bent double and the thin line strained almost to breaking, while on the waters of Jordan a great fish splashed and rolled.

"I cannot pull him in," he cried. "The line will never bear it and the bank is steep. Oh! Miriam, we shall lose him!"

Then there was a splash, and, behold! the girl at his side had sprung into the swiftly running river. Though its waters, reaching to her neck, washed her down the stream, she hugged to her young breast that great, slippery fish, yes, and gripped its back fin between her teeth, till with the aid of his reed rod he drew them both to land.

"I will buy that lamp," said Caleb presently. "The design pleases me. What artist made it?"

The merchant shrugged his shoulders.

"Sir, I do not know," he answered. "These goods are supplied to us with many others, such as joinery and carving, by one Septimus, who is a contractor and, they say, a head priest among the Christians, employing many hands at his shops in the poor streets yonder. One or more of them must be designers of taste, since of late we have received from him some lamps of great beauty."

Then the man was called away to attend to another customer and Caleb paid for his lamp.

That evening at dusk Caleb, bearing the lamp in his hand, found his way to the workshop of Septimus, only to discover that the part of the factory where lamps were moulded was already closed. A girl who had just shut the door, seeing him stand perplexed before it, asked civilly if she could help him.

"Maiden," he answered, "I am in trouble who wish to find her who moulded this lamp, so that I may order others, but am told that she has left her work for the day."

"Yes," said the maiden, looking at the lamp, which evidently she recognised. "It is pretty, is it not? Well, cannot you return to-morrow?"

"Alas! no, I expect to be leaving Rome for a while, so I fear that I must go elsewhere."

The girl reflected to herself that it would be a pity if the order were lost, and with it the commission which she might divide with the maker of the lamp. "It is against the rules, but I will show you where she lives," she said, "and if she is there, which is probable, for I have never seen her or her companion go out at night, you can tell her your wishes."

Caleb thanked the girl and followed her through sundry tortuous lanes to a court surrounded by old houses.

"If you go in there," she said, pointing to a certain doorway, "and climb to the top of the stairs, I forget whether there are three or four flights, you will find the makers of the lamp in the roof-rooms—oh! sir, I thank you, but I expected nothing. Good-night."

At length Caleb stood at the head of the stairs, which were both steep, narrow, and in the dark hard to climb. Before him, at the end of a rickety landing, a small ill-fitting door stood ajar. There was light within the room beyond, and from it came a sound of voices. Caleb crept up to the door and listened, for as the floor below was untenanted he knew that none could see him. Bending down he looked through the space between the door and its framework and his heart stood still. There, standing full in the lamplight, clothed in a pure white robe, for her rough working dress lay upon a stool beside her, was Miriam herself, her elbow leaning on the curtained window-place. She was talking to Nehushta, who, her back bent almost double over a little charcoal fire, was engaged in cooking their supper.

"Think," she was saying, "only think, Nou, our last night in this hateful city, and then, instead of that stifling workshop and the terror of Domitian, the open sea and the fresh salt wind and nobody to fear but God. *Luna!* Is it not a beautiful name for a ship? I can see her, all silver—"

"Peace," said Nehushta. "Are you mad, girl, to talk so loud? I though I heard a sound upon the stairs just now."

"It is only the rats," answered Miriam cheerfully, "no one ever comes up here. I tell you that were it not for Marcus I could weep with joy."

Caleb crept back to the head of the stairs and down several steps, which he began to re-ascend noisily, grumbling at their gloom and steepness. Then, before the women even had time to shut the door, he thrust it wide and walked straight into the room.

"Your pardon," he began, then added quietly, "Why, Miriam, when we parted on the gate Nicanor, who could have foretold that we should live to meet again here in a Roman attic? And you, Nehushta. Why, we were separated in the fray outside the Temple walls, though, indeed, I think that I saw you in a strange place some months ago, namely, the slave-ring on the Forum."

"Caleb," asked Miriam in a hollow voice, "what is your business here?"

"Well, Miriam, it began with a desire for a replica of this lamp, which reminds me of a spot familiar to my childhood. Do you remember it? Now that I have found who is the lamp's maker—"

"Cease fooling," broke in Nehushta. "Bird of ill-omen, you have come to drag your prey back to the shame and ruin which she has escaped."

"I was not always called thus," answered Caleb, flushing, "when I rescued you from the house at Tyre for instance, or when I risked my life, Miriam, to throw you food upon the gate Nicanor. Nay, I come to save you from Domitian—"

"And to take her for yourself," answered Nehushta. "Oh! we Christians also have eyes to see and ears to hear, and, black-hearted traitor that you are, we know all your shame. We know of your bargain with the chamberlain of Domitian, by which the body of the slave was to be the price of the life of her buyer. We know how you swore away the honour of your rival, Marcus, with false testimony, and how from week to week you have quartered Rome as a vulture quarters the sky till at length you have smelt out the quarry. Well, she is helpless, but One is strong, and may His vengeance fall upon your life and soul."

Suddenly Nehushta's voice, that had risen to a scream, died away, and she stood before him threatening him with her bony fists, and searching his face with her burning eyes, a vengeance incarnate.

"Peace, woman, peace," said Caleb, shrinking back before her. "Spare your reproaches; if I have sinned much it is because I have loved more—"

"And hate most of all," added Nehushta.

"Oh! Caleb," broke in Miriam, "if as you say you love me, why should you deal thus with me? You know well that I do not love you after this sort, no, and never can, and even if you keep me from Domitian, who does but make a tool of you, what would it advantage you to take a woman who leaves her heart elsewhere? Also I may never marry you for that same reason that I may not marry Marcus, because my faith is and must remain apart from yours. Would you make a base slave of your old playmate, Caleb? Would you bring her to the level of a dancing-girl? Oh! let me go in peace."

"Upon the ship *Luna,*" said Caleb sullenly.

Miriam gasped! So he knew their plans.

"Yes," she replied desperately, "upon the ship *Luna,* to find such a fate as Heaven may give me; at least to be at peace and free. For your soul's sake, Caleb, let me go. Once years ago you swore that you would not force yourself upon me against my will. Will you break that oath to-day?"

"I swore also, Miriam, that it should go ill with any man who came between you and me. Shall I break that oath to-day? Give yourself to me of your own will and save Marcus. Refuse and I will bring him to his death. Choose now between me and your lover's life."

"Are you a coward that you should lay such a choice upon me, Caleb?"

"Call me what you will. Choose."

Miriam clasped her hands and for a moment stood looking upwards. Then a light of purpose grew upon her face and she answered:

"Caleb, I have chosen. Do your worst. The fate of Marcus is not in my hands, or your hands, but in the hands of God; nor, unless He wills it, can one hair of his head be harmed by you or by Domitian. For is it not written in the book of your own Law that 'the King's heart is in the hand of the Lord, he turneth it whithersoever he will.' But my honour is my own, and to stain it would be a sin for which I alone must answer to Heaven and to Marcus, dead or living—Marcus, who would curse and spit upon me did I attempt to buy his safety at such a price."

"Is that your last word, Miriam?"

"It is. If it pleases you by false witness and by murder to destroy the man who once spared you, then if such a thing be suffered, have your will and reap its fruits. I make no bargain with you, for myself or for him—do your worst to both of us."

"So be it," said Caleb with a bitter laugh, "but I think that the ship *Luna* will lack her fairest passenger."

Miriam sank down upon a seat and covered her face with her hands, a piteous sight in her misery and the terror which, notwithstanding her bold words, she could not conceal. Caleb walked to the door and paused there, while the white-haired Nehushta stood by the brazier of charcoal and watched them both with her fierce eyes. Presently Caleb glanced round at Miriam crouched by the window and a strange new look came into his face.

"I cannot do it," he said slowly, each word falling heavily from his lips like single rain-drops from a cloud, or the slow blood from a mortal wound.

Miriam let her hands slip from her face and stared at him.

"Miriam," he said, "you are right; I have sinned against you and this man Marcus. Now I will expiate my sin. Your secret is safe with me, and since you hate me I will never see you more. Miriam, we look upon each other for the last time. Further, if I can, I will work for the deliverance of Marcus and help him to join you in Tyre, whither the *Luna* is bound—is she not? Farewell?"

Once again he turned to go, but it would seem that his eyes were blinded, or his brain was dulled by the agony that worked within. At least Caleb caught his foot in the ancient uneven boards, stumbled, and fell heavily upon his face. Instantly, with a low hiss of hate and a spring like that of a cat, Nehushta was upon him. Thrusting her knees upon his back she seized the nape of his neck with her left hand and with her right drew a dagger from her bosom.

"Forbear!" said Miriam. "Touch him with that knife and

we part forever. Nay, I mean it. I myself will hand you to the officer, even if he hales me to Domitian."

Then Nehushta rose to her feet.

"Fool!" she said, "fool, to trust to that man of double moods, whose mercy to-night will be vengeance to-morrow. Oh! you are undone! Alas! you are undone!"

Regaining his feet Caleb looked at her contemptuously.

"Had you stabbed she might have been undone indeed," he said. "Now, as of old, there is little wisdom in that gray head of yours, Nehushta; nor can your hate suffer you to understand the intermingled good and evil of my heart." Then he advanced to Miriam, lifted her hand and kissed it. With a sudden movement she proffered him her brow.

"Nay," he said, "tempt me not, it is not for me. Farewell."

Another instant and he was gone.

It would seem that Caleb kept his word, for three days later the vessel *Luna* sailed unmolested from the port of Ostia in the charge of the Greek captain Hector, having on board Miriam, Nehushta, Julia, and Gallus.

Within a week of this sailing Titus at length returned to Rome. Here in due course the case of Marcus was brought before him by the prisoner's friends, together with a demand that he should be granted a new and open trial for the clearing of his honour. Titus, who for his own reasons refused to see Marcus, listened patiently, then gave his decision.

He rejoiced, he said, to learn that his close friend and trusted officer was still alive, since he had long mourned him as dead. He grieved that in his absence he should have been put upon his trial on the charge of having been taken captive, living, by the Jews, which, if Marcus upon his arrival in Rome had at once reported himself to him, would not have happened. He dismissed all accusations against his military honour and courage as mere idle talk, since he had a hundred times proved him to be the bravest of men, and knew, moreover, something of the circumstances under which he was captured. But, however willing he might be to do so, he was unable for public reasons to disregard the fact that he had been duly convicted by a court- martial, under the Prince Domitian, of having broken the command of his general and suffered himself to be taken prisoner alive. To do so would be to proclaim himself, Titus, unjust, who had caused others to suffer for this same offence, and to offer insult to the prince, his brother, who in the exercise of his discretion as commander in his absence, had thought fit to order the trial. Still, his punishment should be of the lightest possible. He commanded that on leaving his prison Marcus should go straight to his own house by night, so that there might be no public talk or demonstration among his friends, and there make such arrangement of his affairs as seemed good to him. Further, he commanded that within ten days he should leave Italy, to dwell or travel abroad for a period of three years, unless the time should be shortened by some special decree. After the lapse of these three years he would be free to return to Rome. This was his judgment and it could not be altered.

As it chanced, it was the chamberlain Saturius who first communicated the Imperial decree to Marcus. Hurrying straight from the palace to the prison he was admitted into the prisoner's chamber.

"Well," said Marcus, looking up, "what evil tidings have you now?"

"None, none," answered Saturius. "I have very good tidings, and that is why I run so fast. You are only banished for three years, thanks to my secret efforts," and he smiled craftily. "Even your property is left to you, a fact which will, I trust, enable you to reward your friends for their labours on your behalf."

"Tell me all," and the rogue obeyed, while Marcus listened with a face of stone.

"Why did Titus decide thus?" he asked when it was finished. "Speak frankly, man, if you wish for a reward."

"Because, noble Marcus, Domitian had been with him beforehand and told him that if he reversed his public judgment it would be a cause of open quarrel between them. This, Cæsar, who fears his brother, does not seek. That is why he would not see you, lest his love for his friend should overcome his reason."

"So the prince is still my enemy?"

"Yes, and more bitter than before, since he cannot find the Pearl- Maiden, and is sure that you have spirited her away. Be advised by me and leave Rome quickly, lest worse things befall you."

"Aye," said Marcus, "I will leave Rome quickly, for how shall I abide here who have lost my honour. Yet first it may please your master to know that by now the lady whom he seeks is far across the sea. Now get you gone, you fox, for I desire to be alone."

The face of Saturius became evil.

"Is that all you have to say?" he asked. "Am I to win no reward?"

"If you stay longer," said Marcus, "you will win one which you do not desire."

Then Saturius went, but without the door he turned and shook his fist towards the chamber he had left.

"Fox," he muttered. "He called me fox and gave me nothing. Well, foxes may find some pickings on his bones."

The chamberlain's road to the palace ran past the place of business of the merchant Demetrius. He stopped and looked at it. "Perhaps this one will be more liberal," he said to himself, and entered.

In his private office he found Caleb alone, his face buried in his hands. Seating himself he plunged into his tale, ending it with an apology to Caleb for the lightness of the sentence inflicted upon Marcus.

"Titus would do no more," he said; "indeed, were it not for the fear of Domitian, he could have not have been brought to do so much, for he loves the man, who has been a prefect of his bodyguard, and was deeply grieved that he must disgrace him. Still, disgraced he is, aye, and he feels it; therefore I trust that you, most generous Demetrius, who hate him, will remember the service of your servant in this matter."

"Yes," said Caleb quietly, "fear not, you shall be well paid, for you have done your best."

"I thank you, friend," answered Saturius, rubbing his hands, "and, after all, things may be better than they seem. That insolent fool let out just now that the girl about whom there is all this bother has been smuggled away somewhere across the seas. When Domitian learns that he will be so mad with anger that he may be worked up to take a little vengeance of his own upon the person of the noble Marcus, who has thus contrived to trick him. Also Marcus shall not get the Pearl- Maiden, for the prince will cause her to be followed and brought back—to you, worthy Demetrius."

"Then," answered Caleb, slowly, "he must seek for her, not across the sea, but in its depths."

"What do you mean?"

"I mean that I have tidings that Pearl-Maiden escaped in the ship *Luna* hard upon a month ago. This morning the captain and some mariners of the galley *Imperatrix* arrived in Rome. They report that they met a great gale off Rhegium, and towards the end of it saw a vessel sink. Afterwards they picked up a sailor clinging to a piece of wood, who told them that the ship's name was *Luna* and that she foundered with all hands."

"Have you seen this sailor?"

"No; he died of exhaustion soon after he was rescued; but I have seen the men of the galley, who brought me note of certain goods consigned to me in her hold. They repeated this story to me with their own lips."

"So, after all, she whom so many sought was destined to the arms of Neptune, as became a pearl," reflected Saturius. "Well, well, as Domitian cannot be revenged upon Neptune he will be the more wroth with the man who sent her to that god. Now I go to tell him all these tidings and learn his mind."

"You will return and acquaint me with it, will you not?" asked Caleb, looking up.

"Certainly, and at once. Our account is not yet balanced, most generous Demetrius."

"No," answered Caleb, "our accounts are not yet balanced."

Two hours later the chamberlain reappeared in the office.

"Well," said Caleb, "how does it go?"

"Ill, very ill for Marcus, and well, very well for those who hate him, as you and I do, friend. Oh! never have I seen my Imperial master so enraged. Indeed, when he learned that Pearl-Maiden had escaped and was drowned, so that he could have no hope of her this side the Styx, it was almost dangerous to be near to him. He cursed Titus for the lightness of his sentence; he cursed you; he cursed *me*. But I turned his wrath into the right channel. I showed him that for all these ills Marcus, and Marcus alone, is to blame, Marcus who is to pay the price of them with a three years' pleasant banishment from Rome, which doubtless, will be remitted presently. I tell you that Domitian wept and gnashed his teeth at the thought of it, until I showed him a better plan—knowing that it would please you, friend Demetrius."

"What plan?"

Saturius rose, and having looked round to see that the door was fastened, came and whispered into Caleb's ear.

"Look you, after sunset to-night, that is within two hours, Marcus is to be put out of his prison and conducted to the side door of his own house, that beneath the archway, where he is ordered to remain until he leaves Rome. In this house is no one except an old man, the steward Stephanus, and a slave woman. Well, before he gets there, certain trusty fellows, such as Domitian knows how to lay his hands upon, will have entered the house, and having secured the steward and the woman, will await the coming of Marcus beneath the archway. You can guess the rest. Is it not well conceived?"

"Very well," answered Caleb. "But may there not be suspicion?"

"None, none. Who would dare to suspect Domitian? A private crime, doubtless! The rich have so many enemies."

What Saturius did not add was that nobody would suspect Domitian because the masked bravoes were instructed to inform the steward and the slave when they had bound and gagged them, that they were hired to do the deed of blood by a certain merchant named Demetrius, otherwise Caleb the Jew, who had an ancient quarrel against Marcus, which, already, he had tried to satisfy by giving false evidence before the court-martial.

"Now," went on Saturius, "I must be going, for there are one or two little things which need attention, and time presses. Shall we balance that account, friend Demetrius?"

"Certainly," said Caleb, and taking a roll of gold from a drawer he pushed it across the table.

Saturius shook his head sadly. "I laid it at twice as much," he said. "Think how you hate him and how richly your hate will be fed. First disgraced unjustly, he, one of the best soldiers and bravest captains in the army, and then hacked to death by cutthroats in the doorway of his own house. What more could you want?"

"Nothing," answered Caleb. "Only the man isn't dead yet. Sometimes the Fates have strange surprises for us mortals, friend Saturius."

"Dead? He will be dead soon enough."

"Good. You shall have the rest of the money when I have seen his body. No, I don't want any bungling and that's the best way to make certain."

"I wonder," thought Saturius, as he departed out of the office and this history, "I wonder how I shall manage to get the balance of my fee before they have my Jewish friend by the heels. But it can be arranged—doubtless it can be arranged."

When he had gone, Caleb, who, it would seem, also had things which needed attention and felt that time pressed, took pen and wrote a short letter. Next he summoned a clerk and gave orders that it was to be delivered two hours after sunset—not before.

Meanwhile, he enclosed it in an outer wrapping so that the address was not seen. This done, he sat still for a time, his lips moving, almost as though he were engaged in prayer. Then, seeing that it was the hour of sunset, he rose, wrapped himself in a long dark cloak, such as was worn by Roman officers, and went out.

Chapter 29

How Marcus Changed His Faith

Caleb was not the only one who heard the evil tidings of the ship *Luna;* it came to the ears of the bishop Cyril also, since little of any moment passed within the city of Rome which the Christians did not know.

Like Caleb, he satisfied himself of the truth of the matter by an interview with the captain of the *Imperatrix.* Then with a sorrowful heart he departed to the prison near the Temple of Mars. Here the warden told him that Marcus wished to see no one, but answering "Friend, my business will not wait," he pushed past the man and entered the room beyond. Marcus was standing up in the centre of it, in his hand a drawn sword of the short Roman pattern, which, on catching sight of his visitor, he cast upon the table with an exclamation of impatience. It fell beside a letter addressed to "The Lady Miriam in Tyre. To be given into her own hand."

"Peace be with you," said the bishop, searching his face with his quiet eyes.

"I thank you, friend," answered Marcus, smiling strangely, "I need peace, and—seek it."

"Son," asked the bishop, "what were you about to do?"

"Friend," answered Marcus, "If you desire to know, I

was about to fall upon my sword. One more minute and I should have been dead. They brought it me with the cloak and other things. It was thoughtful of them, and I guessed their meaning."

Cyril lifted the sword from the table and cast it into a corner of the room.

"God be thanked," he said, "Who led my feet here in time to save you from this sin. Why, because it has pleased Him to take her life, should you seek to take your own?"

"Her life?" said Marcus. "What dreadful words are these. Her life! Whose life?"

"The life of Miriam. I came to tell you. She is drowned upon the seas with all her company."

For a moment Marcus stood swaying to and fro like a drunken man. Then he said:

"Is it so indeed? Well, the more reason that I should make haste to follow her. Begone and leave me to do the deed alone," and he stepped towards the sword.

Cyril set his foot upon the shining blade.

"What is this madness?" he asked. "If you did not know of Miriam's death, why do you desire to kill yourself?"

"Because I have lost more than Miriam. Man, they have robbed me of my honour. By the decree of Titus, I, Marcus, am branded as a coward. Yes, Titus, at whose side I have fought a score of battles—Titus, from whom I have warded many a blow—has banished me from Rome."

"Tell me of this thing," said Cyril.

So Marcus told him all. Cyril listened in silence, then said sternly:

"Is it for this that you would kill yourself? Is your honour lessened by a decree based upon false evidence, and given for reasons of policy? Do you cease to be honourable because others are dishonourable, and would you—a soldier—fly from the battle? Now, indeed, Marcus, you show yourself a coward."

"How can I live on who am so shamed?" he asked passionately. "My friends knew that I could not live, and that is why they wrapped a sword in yonder cloak and sent it me. Also Miriam, you say, is dead."

"Satan sent it to you, Marcus, desiring to fashion of your foolish pride a ladder down which you might climb to hell. Cast aside this base temptation which wears the mask of false honour; face your trouble like a man, and conquer it by innocence—and faith."

"Miriam! What of Miriam?"

"Yes, what of Miriam? How would she welcome you yonder, who come to greet her with your blood upon your hands? Oh! son, do you not understand that this is the trial laid upon you? You have been brought low that you might rise high. Once the world gave you all it had to give. You were rich, you were a captain among captains; you were high- born; men called you 'The Fortunate.' Then Christ appealed to you in vain, you put Him by. What had you to do with the crucified carpenter of Galilee? Now by the plotting of your foes you have fallen. No longer do you rank high in your trade of blood. You are dismissed its service and an exile. The lesson of life has come home to you, therefore you seek to escape from life rather than bide in it to do your duty through good and ill, heedless of what men may say, and finding peace in the verdict of your own conscience. Let Him Whom you put by in your hours of pomp come to you now. Carry your cross with your shame as He carried His in His shame. In His light find light, in His peace find peace, and at the end her who has been taken from you awhile. Has my spirit spoken in vain with your spirit during all these many weeks, son Marcus? Already you have told me that you believe, and now at the first breath of trouble will you go back upon that which you know to be the Truth? Oh! once more listen to me, that your eyes may be opened before it is too late."

"Speak on, I hear you," said Marcus with a sigh.

So Cyril pleaded with him in the passion of one inspired, and as Marcus hearkened his heart was softened and his purpose turned.

"I knew it all before, I believed it all before," he said at length, "but I would not accept your baptism and become a member of your Church."

"Why not, son?"

"Because had I done so she would have thought and you might have thought, and perhaps I myself should have thought that I did it, as once I offered to do, to win her whom I desired above all things on earth. Now she is dead and it is otherwise. Shrive me, father, and do your office."

So there in the prison cell the bishop Cyril took water and baptised the Roman Marcus into the body of the Christian Church.

"What shall I do now?" Marcus asked as he rose from his knees. "Once Cæsar was my master, now you speak with the voice of Cæsar. Command me."

"I do not speak, Christ speaks. Listen. I am called by the Church to go to Alexandria in Egypt, whither I sail within three days. Will you who are exiled from Rome come with me? There I can find you work to do."

"I have said that you are Cæsar," answered Marcus. "Now it is sunset and I am free; accompany me to my house, I pray you, for there much business waits me in which I need counsel, who am overborne."

So presently the gates were opened as Titus had commanded, and they went forth, attended only by a guard of two men, walking unnoted through the streets to the palace in the Via Agrippa.

"There is the door," said the sergeant of the guard, pointing to the side entrance of the house. "Enter with your friend and, noble Marcus, fare you well."

So they went to the archway, and finding the door ajar, passed through and shut it behind them.

"For a house where there is much to steal this is ill guarded, son. In Rome an open gate ought to have a watchman," said Cyril as he groped his way through the darkness of the arch.

"My steward Stephanus should be at hand, for the jailer advised him of my coming—who never thought to come," began Marcus, then of a sudden stumbled heavily and was silent.

"What is it?" asked Cyril.

"By the feel one who is drunken—or dead. Some beggar, perhaps, who sleeps off his liquor here."

By now Cyril was through the archway and in the little courtyard beyond.

"A light burns in that window," he said. "Come, you know the path, guide me to it. We can return to this sleeper."

"Who seems hard to wake," added Marcus, as he led the way across the courtyard to the door of the offices. This also proved to be open and by it they entered the room where the steward kept his books and slept. Upon the table a lamp was burning, that which they had seen through the casement. Its light showed them a strange sight. An iron- bound box that was chained to the wall had been broken open and its contents rifled, for papers were strewn here and there, and on them lay an empty leathern money-bag. The furniture also was overturned as though in some struggle, while among it, one in the corner of the room and one beneath the marble table, which was too heavy to be moved, lay two figures, those of a man and a woman.

"Murderers have been here," said Cyril with a groan.

Marcus snatched the lamp from the table and held it to the face of the man in the corner.

"It is Stephanus," he said, "Stephanus bound and gagged, but living, and the other is the slave woman. Hold the lamp while I loose them," and drawing his short sword, he cut away the bonds, first of the one and then of the other. "Speak, man, speak!" he said, as Stephanus struggled to his feet. "What has chanced here?"

For some moments the old steward stared at him with round, frightened eyes. Then he gasped:

"Oh! my lord, I thought you dead. They said that they had come to kill you by command of the Jew Caleb, he who gave the evidence."

"They! Who?" asked Marcus.

"I know not, four men whose faces were masked. They said also that though you must die, they were commanded to do me and this woman no harm, only to bind and silence us. This they did, then, having taken what money they could find, went out to waylay you. Afterwards I heard a scuffle in the arch and well-nigh died of sorrow, for I who could neither warn nor help you, was sure that you were perishing beneath their knives."

"For this deliverance, thank God," said Cyril, lifting up his hands.

"Presently, presently," answered Marcus. "First follow me," and taking the lamp in his hand, he ran back to the archway.

Beneath it a man lay upon his face—he across whom Marcus had stumbled, and about him blood flowed from many wounds. In silence they turned him over so that the light fell upon his features. Then Marcus staggered back amazed, for, behold! they were Caleb's, notwithstanding the blood and wounds that marred them, still dark and handsome in his death sleep.

"Why," he said to Stephanus, "this is that very man whose bloody work, as they told us, the murderers came to do. It would seem that he has fallen into his own snare."

"Are you certain, son?" asked Cyril. "Does not this gashed and gory cheek deceive you?"

"Draw that hand of his from beneath the cloak," answered Marcus. "If I am right the first finger will lack a joint."

Cyril obeyed and held up the stiffening hand. It was as Marcus had said.

"Caught in his own snare!" repeated Marcus. "Well, though I knew he hated me, and more than once we have striven to slay each other in battle and private fight, never would I have believed that Caleb the Jew would sink to murder. He is well repaid, the treacherous dog!"

"Judge not, that ye be not judged," answered Cyril. "What do you know of how or why this man came by his death? He may have been hurrying here to warn you."

"Against his own paid assassins! No, father, I know Caleb better, only he was viler than I thought."

Then they carried the body into the house and took counsel what they should do. While they reasoned together, for every path seemed full of danger, there came a knock upon the archway door. They hesitated, not knowing whether it would be safe to open, till the knock was repeated more loudly.

"I will go, lord," said Stephanus, "for why need I fear, who am of no account to any one?"

So he went, presently to return.

"What was it?" asked Marcus.

"Only a young man, who said that he had been strictly charged by his master, Demetrius the Alexandrian merchant, to deliver a letter at this hour. Here is the letter."

"Demetrius, the Alexandrian merchant," said Marcus as he took it. "Why, under that name Caleb who lies there dead passed in Rome."

"Read the letter," said Cyril.

So Marcus cut the silk, broke the seal, and read:

"To the noble Marcus,

"In the past I have worked you evil and often striven to take your life. Now it has come to my ears that Domitian, who hates you even worse than I do, if for less reason, has laid a plot to murder you on the threshold of your own house. Therefore, by way of amends for that evidence which I gave against you that stained the truth, since no braver man ever breathed than you are, Marcus, it has come into my mind to visit the Palace Fortunate wrapped in such a cloak as you Roman captains wear. There, before you read this letter, perhaps we shall meet again. Still, mourn me not, Marcus, nor speak of me as generous, or noble, since Miriam is dead, and I who have followed her through life desire to follow her through death, hoping that there I may find a kinder fortune at her hands, or if not, forgetfulness. You who will live long, must drink deep of memory—a bitterer cup. Marcus, farewell. Since die I must, I would that it had been in open fight beneath your sword, but Fate, who has given me fortune, but no true favour, appoints me to the daggers of assassins that seek another heart. So be it. You tarry here, but I travel to Miriam. Why should I grumble at the road?

"Caleb. "Written at Rome upon the night of my death."

"A brave man and a bitter," said Marcus when he had finished reading. "Know, my father, that I am more jealous of him now than ever I was in his life's days. Had it not been for you and your preaching," he added angrily, "when he came to seek Miriam, he would have found me at her side. But now, how can I tell?"

"Peace to your heathen talk!" answered the bishop. "Is the land of spirits then such as your poets picture, and do the dead turn to each other with eyes of earthly passion? Yet," he added more gently, "I should not blame you who, like this poor Jew, from childhood have been steeped in superstitions. Have no fear of his rivalry in the heavenly fields, friend Marcus, where neither do they marry or are given in marriage, nor think that self-murder can help a man. What the end of all this tale may be does not yet appear; still I am certain that yonder Caleb will take no gain in hurrying down to death, unless indeed he did it from a nobler motive than he says, as I for one believe."

"I trust that it may be so," answered Marcus, "although in truth that another man should die for me gives me no comfort. Rather would I that he had left me to my doom."

"As God has willed so it has befallen, for 'man's goings are of the Lord; how then can a man understand his own way?'" replied Cyril with a sigh. "Now let us to other matters, for time is short and it comes upon me that you will do well to be clear of Rome before Domitian finds that Caleb fell in place of Marcus."

Nearly three more months had gone when, at length, one night as the sun vanished, a galley crept wearily into the harbour of Alexandria and cast anchor just as the light of Pharos began to shine across the sea. Her passage through the winter gales had been hard, and for weeks at a time she had been obliged to shelter in harbours by the way. Now, short of food and water, she had come safely to her haven, for which mercy the bishop Cyril with the Roman Marcus and such other Christians as were aboard of her gave thanks to Heaven upon their knees in their little cabin near the forecastle, for it was too late to attempt to land that night. Then they went on deck and, as all their food was gone and they had no drink except some stinking water, leaned upon the bulwarks and looked hungrily towards the shore, where gleamed the thousand lights of the mighty city. Near to them, not a bowshot away indeed, lay another ship. Presently, as they stared at her black outline, the sound of singing floated from her decks across the still, starlit waters of the harbour. They listened to it idly enough at first, till at length some words of that song reached their ears, causing them to look at each other.

"That is no sailor's ditty," said Marcus.

"No," answered Cyril, "it is a Christian hymn, and one that I know well. Listen. Each verse ends, 'Peace, be still!'"

"Then," said Marcus, "yonder must be a Christian ship, else they would not dare to sing that hymn. The night is calm, let us beg the boat and visit it. I am thirsty, and those good folk may have fresh water."

"If you wish," answered Cyril. "There too we may get tidings as well as water."

A while later the little boat rowed to the side of the strange ship and asked leave to board of the watchman.

"What sign do you give?" asked the officer.

"The sign of the Cross," answered Cyril. "We have heard your hymn who are of the brotherhood of Rome."

Then a rope ladder was thrown down to them and the officer bade them make fast and be welcome.

They climbed upon the deck and went to seek the captain, who was in the afterpart of the ship, where an awning was stretched. In the space enclosed by this awning, which was lit with lanterns, stood a woman in a white robe, who sang the refrain of the hymn in a very sweet voice, others of the company, from time to time, joining in its choruses.

"From the dead am I arisen"

sang the voice, and there was something in the thrilling notes that went straight to the heart of Marcus, some tone and quality which were familiar.

Side by side with Cyril he climbed onwards across the rowing benches, and the noise of their stumbling footsteps reaching the singer's ears, caused her to pause in her song. Then stepping forward a little, as though to look, she came under the lantern so that its light fell full upon her face, and, seeing nothing, once more took up her chant:

"Oh ye faithless, from the dead am I arisen."

"Look, look!" gasped Marcus, clutching Cyril by the arm. "Look! It is Miriam, or her spirit."

Another instant and he, too, had come into the circle of the lamplight, so that his eyes met the eyes of the singer. Now she saw him and, with a little cry, sank senseless to the deck.

So the long story ended. Afterwards they learned that the tale which had been brought to Rome of the loss of the ship *Luna* was false. She had met the great gale, indeed, but had sheltered from it in a harbour, where the skill of her captain, Hector, brought her safely. Then she made her way to Sicily, where she refitted, and so on to one of the Grecian ports, in which she lay for eight weeks waiting for better weather, till a favouring wind brought her somewhat slowly to Alexandria, a port she won only two days before the galley of Marcus. It would seem, therefore, that the vessel that had foundered in sight of the *Imperatrix* was either another ship also called the *Luna,* no uncommon name, or that the mariners of the *Imperatrix* had not heard her title rightly. It may have been even that the dying sailor who told it to them wandered in his mind, and forgetting how his last ship was called, gave her some name with which he was familiar. At the least, through the good workings of Providence, that *Luna* which bore Miriam and her company escaped the perils of the deep and in due time reached the haven of Alexandria.

Before they parted that happy night all their tale was told. Miriam learned how Caleb had kept the promise that he made to her, although when he thought her dead his fierce and jealous heart would suffer him to tell nothing of it to Marcus. She learned also how it came about that Marcus had been saved from death at his own hand by Cyril and entered the company of the Christian brotherhood. Very glad were both of them to think in the after years that he had done this believing her to be lost to him in death. Now none could say that he had changed his faith to win a woman, nor could their own consciences whisper to them that this was possible, though even at the time he knew it not.

So they understood how through their many trials, dangers, and temptations all things had worked together for good to them.

On the morrow, there in the ship *Luna,* Marcus and Miriam, whom the Romans called Pearl-Maiden, were wedded by the bishop Cyril, the Captain Gallus giving the bride in marriage, while the white-haired, fierce-eyed Nehushta stood at their side and blessed them in the name of that dead mother whose command had not been broken.

www.ingramcontent.com/pod-product-compliance
Lightning Source LLC
Chambersburg PA
CBHW030349310726
48979CB00001B/237

* 9 7 8 1 4 3 4 1 1 7 4 1 0 *